W9-CDW-838

PASSOVER

JEFF YOCUM

AUTHOR OF *THE EYES OF GOD*

PASSOVER

This is a work of fiction. All of the characters, names, incidents, organizations, and dialogue in this novel are either the products of the author's imagination or are used fictitiously.

iUniverse books may be ordered through booksellers or by contacting:

iUniverse
1663 Liberty Drive
Bloomington, IN 47403
www.iuniverse.com
1-800-Authors (1-800-288-4677)

ISBN: 978-1-5320-7362-5 (sc)
ISBN: 978-1-5320-7364-9 (hc)
ISBN: 978-1-5320-7363-2 (e)

Library of Congress Control Number: 2019905190

Print information available on the last page.

iUniverse rev. date: 04/30/2019

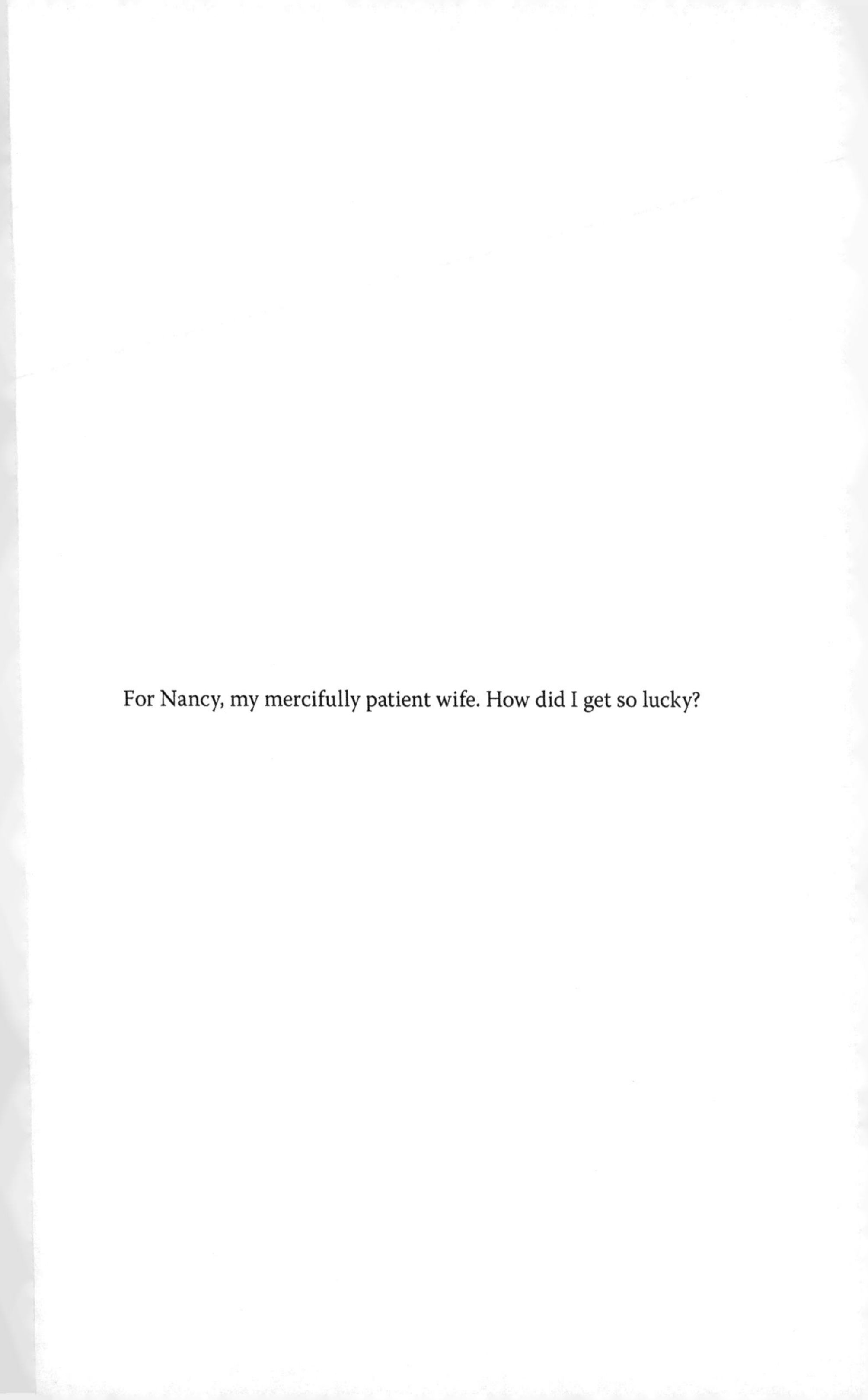

For Nancy, my mercifully patient wife. How did I get so lucky?

ACKNOWLEDGMENTS

I'd like to thank a number of people who made themselves available as sounding boards for proofing and support. J.J. Morgan, Erin White, Apryl Maxson, Mark Farbman, Cindy Stark, Heidi Feig, and Lois Stern all offered me much needed help and advice. I am grateful to Eva Moses Kor for sharing aspects of her experience at Auschwitz, particularly with Josef Mengele.

CHAPTER 1

MARCH 19, 2019

Dr. Chris Malone watched through the portal as the Gulfstream III maneuvered its way between the towering mounds of dirty snow toward the edge of the taxiway. Four SUVs and a police cruiser waited just outside the fence line. The sodium lights lining the surrounding hangars painted a world that had only indigo, yellow, and violet in its color spectrum. Malone's eight-person team descended the steps all with duffel bags and large trunks. A pyramid of gear formed just beyond the wingtip.

Malone saw three winter-clad occupants emerge from one of the vehicles and approach the new arrivals. The leader removed the glove from her hand and extended it to the person who was the first to get off the plane. "Dr. Malone? Dr. Kelly Simmons."

Rather than shaking hands, the man pointed to Malone. "I'm Lawrence Sanders. That's Dr. Malone."

"Hi. Chris Malone. Thanks for meeting us here." Malone extended her ungloved hand. She saw Simmons's embarrassment for assuming she was a man. It wasn't the first time. Malone, still holding the handshake, leaned in. "Don't worry. Happens all the time. My father wanted a boy, so he gave me one of those gender-neutral names as his consolation. Mom got even with him and gave him four sons after me."

A gust nearly knocked Simmons over.

"Have you had any more reported fatalities?" asked Malone.

"Not for about"—Simmons tugged at the sleeve of her parka to expose her watch—"sixteen hours. It appears that all twenty-seven of the victims died within twenty-four hours. Actually, all within twenty-one hours."

In a voice loud enough to be heard over the wind and the waning jet noise, Malone said, "This is my team. Dr. Sanders, my assistant, and Wiley Colfax, who keeps the ship aright." She pointed to all the other members of her team as she introduced them.

Simmons tried to acknowledge and shake hands as each was introduced, but it quickly became awkward. She motioned to the two people with her. "This is John Oronsky and Calvin Larson, Department of Health technicians."

Everyone shook hands and exchanged introductions as they clustered in a knot. Their collective breath fogged for a moment and was blown away by the relentless wind. The newly arrived from the Atlanta home of the Centers for Disease Control and Prevention shivered as repeated gusts swept across the airfield.

Malone counted heads and turned to Dr. Sanders and Wiley. "We got everything?"

Sanders nodded, too cold to speak, and gave a thumbs-up. Malone had come to depend upon him for his organizational skills and ability to solve technical problems. Wiley was her red tape master. She had made a point of taking care of her administrator knowing she'd be lost in a sea of paperwork if it weren't for Wiley Coyote, as she was known.

"Well, what say we get out of this cold? Let's see ... there are eleven of us all together." Malone looked at the vehicles as if she were going to assign each of them a seat, but she halted. "Are those company vehicles ... with drivers? And what's the police car for?"

Simmons strained to be heard over the wind and jet noise. "They're from GenStar Mining. It's pretty much their town. They loaned them to us at no cost along with the drivers. The cop is the sheriff's idea. People are pretty nervous. GenStar said whatever we needed they would be pleased to provide."

"Do they really think a convoy of vehicles with a police escort driving through town will settle folks' nerves?" She paused as she contemplated the situation. "Have the drivers ride back to wherever they need to go with the police. I don't want any of them."

Simmons opened her mouth to protest, but Malone cut her off. "When you spoke to Wiley on the phone, you said all the arrangements had been made. I didn't think I was being catered by a company. That could put this investigation in an awkward position."

Simmons responded in her defense, "My department is under severe budget constraints, so I was grateful for the offer of assistance."

Having dealt with such bureaucracies, Malone understood her dilemma. "Oh, all right. They did say whatever I needed. Well, I need tight control on everything we discuss, and I need as low a profile as possible until we get a handle on this. What I don't need is a driver overhearing a discussion he doesn't understand and taking it back to whomever to gum up the works." She barked at Sanders, "Keep track of the time of use, gas, that sort of thing. I want to reimburse the company. I don't want them thinking I owe them any favors." She turned to Simmons. "Dr. Simmons, I'd like you to ride with me and fill me in on your latest information." Turning to the rest of her team and in a louder voice, she said, "You guys get your gear loaded into the other vehicles."

Simmons parted to talk to the drivers. Malone saw there was a little animation among the group. She broke away from her team and joined Simmons. "Is there something wrong?"

"They've been given directions to drive and assist you in whatever way you need. They're concerned they'll be in trouble if they just turn the vehicles over to you."

Malone paused and smiled. "Guys, I understand your concern, but I have a protocol I must follow." She didn't, but they didn't know that. "I'll speak to your supervisors and vouch for you, but I cannot have unnecessary personnel involved." She caught herself from saying, "... until we know what we're dealing with."

The two younger drivers turned to an older, more senior-looking fellow for direction. He did not appear to be happy with the impasse. Malone suspected he was not just some guy pulled out of the motor pool. He had a mission.

Malone addressed the senior driver. "It has to be this way. I appreciate the assistance your company has offered, but if necessary, we'll procure our own transportation."

"From where? Do you know where you are? Fargo is the closest town big enough to have rental cars. It's more'n a hundred miles from here. We're it."

Without malice in her voice, Malone said, "I'm sorry. What's your name?"

"Mike Gunderson."

"Mr. Gunderson, I represent the US government, and I'm trying to determine why twenty-seven people suddenly died in this garden spot. I'm trying to do it with as little commotion as possible. But I can have the National Guard, FBI, EPA, Homeland Security, or whoever else I want here by morning. Do you think that will be in your company's best interest?"

It was all a bluff, but it was one she had honed to perfection.

Gunderson turned to the others and said, "Get in the cruiser, guys. We're done here." Under his breath but still audible, he said, "Ball breaker."

Malone was left with Simmons. She turned to her and gestured to the lead vehicle. "After you, Dr. Simmons."

Malone looked back at the departing drivers and considered Gunderson as just another guy who thought he could bulldoze her. What Gunderson and many guys before him did not know was that Chris Malone was the eldest and only daughter of five kids. Her father referred to her as his enforcer—the one who got the boys to fall in line. Her five-foot-two stature and pretty smile hid an iron fist beneath.

The Gundersons in her life had not watched her best high school basketball game in which she had scored only four points and made just two rebounds. That had not been her assignment. Her five-two body had been given the task of keeping the conference's leading scorer and rebounder out of the lane despite her thirteen-inch height advantage. That night, the superstar scored only four points and fouled out in the middle of the fourth period for too many over-the-back fouls. The last foul was a technical issued for taking a frustrated swing at Chris's head. Chris's team had been the one loss that year for that team, which later went on to win the state championship.

The Gundersons of the world had not seen her preparing specimen slides with a two-month-old asleep in a pouch strapped to her chest. She was doing what she had to to finish her doctoral thesis. They did not know she had been selected for the Drake Award given each year to the most outstanding doctoral candidate. She had used the prize money to pay her mounting pediatrician bills.

Malone was the last to get into the SUV. Before climbing in, she signaled for the other three vehicles to follow her. The warmth of the interior of the vehicle was welcome. Sanders shifted into drive, and the small caravan departed the airfield.

Malone unzipped the top of her coat and arranged herself until she was comfortable in her winter garb.

"Where we headed, boss?" Sanders asked.

"Dr. Simmons?" Malone was being deferential.

"I thought I'd take you to the makeshift morgue we set up. Dr. Pilsner, one of our pathologists, is there. Let you see where we're operating from. It's pretty much on the way to the motel. Just head straight out that gate and turn left."

"Just out of curiosity, what's a motel doing way out here?" asked Malone.

"It's part of a truck stop complex on the east-west route."

Ugh. Another fleabag motel, Malone thought.

The convoy sped away into the prairie.

After a while, Malone turned to her counterpart. "Dr. Simmons, let's talk. But before we do, I want to understand your role. As I understand it, you're an investigator with Minnesota. Do I have that correct?"

"Yes. Department of Public Health. I'm a pathologist with a background in epidemiology."

"Very good. Someone who understands. So what can you tell me?"

Simmons cleared her throat. "As I said, we haven't had any deaths reported in the past sixteen hours. Most of the victims, nineteen out of the twenty-seven, were male, white, but that's not a real discriminator here since the population is mostly white. Ages range from midteens to fortyish." She paused and her brow furrowed a bit. "Except for one elderly woman. Seventy-three. Victims worked at various occupations scattered across the area. No discernable clusters except in a couple of households."

"Symptoms?"

"Some were witnessed to have agonal breathing, chest discomfort, unconsciousness, seizures, then ... Well, most were just found dead. Some were witnessed to have just collapsed." Simmons pulled her notepad from her coat pocket and flipped through several pages. "Only five victims actually presented to the ER. The attending physician confirmed the general consistency with several of those who had expired without an attendant. Agonal respiratory, chest pains ... pupils reacted normally, which points away from overdose. Odd."

Malone was expressionless. "Were the victims loners? You know, by themselves?"

"Some, but most were in households with other family members or roommates. One of the witnesses stated that it was as if someone had just flipped a switch off."

Malone was trying to establish the boundaries of the malady. "Any secondary contaminations? Family? First responders?"

"No, though there were a few cases where two or three were found together. But that wasn't the case with the majority. The physicians for the five victims who did make it to the ER noted that there seemed to be a lack of symptoms. No fever, no sore throat, headache, that sort of thing. Most were described to have been fine just before their demise. Except for the elderly woman. She had been in declining health."

"Any chance she's just an anomaly? Just happened to die at the same time as the others?"

"Possibly. The more I think about it, probably. But at the time, the first responders were being overwhelmed."

Malone thought about the remote, rural nature of the area. "I can see that. Probably more deaths in twenty-four hours than usually in a whole year."

"We've had less than a day to sort through this."

"So have tissue samples been taken? Blood work?" Malone asked.

"Yes. And they've been sent to Saint Paul. Somebody got ambitious, and we have some early results."

"And?"

Simmons cleared her throat again. "Nothing, nothing that stands out. It'll take a few more hours for the cultures."

Malone was groping. "Chemical?"

"Mass spectrometer tests are being run, but that'll take a little more time as well."

Malone turned in her seat and looked at the wintry Minnesota landscape. Early spring thaws and refreezing had caused the snow to have a sort of glazed appearance that reflected the light of a gossamer moon. It made the entire landscape appear as though it were flooded. She pondered what she had just heard. It was consistent with the other two sites. Same symptoms, same time, only in different small towns. Remote and isolated. One was in Bonners Ferry, Idaho, and the other in Renovo, Pennsylvania. CDC teams were sent to those locations as well though the death tolls were not as high.

As an epidemiologist, Malone was trained to methodically sort through all the details and data. The purpose was to ensure all the pertinent facts were captured and vetted. Even so, her mind was drawn to one bizarre fact that stood out from all the rest—all the deaths from three separate sites thousands of miles apart occurred in the same twenty-four-hour period. And then no more. It was just as Simmons had said—as if someone had flipped a switch.

Simmons continued her briefing. "Dr. Pilsner has been doing preliminary, noninvasive examinations at the garage."

"Garage?" Malone asked.

"The hospital is rather small, really just a clinic, and there's just one funeral home in the area. They were overwhelmed pretty quickly, so we had to set something up as fast as possible. We set up a temporary morgue in a garage where we can control the temperature to just above freezing and have enough room for twenty-seven bodies. It's fairly remote, and—"

Malone interrupted her. "Let me guess. It belongs to GenStar."

"Well, yes. There are no other options unless we transport everything to Saint Paul. Even so, we'd need a staging area—"

Malone stuck her hands up as if to surrender. "Okay, okay, I get it."

"On the plus side, the garage is in a fenced, controlled area limiting access."

"That's a positive. When the media catches up to this, control will be critical. The last thing we need is a bunch of photos and videos going viral."

"They're already here. A TV news crew out of Minneapolis," Simmons said with a slight smile.

"Swell. Why hasn't a vaccine been developed for this?" Malone asked, mocking the stupid questions she anticipated being asked.

"More are probably on the way. Dr. Pilsner has given them a statement assuring them that there is no immediate danger, that you guys were on the way and would be part of the investigation. Pretty pat stuff so far."

"Any questions or statements about terrorism?"

"I believe he did say something to the effect that there was nothing to suggest terrorism played a part in this," Simmons replied.

"You all did a pretty good job getting on top of this given the circumstances," Malone said, trying to be conciliatory. She knew she'd have to work through some tough issues and warring agendas in the next few days. *At least try to have a good working relationship with the ones in the trenches with you,* she told herself.

The conversation stalled. Malone reflected on the timing of the three incidents. Normally, she could develop two or three working theories, straw men on which she could hang facts and subtheories until a plausible picture emerged, but not that time. Nothing from her background could even begin to be hammered into a theory.

The four SUVs pulled up to the guard shack. A guard leaned into the lead vehicle, spoke briefly to the driver, and signaled all four vehicles to proceed. A tarp covering the GenStar logo on a large sign flapped crazily in the freezing gusts. The garage was just beyond the office structure. A sheriff's department cruiser sat outside the metal, industrial-looking building along with one other official-looking vehicle.

Malone was relieved to see that the building was not some run-down shack but a rather substantial looking place, even neat. The occupants climbed out and hustled in.

A deputy sheriff greeted them from behind a desk in the foyer. "How can I help you?"

Simmons led again. "I'm Dr. Simmons from the Minnesota Department of Health. These folks are from the CDC."

The deputy stood. "Good. I was told you'd be here this evening. Kind of glad you're here."

"Something wrong?" Simmons asked.

"No! No! It's just ... you know, kind of creepy with ..." His voice trailed off. He nodded toward the garage bay. "There's someone else in there. Pilsner? I think that's his name."

"Well, we'll be here for a little while," Simmons said reassuringly.

The deputy managed a smile at that. He pulled a key from the desk and unlocked the door. The group moved toward the next room as the deputy held the door for them.

"Looks like I may be out of a job," the deputy quipped as Malone and Simmons entered the doorway.

"Pardon?" Malone asked.

"Out of a job," the deputy repeated, blushing at the realization his little joke may have been really inappropriate considering the circumstances.

"What do you mean?"

He hesitantly pointed to the makeshift morgue. "It's just that almost every crackhead and stoner in the county is in that room."

"You're saying those people were known drug users?"

"Well, except for Mrs. Lane, the old woman."

"Really? Interesting. That's useful. Thank you." A big piece of the puzzle, but Malone needed verification.

Simmons pushed her way to the front of the group to address them. "We've made a makeshift changing room in this office," she said, pointing left. "You can take off your coats and put your bunny suits on in there. You'll find what you need along the front wall. About three at a time can fit in there."

A tall, thin man wearing a white Tyvek suit approached the group and introduced himself. "I'm Dr. Pilsner from the Minnesota Department of Health. Welcome to Kayford, Minnesota. I'm sure you've been briefed on the situation here. Blood and tissue samples are being processed, but the volume of victims is causing a bit of a delay. The bodies will be transferred for autopsy tomorrow." Pilsner checked his watch and corrected himself. "This morning."

Malone studied Pilsner not so much for the information he was giving but for the little indicators of the inevitable jockeying for authority she had experienced nearly every time she had been called into a situation involving state and federal agencies. She knew she was a good epidemiologist, but she also knew that her ability to read situations and keep everyone's feathers from being ruffled had put her in such demand by the CDC. Her talent for group management was the reason she was constantly being jerked away from her normal routine and thrown into some rising health crisis. Her bosses had told her as much. Life in the field had become the norm; a routine life had become nonexistent.

But she didn't see much federal/state tension there. Malone saw in Pilsner a man worn out from the immediate work of the past day or so. More than that, she saw fatigue brought on by more responsibility than authority or funding would allow for. She saw a man who would be grateful for reinforcements to help with the investigation and handling the inevitable media scrutiny.

"We've ruled out viral or other biological causes, but please suit up before I take you in to view the victims," Pilsner said.

The group donned masks with filters and other protective apparel. After a brief look to see that everyone was properly suited, Pilsner led them into the temporary morgue. Sawhorses supporting doors formed tables that covered the entire open floor of the shop area. The tables were arranged in a six-by-five pattern. Ominously, all but three had long, black plastic bags stretched out on them.

"Twenty-seven victims, ladies and gentlemen." Pilsner walked between two rows spreading his arms for emphasis. "The vector mechanism on this one is something of a mystery. Some of the victims were handled before and after death by their friends and relatives with no apparent infection. Some were complete loners. There was one cluster of four victims in a single house but no victims from the surrounding houses." Pilsner opened one of the bags. The group looked at a remarkably placid body.

"Have you found any common threads?" Sanders asked.

Pilsner contemplated for a moment before responding. "No. They're mostly in their twenties, but one victim is a seventy-three year-old grandmother. Most, almost two-thirds, are male, but that's pretty much true of the population here. Most but not all worked for GenStar, but that's not a real discriminator either since just about everyone here does in one capacity or another. That's where you'll begin tomorrow—looking for the thread that ties them all together. Dr. Malone, I believe you may want to say something at this point."

Malone stepped forward just a little. "You've all been trained how to conduct environmental-causes investigations. The question sheet, the Subject Environmental Inventory form, the SEI, to perform that investigation is three hundred questions long." Malone paused. "That's a lot of questions to throw at grieving friends and relatives. People will be testy, angry, and liable to be verbally abusive. Don't get drawn into their emotions. Reassure them it's all necessary to find what took their loved ones' lives so it can be prevented from doing that to others. There'll be a law-enforcement officer assigned to each of the teams. Keep them away from the actual conversation but close enough that their presence is known. Hopefully, that will be enough to stop any physical manifestation of the frustrations these folks are no doubt feeling."

Malone leaned against one of the empty tables and crossed her arms. She collected her thoughts before she continued the briefing. It was a chance for questions, but none came. That she knew indicated that the team was exhausted. They had all worked a full day at their routine functions at the CDC before being scrambled onto a field investigation team and flown to the outback of wintertime Minnesota.

"There's not much more we can do tonight. Tomorrow, we'll start looking for environmental commonalities of the victims. The people we want to talk to are no doubt asleep. We'll go at them in the morning. We'll get you to your motel rooms as soon as we can. I want you to get some rest. I don't need to tell you to watch your conversations. Folks are already spooked, and the media is here to scare them even more. So if

Dr. Pilsner doesn't have anything to add, let's get out of here for tonight and get some rest."

Pilsner shook his head, so the group made for the makeshift dressing room to take off their protective clothing. Within fifteen minutes, they were getting into the vehicles to head across the frozen landscape for the ride to the Great North Motel.

Malone got into the vehicle with Simmons, Wiley, and Sanders. They'd use the time getting to the motel for a little more planning.

"Dr. Simmons, I'd like to—"

"Call me Kelly," Simmons said. "I think we're going to be joined at the hip for the foreseeable future. Might as well dispense with the formalities."

"Thank you. Couldn't agree more. Call me Chris. Anyway, I'd like to pair up your guys with mine tomorrow at least as much as we can. There may be some benefit to having some hometown folks present to assuage any fear of outsiders."

"I concur, but I suspect anyone who's not at least third-generation Kayford is considered an outsider."

"You're probably right. I'd like your guys to be the lead. Hopefully, they all have that charming upper-Midwest accent."

"Not a problem."

Chris turned to Wiley. "Call the sheriff's office as soon as you can and arrange to have five escorts tomorrow morning. We have enough for four teams. I have an idea for one other team for another purpose."

"Let me call the sheriff's office," Kelly said. "It may go over better at this hour if they heard my charming Midwestern accent." She smiled.

Chris returned the smile appreciating the joke. "Thanks. You'll need to ask him for more help. There may be more victims not yet accounted for."

"Chris, what do you mean?" asked Kelly.

"The deputy at the garage said something to me that may be significant. He said something about all the victims being known drug users except the elderly woman. Given the rural, isolated nature of the population here, there may well be some victims we haven't found yet."

"The sheriff hopefully has a list of known offenders with addresses," Kelly said, following the logic.

"Precisely. I don't want to put all our efforts into this unless we start finding bodies everywhere."

Chris made a mental note to keep Kelly in mind should she need to recruit someone in the future. She wondered how easy it would be to lure her away from this winter wonderland to the balmy climes of Atlanta.

"Do you think there would be any merit to having Dr. Pilsner go along on a scouting team? He's a very competent pathologist. He may be of benefit at the scene if they do come across more victims," Kelly said.

"Good suggestion. Think he'll go for it?"

"I think he'd jump at a chance to get out."

"Good. I hope I'm wrong, but ..."

Kelly pulled out her cell phone and called the sheriff's office. Chris discussed with Lawrence who would go with whom in the morning. Wiley was working away on her laptop. Chris didn't have any idea what she was working on but was sure she wasn't just surfing the internet. Some potential logistical problem was no doubt being averted at that very moment.

The small convoy pulled into the parking lot of the Great North Motel. It was indeed a truck stop with the motel off to one side. The red neon lighting made the ice-encrusted surroundings look pink. A burned-out section of the sign that included the letters *r-t-h* rendered the motel's name Great No ... Motel. Sanders took a picture of it with his cell phone.

Simmons and Malone were the only ones to get out when the convoy pulled up to the lobby door. It took a few minutes to get the night manager to the front. The elderly manager looked alarmed as he looked out and saw the number of people.

Malone and Kelly came back to the vehicles and distributed keys. No one seemed to care who got which room just as long as it had heat, a bed, and a bathroom.

Before everyone disappeared into their rooms, Malone told them, "We meet for breakfast at six thirty. There will be five police escorts here tomorrow at seven thirty, one for each team of two. Lawrence and Wiley will run things from here. Get some rest and be ready to go in the morning. Goodnight."

The group dispersed to get out of the frigid wind. Malone collected her bag and headed for her room on the second level, which was as unremarkable as the hundred others she'd been in during the last six years. Considering her state of exhaustion, that didn't matter. She dropped her bag on the chair, fished out her toiletries kit, and found her clock. It wouldn't do if she were the late one in the morning.

She shed her clothes to prepare for a short night's sleep. She set the clock. Put out the clothes she would wear. Brushed her teeth. Checked her cell phone for messages—one missed call and one text message: "Call home. Urgent."

Malone looked at her watch; it was 1:13 a.m. Sam would really be upset if she called that late. Besides, her exhaustion told her, there was nothing she could do at such a late hour. She elected to call first thing in the morning.

CHAPTER 2

MARCH 20, 2019

Malone awoke from what felt like only a moment of sleep to the incessant buzzing of her travel alarm. The alarm clock app on her cell phone joined the chorus. Ever the cautious woman. She was awake but couldn't quite gather herself to move in any meaningful way. She looked at the window and saw it was still dark.

The fog of sleep cleared, and she sorted out the demands of the day ahead. First, meet with her team for breakfast and go through the day's assignments. Next, meet with the MDH folks to discuss the protocol for handling the bodies.

A thought occurred to her; she would have GenStar line up several of their large dump trucks in front of the garage where the bodies were being kept to provide a visual screen from the road and obscure the view for cameras. *What was that guy's name? Mike? Mike Ferguson? No. Something Scandinavian. Gunderson. Mike Gunderson. GenStar's eager to help. Here's something they can do that will actually be helpful. The line of trucks will look natural enough for a mine operation. Plausible deniability against accusations of trying to hide something.*

She reflected a moment on what she had become—a bureaucrat. She was spending most of her energy not on the science of problems but on the people issues of those problems.

A moment more of lamenting the demise of her integrity passed before another thought pushed its way to the forefront of her consciousness—*Call home.* She groaned at the thought. She looked at the clock. She had only twenty minutes before she was supposed to meet her team for breakfast. She elected to shower and dress before she made the call. She'd be more awake and alert afterward she reasoned.

With just a couple of minutes to spare, she walked out of the hotel into the bitter bite of a March Minnesota morning. She took a deep breath and called her husband, Sam, as she walked from her room at the back of the motel toward the front, where the diner was.

"Why didn't you call?"

Chris opened her mouth to speak but was cut off.

"Erika didn't come home last night until this morning. I've had it with her. It's like an alien has taken over her body."

"I'll talk to her as soon as I get—"

"Talk to her? When, Chris? You're never here. You're always out saving the world!"

Chris rounded the corner and was greeted with a view of the parking lot nearly full of news vans. "Oh crap!"

"What?" Sam asked.

"No. Not you. I just saw something here that's not going to make any of this any easier. Listen, I have to go. I'll call you later this afternoon." She disconnected. A mistake, she thought, but one she'd deal with the consequences of later.

Malone took a quick glance around for the ambush reporter but saw none. She hoped all the news guys were still asleep. Being the only motel within a hundred miles naturally put her and them in such proximity. *I'll have to be extra vigilant. So will everyone else.*

She walked into the little diner and saw only her team members, Kelly's team, and a few others who looked like locals. Originally, she had wanted to meet with her team over coffee and breakfast. That wouldn't do at that point with representatives of every major news outlet snoozing just a few yards away. *Okay, let's order breakfast to go and eat it in the garage.*

She could tell that didn't sit well with the team, but there were no audible protests. No one including herself relished the idea of eating in a garage with a bunch of bodies in the next room. Visions of platters of eggs and bacon gave way to orders of egg, bacon, and cheese sandwiches and coffee in polystyrene cups.

Chris pulled Kelly to the side and explained in hushed tones, "We're in a nest of news crews."

Everyone got bagged breakfasts and headed to the line of parked SUVs. Wiley and Sanders got into Malone's vehicle to get a jump on their assignments. Within a couple of minutes, the caravan headed out of the parking lot. Kelly and Malone were riding together again. Malone noticed some of the media folks emerging from the hotel.

Malone addressed Wiley. "As soon as we get to the garage, get hold of that Gunderson fellow and ask him if he can park some of his large trucks and equipment in front of the garage along the fence. Those camera crews will be with us pretty quick once they figure out where everything is."

"I have a signal here. I'll call him now. I have his number."

"Tell him not to do anything if there are news crews already there." *Ever the artful bureaucrat* Malone thought.

The convoy sped through the prairie toward the makeshift mortuary. The faintest purplish-gray light appeared on the horizon. The frozen landscape reflected the narrow band of dawning light giving it that appearance of water she had noticed the night before. As they rounded a long, sweeping curve, Malone looked back past the end of the convoy to see if they had picked up any company. She saw just the three vehicles that were with hers.

"Did you get hold of Gunderson?" she asked Wiley.

"No answer. I left a messag—"

Wiley's cell buzzed. She held up a finger telling Malone it was Gunderson.

"Mr. Gunderson, yes. Thank you for getting back to me so quickly."

Wiley paused as Gunderson replied. Malone motioned for Wiley to hand her the phone.

"Hi, Mr. Gunderson. This is Dr. Malone. We met last night. You offered your company's services. I need your help. Is it possible to park some of your big dump trucks and equipment between the garage and the fence along the road? I think it would be better if the garage weren't so exposed. News crews are already in town and will likely be setting up shop just outside your gate pretty soon ... Thank you, Mr. Gunderson. Your assistance is most appreciated. If the news vans are already there or if they show up, please cease. I don't want them making out that we're trying to hide something. I'm sure you understand ... Yes ... Again, thank you, Mr. Gunderson. We should be there in fifteen or twenty minutes."

Malone asked Kelly, "How'd you make out with the sheriff?"

"He whined a little but came around."

Malone sensed there was more to the story. "Came around?"

"Well, I painted a picture of finding bodies weeks from now that had frozen and thawed repeatedly and how bad it would look if it came out that he had rejected a request to find those very bodies weeks earlier ... all in my charming Midwest accent."

I gotta find a place for her with the CDC, Malone thought.

"I made a couple other calls last night. I even got my boss to get the governor involved. That lit some fires under some butts, and apparently, someone worked all night because I had tox reports in my inbox this morning." Kelly waved a stack of reports.

"Super!" exclaimed Malone hoping it might point in some direction toward a culprit.

"Except for a couple of victims having nonthreatening levels of alcohol and THC in their blood, none had any significant levels of other drugs in their blood. That rules out overdoses," said Kelly.

"What?" Malone asked astonished. "I was sure there'd be a drug connection to this."

"The sheriff confirmed the drug-related histories of most of the victims, but drugs don't appear to be the culprit here," Kelly said with a shrug.

Malone took the reports from Kelly and leafed through them. It wasn't that she didn't trust Kelly's word; it was just that she had been so sure of her suspicions. Malone was still scanning the reports when they rolled up to the guard shack at the GenStar gate. Large trucks and heavy equipment pieces were moving about everywhere making even the interior of the SUV shake. Malone saw Gunderson directing the mammoth pieces into position. She looked about to see if any camera lights were among the other bright lights but saw none. She was grateful for that small favor.

The convoy wove its way around the confusion and pulled into whatever spaces were available around the garage. They joined a sheriff's department SUV. Malone got out and looked back toward the fence line. The visual screen was coming together nicely. It wasn't completely airtight, but it looked natural enough. *Plausible deniability,* Malone thought as she rushed into the garage.

A different deputy met them in the front office. Kelly produced her credentials for him. He studied them for a moment and handed them back. "Good morning, Dr. Simmons."

Kelly smiled. "Good morning. I can vouch for the rest of these folks." Her arm swept the room. "I appreciate your checking."

"I just got a radio call telling me your escorts are on their way here. This is about time for shift change, so they're all being briefed."

"Excellent. Thank you."

Kelly turned to the teams and told them they might want to shed their parkas since it would be an hour or so before they headed out. The team members took the opportunity to do so. The deputy unlocked the door to the garage-bay mortuary. They gathered at the empty end of the bay.

Malone addressed them. "We're going to send out four teams to do the environmental causes. We're going to do it a little bit differently by teaming each CDC person with an MDH person. I want the MDH folks to initiate the interviews. You guys from Atlanta may scare folks with your southern accents." A mild chuckle rippled through the small cluster of scientists.

"Dr. Pilsner and Dr. Adamavich, we have a special assignment for you two." Malone looked for both men, and once making eye contact with them, she addressed the whole group. "We have some reason to suspect drugs may have played a role in this. Until twenty minutes ago, I would have bet money that that was the case. Almost all the victims in this room had drug histories, but Dr. Simmons has in her possession a stack of fresh tox reports indicating otherwise. To be prudent, I've asked the sheriff to provide a list of known users in the county and a deputy. I want you two to go with the deputy and check the names on that list that are not those of any in these body bags. This is a very rural, isolated region. I want to make sure we're thorough. We don't need more bodies showing up repeatedly over the next two weeks."

Dr. Pilsner raised his hand as if he were in school. "And if we do find another victim?"

Malone thought about that. "Have the deputy call it in by phone. Don't use the radio. I don't want the media picking that up and swarming all over the place. Have them call it in, and we'll see if we can dispatch EMTs to recover the body and bring it back here under the radar."

Lawrence Sanders injected, "I'll check to see if there's a back entrance here."

"Good idea. I hope all of this can be accomplished by the end of the day. If we find more bodies, I'll include that information at a press conference that I'm sure we'll have before the end of the day. Better yet, the sheriff can make that announcement. We may get lucky and not find any more."

Kelly said, "When the police escorts get here, perhaps we should have them park around back. And if Lawrence finds a backway in, the teams and the escorts could leave that way."

Malone was about to agree but changed her mind. "That's good, but using the backway now will just encourage the news guys to find it and stake it out. I'd rather keep that in case we find more bodies. Let's send the teams out now and have them wait somewhere off-site to meet up with the escorts. That way, we won't have a parade of SUVs and police vehicles tearing out of here en masse."

"Good point. There's a parking lot on the east side of town. It's easy enough to find," Kelly said.

"You and I will brief the deputies when they arrive," Malone said to Kelly privately. She turned to the group. "Let's get past all this cloak-and-dagger crap and do what we came here for. Before you leave, check your tablets to make sure you have version three of the SEI form. You don't want to be forty miles from here and discover you have the wrong tools. Also, Wiley has extra batteries for your tablets. Same reason. Any last remarks or questions?" She paused but got no response. "Also, get the number of the phone to this building. Landlines may be our best option out here."

Everyone paired up, pulled on winter wear, and headed out.

Later that morning, CDC investigator Kyle Adamavich was with Dr. Mike Pilsner, the MDH pathologist. They had been assigned to the northern section of the county. A sheriff's deputy escorted them down a desolate stretch of Route 33. Adamavich sensed Pilsner wasn't comfortable with the deputy's seventy-five-mile-an-hour pace on the narrow, wintry road. It was their third call of the morning on known drug users. There were no flashing lights. No need. They were the only ones on the road coming or going.

The previous two visits were interesting, but the occupants were alive. They had given their testimonials about their newfound sobriety complete with exact information about how long they had been clean—eight months, three weeks and ten months, one week. "Taking it one day at a time. Praise God."

Morris, the deputy, slowed down along a fence line that seemed to run off to the horizon in both directions. Adamavich couldn't see what he was slowing for until the deputy turned into a drive that abruptly intersected the main road. Across the open field, a small house sat; several cars were in front. The cruiser stalled for a moment as it encountered tall snowdrifts on the drive. Adamavich felt the SUV engage all four wheels. Pilsner followed as best he could in the deputy's tracks.

As they got closer, Adamavich made out more details of the house and surroundings. The house was sided with gray-blue asphalt shingles in a brick pattern that had been popular in the fifties. Rips in the skin revealed well-worn clapboards beneath. Plastic sheeting substituted for storm windows. A satellite dish clung tenuously to one corner of the house. Three vehicles adorned the yard. Two were clear of snow as though they had been driven since the last snow. The third vehicle looked as though it had been rooted to the frozen ground for many winters. A snow-covered plastic jungle gym and slide sat in the side yard under a ragged, barren tree.

The deputy got out and stood, his hand resting on his sidearm. He scanned the house for any sign of activity. Adamavich and Pilsner joined him but at a distance. The small stoop at the center of the house's front didn't look like it could hold the weight of even one man. The deputy ascended the steps as gingerly as he could. He gave the door three firm knocks and waited shifting away from the center of the door. No answer.

He knocked louder three more times. No answer. His unease was apparent. He tugged at his sidearm to loosen it a bit from its holster and banged on the door again.

"Sheriff's department! We just need to talk! I don't have any papers or warrants. We just need to check and make sure you're okay."

Still no answer. Pilsner and Adamavich drew closer. All three men froze to listen for the slightest sound. There it was. A child's wail.

Deputy Morris banged on the door again. "Sheriff's department! Open up!"

Still no response. Just louder toddler cries from within. The deputy hopped off the stoop and ran to the nearest window. With one strong tug, he ripped the cloudy plastic film away from the frame. He pressed his face as near the pane as he dared and cupped his hands around his face to see through the grimy glass. Nothing. He ran around to the back. Adamavich and Pilsner followed. Again, the deputy tore away the plastic and peered in. Without explanation, he ran to the back door and tried the handle; the door was locked. One tremendous shove broke the latch side of the door away from the frame. He entered the kitchen.

Adamavich looked through the window to see what had caused the deputy to do what he had done. Lying across the bed of the back bedroom was the lifeless, partially clad body of a woman. A man sat slumped in a chair in the corner. Most disturbing were the terrified figures of two girls clutching each other. The men saw the officer rush in. The girls scurried into a corner away from him and huddled there.

Adamavich turned to Pilsner. "Come on." He motioned for him to follow him through the back door.

"What is it?"

They met Morris coming out of the bedroom and into the kitchen carrying both girls, who were clad only in pajamas and were shivering. The house was frigid. The children clung to the deputy. One looked to be four or five, and the other was barely more than a toddler, perhaps two.

Morris sat on a kitchen chair to better hold the two girls. He rubbed their backs to help warm them.

"In the trunk of the cruiser on the left side are a couple of blankets. The trunk release is on the driver's door. Would you get them?" He was not so much asking Adamavich as telling him.

Adamavich complied and pulled Dr. Pilsner out with him. They headed to the vehicles.

"Dr. Pilsner, I think we should get our bunny suits on before we go into that bedroom. Actually, we shouldn't even go into that house without proper protection. Can't take those kids out into this cold though," Adamavich said as he rummaged through the trunk of the cruiser.

"I don't think that'll be a problem. We're already exposed. The two girls have been exposed. It may be a good idea to wear them to preserve evidence though." Pilsner pulled out his cellphone and held it up at different angles. "No signal. How about yours?"

Adamavich tucked the blankets under his arm and fished his phone from his pants pocket. "No, no signal either." He looked at the wires going into the house and pointed at one of the lines. "They have a land line. Hope they paid their bill." He headed back into the house.

Adamavich entered the kitchen and helped Morris wrap the girls up in the blankets. The little one needed her diaper changed. The two men looked at each other. "I'll do it," Morris sighed.

He turned to the older sister. "Can you help me change your sister's diaper, sweetie? Just show me where her diapers are. I'll do it."

The little girl slipped from his lap and led him by the hand into a room on the opposite side of the kitchen. The three of them disappeared through the doorway.

Adamavich pulled out rubber gloves from his coat pocket and pulled them on. Pulling the notepad from his coat pocket, he looked about the kitchen and saw the wall phone. He felt relief when he lifted the receiver and heard the dial tone. With his arm stretched to its full length to read the number he had on a piece of paper, he dialed it.

"Hello?"

"Hi. This is Dr. Adamavich with the CDC. I need to speak to Dr. Malone please."

"Just a moment. I'll see if I can locate her."

A loud bang as the phone was apparently dropped caused Adamavich to jerk his head away from the receiver.

Deputy Morris returned with the little girls in his arms while Adamavich stood waiting. They returned to the table and sat. Both girls had clothes in their hands. Morris helped them pull on their pants and sweaters. "It's even colder in the bedroom," he said.

"I'm calling the garage to let them know what we've found. Cell phones don't work out here, and we shouldn't broadcast this on the radio," Adamavich told the deputy.

"I need to call this in as well. We need Child Services and an ambulance."

Adamavich held up one finger toward Morris as he asked, "Chris?"

"What do you have?"

"We've found two more. The deputy has names and a location but hasn't called it in yet. He'll do that as soon as I get through here. There are two small children as well. Girls. They appear healthy, but we need to take care of them first. We'll need to use the back entrance as we discussed this morning. Can you coordinate with the sheriff's people please?"

"Will do."

"Well, probably should make that call pretty quick. Get ahead of it. I'll get back to you as soon as I can."

An hour passed after Deputy Morris called the sheriff's office with the news of two more victims before anyone turned onto the nearly hidden drive. Morris took the two girls to the SUV so they could warm up. At least that was the reason he told them to get them to leave the house. Pilsner and Adamavich didn't want the girls present while they examined their dead parents in the next room.

The first to show up was the sheriff. He pulled his cruiser beside Morris's SUV so both driver-side windows were within arm's reach of each other. Both windows rolled down. Sheriff Knutsen carefully handed over a sack to Morris.

"The coffee's hot. Be careful. There's a couple orders of chicken nuggets and fries for the girls. Most kids like those."

Indeed they did; the girls tore into the food with abandon. Both lawmen watched with a small amount of pleasure.

"Where're your doctors?"

Morris, having just taken a swallow of the coffee, couldn't answer right away. He just pointed to the house and swallowed hard. The hot coffee made his eyes tear a little. "They're in the house. One of them is a state pathologist."

"Just as well. We don't have the means to properly investigate this." Sheriff Knutsen sighed. "I hope this thing comes to an end soon."

Morris looked over at Knutsen. His eyes sagged. He had stubble from a day's growth on his face. Not like Knutsen, a former military man who always looked crisp. The toll was mounting.

"Me too. People are starting to talk about Armageddon and ..." He stopped talking as he looked over at the two girls. They were fully focused on their first meal in a couple of days. He pulled his cruiser up a few feet forward so he could open the door. He got out and walked back to the sheriff's car.

"Have you heard anything about what this is? I asked these guys," he pointed to the house, "but they said they hadn't had time to draw any conclusions."

"That's pretty much the story I'm getting as well. They really haven't been here that long. It takes so long to cover all this open space."

"Is it true there were outbreaks in other parts of the country?"

"Apparently. One in Idaho. Another in Pennsylvania. Both remote, isolated, small towns just like Kayford."

"Haven't they figured out what caused the deaths in those other places?"

"Haven't had any more time than we've had here. They all happened pretty much at the same time."

"Holy crap!"

"Yeah, holy crap." The sheriff looked out over the open prairie. "My gut tells me that there's a bad batch of drugs even if the drug screens did come back virtually clear on just about all of them. You and I know not many dopers get religion and get clean all at the same time."

Across the field out on the highway, an ambulance crested a rise in the road. Knutsen turned his lights on so they'd see where they needed to turn. The ambulance missed the drive anyway and had to back up several feet. Any other time, the two officers would have been amused. Not that day.

With some effort, the ambulance made it to where the patrol vehicles were parked. Two EMTs emerged and walked to the sheriff and Morris.

"What's the story? They didn't give us much information, and we were told to stay off the radio. They just told us to get out here."

"The story is we have a couple more bodies. But before we get to that, I need you to look at the two little girls who were also in the house." The sheriff pointed to the other patrol vehicle. "They've been sitting in there to warm up. There's no heat in the house. I brought something from town for them to eat."

The younger of the two EMTs said, "Sheriff, you probably shouldn't have oughta done that. They may be suffering from some sort of internal organ distress."

The older one rolled his eyes.

"Internal organ distress? Yeah, hunger. They probably haven't eaten in two days. Just let Deputy Morris get the girls and put them in the ambulance so you can check them for frostbite or anything else. Geez!"

Morris headed back to his cruiser and opened the door. "Did you get enough to eat?"

They shook their heads.

"Well, we'll get you some more in a little while. Right now, I need you to let me carry you to that big ambulance so you can see the neat stuff inside, okay?"

The older one withdrew, and the little one followed her lead. Their hollow eyes showed the fear that their blank expressions hid.

"Nothing's going to happen, sweeties, I promise. Some nice people just want to make sure you're not hurt. I'll stay with you the whole time, okay?"

Neither answered, but the older one wrapped her slender arms around the deputy's neck. Seeing that, the younger one allowed Morris to scoop her up as well.

The sheriff waited a little longer for the Child Services folks, but not seeing them coming along the road, he went inside to see what was going on there. Morris left the girls with the EMTs and joined him. They followed the tracks to the back stoop and banged on the shattered door.

"You guys doing all right?" the sheriff hollered.

Adamavich appeared in the bedroom doorway. The sight of a figure decked out in a white Tyvek suit was enough to cause both officers to go no farther into the house than the doorway.

Adamavich pulled his cap off. "We're about done here. You can call the EMT guys in a few minutes and have them transport these two out."

"At the moment, they're examining the two girls. Shouldn't be much longer. They didn't appear hurt, just cold and hungry."

"Can you tell anything yet?" Knutsen asked.

Adamavich turned to the sheriff. "They both seem to fit the pattern of all the rest. Evidence of agonal breathing, sudden collapse." Adamavich shrugged. "We did find what looks like might be their drug stash. It was out in the open. We left it alone."

"Time of death?"

"We think it falls within the same time frame as the others, about a day and a half ago. We had to make some assumptions about the ambient temperatures."

The sheriff turned to exit. "I'll send the EMTs in when you're done. Let me put their stash in an evidence bag."

Morris went out to gather the girls and get them into his cruiser. He saw another vehicle coming across the field and hoped it was Child Services. Morris put the girls in his cruiser. When the car pulled up to the other vehicles, a slight woman emerged and approached the sheriff and Morris. "Joan Smalls, Child Protective Services." She extended her hand to shake the men's hands.

"Yes, I think we've met before," said Morris.

"No doubt."

"You by yourself?" the sheriff asked.

"Unfortunately yes. Budget cuts."

Morris briefed Smalls on the situation. "We found the two girls in the house. There are two deceased adults in the house we assume are the parents. The heat's off in the house, and it didn't appear they'd eaten in a while. We did give them something to eat."

The sheriff spoke. "There are two specialists in the house now doing a preliminary survey. They told me it looks like the deceased have been dead for a day and a half. So it looks like the girls were left alone with their dead parents for quite some time."

Morris waited to see if the sheriff had any more information before he continued. "The paramedics gave a cursory examination but didn't find anything."

"Thank you for the update, Deputy. Do you have the girls' names?"

"Uh, no. They didn't want to talk much. I didn't push it. The two adults were Brian Wilson and Janice Halprin."

"We'll check the records starting with the mother. For now, getting them away from this is the priority."

Morris opened the door to get the two girls out. Seeing the two adults coming for them, the older girl shrieked and jumped to the opposite side of the vehicle. The younger girl imitated her sister. Smalls tried capturing them from the other side. Both girls fought back with blind rage. Smalls retreated and closed the door. Morris did as well. They looked at each over the top of the cruiser.

"Any suggestions?" asked Morris.

"Tranquilizer gun maybe," Smalls retorted.

"Look, they were settled down pretty good until we tried to take them out of the cruiser. How about I drive them to wherever you need to take them and perhaps they'll calm down. They seemed to trust me for a while there," Morris offered.

"Worth a try," Smalls said.

"Sheriff!" Morris summoned Sheriff Knutsen over to his cruiser. "I probably need to transport these girls. They just went berserk when we tried to pull them out. I think I can keep them calm if they stay with me. Can you pull someone else to escort those two guys around?"

Knutsen nodded. "Yeah. I'll have another patrol meet them after they leave here. I'd escort them around myself, but I need to get back to the office. I'm sure the governor's office will want to get in the middle of this. They've already set up a press conference for four this afternoon. Just what we need."

Walter Aiken from the CDC watched as John Oronsky of the MDH parked the SUV as best he could among the piles of snow along the curb. The patrol car found an opening a little farther down the street. Aiken took note of the small neighborhood of modest, single-story, mostly neat houses that had probably been built in the fifties or sixties. He and Oronsky were one of two teams assigned to contact the aggrieved families in town since most of the victims lived there. The other teams had been given either the northern or southern parts of the county.

They met the deputy at the end of the drive. Aiken glanced up and down the street. He noticed a curtain in the front window of the house across the street suddenly jerk closed. The three men walked to the door. The deputy knocked on the door. Momentarily, a wary woman cracked the door enough to see who was interrupting her solitude.

"Yes?" she asked from behind the storm door.

The deputy spoke. "Good morning, Mrs. Lansky. Sorry to disturb you. I'm Deputy Sorenson. These gentlemen with me are from the Minnesota Department of Health and the Centers for Disease Control and Prevention. They need to ask you some questions related to the death of your son. They'd appreciate it if you would allow them in to talk to y—"

Mrs. Lansky slammed the door. To Aiken's relief, it was only to remove the chain latch. She opened the door fully and unlocked the storm door. Without another word, she turned and walked back into the darkened interior. The three men took it as an invitation to enter and followed her.

She led them to the front room that appeared to be the living room. There was a blanket on the sofa that looked as though someone had just gotten up. The television blared with some talk show featuring people arguing about some sort of nonsense. Thankfully, the woman picked up the remote and turned it off.

Aiken watched the woman. She looked to be in her early to midforties; it was hard to tell in the dim light. She was still in her nightclothes and gown, slippers on her feet. She looked exhausted. Exhausted wasn't the right descriptor though. Perhaps despondent.

Mrs. Lansky bundled up the blanket and motioned for everyone to have a seat. Aiken and Oronsky complied, but Deputy Sorenson held back and elected to stand just outside the room in the hallway.

Oronsky spoke. "Mrs. Lansky, this is Dr. Aiken from the CDC, and I'm John Oronsky from the state department of health. First, let me express our condolences for your loss." He paused a moment. "As you are probably aware, your son, Robert, was—"

"Robbie. Everyone calls him Robbie," Mrs. Lansky broke in.

"Yes. Sorry. Robbie." Oronsky cleared his throat. "Robbie was one of a number of victims. We're here to try to determine what may have caused these unfortunate deaths."

Aiken looked around the living room. On almost every flat surface was a framed picture of a young boy he assumed was Robbie—in a Little League uniform, with missing front teeth, with a young lady in a formal dress and wearing a big corsage. One frame lay facedown on the coffee table just in front of Mrs. Lansky. A pictorial history of a young life.

"Mrs. Lansky, we have a number of questions to ask, but before we get started on that, could you tell us a little about Robbie?" Aiken asked wanting to help ease her into the long interrogation but also as a reminder to himself that the subject of his inquiry had been a real, living person, not just a specimen.

The woman sat motionless, speechless. She seemed focused on some far-off point in space visible only to herself.

"Mrs. Lansky?"

Her stare focused sharply. Her glare penetrated Aiken. She sprang to her feet and swept past all of them nearly pushing Deputy Sorenson over as she headed down the narrow hallway. Oronsky and Aiken stood; they were uncertain about what to do. Sorenson instinctively placed his hand on his sidearm and stepped partially into the living room doorway for a shield.

After some banging around in a room at the end of the hallway, Mrs. Lansky reappeared and charged back into the room with a shoebox in her hands. She stopped at the coffee table and dropped the box on it spilling its contents.

Aiken looked at the scattered contents. Syringes. Pipes. Plastic bags of a grayish powder.

"Drug paraphernalia," Deputy Sorenson explained.

"This is all you need know about my son!" Mrs. Lansky screamed. "This is the hell he's put me through for the past two years!"

She picked up the photo on the coffee table and thrust it at Oronsky. "One day he's asking for money to help buy a car. The next he's a crackhead. I tried everything to help. Even got into that national rehab program, the Tudos program." She collapsed to her knees and wept.

Oronsky looked at Aiken and shrugged.

"I'll explain later," Aiken said.

Aiken knelt beside her and put his arm around her in an effort to console her. Her sobs subsided. He and Oronsky helped her to the sofa again.

"Let me go to the car and get an evidence bag. You okay with her until I get back?" Sorenson asked.

Aiken nodded, and Deputy Sorenson left.

"Mrs. Lansky, is there someone we can call to come and be with you? A neighbor? Family? Anyone?" Oronsky asked.

"No," she replied in a barely audible voice.

The three men eventually got Mrs. Lansky settled and back under the sofa blanket. They made their departure without getting any answers for the survey. They did, however, have something that might provide more answers than a dozen surveys.

"If all the interviews go like that, we'll be here for a month," said Aiken. "Before we go to the next family, we should get that bag back and analyzed."

"Let me call the watch commander before we do that," Deputy Sorenson said. "I don't want to create a chain-of-custody screwup if this turns into a criminal investigation."

Aiken looked at Oronsky, and they nodded in agreement. "Probably prudent, but we need to expedite this," Oronsky said.

Sorenson reached for the radio mic clipped to his shoulder and requested the watch commander to come to his location.

A voice returned and acknowledged the request and address. "What's the nature of the issue?"

"A chain-of-custody issue. Rather not give more details."

Aiken felt a little relief that Sorenson had stopped short of radioing too much information.

After a pause, they heard, "Roger. On my way."

Outside, Sorenson rested the bag on the hood of his cruiser and wrote out his name, time, date, location, Mrs. Lansky's name, and the name of the two witnesses, Oronsky and Aiken, on the bag. However, he did not seal it. "I'll wait for the watch commander before I seal it. He'll want to take a field test on it."

The three men stood waiting awkwardly at the hood of the cruiser.

"What was that about a national rehab program?" Oronsky asked jerking his thumb over his shoulder toward the Lansky house.

Aiken looked at the deputy to see if he wanted to explain, but he saw no indication the deputy wanted to. "Tudos Pharmaceuticals started a low-cost program, Campaign of Hope or something like that, to help addicts kick their habit. They offered a new drug that suppressed the desire for drugs. It had some success. The company's owner, a guy named

Jakob Bauer, got into a jam with the shareholders because he didn't want the company to make any profits on the drug sales."

"How do you know all that?" Oronsky asked.

"I play the market. Try to keep up with the business news. Gotta couple of kids heading to college in a couple of years," Aiken said.

Five minutes passed before Sergeant Davis, the watch commander, pulled up in his SUV cruiser. He and the deputy conferred for several minutes as Sorenson gave him the story of what had transpired in Mrs. Lansky's living room. Davis got a small kit out of the back of his cruiser and returned to the hood of Sorenson's cruiser. Aiken watched from a respectful distance as Davis took a small sample and placed it in a small vial. He shook it, looked at it, and shook it again.

Aiken heard him say, "There's some presence, but it's awful weak."

Aiken stepped closer. "May I look at that please?"

The sergeant turned to look at Aiken as if to ask, *Who are you?* Sorenson immediately introduced the two bystanders. "This is Dr. Aiken from the CDC, and that is Mr. Oronsky from the Minnesota DOH."

The sergeant hesitantly handed the small vial to Aiken, who swirled it again. The clear liquid had a faint pink tint. There was a precipitant in the bottom.

"Is this what they usually look like when you do these field tests?" he asked.

"Usually they're a darker pink, almost red," Davis said.

"Do you often get that precipitate, that dark stuff at the bottom?"

"I know what precipitant is, and no, not usually. In fact, this is the first time I've ever seen it," Sergeant Davis replied testily.

"This is a test for what, opiates?" Aiken asked trying to convey more respect.

"Yes."

Aiken handed the vial back to the sergeant. "Thank you."

Sergeant Davis sealed the bag with tape and wrote his name across the seal as did Deputy Sorenson. "I'll take this to the station and get it out to the state lab in Saint Paul first thing."

Aiken stepped toward the watch commander. "Sergeant, it would be better if that were turned over to the CDC for analysis. This isn't your typical drug bust."

Davis stopped. He was turning red. "This is the proper protocol, Doctor. Stand aside."

"Yes, I appreciate the need for following protocol, but this is a health emergency. We need to get to the root of it before"—Aiken paused, searching for words that wouldn't convey doomsday—"before there are other deaths. Time is our enemy here."

"Step aside, Dr. Aiken, before I arrest you for obstruction!"

Aiken stepped back. Davis climbed into his cruiser and sped away as fast as the slushy street would allow.

Aiken and Oronsky turned to Sorenson with puzzled looks.

"His son-in-law is in one of those body bags back at the garage," Sorenson explained clearly embarrassed.

Aiken sighed. "Is there a pay phone near here somewhere? My cell phone doesn't have any service here. I need to relay all of this to the boss."

Sorenson headed back to the cruiser. "Follow me."

CHAPTER 3

JUNE 17, 1944, BEFORE DAWN

The railcar lurched to a halt just as the brakes' screeching reached a crescendo. A moment of utter quiet was suspended over the car's occupants—not a calm quiet but a quiet of breathless dread of what was to happen next. Even the children clutching their mothers in the dark held in their whimpers.

After being sealed for six days, the sliding door of the cattle car slammed open to a burst of brilliant light that blinded the ninety-some occupants. The interior of the car exploded with chaos and noise. Four-year-old Jakob Bauer held onto his mother to the point of choking her. His two sisters, Rachel and Leah, did the same, and the four fell backward to the filthy floor. Jakob's father helped them up and to their feet.

Shouts of "Raus! Raus!" filled the air along with dogs barking, children crying, women screaming, and names being called out in desperate searches for loved ones. Soldiers ran in and out of the swelling crowd pushing and shoving the bewildered arrivals. Above the cacophony of chaos, the melody of Mozart's *Eine Kleine Nachtmusik* blared from speakers on tall poles up and down the length of the train.

Jakob's fear was countered briefly by the relief of fresh, cool air rushing into the grim confines of the railcar. The stench of urine and excrement quickly gave way to a new smell just as foul. The occupants made their way to the one door. The more able bodied helped the less capable make the jump of more than a meter from the railcar to the ground. Six days of confinement had rendered them all stiff and unsteady.

As he was lowered to the ground, Jakob looked back at the interior of the railcar and in the dim light saw that several people had not moved toward the exit. *Why don't they want to leave?* His young mind did not comprehend those souls were beyond caring about what happened next. Before he could ask, his mother handed him to his father on the ground, and he was immersed in yet another world. Rachel and Leah soon stood next to him, and the three towheaded siblings held each other's hands as they had been taught to do their entire young lives. In another instant, his mother was with them again and grabbed the three children's free hands. Father lifted the family's only possession, a suitcase, and the five turned to face their fates.

Armed soldiers passed through the crowd shouting orders for men to move to the right and women to the left. An anxious cry arose, and the guards scurried about creating a separation. A smiling soldier appeared before the Bauer family stating as if obviously logical, "We must separate the women from the men so you can shower and be deloused! All children under twelve with your mothers to the left!"

Another soldier worked his way through the throng separating the sexes pushing left, pushing right. Jakob's parents fussed about who was to take the suitcase.

"You take it! You have the children!" his father insisted.

"I can't carry it and hold the children as well!"

A soldier stepped in and pushed the bag into the father's arms. "You take it. You will all be reunited after delousing." He handed him a piece of chalk. "Put your name on the side and stack it over there with the others. You can reclaim it after you have showered."

Jakob's father wrote Bauer on the side in big letters. As soon as he finished, a man tapped him on the shoulder and asked for the chalk to do the same to his luggage.

"You must move to the right!" This time the soldier held up his rifle across his body and used it to drive the two men from their wives and children.

The other man protested, "If we are separating for showers, why are the old men on that side with the women?" The soldier answered with a glancing blow to the man's head with the butt of the rifle. The man fell to the ground, and Isaak Bauer quickly helped him to his feet.

Husbands gave last instructions. Wives stood paralyzed in fear. All up and down the rail siding, similar scenes were occurring. The long, narrow crowd running the length of the forty-some railcars slowly split into two distinct sides in a fashion resembling the mitosis of an organism. Jakob looked around and just as quickly lost sight of his father in the other line.

Once the mitosis was complete, the line of women, children, and old men lurched forward. Jakob's field of view did not allow him to see where they were all moving. He could see only his sisters, mother, and those immediately around him. He could however see up into the night sky. Beyond the brilliant glare of the lights, he saw a red glow reflecting off the early morning mist. It seemed brightest in the direction to their left. At some distance beyond a stand of trees, Jakob made out the tops of two chimneys that were belching a dense, black smoke that alternated with bursts of orange-red flames. He tugged on his mother's sleeve and pointed to the fire.

His mother looked at him. "Yes. I see. It must be a factory."

"Zwillinge!" "Twins!" a soldier came down the line ahead of them shouting and looking at the children in line. Jakob's mother jerked her three children behind her.

"Twins!" the soldier called again.

"They will live!" A whisper. Jakob's mother looked around to see from where it had come. A man in striped pajamas stood next to her wrestling with a large trunk that had come off one of the cattle cars. She looked at him as if to ask, *What?*

Without looking at her but at the three hidden children, he repeated, "They will live."

This time she asked aloud in an exasperated voice, "What do you mean?"

The man, annoyed at the woman's stupidity, repeated, "They will live!"

A second striped man approached and whispered, "*Malekhamoves*!"

Ilsa recoiled. "What are you saying? I don't speak Yiddish."

The first striped man reddened in anger at both the other prisoner and Ilsa. "There is your Angel of Death!" pointing at the orange-red glow.

Aghast, Ilsa asked, "Angel of Death?" A terrible moment was suspended like a lifetime. She looked for her husband's help but saw only the line of men marching away. A soldier dragged an old man from the line of men and shoved him into the line for women and children.

They kicked another one toward the women. Only the strongest stayed with the all-male line.

"I have triplets! Here!" Ilsa cried out in German.

A soldier was beside her in an instant. Jakob was startled when the soldier grabbed his mother, and the four were led to the front of the line. There they stood before another soldier. Even Jakob could tell that this soldier was someone special.

"Herr Hauptsturmfürher, Drillinge!"

The captain rotated to address the soldier and returned the soldier's salute. "Did you say triplets?"

The soldier, flush from the exertion of separating out the transport, answered, "Yes sir. This woman says these three are triplets." He pushed Ilsa forward toward the handsome, immaculately dressed officer in a white clinic coat.

The officer smiled reassuringly at Ilsa. He gently held each child's chin to get them to look up at him. Jakob was the last of the three. The captain looked longer at him than he did at Rachel or Leah.

"Is this child a boy?" The soldier moved to grab Ilsa again.

"Yes!" she replied firmly. "They were all born at the same time!"

The officer smiled again. "You wouldn't try to fool a doctor, would you?"

"Doktor? Nein, Herr Doktor! I swear these are triplets. All born on the fifth of May 1940."

The officer doctor examined each of the children's faces again. He turned their faces toward the light making note of their fair features and startling blue eyes. He turned back to Ilsa. "You are a Jew, no?"

"Nein, Herr Doktor. My husband is Jewish."

"But you are Hungarian?"

"I am German."

Jakob saw fear in his mother's face.

"German! You're married to a Jew?"

"Ja, Herr Doktor. I converted to Judaism."

The doctor stood for a moment with a trace of a smile. "For love, Frau ...?"

"Bauer. Ilsa Bauer. Yes, I love my husband."

The doctor nodded. The noise surrounding them died down as the transport arrivals headed off to their fates. The music from the loudspeakers could be heard clearly. The doctor's gaze upon Jakob's mother lingered a long moment. He returned to examining the children.

Jakob had seen doubt on other adult faces before, those who were skeptical that he and his sisters were triplets. Jakob sensed this man, unlike others, threatened them all with great harm. He wasn't just another skeptic. Jakob pulled away from his mother's reach and tugged on the officer's trousers.

"Jakob! No!"

The soldier seized Ilsa as she lunged for Jakob.

Jakob looked up at the startled officer. "Mozart," he said, pointing to the speaker.

The officer did not move or speak for another eternity. He broke into a broad smile. "Yes, Mozart. Do you know the name of the piece being played?"

With evident pride, Jakob said, "Eine Kleine Nachtmusik."

"Bravo! What a clever lad indeed!"

The doctor turned to the soldier. "Sergeant, get someone to register these children."

"Jawohl, Herr Doktor Mengele. And the woman?"

The officer snapped his thumb in a motion to the left and walked away exclaiming, "She wishes to be one of the chosen people. Now she truly is."

Another soldier pushed his mother into the line of women, old men, and small children. She turned and looked at her children. The soldier pushed her again, and she was swallowed up by the crowd.

The sergeant led Jakob and his sisters away from the commotion of the ramp and handed them over to the care of a man wearing what looked to Jakob like dirty, coarse pajamas. The man said nothing other than short, terse directions in a language Jakob did not understand. It sounded like the language used by the soldiers who had so recently became prominent in his life.

Jakob saw that the man's sullen, grim demeanor frightened his sisters. He put himself between them and the grimy man. The siblings held each other's hands as they never had before as he led them away. After a short distance, they crossed the railroad tracks away from the throng of people. They were made to wait just outside a tall, metal-framed gate. Pointing to the several strands of barbwire attached to porcelain knobs, the grim-faced pajama man shook his head and drew his finger across his throat. The children clustered even tighter understanding well enough that the fence was bad and not to be touched.

Jakob looked back at the crowd and searched the chaotic activity for familiar faces. Under the glaring carbon-arc searchlights, two large lines had formed—one for just men and one for women, other children, and old men. The lines shuffled forward toward two men in uniforms. Jakob recognized one of the two men as the one who had spoken to him and his mother just a few minutes before. The man motioned with his hand to the left and right keeping rhythm with the music falling over the scene. It reminded Jakob of how his father had entertained him and his siblings as well as the other children in the Miskolc ghetto by playing records of great musical masterpieces. He showed the children an illustration of a conductor standing before an orchestra. Using a slightly crooked stick as a baton and with exaggerated movements that drove the children to tittering delight, he demonstrated how the conductor led the orchestra.

Jakob loved listening to the music. The pride he felt for his father swelled in his chest. So starved were they all for learning something other than the harsh realities of the ghetto. Mr. Bauer's demonstration and explanation of the scratchy music emanating from the hand-cranked record player transported them away to a place of beauty.

This man looked just as his father had although a little less animated. He wore a confident smile, a smile of achievement. Jakob saw some of the same children his father had made laugh crossing the tracks with their mothers and heading down a long, dirt road paralleling the tracks. Jakob wanted to join them. Perhaps they could take him to his mother.

The area between the tracks was clearing of the people who had arrived with Jakob and his family. Jakob caught sight again of the uniformed man who had spoken to him. He and the man at the head of the other line climbed into a car with a big red cross painted on the door. It sped off in the same direction that most of the old men, women, and children had taken. He followed the car as best he could into the distance where he could just make out some sort of buildings, one on each side of the tracks. An orange-red glow above the buildings silhouetted the chimneys.

A locomotive without any railcars chuffed toward him out of the darkness between the two orange glows. He loved watching the activity around the rail yards. Until these past few days, he had yearned to ride one.

Jakob felt Leah's hand pull out of his, and he turned to look at her. She covered her face with her hands and sobbed uncontrollably. The pajama man grabbed her by her shoulders and shook her. "Nicht!" He was seething. "Nicht!"

Leah froze as if paralyzed as did Jakob and Rachel. The pajama man said something else Jakob could only take to mean, "You must not cry!"

Though he was only four, Jakob from that moment on understood this place was a place of evil and their lives were in danger. He didn't know why, or by whose hands, or for what reasons they were in peril, but he comprehended at a primordial level that life there would be contended for savagely.

Jakob, having received the message and looking to break the tension, returned his gaze to the rail platform. He continued looking in hope of finding a familiar face—any face. All he saw were many other grim-faced pajama men loading onto trucks suitcases, bundles, pots of every description, baby carriages, and things he did not recognize.

The people who hadn't moved when Jakob had climbed out of the railcar came flying out and onto the platform. Others flew out of the other cars as well, two or three from every car. Pajama men picked them up by the arms and legs and swung them onto the bed of another truck.

One of the flying men fell back to the ground. A short, stout man in a gray-green uniform screamed at the two pajama men. He struck them alternately with some sort of short, stiff whip. The two pajama men absorbed the blows while trying to pick up the flying man. The blows ceased, and the pajama men gave a mighty effort to make the man fly to the top of the stack of other flying men.

Farther up the tracks, Jakob heard the plaintive cries of an infant. Among the clutter and debris, he made out a baby sitting with outstretched arms. Jakob saw the pajama men look at the child and then scurry off to some other urgent task. A uniform man stomped toward the wailing baby and grabbed it by an ankle. He turned and walked back toward the truck, passing behind the side opposite from Jakob's view. The cries became a shriek until Jakob heard a thud. Abrupt quiet. The limp child flew over the side joining the stack of flying men.

"Are these the girls?"

Jakob and his sisters wheeled around to see a woman with hair cut short like a man's approach them. She spoke Hungarian, which gave the children a momentary sense of relief. Jakob looked at her face hoping to find kindness, but what he saw was the same grimness the pajama man possessed.

The pajama man understood her even though he did not speak Hungarian. He grabbed the two girls by their wrists and handed them over to the woman. Leah and Rachel resisted; the woman spoke to them in a gentle voice.

"It will be all right. We are going to a place where there are lots of children, all girls, just like you."

Jakob lunged to go as well, but the pajama man held him back. In the same, gentle voice, she spoke to him. "You are going to be with many other boys just like you. You'll see. You will have many playmates."

In less than half an hour, every person he knew—his mother, father and even his sisters—had been being pulled away. He screamed, "Nem!"

The pajama man seized him by the shoulders. "Nicht!"

Once more, fear of the man gripped Jakob, and he stopped his protest. The man grabbed his wrist and marched him at a pace his little legs could not match. They crossed back over the three sets of tracks toward the gate on the opposite side. The guard moved to challenge the man, but the pajama man uttered, "Mengele," and he opened the gate instead. Behind them, Jakob heard the railcars lurch and rumble. Farther up the tracks, a locomotive gave two short toots, and the railcars he and everyone he had ever known had arrived in rolled back the direction they had entered. To Jakob's amazement, the whole train passed through a long, brick building as if it were a tunnel.

Having passed the guard by several meters, Jakob and the pajama man were more or less by themselves on a dirt road that passed between two fence lines. The pajama man ceased dragging Jakob and settled into a pace Jakob could sustain. Intermittently placed lights cast light on the humming fence line running to the horizon. Jakob had never seen fences like those before. The fence posts reminded him of a picture his mother had once shown him that illustrated a story about a shepherd boy. The boy held a long staff with a crook at the top. His mother told him the staff was called a shepherd's crook. He didn't remember much of the story, only that the boy acted stupidly and a wolf ate him as a result.

The enveloping darkness caused panic to grip him and made him recoil from it all. He quickly composed himself when the pajama man turned to upbraid him. The man withheld his hand. Jakob was learning.

Jakob and the man walked on into the night with the humming fence line always about them. Less than an hour before, he had emerged from a railcar in which he had been locked for six days with so many other people; no one had had room to move about. And then, walking for what seemed kilometers, Jakob felt exhaustion to the point of pain as he had never before experienced.

The pair came to another gate and another guard. The pajama man uttered the name "Mengele" again, and the gate swung open. They were surrounded by woods on either side of the road. The only lights were on the other side of the wood line. The glow of two more chimneys not as large as the other two lent their red to the spectrum of light silhouetting the trees. Figures, people, moved among the trees. Jakob pulled to the center of the road. The pajama man clutched him tighter.

A slight breeze drove the smoke plume from the chimneys toward the ground, through the woods, and toward Jakob. It was the same odor he had smelled when the train had pulled into the place. It gagged him. Had he had anything in his stomach, he would have vomited. As it was, he just heaved painfully. He felt a greasy ash flake fall lightly on his cheek.

Still they walked. They passed an area where other pajama men and bald women unloaded trucks of suitcases and bundles under harshly bright white lights making the men and women look like ghosts. They made a mountain of suitcases taller than Jakob thought possible. And still Jakob walked.

Ahead, another building appeared. A queue of men spilled out the door. To Jakob's relief, it seemed to be their destination. He and the pajama man entered a different door. Another pajama man sat behind a small table at what appeared to be the head of the line running out the door. His escort pushed in front of the first man in the queue, spoke briefly to the man behind the table, pointed at Jakob, and disappeared.

The man behind the table looked at Jakob. "Do you know your name?"

Jakob blinked mutely.

"Your name. Do you know your name?"

He swallowed. "Jakob."

"Your surname."

Jakob stared blankly.

"Your last name. What is your last name?"

He stammered, "Jakob Bauer."

The man wrote the name on an index card. Another man appeared, took the card, and grabbed Jakob by the wrist. The man pulled Jakob into another room with several lines of naked men. They were wet and covered with a white powder giving them the appearance of spirits. The man led him to the head of one of the lines. He pushed a naked man out of the way and presented Jacob to the man behind the table.

"Mengele," was all he said.

The other man paused briefly, looked at Jakob, and motioned with his hand. Another pajama man jerked Jakob's left arm across the table and pulled up his sleeve past his elbow. The man behind the table placed some sort of instrument against his forearm.

The flash of pain was so intense that Jakob could not scream. He tried to recoil, but the other man held him with his weight pinning his arm flat against the table. A uniformed guard stepped forward but was not needed.

Jakob looked at his stinging arm. A ragged A-25160 stood out against the backdrop of scarlet flesh. Tears welled in his eyes, but he made no sound—not even a whimper. Jakob was learning.

Another man grabbed his wrist and led him out of the building. Jakob dreaded another long march in the dark. By then, the sky had turned a depressing shade of gray. Outside the building, men were assembling like soldiers.

His handler led him back the way he had come. Jakob found it a little easier to see. They passed the building with the suitcase mountain. There were many more people. They swarmed at the base of the mountain like locusts consuming it.

Again, Jakob passed the little wood. The fire above the buildings on the other side glowed brighter even though day was breaking. *Where are the people, those dark figures I saw earlier? Perhaps they were ghosts after all.*

The lights above the fence lines blinked off in sections as the brightening sky made the morning mist visible. Jakob saw row upon row of gray-brown huts out of which swarms of pajama men poured and formed lines. The noise rose in proportion to the reddening of the morning sky. Shouts, curses, dogs barking. A gunshot in the distance. A train's whistle. It was a city. A very strange city.

Jakob's arm, feeling as if it were ablaze, distracted him from the ache in his little legs. His escort diverted from the path Jakob had come by earlier. He hoped he was near to wherever he was being taken. Out of some of the gray-brown buildings, several pajama men carried naked men by their arms and legs and tossed them onto carts just as he had seen by the railcars.

They approached the next-to-last building in the row and finally stopped. Children—boys—came stumbling out. They were of all ages and heights and were all dressed differently—regular clothes, not the drab, striped pajamas. A tall, young man led them. The man holding Jakob's wrist let go with a tug toward the young man and handed the tall, young man an index card.

"From last night's transport."

Jakob looked up at the new interloper in his life. For the first time since arriving, he recognized compassion.

"Hello. I'm Zvi Spiegel. They call me the Zwillingsvater. That means the twins' father," the young man said, speaking as if he were much older. "So you are Jakob Bauer."

Jakob nodded and extended his hand to shake as he had been taught but said nothing. Zwillingsvater took his hand and gently shook it. It was early morning, but Jakob had been awake for several hours. He had walked for what seemed like ten kilometers through the night in this strangest of places. At some point, he had been tattooed. He was hungry and exhausted to the point of delirium, but above all, he was confused. He rubbed his arm making it an even angrier red.

Zwillingsvater took Jakob's hand and led him to eat breakfast with the other boys. Breakfast wasn't much more that a thin, greasy soup, but it was more than Jakob had had in days. He finished it and wiped the interior of the bowl with a sliver of stale bread. He craved more, but none was to be had.

The bowls were collected, and the company of boys hustled about cleaning and straightening. Unfamiliarity with the routine, sleep deprivation, and sheer exhaustion combined to immobilize Jakob. With the pangs of hunger blunted, Jakob's body could muster no effort for anything other than sleep. He slumped in a corner and immediately fell unconscious. The other boys stopped aghast.

"Jakob! Jakob! You must wake up!" Zwillingsvater said. He lightly slapped Jacob's cheeks. "You must remain awake a little longer."

Jakob did wake although even more bewildered. He stared at his tormentor.

"Jakob, you must stay awake. The doctor will be here soon. You must be awake."

There was a commotion in the adjacent room, and the other boys scurried about as they lined up in front of the bunkbeds. Zwillingsvater held Jakob up as the doctor entered the room.

"What do we have here?"

"He is a new arrival from last night. He just arrived less than an hour ago, Herr Doktor." Zwillingsvater lowered Jakob to stand on his own.

The doctor leaned over to observe the boy closer. Jakob recognized the doctor as the one who had spoken to his mother at the train. Cupping the boy's chin in his hand, he said, "Ahh yes. The Mozart lover."

Jakob brightened a little at the recognition.

Still holding the boy's chin, he said, "Such blue eyes! Gold hair! So clever as to recognize Mozart! You Hungarians have a word for a person such as yourself. Tudos. Do you know what that means?"

Jakob shook his head.

"It means savant, a very intelligent person. Are you a tudos, my little friend?"

Jakob, unsure whether to answer or not, chose to say, "Tudos? Yes."

Mengele studied the boy's features intently. "Indeed you may be." He turned to Spiegel, the Zwillingsvater. "You've taken care of him?"

"Yes, Herr Doktor. He just ate. He is very tired though. He has been awake quite some time." Spiegel was careful not to make the conclusion for the doctor that the boy needed to sleep.

The doctor took note of Jakob's bleary eyes. "Get him settled, and let him sleep. This one is special."

"Yes, Doctor Mengele."

"Have the rest taken to the clinic for blood work."

"Yes, Herr Doktor."

Before exiting the barracks, the doctor handed Jakob a candy wrapped in wax paper. Jakob clutched it in his small fist.

JUNE 17, 1944, AFTERNOON

Jakob broke his slumber. He sat up disoriented and dazed. He looked about the bleak barracks. The drab surroundings gave him no clues as to where he was. From outside came the noises of what sounded like a city—trains rumbling along tooting their whistles, people shouting, dogs barking, babies wailing.

Where am I? he wondered. He looked at his hand and found that the candy, still in its wrapper, had softened by the warmth of his hand. He started to unwrap it, but a searing pain in his arm caused him to drop the candy as he let out a yelp. He looked with terror at his swollen, inflamed arm. It was from the thing those men had done to him in the night. He sobbed.

An arm wrapping around his shoulder caused him to completely break down and sob. He heard a gentle voice, a man's voice, a consoling voice. "It'll be all right. Here, let me put this salve on it."

Jakob looked up and saw the young man who had taken him in from the pajama man. This man was thin, lanky, dark haired. He wore regular clothes with a vest. Jakob extended his throbbing arm to him instinctively knowing that the man would help him.

The man cleaned the wound as best he could, applied a thin layer of salve, and wrapped it in a cloth bandage. "There you go. It will be better in a day or two," he said, smiling. "Do you remember me from this morning? I'm Zvi Spiegel, Zwillingsvater."

Jakob nodded as he wiped tears from his eyes.

Zwillingsvater picked up the candy still in its wrapper and handed it to Jakob. "You better eat this before the others return."

Jakob nodded again and wrestled the wrapper from the sticky treat.

Zwillingsvater patted the boy on the knee and stood. "Would you like to come outside with me? The sun will be good for you."

Sheepishly, Jakob nodded and slid from the bunk to the floor. He took Zwillingsvater's offered hand, and they walked outside. The brilliance of light blinded Jakob, but he adjusted soon enough.

"I need you to wake up, Jakob. I have some papers I need to fill out for the doctor. We'll walk around for a few minutes, and you can help me heat some water for the wash. We'll come back inside in a little while," Zwillingsvater explained patiently to the child.

Zwillingsvater started a small fire with a few chunks of wood. The fire was directly under a large basin of gray water. Once the fire was going on its own, they walked about. He strictly warned Jakob to stay well clear of the fence. Zwillingsvater pointed out an adjacent section of the camp that housed whole families of Roma, Gypsies. A number of children scurried about. Even from a distance of fifty meters, Jakob saw terrible sores on some children's faces. One dark-haired boy about the same age as Jakob smiled, waved, and walked toward the edge of the road that separated them. No fence stood between them, but Zwillingsvater told Jakob that he was not under any circumstances to cross the dirt road.

Though the rail yard was the most prominent feature in the vicinity, Zwillingsvater made no mention of it though it was just a few meters from where they stood. It was empty of trains at that moment, but a crew of pajama men gathered up scraps of clothing and other debris. At the near end of the tracks was a large redbrick building with a square chimney. Jakob recognized it from the night before. Only thin wisps of smoke drifted from it at the moment—none of the angry red glare of the night before. Just a few meters to the side of that building was another one just like it. It was directly behind his barracks. It too seemed idle like a locomotive waiting to move.

Jakob heard the shrill tweet of a locomotive in the distance beyond the large building with the tower at the other end of the tracks. A moment later, a loud whirring noise started up at one of the buildings with the chimneys. The wisp of smoke drifting skyward shot up with a whoosh. Jakob felt a wave of fear. He stepped back behind Zwillingsvater's legs. Just as the whining noise reached a sustained pitch, the other building with the square chimney came alive too. Soon, its whine came to a crescendo and leveled off at the same high pitch as the first building. To Jakob, it was as if two giants had awakened.

"Jakob, let's go back inside and answer some questions for the doctor. You seem to be well awake now," Zwillingsvater smiled and directed the boy toward the barracks.

Inside at a small table near the front door, Jakob sat nibbling on a piece of bread crust Zwillingsvater had given him. Zwillingsvater scribbled for a moment on a form.

"Jakob, do you know your birthday?"

"May 5, 1940."

"Very good! Do you know your father's name?"

"Isaak Bauer."

"And your mother?"

"Ilsa Woeffel Bauer."

"That's very good indeed. How does such a young boy know his mother's maiden name?"

Jakob stared blankly at Zwillingsvater. He had always known it. His parents had entertained him and his sisters with many stories of their youths. Stories about their grandparents whom they had never met. Stories about fantastic places they had traveled.

"You are quite a clever boy, Jakob Bauer," Zwillingsvater observed in a tone tinged with amazement and without any trace of patronization.

The boy said nothing.

"Doctor Mengele will be back sometime this afternoon. He will want to talk to you and ask you more questions. I will be there to help you understand the doctor." Zwillingsvater paused. "Jakob, it is very important that you answer all the doctor's questions as best you can. You must not provoke him in any way. Show him how smart you are. He really likes boys who are as clever as you are."

Jakob nodded.

"What did the doctor mean when he called you 'Mozart lover' this morning? Do you remember?"

"The music that was playing by the train. It was Mozart."

"Good, good. When the doctor speaks to you, tell him you like Mozart. The doctor likes Mozart as well."

He patted the boy's head, collected the forms, placed them squarely on the clipboard, and hung it on a nail over the table. He turned to exit and motioned for Jakob to follow. Once outside, he checked the temperature of the washbasin of linens and clothes and stirred them with a board shaped like a paddle. The clothes all looked dull and gray to Jakob.

Although he never strayed too far from Zwillingsvater's side, Jakob did look about at his new surroundings. All the fences were strung on shepherd's crook posts with white porcelain knobs. He had seen them the night before on his trek to that place, but in the daylight, he saw they stretched to the horizon in all directions. Just beyond the closest fence was the railroad. That was of the utmost interest to Jakob.

He couldn't see the locomotive behind the row of railcars, but Jakob followed the smoke from its stack it as it chuffed up the tracks. When it reached the long brick building with the tower in its center, it stopped. A short toot from its whistle preceded its moving again. The railcars before him jerked with a great clatter all along the line. That was Jakob's favorite thing to see in the rail yards his father had shown him.

Slowly, the whole line of boxcars rolled toward the large building at the far end of the tracks. Jakob saw them pass through the opening in the building just as he had seen the night before. As the end of the train passed, another line of boxcars sat on the next track over. Pajama men were scurrying about loading all manner of items onto trucks. He had seen that activity the night before, but it looked so different in daylight.

In the tiny openings at the upper corners of the boxcars, Jakob saw faces and hands moving. A line of soldiers walked down the line of cars with one stopping at every door. Some of the soldiers had large brown dogs that looked like the wolves he had seen in the story about the little shepherd boy. Jakob was transfixed with what was happening before him just a few meters away. It occurred to him that there was no music.

He felt the arm about his shoulder again, this time firmer as it turned him away from the tracks. "Jakob, why don't you come help me with this heavy laundry. I need help hanging it, and you are so strong." Zwillingsvater led Jakob away from the tracks and in between two barracks to where a basin with heavy, wet laundry sat. Several wires spanned the two structures. Jakob yielded without a fuss. He was happy to show Zwillingsvater how strong he was.

A little later, a truck pulled up to the barracks and stopped. From the back jumped several boys who were older than Jakob. They reached back into the truck and helped several younger boys climb down. To Jakob's amazement, they were all twins. For all of his four short years, people had always made a fuss over Jakob and his sisters even in the ghetto. He saw a dozen or more twins and thought that it was indeed a special place.

Jakob was excited to see that some of the boys were not much older than he was, but his excitement faded as he noticed their listlessness. The boys plodded toward the barracks. Some were rubbing their arms. As they passed, Jakob saw the bruises at the crooks of their elbows that contrasted prominently with the unnatural pallor of their skin. Zwillingsvater stood beside him and counted as they filed past. As the last one entered the barracks, Zwillingsvater followed the boys into the barracks leaving Jakob alone.

Not knowing what to do, Jakob stood for a moment at the door before deciding not to go in. He was drawn to the trains once again and edged in the direction of the tracks to watch the commotion. So many things were happening just before his eyes. He didn't know where to look. It was just like what he had seen the night before, but he was then on the outside looking in.

He saw women crying after their husbands and children, a man in uniform savaging a man in an overcoat, two lines of people forming along the tracks. And at the head of the lines were two men in gray-green uniforms, not the ones he had seen the night before, pointing to the left and right. As they passed before these two uniformed men, the people in the lines turned toward the way they had been directed. Jakob saw a pattern develop. Old men, women, and children went one way. Young men went the other. Jakob was transfixed by what was happening right before him.

"Spiegel! Spiegel! Get out here!"

The shouts startled Jakob and broke his daze. He whirled about to the see the doctor who had given him the candy that morning. Spiegel tore from the building to stand before the doctor, head bowed and cap removed.

"Why is this boy out here alone?" The doctor raised his hand to strike Zwillingsvater but withheld the blow. His face was beet red, and he breathed through clenched teeth. Zwillingsvater never raised his head or spoke.

Jakob stood paralyzed. His heart pounded in his chest.

"Have him in my office in five minutes!" The doctor stormed off toward the adjacent building.

Zwillingsvater took the boy's hand and firmly led him toward the barracks with the other boys. Jakob felt all their eyes on him as he entered. Nothing was said, but Jakob was doubly terrified. Without fully comprehending what had just occurred, he felt the guilt of responsibility. His eyes welled with tears.

"It's all right, Jakob. It will be all right. Nothing really happened. Dr. Mengele just got angry."

Jakob broke down and sobbed. "I don't want you to be hurt!" he wailed.

"It's all right, isn't it, boys?" Zwillingsvater turned and enlisted the help of the other boys, who all chimed in with encouragement. Jakob calmed down a little.

"Remember what we talked about earlier today? You must answer the doctor when he talks to you. You must not be afraid. He won't hurt you. He was upset at me because he thought I had let you be in danger. I'm sorry. Please forgive me."

Jakob sniffled and hugged Zwillingsvater.

"You must be a big boy right now, Jakob. You must be strong and talk to Dr. Mengele so he won't be mad at me again. Do you understand?"

Jakob nodded and composed himself as if he truly did understand. Zwillingsvater wiped the boy's face with a wet cloth and combed his yellow hair. He took the clipboard from the nail, grabbed the boy's hand, and headed out the door with him.

Jakob stood shaking at the doorway of the adjacent building as Zwillingsvater knocked. From within and over music being played came, "Enter!"

Zwillingsvater pushed the door open and led Jakob to stand before the doctor, who was in a white coat. Without a word, he handed the doctor the clipboard. He gave Jakob an almost imperceptible pat on the shoulder. The doctor remained at his desk without looking up. A minute passed. Then another.

"Schubert," Jakob said.

The doctor looked up. "What did you say?"

Spiegel froze.

Jakob pointed at the phonograph. "Schubert."

Mengele set his pen down and studied the boy. Another minute passed. The doctor's eyes narrowed as if he were contemplating something. "Did he tell you to say that?"

Spiegel translated the question from German into Hungarian concluding with pointing to himself.

Jakob shook his head. The doctor stood, looked at Spiegel, and then walked over to the phonograph. He sorted through a short stack of records until he came to one in particular and placed it on the turntable. He carefully placed the needle on the groove. A bold measure thundered from the box. *Da da da daaaa!* "Do you recognize this?"

Before Spiegel could translate, Jakob said. "Beethoven. I like Mozart." He exchanged eye contact with Zwillingsvater.

After hearing the translation, the doctor said, "Wunderbar! I like Mozart as well!"

Mengele crossed back over toward his desk to get the clipboard. He looked at it momentarily. "Your name is Jakob? You are how old?"

Jakob held up three fingers and his thumb before extending his hand to shake.

Mengele took the boy's hand and shook it vigorously. "Indeed you are. Tell me, young Jakob, do you know where your mother was from?"

Recalling his mother's stories of her girlhood, he said, "Joachimstal."

"Joachimstal? In Czechoslovakia?"

Jakob nodded.

Mengele scratched furiously at his notes. Jakob and Spiegel stood patiently.

"Tell me, Jakob, do you know anything about your mother's parents?"

Jakob nodded.

"Did they live in Joachimstal?"

Jakob shook his head.

"They didn't? Where did they live?"

"Deutschland."

"They were Germans?"

Jakob nodded. "Anya left Germany and went to work at a spa when she was eighteen and met Papa. Then they got married and lived happily ever after in Hungary, where Papa lived."

Mengele turned to Spiegel for the translation. "Anya?"

"His mother worked at a spa, met his father, and they married and settled in Hungary."

Through Spiegel, Mengele asked, "You know what a spa is?"

Jakob recalled his image of a spa as a big beautiful building with hundreds of white, gleaming bathtubs. It made no sense to him, but it was how his mother had described it to him when he had inquired. "A big building with lots of bathtubs."

Upon hearing the translation, Mengele roared with laughter. He observed the boy. "How is it you know so much? You are such a small boy."

Jakob had no answer and so made no reply.

The doctor took Jakob's bandaged arm in his hand and unwound the dressing. Drawing a light over the inflamed area, he examined it closely. "You dressed this?" he asked Spiegel.

Spiegel braced himself. "Yes, Herr Doktor."

"Good." He reached in a drawer and retrieved a small tube of ointment and some clean gauze. "Here. Use this in the future. I do not want that infected. Do you hear me?"

"Yes, Herr Doktor."

Mengele wrote out a long note and handed it to Spiegel. "I have transport duties tomorrow morning and will not be able to be here in the morning. Have him at the clinic tomorrow at one o'clock. I will have my auto sent around. These are instruction for extra rations from the kitchen. And some soap to wash that tattoo." Mengele handed Spiegel a paper.

Hesitantly, Spiegel asked, "Should I accompany the boy?"

Mengele looked at him for what felt like a minute before he tersely said, "No. Just have him ready. Now take care of him." He pulled another candy from his pocket and handed it to Jakob.

Zwillingsvater put his hands on the boy's shoulder and guided him out the door. Once outside and out of earshot, he said, "You did very well, Jakob. Very well! Eat your candy."

CHAPTER 4

JUNE 18, 1944

The gauzy gray of morning light found Jakob stirring to life with the other boys of his barracks. Zwillingsvater had introduced him around the evening before. Of all the pairs of twins, only one pair was near his age. The rest were six, seven, perhaps nine. A few were even older, in their early teens. They showed the least interest of all in Jakob. All the twin pairs seemed to associate almost exclusively with each other. Zwillingsvater did his best to help Jakob fit in.

The first order of business at Zwillingsvater's insistence was to wash themselves. On that morning, that meant their entire bodies. A bar of coarse soap had appeared mysteriously overnight. They all lathered up while Zwillingsvater poured water over their heads to rinse. He had to caution them not to let their excitement be heard outside. Nothing good would come from piquing the attention of guards, the kapos, even if the boys were Mengele's pets.

There were no towels to dry themselves, but that did little to dampen the boys' spirits. The rising warmth of the summer morning had them dry soon enough. Zwillingsvater was careful to wash Jakob and in particular his wound. Afterward, he dressed it properly with the new ointment and a clean bandage. The swelling had receded, but it itched Jakob. Like a mother, Zwillingsvater sternly cautioned him not to scratch or rub it if he didn't want it to get infected. Jakob obeyed—when he was watched.

Breakfast came next, and the boys were ignited again in their enthusiasm. There were distinctively a few more vegetables and small bits of meat in the usually thin soup. Once again, Zwillingsvater admonished them to celebrate silently. An extra wedge of bread with something resembling butter was in Jakob's bowl.

The morning meal did not last very long; the boys, at the edge of hunger, seldom lingered over their food. The bowls were cleared and rinsed as clean as possible in boiling hot water. Without dish soap, it was the best Zwillingsvater could manage to help prevent dysentery, a condition of epidemic proportions in most of the camp. The smell of it contributed a significant portion of the effluvia pervading the prisoners' world.

The boys not engaged in rendering the metal bowls clean scurried about sweeping, dusting, and straightening. Jakob joined in by straightening his bed. Calling it a bed was a generous description. In reality, it was nothing more than a deep shelf, one of three stacked atop each other.

"Doctor Mengele will not be joining us this morning, so we'll work on our reading. If you're very diligent, we'll go outside for some football later."

A smattering of moans bounced about the group.

"Don't complain. You are the only ones allowed this privilege," Zwillingsvater admonished them gently.

Their reading material consisted of discarded cartons, old newspapers, and one dog-eared book. Zwillingsvater turned to the oldest pair in the room to help younger pairs read aloud the various texts. Zwillingsvater attended to the very young, a subgroup comprising Jakob and a pair of six-year-old twins. They were to learn the alphabet one letter at a time.

The twins pronounced each letter as they scratched them out on the concrete floor with a rock. Jakob said nothing but followed what was being said and done.

"Jakob, would you like to try?" Zwillingsvater asked.

"*A, B, C, D, E, F …*" Jakob responded, rattling off all the letters.

"That's very good, Jakob." Zwillingsvater reached for a section of old newspaper from the older group and handed it Jakob. "Can you read this?"

Jakob read aloud an article in Hungarian about Miklos Horthy, Regent of Hungary. He stumbled over a few difficult words, but he sounded them out syllable by syllable and pressed on to finish the article. After completing the text, he handed the newspaper back to Zwillingsvater. Drawn to the demonstration taking place in their grim little world, the older boys ceased their studies and watched the new boy perform his feat.

"All right. Everyone back to your studies," Zwillingsvater said to them. "Jakob, do you understand what you just read?"

"Regent Horthy welcomed back the Fifty-Sixth Infantry Regiment from the war with the Bolsheviks," Jakob replied matter-of-factly.

"Yes, that's correct."

Zwillingsvater rose and walked to the door to see if the transport train had left. He wanted to shield the boys from the drama that played out with each transport and each selection. As good as his intentions were, the boys, and even Jakob, who had been there for only slightly more than a day, knew what was occurring.

The train readied to pull away from the selection ramp. Only the Kanada prisoners remained gathering the spoils left by the previous transport. Kanada was the part of the camp that processed the belongings brought to Auschwitz by the unsuspecting prisoners. The Nazis made great enterprise of the loot—clothing, shoes, cookware, gold teeth, everything. Even hair was bundled and sent to feed the war machine. Nothing was wasted.

Zwillingsvater looked at the columns of smoke rising from the chimney of Crematoria II and III and noted that the slight morning breeze from the south and east carried the smoke away from their barracks. The boys were able to take advantage of the favorable conditions and play outside.

A football made of rags was produced from a bin and carried outside with youthful exuberance. Two teams quickly formed, and they included the six-year-olds. Though it was football, it better resembled a scrum kicking a ball in all directions with all players in wild pursuit, all except Jakob. He chose to observe. Zwillingsvater left him alone. He was new to that, and Zwillingsvater instinctively knew Jakob needed time to comprehend his new reality regardless of his obvious intelligence. He was still just a four-year-old boy having been stripped of almost everything and everyone he had known.

As the older boys played, Zwillingsvater continued to contemplate his newest ward. Paramount to all such musings regarding each of the boys was his central question, *How best can I help this one survive?*

The two most blatant traits of Jakob were his intelligence and his Aryan features. He had seen Mengele show favoritism before to boys who displayed uncommon intelligence. Mengele's errand boy, Marc Berkowitz, was a case in point. It would be even more of an advantage for Jakob if he learned to speak German. Zwillingsvater resolved to teach him some rudimentary phrases. Given his Nordic looks, Jakob's speaking German could be the straw that tipped the balance in his favor.

Zwillingsvater saw Jakob's attention had drifted from the game and the other boys to the Roma families just a few meters across the dirt road from their barracks. Mothers, fathers, grandparents, and even children lay about in the sun watching the twins' football game. A dark-haired boy broke away from his family and walked to the edge of the road to wave at Jakob. A couple of panicked adults with the same dark hair and features dragged the boy away. Jakob waved back, but the boy did not see that.

The shrill tweet of another transport train announced its approach. Zwillingsvater had never seen so many transports as he had seen in the last four or five weeks. He pulled out the pocket watch Mengele had provided him. It was past noon, and the boys had been at play for a little more than an hour. Exercise was good for them physically and mentally, but he knew the meager rations and the constant blood sampling were taking a toll on their endurance and ability to fight off infections.

"All right boys, time to return for your afternoon studies." They complied without protest; he suspected they were near their limits. "Jakob, time to get ready to see the doctor."

Jakob continued watching the Roma for a bit before turning back to the barracks. Zwillingsvater stood at the door until all the boys made their way inside. He told one of the two oldest boys to start the multiplication table drills while the other was to help the younger ones with their counting.

Zwillingsvater stopped Jakob at the door. "I want to change your dressing before Dr. Mengele sends his car around to pick you up."

Jakob yielded up his arm but said nothing. The inflammation was nearly gone. Zwillingsvater debated leaving it undressed, but he decided to let Mengele make that decision. He was sure to check it. Other than checking the bandage, Zwillingsvater wanted to coach Jacob some before his appointment with the doctor.

"Jakob, your reading skills are quite remarkable. Dr. Mengele really likes boys who can read. When you are in his office, see if you can find something to read aloud. Anything. A sign on the wall, a paper on the desk—anything." Then it occurred to Zwillingsvater that everything would be in German rather than Hungarian. He tore a page from the one book in the barracks, a poem, and stuffed it in Jakob's pocket. "Here, read this."

Again, the boy said nothing. Though Jakob was mute, Zwillingsvater perceived he assimilated all of what was being said. Something in the boy's robin's egg blue eyes suggested uncommon comprehension.

"I want you to learn a few things to say in German for the doctor. If he gives something, say a candy, say 'Danke.' That means 'Thank you.' When you leave, say, 'Auf Wiedersehen, Herr Doktor.'"

Jakob nodded. Zwillingsvater wished he had had more time to teach him a few more phrases, but it was nearing one o'clock. He washed Jakob's face again, wetted his hair, and combed it.

A few minutes after one, a car with a big red cross on the side pulled up to the barracks. Zwillingsvater escorted Jakob out to the car and opened the door for him to climb in. The driver, a surly kapo assigned to the Sonderkommandos housed in Crematorium IV, leaned over and told Zwillingsvater to get in as well.

Zwillingsvater protested, but the driver cut him off. "Are you Spiegel? If so, get in. Mengele wants you to come along. Get in or I'll leave you here and let you explain to the good doctor why you didn't come."

Zwillingsvater climbed in as quickly as possible. The other boys would have to do without him for a while. The car took off creating a cloud of dust before the door was shut causing Zwillingsvater to fall into the seat.

The car slowed at three gates where the driver leaned his head out and shouted, "Mengele!" They didn't have to come to complete stops as the guards were so quick to open the gates. A short, two-kilometer drive and they were at another facility surrounded by barbwire hung on porcelain knobs.

That time, the car stopped at a gate with a black and white–striped guard box and a large rail gate that stretched across the drive. An iron span arched overhead.

Zwillingsvater watched Jakob sounding out the words imbedded on the arch, "Ar ... beit ... Macht ... Frei. Arbeit Macht Frei." Jakob looked to Zwillingsvater for an explanation.

"Work Makes You Free."

The driver uttered the magic name again, and the gate lifted allowing the car to pass. The place looked different to Jakob. He saw substantial buildings of redbrick and even trees with white bark. The same pajama men plodded about as in the other place all with the same grim faces. He saw more soldiers.

The car drove forward a short distance and turned right before stopping at the next-to-last building on the narrow street. Block 10 read a sign above a door. Zwillingsvater got out and assisted Jakob from the car, which sped off almost before they were clear of it. Holding each other's hand, they climbed the few steps to the entryway.

The building they were entering was connected to the adjacent building by a high wall with a large gate in the middle. Zwillingsvater tried not to look at the other building, Block 11. Other than the crematoria, Block 11 was the most feared building in the entire world of Auschwitz. Prisoners knew it as the punishment block. Death was mercifully quick in the crematoria. Not so in Block 11.

Inside, a corridor with rooms off to each side. Zwillingsvater went to the second door on the left, knocked, and waited for a reply.

"Enter."

Zwillingsvater opened the door allowing Jakob to enter ahead of him. Mengele sat at a desk scribbling notes on a chart. A young girl about eight years old stood naked at the side of his desk. She tried covering herself as best she could.

"In a moment," was all the doctor said without looking up.

He took a syringe off his desk and squeezed a jet of liquid from it to get the bubble of air out. He grasped the girl's frail arm and injected the contents into it. She flinched and teared up but made no sound. The doctor pointed toward the door to the adjacent room. Zwillingsvater saw another girl with exactly the same features and just as naked as the girl just injected. *Her twin,* he surmised.

Mengele swung about and gave his attention to Jakob. "Ahh, my music lover!"

"You wanted me as well, Herr Doktor?"

"Yes, Spiegel. Your German is better than Berkowitz's, and he's just a kid. I may need a little more maturity in translating. I want to talk to this young fellow." He cupped his hand under Jakob's chin and squeezed affectionately.

Mengele rose from his desk and crossed the hallway to a larger room that had a number of exam tables, scales, wall charts, medicine cabinets, and all manner of other examination equipment. Seated on a table were Leah and Rachel. At the sight of his sisters, Zwillingsvater saw

Jakob show real emotion for the first time. His excitement was quickly tempered. They were naked as the other girl had been.

"Have him remove his clothing."

In Hungarian, Zwillingsvater said, "Jakob, the doctor needs you remove your clothes as well."

Jakob recoiled. Zwillingsvater knelt and in an almost inaudible tone said, "It will be all right. No one will see you except the doctor." Zwillingsvater locked eyes with the boy hoping to convey to him how desperately important it was for him to comply. And Zwillingsvater saw the same intense comprehension in Jakob he had seen earlier that morning. The boy understood and allowed Zwillingsvater to help him undress. Zwillingsvater drew Jakob's attention to a large mural of Snow White and the Seven Dwarves to distract the boy from his shame.

Mengele began with an eye chart made up of every imaginable shade of eye color. One tab was for brown eyes. Another for green. The blue eye card was the one being closely compared to the three children. Zwillingsvater saw that the two girls' eyes were somewhere in the middle of the range. Jakob's eyes, however, were well to one end of the blue spectrum. That obviously impressed Mengele.

Zwillingsvater felt awkward standing in the middle of the room, so he retreated to the near wall and made himself as inconspicuous as possible. The doctor no longer talked to the children but more or less to himself. A nurse entered the room to take notes; she was a Hungarian Jew who was fluent in German; she had been pulled from one of the transports. Zwillingsvater saw that she struggled to hear the doctor's mutterings.

The children's hair was the next item to be categorized. Mengele held a long paddle with locks of various shades of hair next to each child's head. He moved the paddle back and forth until he located the perfect match for each child's hair. Again, the girls' hair fell midrange of the preferred Aryan hair trait while Jakob's hair matched the samples near the end of the spectrum of color.

"Marvelous," Zwillingsvater heard Mengele murmur.

The examination next included weighing the three and measuring their height. Zwillingsvater thought it odd that Mengele hadn't done that first, but he suspected the doctor was so eager to evaluate the obvious Aryan traits that he couldn't wait to do that.

The rest of the afternoon included more measurements of all the triplets' body features with large pincer-like calipers and other devices.

The nurse faithfully transcribed the doctor's every word; Zwillingsvater's translation services were not required. He kept time by looking at a wall clock in the next room; he dared not look at the pocket watch.

A little after three, Mengele concluded his evaluation and said, "Send Berkowitz to tell Gottliebova to go to the boys' barracks tomorrow before she goes to the Roma camp and have her paint this boy. Tell her I particularly want his eyes captured."

"Yes Doctor." The nurse disappeared to type up the copious notes.

To the children, he said, "Get dressed."

Hearing Zwillingsvater's interpretation, they were more than happy to comply.

He told Spiegel, "Take them back to Birkenau." He left the room.

"Forgive me, Herr Doktor, but I will need a pass."

Visibly irritated, Mengele scratched out the form and threw it in Spiegel's face. Before he reached the door, he heard a child's strong voice behind him. "Auf Wiedersehen, Herr Doktor. Arbeit macht frei."

Mengele wheeled about and saw Jakob waving at him. "Auf Wiedersehen, my intelligentsia!" He cupped and squeezed the boy's chin. From his pocket, he pulled a candy and handed it to the boy. He left.

Zwillingsvater knelt beside Jakob and asked him to introduce him to his sisters. He reasoned they would trust him more and hence be more cooperative if they felt Jakob trusted him. The two girls nodded, looked up at Zwillingsvater, and extended their small hands to him.

Zwillingsvater left Block 10 with his three charges. Never had he been allowed to leave a secure area without a guard or escort. He gathered his nerve as he approached the gate to test the weight of Mengele's signature. He must not appear nervous.

The guard took the pass from his hand and examined it closely. He looked at the three children holding hands. "Where are you taking these children?"

"Back to their barracks in Birkenau."

The private called for the officer of the watch to come to the door. Momentarily, a lieutenant appeared at the guard shack. "What is it?"

"This Jew has a pass to take these children to Birkenau."

The lieutenant looked at the pass trying to decipher the signature. "Whose signature is this?"

"Doctor Mengele's. These children are in his custody," Zwillingsvater explained, trying to project confidence.

The moment was suspended in time as the officer inspected the pass again. Jakob let his sisters' hands go and fished the candy treat from his pocket. He stepped forward showing the officer his prize.

Zwillingsvater's head felt as it were about to explode but said nothing; he looked only at the officer for his reaction.

He said brusquely, "Let them pass."

As they passed beneath the gate, Zwillingsvater heard the lieutenant ask the private, "Who else gives candies to little Jews?"

It was two kilometers back to Birkenau, Auschwitz's largest camp, the one designed from the ground up for industrial-scale murder. While in Mengele's service, Zwillingsvater had been to most of the camp's sections. Birkenau was an immense factory spread out over more than two square kilometers and was expanding.

Zwillingsvater relished the opportunity to walk outside the wire without escort though he knew they could be stopped at any moment. Not having to wear the striped prison garb of the other inmates helped deflect some of the attention from them. The three children were happy to be together for the afternoon even if it required sitting through the ordeal of physical examinations.

Jakob pulled the poem from his pocket and showed it to Zwillingsvater.

"Oh yes. You didn't have an opportunity to read it, did you? It was in your pocket while you were ... Never mind though. I think the doctor was quite impressed all the same. Save it for another time to read to the doctor," said Zwillingsvater.

Jakob tucked it back into his pocket.

About half an hour later, the tiny group approached the large building that cars and trains passed through. Zwillingsvater showed his pass to the sentry on duty and was allowed to pass unchallenged. He supposed the guard figured no one would break into such a place.

As they passed through the gate, another fear swept over Zwillingsvater. A transport sat on the tracks ahead of them. He was afraid that he and the children would get swept up in the selection. The guards and kapos were at their most brutal during the selections of the new transport arrivals. Pass or no pass, they would not listen. He slowed their gait to see how far along into the process the selection had proceeded. At the far end of the ramp, he could not see any of the new arrivals heading for either Crematorium II or III. That could mean they were headed to Crematoria IV and V, or it could be that they had not yet started the selections. In that case, the guards and kapos would be around for another half an hour or so. Then to his relief, he saw the locomotive heading back up the ramp to couple itself to the transport so it could pull it out of the selection yard. The soldiers would be gone soon, and they could then pass.

Oblivious to Zwillingsvater's concerns regarding their safety, Jakob was awestruck by the sheer size of his new world. Looking along the tracks toward the far end to the buildings with the glowing chimneys, they seemed tiny in scale, almost indiscernible to him. The ubiquitous fence lines ran to infinity. All along both sides of the rail line were row upon row of bleak, brown barracks that were little more than shacks. The end of each row was beyond the horizon. Jakob understood that this place was an infinite world. Infinitely large. Infinitely cruel.

The women's camp, where his sisters' barracks was, was on their left as they walked along the camp road. Jakob's attention was drawn to the shaved heads of the women. Only their shabby gray dresses gave any clue that they were indeed women. They all plodded about as grimly as the men did. *Is my mother among them?*

The men's camp lay to their right beyond the three railroad tracks. The locomotive passed them on the nearest track and soon coupled to the transport. In a few minutes more, the cars of the transport jerked as they exited the camp to make room for the next transport of four or five thousand souls.

Zwillingsvater led the triplets into the women's camp easily enough and headed toward Mengele's barracks for twin girls. While they were passing a work crew of women digging a drainage ditch, one female inmate dropped her pick and ran toward them shouting, "Kinder! Where are all our children? Have you seen my daughters?"

Jakob watched in terror as a large wolflike dog from the other end of the work crew charged and fell upon the woman ripping at her neck and face. Her scream turned into a gurgle as blood spurted from her neck. A kapo wielding a short club ran up and bludgeoned the woman. The woman soon lay motionless. The kapo summoned two women from the work crew to take the body away.

Zwillingsvater tried to shield the children from the ghastly scene but was impotent to do so. It all had happened so quickly and almost at their feet. Rachel and Leah cried inconsolably. Jakob withdrew quietly behind

Zwillingsvater as he quickly got them away from the area. Eventually, the children calmed down.

Jakob watched as Zwillingsvater delivered the girls to the woman in charge of the barracks. She seemed an unpleasant woman—brusque and scowling at his sisters, who had no protectorate like Zwillingsvater. They would largely be left to their own devices. He could not help them.

Later that evening, as the boys' barracks was ready for sleep, Zwillingsvater came to Jakob's bedside. "Are you all right?"

Jakob wiped tears from his eyes and nodded. He soon succumbed to the exhaustion of the day.

CHAPTER 5

MARCH 20, 2019, AFTERNOON

Malone stood with Simmons in the small front office of the makeshift morgue. Through the front window, she saw a dark, official-looking sedan pull up. Two men got out and entered the front door. The two women stopped talking and closed their notes before going to greet the two men.

"Alex Lamar, public affairs director for Governor Stevenson." The young man extended his hand to Simmons and Malone. A deputy sat behind the desk, and another man who had arrived with Lamar—presumably security—stood to one side. Simmons and Malone introduced themselves and their respective agencies.

"Is there somewhere we can talk privately?"

Simmons pushed open the door to the back of the garage. "Sure. This way."

"I ... I ..." Lamar stammered thinking she was leading him into where the bodies lay motionless on the makeshift tables.

"There's a dressing room we can use just inside here." Simmons was careful not to display anything other than the highest level of professionalism.

Malone recognized immediately Simmons's gambit—get the upper hand on this interfering little bureaucratic wonk. She really needed to find a job for Simmons with the CDC. *You can never have too many savvy people,* she thought. Simmons had rocked this suit back on his heels in less than a minute.

The three left the front office to make their way into the even smaller dressing room. Malone saw that Lamar couldn't resist looking out into the bays at the neatly aligned tables with black body bags atop. He quickly averted his eyes and hastened his pace. Under the dim fluorescent lights of the changing room, Malone couldn't tell if it was the lighting or if the blood had drained from Lamar's face.

He cleared his throat. "As I said, I'm the governor's public affairs director. I'm here because as I discussed earlier with Ms. Simmons—"

"Doctor Simmons," Malone injected.

"What? Oh yes. Doctor Simmons. As I discussed with Dr. Simmons earlier, the governor is coming here to Kayford this afternoon to conduct a press conference at four. I've already made arrangements with the sheriff's department to use the high school auditorium. I need to brief the governor before that happens on what this ..." Lamar paused as he searched for the perfect, nonfrightening, politically safe term for what had happened.

"Incident?" Simmons offered.

"Yes. This tragic incident."

She would have offered up *disaster,* but that probably would have caused Lamar's head to implode. He reminded her of a bomb-disposal guy in a room full of ticking clocks.

"Anyway, the governor will convey his condolences to the families and briefly describe the time line of events, the death toll of twenty-seven, the—"

"Twenty-nine as of just a little while ago," Simmons said.

"People are still dying?" Lamar exclaimed visibly shaken. He covered his nose and mouth with a handkerchief.

Despite the guy's edginess, Simmons continued. "Preliminary examination places the two new victims' deaths at approximately the same as the others. They were a couple living well outside town. Remote. We may find more. One of our teams is working with the sheriff's department to locate other possible victims."

"Hasn't everyone been accounted for?" Lamar asked.

"It's a huge area to cover. Fortunately, it's winter, and most people are in their homes and not out and about, but it takes time to knock on doors," Simmons said. She pulled her notepad out and wrote a note to herself to have the team check any ice-fishing shacks.

"That may take forever. Can't it be sped up?"

"We believe the victims are from the drug users' community. The sheriff has provided the addresses of known users, and that's narrowed our search some. That's what led us to the two additional victims."

"Drug users? You're saying all the victims were crackheads?"

"According to the sheriff, most of the victims had histories of drug use of some form, but not all. However—"

"However what, Dr. Simmons?" Lamar had found his legs again.

"However, tox screens from Saint Paul show virtually no trace of drugs."

Lamar digested this last bit of information for a moment. "So you don't have a clue about what caused this?"

"We will. It's been only about forty-eight hours," Malone said, stepping into the conversation.

"Well, what *do* you know, *Doctor* Malone? I can't have the governor go on national television, shrug his shoulders, and say, 'Gee, we don't know.' That doesn't play well at home. And believe me, if we don't provide answers, every conspiracy theory nutcase will be more than happy to provide some."

Ahh. A pissing contest. Malone realized she had to get this guy on task. "This is what we do know, Mr. Lamar: Twenty-nine people died within a twenty-four-hour period from a cause yet to be determined. Other incidents occurred in roughly the same time frame in small towns similar to Kayford in two other states. Most of the victims had histories of drug use, but you can't say that publicly since the tox screens came back negative. The victims' families would sue you into oblivion.

"The cause doesn't appear to be a biological agent such as a bacterium or a virus though that hasn't been completely ruled out. More answers will be forthcoming once complete autopsies have been conducted. The first of the victims were sent out at noon today to the MDH laboratory in Saint Paul. The resources of the MDH, the CDC, and the health departments of two others states are fully committed to accurately determining the cause of this tragedy and preventing it from happening again."

Lamar blinked. "Well, that's something. I can work with that. The governor will make his introductory remarks. The technical stuff will be left up to you two."

"I think Dr. Simmons should be the lead in that regard. It's your state. The home team plays better," Malone said.

"Yes. That sounds good," Lamar said.

"We'll emphasize what's been done to date, the ongoing lab work, the cessation of further casualties, and the lack of evidence pointing to a biological vector," Simmons said. "The wild card will be the questions. If they ask about the victims' drug histories, we'll refer to the tox reports."

"How would they know about the victims' records? That information hasn't been released." Lamar said.

Geez. How'd this guy get this job? Kelly thought. With restraint, she answered, "It's a small town, Mr. Lamar. It's almost a certainty that all those reporters have been shoving microphones into the locals' faces trying to get that perfect soundbite."

Lamar yielded.

Simmons continued. "If they ask about the contagious nature of whatever this pathogen is, we'll cite the large number of first responders, witnesses, and family members who do not show any signs of the symptoms. Conspiracy theorists are still going to work overtime coming up with end-of-the-world scenarios, but that can't be helped."

"Pathogen?" Lamar asked.

"What?" Simmons asked reflexively.

"You said, 'whatever this pathogen is.'"

"Causative agent," Kelly replied.

"Use that. Pathogen sounds too sinister. And don't refer to it as 'whatever this is.'"

Malone resisted rolling her eyes.

Kelly continued. "They'll probably ask about the most recent victims discovered this morning. We'll emphasize that the time of death appears to be within the same time frame as the others."

Lamar relaxed. "Very good. I need to get back. If you have any difficulty, I'll be available as well. I need to head to the high school to make sure things are ready there."

Seeing Lamar get into the back seat and be driven away, Chris turned to Kelly and with a straight face said, "If we have difficulty, we have Mr. Lamar for backup." The women held their poker faces about half a second before they broke into snorting laughter. Given the depth of all the tragedy that had surrounded them for the previous two days, they laughed until tears ran down their cheeks. The comic relief was exactly what they had needed.

Malone glanced at the deputy at the desk and thought she detected something of a smirk.

"How long does it take to get to the high school?" she asked the deputy.

"From here? Oh, about half an hour."

Chris looked at her watch and addressed Kelly. "We probably want to leave in a few minutes. I need to freshen up before we go. We may not get a chance when we get there, and I look like death on a cracker."

"Yeah, me next."

Having completed their grooming, the two women donned their heavy coats and made for the door. On their way out, Chris called out over her shoulder to the deputy, "We probably won't see you by the time we get back. Have a good evening."

"Good luck with the news conference. If I run into any trouble, I'll call Mr. Lamar."

That sent the women into another round of laughter although subdued. Laughing while coming out of a morgue would have been a poor visual had there been some enterprising freelance photographer with a zoom lens somewhere about looking for a money shot.

Simmons and Malone arrived at the high school to find several news vehicles in front of the building. They presented their credentials to the deputy posted at the front door. Kelly stepped into the lobby with Chris and asked the deputy where things had been set up. He pointed down the hall toward three sets of double doors. *Probably the auditorium*, Malone thought. They thanked him and headed in that direction.

From the back of the auditorium, Kelly saw chaos. A number of news crews were still jockeying for position while technicians were busy running wiring to their equipment. Reporters warmed up their voices and on-screen faces, scribbled their final notes, and primped. Simmons knew that it would be the final moment of anonymity for Malone and herself. After the news conference, their time in Kayford would be subjected to ambush interviews, sniper-range photos, and all manner of eavesdropping. They backed out of the auditorium.

"I need to call home before we do this. If you'll excuse me," Chris told Kelly as she pointed toward a secluded area across the lobby.

"Sure. We have some time."

Chris turned to walk away only to run into Lamar.

"Ladies! I was beginning to worry. Listen, we can take this hallway and enter at the stage. Avoid all those folks in there. I'd like Dr. Simmons to lead when the two of you are speaking."

Chris nodded. "I have to make a call. I'll be there in time. Don't worry."

Lamar opened his mouth to insist she come along just as the *whump whump whump whump* of helicopter rotors reverberated throughout the building. "I need to leave." He turned to Simmons. "Make sure she's there before the governor." He scurried off in the direction of the rotor noise.

Simmons looked at Malone. "Take your time. I'll see you there in a few minutes."

Kelly watched Chris for a moment. Chris's free hand waved about as she paced the small, secluded area. Based on Chris's body language, Kelly could tell it was not a pleasant conversation. Not wanting to invade her privacy even from across the lobby, Kelly made her way along the back corridor to the backstage entrance. A state trooper met her at the door. She showed him her badge, and he held the door for her. Just as she was about to enter, a phalanx of state troopers came down the hallway ahead of an entourage. Lamar was just half a step behind the governor. He made eye contact with Kelly.

"Governor, this is *Doctor* Kelly Simmons from the Department of Health, and this is ... Where's Dr. Malone?"

Without skipping a beat, Kelly extended her hand toward the governor. "Pleased to meet you, Governor. My counterpart from the CDC is making a call to Atlanta. She'll be here in a moment."

Lamar's face reddened as the governor addressed Kelly. "Mr. Lamar tells me you'll field the technical questions after my remarks. Answer the questions but keep 'em as vague as possible." He brushed by her.

Kelly positioned herself by the door to watch for Chris but still to be able to hear and see the governor. She was getting antsy. *Where's Chris?* The governor was already speaking. To her relief, Chris hurried down the hallway with a cellphone still to her ear. Kelly saw that Chris appeared to be crying. She fished a tissue from her pocket for her.

"We're almost on," Kelly whispered.

Simmons caught Lamar's eyes as he glared at her from behind the governor. She watched Chris terminate the call just as they sidled toward the edge of the stage.

As press conferences go, Simmons thought that one was going fairly typically. Some of the reporters asked reasonable questions so they could construct informative stories for their audiences. Some tried for the gotcha questions they hoped would create buzz. The politicians wanted to look as though they were on top of the crisis. She and Malone, the only scientists onstage, were repeatedly asked to form conclusions in spite of the absence of verifiable facts.

Sure enough, the question about the victims' histories with drugs did come up. When it did, Malone started to answer when the governor intervened and answered in the appropriate way. "We have no reason to believe these deaths were drug related. The tox screens were all virtually negative." Simmons caught Lamar's glance in her direction.

The news of the latest two victims generated quite a bit of inquiry and required considerable effort to make it clear that the deaths had occurred at about same time as the others; they simply hadn't been found until later. The desired conclusion was that the unknown malady had passed over and was no longer taking lives.

To his credit, Simmons thought Lamar had well prepared the governor to lead the reporters into focusing more on the fate of the two girls found at the house with their dead parents. Although that was tragic, questions regarding their fate were immeasurably easier to answer, and most important, they gave the impression that something good was being done.

After more than an hour, the questions started repeating. Simmons was grateful when Lamar interrupted the governor to remind him that he had another engagement back at the capital and that they needed to conclude the press conference. Simmons and no doubt the reporters knew that was bogus, but they acquiesced graciously having deadlines of their own. The governor wrapped things up with assurances that the tragic incident was being handled properly and solutions were being pursued vigorously.

Chris waited until she made it back to the hotel room before attempting to address the queues of text messages, emails, and voice mail. Modern communication technology enabled any and all to stay in the loop. At that moment, the loop of the CDC bureaucracy felt more like a noose for Chris.

In that respect, the latest incident was following a very familiar pattern: local politicians (governors, members of congress, and so on), news outlets, and executive office agencies were probing their contacts in the CDC including its Office of Public Affairs. In turn, not wanting to disappoint, these internal contacts went directly to the man on the ground, in this case, her, to get the real story.

She remembered that earlier in her career as a team leader for field investigations, that peculiarity of field investigations had threatened to derail her. She had learned through trial by fire that neither answering every inquiry nor ignoring all of them was a viable option. So she learned the art of replying with one-size-fits-all emails. Her replies were typically informative but did not divulge much more than what had already been released to the public. She used technical phrasing wherever possible because the informed ones understood and the less-informed ones were reluctant to ask her for a translation fearing their ignorance would be exposed. She always cc'd her immediate chain of command and sent them by separate confidential emails all the other information that was not yet ready for general consumption.

The confidential messages invariably concluded with a request that her superiors provide more cover from the myriad of requests for inside information. That was an irritant to some of her bosses but was allowed due to her effectiveness in difficult situations. As a reward for her proficiency in the field and perhaps as punishment for her temerity, she drew more than her share of problematic field assignments.

She looked at her watch and was amazed at how quickly the day had gotten away from her. It was a little after six, and she still had a mountain of things to do. The teams were coming back. She'd need to meet with them and see if there were any easily discernable patterns, "actionable information" as it was currently referred to. She peeked out her window and saw quite a bit of activity in the hotel parking lot. A number of the news crews were packing up and heading home. *Good. Less interference.*

Home was where she wanted to be, but of all the things she needed to do that evening, calling home was the one she dreaded most. Her once-docile daughter had turned into a stranger with a venomous tongue bonded to a demonic attitude. She had no sisters, so her husband, Sam, was ill prepared for his daughter's voyage to the dark side of the moon.

Chris pulled the rickety chair from the small table and sat down. She had stopped. The day's fatigue caught her. Her hand trembled. She had not eaten since the takeout breakfast at the makeshift morgue. The bottom of her carry-on bag yielded up a granola bar that she decided would have to do. She scanned her cell for voice mails and surprisingly found just one, which was from Dr. Patterson, her boss. Nothing from home.

Dr. Patterson's voice was always at the same level and pitch whether he was telling someone his house was on fire or was reciting the ingredients in a jar of mustard, and that voice mail was no exception. "Chris, I'm watching your press conference and know you can't answer right now. Give me a call this evening when you get a breather. We're bringing you back to Atlanta. We want you to run the overall investigation on this one. Leave your team there for as long as they need. Let Sanders run the show there. Talk to you later ... And good job on the presser. It struck just the right tone."

Chris deleted the voice mail and paused to consider this latest news. Her hope was that it was the beginning of a new phase in her career. *Am I finally being moved up? Am I being pulled off the road? Too bad this hadn't come a couple of years earlier.*

She flopped on the bed, took a deep breath, and dialed home.

"Hello?"

"It's me. How are things going there?"

"Everything's quiet right now. Not much drama today ... but the evening's young."

"Where is she?"

"Up in her room doing her homework."

"Really?" Chris sat up.

"Well, she's in her room, and it's quiet ... except for the music."

There was a pause before Sam said, "Saw you on national news this evening."

"Yeah? How'd I look?"

Another pause. "Tired."

"That obvious, huh?" Chris lay back down.

"So how bad is this one?"

"Bad, but not just bad. Weird. I can't think of anything that parallels it."

"Scary. Terrorist?"

"Nothing points to that. But the way it came. Laid out twenty-nine people here, another forty some at the other two sites, and then left. It's like a four-dimensional jigsaw with a bunch of pieces missing."

"And guess who gets to put it together."

"Right. Oh, good news. Looks like I'll be home sooner than later. Patterson's bringing me back home to run the investigation at the national level. This might be my chance to get off the road."

"Sure, nine to five, no weekends, holidays off, six weeks of paid vacation."

"Stop. It has to be an improvement. At least I'll get to sleep in my own bed ... with you." Chris stood up and paced the room.

"Do I have to kick my girlfriend out?"

"Oh she can stay, but you'll be a soprano."

"Ow!"

Another long awkward pause before Chris grew serious. "Thanks for listening, Sam. I really needed to hear your voice and laugh. I can't get home soon enough. Give Erika my love. I gotta go."

"When are you coming?"

"I gotta call Patterson and see what he has in mind. I suspect I'll probably be home tomorrow. I'll text you when I find out."

"Good. See you then. Love you."

"Love you too. Tell Erika I love her too."

Chris hung up but sat motionless on the bed. She thought about taking a shower but concluded she was just too beat to expend the effort. After a few minutes, she called Dr. John Patterson.

"Patterson."

"Dr. Patterson, Chris Malone. You wanted me to call."

"Yes. Caught your presser. You and your Minnesota companion handled things well. Those things can be difficult."

"Thank you."

"Listen, as I told you in my voice mail, we'd like to bring you here to coordinate all the field investigations on this one."

"Okay. When do you want me there?" Chris stood and paced.

"As soon as possible of course. You probably need a little time to get the team there coordinated."

"That won't take long. Lawrence has done this enough times that he could do it blindfolded." Malone replied giving Dr. Sanders a plug.

"Think you can make it back by tonight? I don't think I can get the Gulfstream sent back for just one passenger."

"I can't get out tonight. It's too late, and we're too far from Minneapolis. I can fly commercial out tomorrow morning. Besides, I'd like to stop at the state coroner's office and see if anything significant is coming out of the autopsies."

"Good. Stop by my office tomorrow when you get in." Patterson paused a moment before continuing, "Chris, we have to get on top of this in a hurry. It's got a lot of folks worried."

"Understood."

Chris terminated the call and tossed her cell on the bed. She continued to pace.

CHAPTER 6

JULY 30, 1944

Zwillingsvater saw the summer's zenith arrive with a vehemence matching the brutality of the guards and kapos. It came along with the rising tide of transports. He had given up trying to shield the boys from the tragic drama arriving with each transport. The barracks became an oven during the heat of the day, and there were too many transports arriving to keep the boys inside while the trains disgorged their human cargo.

He was amazed at the number of new arrivals wearing their winter coats. He marveled at their naïve optimism that they would need them for the coming winter. The coat bearers fell from the transports barely able to stand let alone walk suffering as they were from thirst and heat exhaustion. They had no way of knowing presenting themselves in such poor physical condition to the SS doctors at the selection would relieve them of ever needing a winter coat again.

The smothering heat stoked the intensity of the ever-present fetid stench of the camp. When God was merciful, an easterly breeze carried the noisome contribution of the chimneys away from the camp leaving only some of the nauseating odors for the inmates. God's mercy seldom came to Auschwitz, where mercy most often manifested itself as a quick death.

Transports came so often those summer days that the boys, including Jakob, gave little notice to them any longer. But an exception to their indifference to the transports occurred a few days earlier. It was not a transport comprising railcars but of trucks from the women's camp. Several trucks roared through the gate and headed toward Crematorium II. The trucks were loaded with women stripped of their clothing. What was unusual was that they were singing the "Ha Tikvah," the Zionist national anthem. Apparently, a selection had occurred in the women's camp. The singing was a rare act of defiance futile as it was. Zwillingsvater could only shake his head.

Six weeks passed since Jakob's arrival—a length of time well above the average survival duration even for those not selected for immediate disposal. He had become a seasoned inmate though he did enjoy rare special privileges and status. He was no longer required to have blood drawn two or three times a week as the other twins had to suffer through, and he did get extra rations, though not a lot. Zwillingsvater managed to use some of those to supplement the diet of the other twins. Jakob's range extended considerably farther, but he never crossed the dirt road to where the Roma boy and his family lived though the boys exchanged salutations almost daily.

Some of the twins in his barracks had come and gone. Nothing was said regarding their whereabouts. When he was still required to give blood, Jakob had seen one of the twins receive an injection in his buttocks. The unfortunate twin's brother had not received the same injection. The injected twin returned to the barracks quite hobbled by the pain. Later that night, the whole barracks was awakened by the boy's fever-driven hallucinations. He was removed the next morning. A day later, his twin left with Mengele. Neither was seen again. It was a pattern repeated several times. The census of the boys' barracks waxed and waned in such a manner from week to week.

Mengele's attention to Jakob increased week by week as well. New to his unique privileges were the almost daily ride-alongs with the doctor in the car with the big red cross. He rode with Mengele for hours at a time. No part of the camp seemed off limits. Once, he even went to one of the buildings with the big chimneys. None of the transport arrivals was there. They had all gone to the crematoria on the other side of the trees and Kanada. Only a team of pajama men called Sonderkommandos scrambled about loading carts with ashes.

Mengele's pathology laboratory was in the building, but they did not enter it. Rather, a man wearing a white coat came to the car and handed Mengele a neatly wrapped box bound with twine. "Your specimens,

Herr Doktor," was all that the man said. Mengele called him Dr. Nyiszli. Jakob took the man to be a prisoner because of the submissive manner he displayed toward Mengele as he approached and talked to him; he was much more deferential than the Nazi prison staff were.

Jealousy further separated Jakob from his barracks mates. Whenever Zwillingsvater was not about, they derided him as the Golden Junge, the golden boy. Zwillingsvater kept the other boys at bay reminding them of the dire if not deadly consequences if Jakob were to show up with a black eye. He was always quick to show them the fruits of Mengele's grace toward Jakob. Although not liking it, the older boys understood the asymmetrical geometry of the situation and enforced Zwillingsvater's protective order.

There were a few days following the time Mengele gave Jakob a new outfit that resentment peaked. It was a nearly new suit cut into a quasi-military fashion that suggested the gray-green, high-collar tunic of the German officer uniforms. Mengele had notified one of the junior officers overseeing the Kanada operations about what he was looking for. Within two or three transports, the young officer acquired the suit hoping to ingratiate himself to the doctor.

Mengele insisted the boy don the suit immediately in front of the others still clad in the ragged clothes they had worn the day they jumped from the transports. Moments after the car with the red cross sped away, taunts of "Golden Junge!" were hurled at Jakob. Zwillingsvater stepped back into the barracks to find boys circling Jakob and poking him.

"Do you want to die, you stupid boy?" Zwillingsvater screamed as he jerked one of the boys up by his collar and slapped the back of his head. The menacing circle melted away.

The morning of the last day of July began as had the days of the last two weeks—hot, dry, and dusty. The heat and lack of rain conspired to dry the usual quagmire of mud normally gripping the camp and its inhabitants. At first, it was a welcomed change, but the heat spawned disease.

Mengele's car rolled up to the boys' barracks at the usual time for the doctor's inspection of his boys. Zwillingsvater had Jakob ready in his uniform with face scrubbed, hair combed smartly, and a few new phrases in German. Jakob's language skills had developed quite well. Besides Zwillingsvater's lessons, he heard it spoken all about him. He had become conversant in the language of the masters of his universe.

The doctor hurried through examining the boys that morning. After his cursory examination, he cupped Jakob's chin and looked as if he were debating whether to take him along. Jakob took the doctor's hand in his and tugged him toward the door. The doctor yielded.

Though it was a short distance from the boys' barracks just across the tracks of the ramp, driving to the women's camp involved taking a rather circuitous route due to the fences and the placement of the many gates. Jakob was relieved the doctor drove himself that morning and not the surly driver from the Sonderkommandos. The doctor smelled particularly nice that morning; Jakob did not know what it was, but it was distinctive and pleasant. Mengele merrily whistled and hummed a lively tune for Jakob. The boy listened carefully and shouted out, "Italian Symphony!"

"Bravo! Bravo, my little prodigy." Mengele beamed. "Now do you know the composer?"

Jakob did not know, but he ventured a guess anyway. He knew from experience with this ritual, which had become a part of their ride-along routine, the answers were almost exclusively German composers. "Schumann?" the boy ventured.

"Nein! Nein! Nein! Nicht Schumann! Mendelssohn. Mendelssohn!" Mengele chastised him good-naturedly. "You should know this. He was a Jew just like you."

Nearly five minutes later, the car with the big red cross entered the women's camp. The doctor navigated the vehicle through the grid of barracks. Everywhere Jakob looked, he saw ghostlike bodies of female inmates lifelessly going about their labors. As on every occasion he went to the women's camp, he hoped to see his mother, something that never happened.

Finally, the car wheeled up to three barracks cordoned off from the rest by a muster of armed guards. A very attractive, very blond female guard approached the vehicle and greeted the doctor. "Herr Doktor! Good to see you again so soon."

"And you as well, Fraulein Grese."

Jakob appraised the woman's dress and mannerisms. Her uniform rivaled Mengele's in fit, form, and perfection. Her tightly coiffed golden hair topped by her garrison cap tilted rakishly over her right eye. She stood erect. Her tall boots were slightly taller at the heel than were those of the other female guards. Even the four-year-old Jakob was enamored with the woman's appearance.

As Jakob tumbled from the car, the woman turned to Mengele. "What is that?"

"That, my dear Irma, is my music prodigy. But not just music. The boy has incredible intelligence. And look at those Aryan features." Mengele cupped his hand under Jakob's chin to lift his face toward the woman.

"A Jew?"

"Half. His mother was a German."

Jakob freed himself from the doctor's grip. His German language skills had advanced enough to appreciate the word *war,* German for "was"—past tense. He dismissed the implications.

"Married to a Jew? How awful."

"Yes, but this boy is extraordinary. He comprehends things better than most adults do, yet he is only four. I believe he is the embodiment of the superiority of Aryan genes."

Mengele's enthusiasm for the boy's abilities failed to infect Irma Grese. She observed the boy a moment longer neither smiling nor frowning before she turned to the business at hand. "We've quarantined Barracks ten, eleven, and twelve just as you ordered. Twelve is the infirmary."

"Yes. Very good. I have trucks coming momentarily."

"Herr Doktor, I understand the need to liquidate Barracks eleven. That is where the typhus was found in most of the women. And Barracks twelve, well, they're useless and a waste of resources trying heal them anyway. But Barracks ten is still healthy. They have certain skills for Farben's Buna Werke factory."

"Skills? My dear Irma, you speak as if these miserable women were highly trained technicians. This is a contagion that could easily swamp our capacity to hold it in check. Monkeys could be trained to do what they do." The doctor paused. "And as it turns out, monkeys unfortunately cost more to maintain," he quipped.

Grese laughed at the doctor's jest.

"Here. Let me demonstrate my young savant's comprehensive abilities."

Jakob was tugged away from his search of the woman's face.

"Master Jakob, my friend here does not understand something," Mengele said as he pointed to the three barracks surrounded by guards. "The people in the middle barracks there are very sick. The people in those two other barracks live very close to the sick people. They will probably get sick too because the sick people are very contagious. They can make other people sick too. The sickness they have is very bad. People will die from it. If they all get sick, then the whole camp, even your barracks, will probably get sick."

Jakob stood absorbing the information. It was the sort of riddle the doctor presented to him many times to test his capacities.

Mengele continued with his elaborate question. "Should I get rid of the few sick people in these three barracks so all the other people in the camp don't get sick? Sacrifice the few for the many? Or should we allow all the people in the whole camp to get sick and die? Sacrifice the many and still lose the few?" The doctor swept his arm in a long arc dramatizing the epic dimensions of the conundrum.

Jakob did indeed understand the cold calculus—a few lost in exchange for saving thousands more.

"All three."

Mengele, elated at the boy's answer, beamed broadly displaying his gap-toothed smile for Fraulein Grese. "You see my dear? Even this child understands my logic."

"Oh you are such a clever boy, Herr Doktor!" Irma teased.

Three trucks loaded with more soldiers rumbled up to the quarantined barracks. Before the trucks came to a complete stop, the soldiers disembarked and reinforced the soldiers forming a perimeter around the three barracks. A phalanx of twenty or more female guards armed with short whips and clubs crossed through the perimeter and entered the barracks. For a moment, Jakob could not see any of what happened inside, but screams from inside left him little doubt of the impending maelstrom.

All the while, Mengele and Grese exchanged flirtatious banter. Occasionally, they took notice of the proceedings. Once, Grese shouted instructions to one of her subordinates. For the most part, the selection was just an opportunity for the couple to be together under the pretext of official business.

The barracks' company of inmates soon formed outside five abreast as if for roll call. Most of them were crying, even wailing. A few stood stoically. Dog handlers joined the melee with barely restrained beasts. The inmates were all numbered. A count short of two women in one of the barracks gave cause to release the dogs. Momentarily, a great crash came from within; Jakob heard shrieks of terror and frenzied growling. A female guard stepped out and selected four inmates to go inside. After a pause, the four inmates carried the bodies of the two missing women out and dropped them by the door. The count then was accurate. All present—2,117.

The inhabitants of the three doomed barracks turned and marched toward the far northern side of the camp—toward Crematoria IV and V. Jakob knew little of the details as to the disposition of the inmates, but later that afternoon, after Mengele returned him to the boys' barracks, he heard shooting off in the distance coming from the direction the women had marched.

The doctor was not seen again until the early evening a couple of days later. Jakob sat at the edge of the dirt road separating the Roma from his barracks. He enjoyed the music from their camp. And so, most evenings, Jakob could be found listening to the plaintive music and watching the Gypsies interact among themselves. Jakob found comfort in the simple, familial activities. And on most evenings, he saw his friend and waved to him.

The evening reveries were arrested by a column of trucks roaring up the dirt road. The car with the big red cross headed the procession. Soldiers sprang from the trucks and formed a line along the road. There was no need to completely surround the Gypsies—the electrified barbwire encompassed the other three sides of the Roma camp. There was no escape.

Jakob instinctively fell back from the road to the barracks. He feared for his friend's life. Zwillingsvater ran about rounding up the twins and hustling them into the barracks. Jakob saw Mengele point and direct two soldiers toward their barracks. The two soldiers ran and grabbed a pair of Gypsy twins recently housed with the other twins; they carried them back toward the Roma camp. Zwillingsvater stepped helplessly aside unable to intervene on their behalf.

From within their barracks, the boys listened to the roundup well into the night. Mothers wailed and pleaded. Children cried and screamed. Men cursed and fought. Guards beat and battered and even shot several. By morning, the Gypsy camp lay empty. Empty of families. Empty of music. Empty of life.

The following day, a hellishly hot day, the doctor came for his usual morning rounds of the boys' barracks. That time, a van accompanied him. Instead of the routine inspections and cursory examinations, all the boys including Zwillingsvater were loaded into the van. All that is except for Jakob and the oldest set of twins, Aaron and Miklos Weisz, teenagers from rural Transylvania.

The boys had heard the induction fans start up earlier that morning in both Crematoria II and III just a hundred meters from their barracks. However, there were no transports on the ramp to be processed. Jakob saw that Zwillingsvater was visibly upset. They had all learned that any deviation from the normal routine such as the fans, the presence of the van, and the fact Zwillingsvater was being forced to go along could not portend anything good.

Zwillingsvater gave desperate last instructions to the two remaining teenagers as he was pushed into the back of the van. Aaron and Miklos were visibly shaken by the morning's events.

Mengele pulled away from the barracks leading the van back down the dirt road. From the door of the barracks, Jakob and the older twins watched the procession through the barbwire and open spaces between the barracks as it weaved its way through the maze of fence lines. At the point they expected to see the vehicles turn right toward the crematoria, it turned left toward the main gate as if headed toward Mengele's clinic in the main camp, the *Stammlager*, just like the usual routine. As often happened in Auschwitz, routines changed for no apparent reason. Sometimes for the worse. Sometimes for no difference. Seldom if ever for good. In hell, good did not exist.

Jakob and the teenaged twins all felt the same rush of relief. The two older boys even managed to laugh. They strolled out of the stifling barracks and sought the shelter of shade from the intensifying sun. There was nothing to do, and there were few people, guards or inmates, anywhere near their immediate vicinity. From their shaded spot, they looked at the forbidden camp of the Roma.

"Let's go see what we can organize from the Gypsy barracks," Aaron suggested.

Jakob had learned the meaning of the word *organize*—to acquire by any and all means necessary—trade, barter, steal—whatever. Organizing was a thin thread tied to survival. Those unable or unwilling to organize did not last very long. But organizing was an activity fraught with perils. To be caught by a guard or a kapo meant almost certain death. Mengele's twins, however, held special sway over the draconian laws prevailing across the Auschwitz world. Few—officer or enlisted, kapo or prisoner—wanted to be seen interfering with Mengele or his precious pets.

"We have to watch Golden Junge here," Miklos replied.

"He can come along."

"They didn't have anything we need. They sure didn't have any food."

"No, but they had some stuff. Mandolins, violins ... stuff we can trade. The Kanada crew hasn't gone through their stuff yet. It'll be hours before the others come back."

"Let's make it quick and get out quick."

The trio headed for the former Gypsy barracks—seventeen of them not counting the kitchen and latrines. Jakob felt terror and exhilaration in equal measures. Whether it was from the devilment or from his inclusion with the big boys of the barracks he could not tell, but once engaged in the act, he was fully in with them.

They entered the first barracks like a team of commandos. In the light from the upper windows, they fanned out in search of booty. Most of what they saw was indeed worthless even in the deprived Auschwitzian universe. They deposited a handful of plunder by the door. The plan was to search each barracks in that manner.

In a little more than an hour, they had searched each barracks. Just as Aaron predicted, there were mandolins, violins, and squeezeboxes. At the far corner of a straw mattress on a bottom bunk, Jakob found two gold rings that solidified his position as a part of the pirate gang.

The three recovered little else of value. Inside a sealed can, Jakob found a curious contraption made of wire and bits of metal that all seemed to be connected to a rusty razor blade at its center. A long coil of wire bound the whole thing. The can was tucked away well out of sight. Jakob's small stature made him ideally suited to ferret out such hidden goods.

Jakob showed it to Miklos, who was puzzled by the device.

Aaron walked up for a closer look. "It's a radio."

"A radio? It can't be. It's just a bunch of wires and bare metal."

"I'm telling you it's a radio. A crystal radio. If you'd paid better attention in school, you'd know that," Aaron teased his brother. "This one uses that rusty razor blade as the crystal—or more precisely, the rust. The ferrous oxide is the crystal. Other metallic crystals can be used, even lead oxide."

"You're such a know-it-all," Miklos shot back.

The radio fascinated Jakob. He imagined listening to broadcast of great symphonies as he and his father had done before their troubles. He didn't care for any of the other loot.

"We'd best be getting back," Aaron said. "They may come back early."

Neither Miklos nor Jakob argued with that; they'd had their adventure. Jakob, for the first time since his arrival, felt a part of the group. The two oldest twins made him a part of their team, and it was he who had found the gold rings—the best currency in the camp.

"We'll walk back to our barracks one at a time. Be sure to walk and take your time. Less likely to draw notice from any guards," instructed Aaron. "Jakob, you go first."

Without hesitation, Jakob cradled the radio can and left the Gypsy barracks closest to his own. Completing his nonchalant act, he picked up a couple of stones in the road and tried to throw them across the fence toward the tracks. He eventually wandered into his barracks. He turned to watch from the doorway as one of the other boys returned with his bounty.

Just as Miklos crossed the road, Mengele's car appeared at the far end of the road heading toward them. Miklos panicked and ran across the road dropping a bowl in the process. The car accelerated and lurched to an abrupt stop stranding Aaron in the Gypsy barracks.

Mengele emerged from the car enraged at the driver, "What do you think you are doing, you fool?"

The driver jumped from the car. "Forgive me, Herr Doktor!" He pointed to Miklos. "I saw this boy running from the Gypsy barracks carrying that bowl." Jakob recognized him as the driver who had taken him and Zwillingsvater to the doctor's office several weeks earlier. He had seen him several times since then driving the doctor about.

Taking in the scene, the doctor focused on Miklos. "What were you doing over there?" Mengele demanded.

Miklos stammered not finding a suitable answer.

Mengele slapped him hard enough to drive him to his knees. Aaron cried out causing Mengele to wheel about and spot the other twin still at the Gypsy barracks.

"Come here at once!"

Aaron didn't move. The doctor, further enraged, pulled his service pistol and pointed it at Miklos's head. Aaron ran to the aid of his brother. Mengele struck Aaron with the butt of his pistol.

Returning from the boys' examinations, the van carrying the other twins and Zwillingsvater pulled up behind the car and unloaded. All the boys gathered at a distance and witnessed the unfolding conflict.

"Empty your pockets!" Mengele screamed.

Aaron and Miklos complied disgorging the loot they'd taken from the Gypsy barracks onto the ground. Each boy's handful included a gold ring resting atop the other trinkets. Mengele's anger escalated to rage at the sight of the gold rings. He lifted his pistol and shot both boys in the head in less than a second.

"Nooo!" Zwillingsvater cried out running toward the doctor.

Mengele lifted the pistol once again toward Zwillingsvater but held his fire. No one moved for the longest of moments. Jakob, watching it all from the door of the barracks, felt as if his heart had burst.

Finally, Mengele told the driver, "You! Get the other driver and load these two into the van. Take them to Dr. Nyiszli and tell him I want the pathology report ready in two hours."

Mengele got into the car leaving his driver to clean up the mess and drove away. Zwillingsvater collected himself. He soothed the boys as he gathered and shepherded them into the barracks.

Jakob, rubbing his tattooed arm, remained at the door watching the two drivers drag the bodies of his newfound friends to the van. They lifted their bodies at the knees and armpits and tossed them flying onto the floor in the back of the van. The van driver got in, turned the van around, and headed directly to Mengele's laboratory in Crematorium II. Mengele's driver stalled a moment longer. He bent down, pretending to tie his shoe, and picked through the two small piles of treasure left on the ground. Before rising again to his feet, he scanned about to see if anyone was watching. Indeed there was. The driver smiled and winked at the boy. Jakob's cheeks flushed hot as he felt a sensation within his chest he had never experienced before.

CHAPTER 7

OCTOBER 7, 1944

The birches along the wood line behind the crematoria attired themselves in their autumn glory. Set against the backdrop of a cobalt-blue sky, the vista would have lifted the spirits of any human anywhere else. In years past, Zwillingsvater thought of autumn as his favorite time of year, God's crescendo of color. But not there. Autumn there was the harbinger of winter—the most brutal season.

Something else pervaded the camp though—a discernable uneasiness not easy for Spiegel to articulate. The running tide of transports disgorging their freight—the Nazi euphemism for the condemned souls brought to the selection ramp, slowed to just two or three a day from the fevered pitch of eight to ten per day. News wrapped in rumor and speculation of Nazi defeats at the hands of the Russians came with the transports from the east. Transports from the west—France, Belgium, Holland—brought reports Paris itself had been liberated in August.

In August, the Buna Werkes, I.G. Farben's plant, was bombed for the first time. It was bombed again in September. Several times a week, air raid sirens wailed as formations of American B-17 and B-24 bombers, using the extensive rail network of the region as navigational aids, flew directly overhead for daylight raids on the Nazi war machine. Dozens of contrails bore witness to the number of planes in each formation. The inmates took some delight in seeing the fence line SS guards cowering in their small, open-front bomb shelters near the towers. For the inmates, a bombing raid on the camp would have been welcomed—even desired.

Casual observers would have been forgiven if they had concluded these events should resurrect hope in the minds of the prisoners. Experience, though, had taught Spiegel that changes to the usually murderous camp routines were portents of even more horrors never before thought imaginable. And so the product of all the augury was an atmosphere of heightened dread.

Mengele sensed the coming day of reckoning as well. It was no secret among the camp personnel. The other SS soldiers—officers and enlisted alike—lined their pockets with the prized pieces of plunder harvested from the freight arriving on the transports. The idea was to put together enough such *douceur* to underwrite a flight to freedom in the postwar world. By contrast, Mengele imagined his path to postwar salvation lay in the immeasurable value of his groundbreaking discoveries yet to be realized. Fewer transports meant fewer prized test specimens—twins—but it also meant less time spent on the ramp overseeing the tedious selection process. And that meant more time in the laboratory. To that end, he redoubled his research.

Twins bore the consequences of his mania as did other prisoners used in medical experiments. Some sets of twins were sent to Block 10 at Auschwitz I directly off the transports. A few sets of twins remained in the boys' barracks. Zwillingsvater's efforts to protect the boys were met with diminishing efficacy. The Nazi monster had been mortally wounded, and Auschwitz, the greatest icon of that beast, was at its greatest lethality.

Zwillingsvater prepared the boys and the barracks that morning ahead of the doctor's visit as per their routine. Young Jakob readied himself for a ride-along should the doctor be so inclined. The morning had a chill about it, so Zwillingsvater conjured up a baggy but clean jacket for Jakob to wear over his uniform. A belt cinched around the waist of the jacket complemented the military look. A cap with a martial bearing and a jaunty tilt low over his right eye completed the ensemble. Jakob liked the baggy jacket. It allowed him plenty of room for organizing—something he had become quite adept at. That day, he had another task to perform known only to himself.

The doctor arrived and performed his usual routine inspections and examinations. When he came to Jakob, he paused and studied the boy as if he were an exhibit in a Berlin museum. Ever perceptive, Jakob stiffened to attention, snapped a crisp salute, and held it as he had seen SS guards do countless times. Another moment passed and the doctor himself snapped to attention and returned a crisp salute. Jakob recovered his salute but still stood at attention.

Mengele applauded his approval of the lad's performance. "My little Prussian! Will you ever cease to amaze me?" He cupped the boy's chin affectionately breaking his stance. "Are you ready for today's adventures?"

"Ja, mein Hauptsturmführer."

Jakob saw the driver holding the passenger door open for the doctor as they left the barracks. It was as he had hoped. He had overcome his fear of the man and was left only with loathing for him because of what he had done to Aaron and Miklos. Mengele had shot his friends, but he was a German. It's what they did. The driver was a prisoner like everyone else. He was the one who had gotten Aaron and Miklos killed.

He had seen the man many times since that day in August, and without exception, he had always given Jakob the same leering smile and a wink. Jakob climbed in first with some assistance from Mengele and found his seat behind the driver. The driver closed the door behind the doctor and scurried around to the front seat.

"Where to, Herr Doktor?"

"The Buna Werkes. I will be there for an hour or so, and then you will take me back to my laboratory."

After a longer, twelve-kilometer drive, the car pulled up to the guard station. The guard looked in, saw Mengele, and waved them through. The driver wove his way through the industrial complex until they pulled up to an office building made of grim, gray block—strictly utilitarian and in keeping with the rest of the facility. Jakob feared this place more than he did the camp. Great mysterious machines towered over him all about. Steam and loud whirring noises enveloped the whole plant.

Mengele opened his door without waiting for the driver. "You stay here with the boy," he instructed. He left the two and picked his way through the mud puddles to the office.

Jakob felt a fright course through his body. He did not want to be left alone with this man. He forced himself to show no fear though. He knew that with animals, fear could invite attack.

The driver stood as he watched the doctor enter the building. He turned to Jakob. "Stay in the car and keep your mouth shut, you little prince."

Jakob obeyed without reluctance. He did not like that place, so staying safely in the car was fine with him. The driver stood by the front of the car smoking a cigarette he had organized from some poor soul on one of the transports. He warmed himself in a shaft of light penetrating the industrial canyon. Jakob looked at the man. He had spent a considerable amount of time pondering how to repay that man for having caused the death of his friends. And right then, the perfect opportunity was at hand.

The same shaft of light that warmed the driver also warmed the car. Jakob entertained himself by watching the activity in the factory. The grim, gray pajama men milled about the base of a furnace. The men poured molten metal from the furnace into a large pot suspended from a huge crane. The metal was then poured into molds. Molds of what Jakob could not tell. A small motorcar on tracks moved the castings to somewhere in the bowels of the factory. Jakob felt quite safe in the car. He took something from the billows of his oversized jacket and slid it snugly beneath the driver's seat.

A pulsing, urgent siren wailed. The pajama men left the furnaces and headed outside toward a shelter some distance from the factory. The driver tossed his cigarette on the ground and joined them leaving Jakob in the car. Looking up through the smoke stacks toward the severely clear sky, Jakob saw the telltale signs of the bombers' contrails approaching. The plant had been bombed before—twice. Long minutes passed. Nothing happened.

Another long wail of the siren signaled the all clear. Men headed back to whatever it was they were doing before the false alarm.

Mengele yanked open the car door. "You were here by yourself?"

Jakob nodded.

"Stupid oaf!"

Walking with a cluster of other men, the driver approached the car casually puffing on another cigarette. Mengele wheeled about to face him.

"You left the boy alone in the car during an air raid?"

He sputtered his only defense. "It was a false alarm, sir."

Mengele, uncharacteristically quiet, said nothing. Jakob saw the doctor's nostrils flare and his jaw muscles bulge. The doctor was much more menacing like that than if he was raging, and the driver knew it. The driver threw his smoke to the ground and hustled to open the door for the doctor.

"Get out of the way you idiot!"

The ride back to Birkenau was oppressively quiet. They entered the camp and were met with the sight of a frantic scramble of soldiers getting onto trucks.

Mengele stepped out of the car and grabbed a soldier. "What's happening?"

"I don't know, sir. There was an explosion at one of the crematoria."

Jakob watched Mengele look frantically toward the direction of Crematorium II, where his laboratory was. Billows of smoke filled the horizon north, perhaps Crematorium IV or V. Sporadic gunfire could be heard.

The doctor jumped back into the car. "Take me there! Hurry!"

The driver wove the car through the fence maze to Crematorium IV. Before they got there, they had to contend with troop-carrying trucks and more filing in behind them. Dozens, perhaps hundreds of SS soldiers scrambled past them. Jakob craned his neck as high as he could to see the chaotic activity.

Mengele jumped out. "Stay with the car!" he ordered.

A fire truck made its way with difficulty through the confusion. Six or seven trucks stood in the way. A second explosion came from the direction of the two crematoria to the south. Mengele's laboratory was in one of the two.

Mengele was almost immediately back at the car. "Get me over there!" he shouted at the driver.

The driver maneuvered furiously to extricate the car from the tangle of military trucks as Mengele slapped the back of the driver's head with a riding crop. "Move, you idiot!"

Back through the maze of fences, the driver dashed at speeds well above what could have been considered safe but was not fast enough for Mengele. They nearly ran over a number of newly arrived prisoners as they crossed the ramp.

"Faster, you idiot!" screamed Mengele whipping the driver like a horse.

Mengele's car pulled up in between the two shooting factions at Crematorium II, where his laboratory was. The doctor jumped out into the melee. Jakob instinctively burrowed as low into the floorboard as he could as did the driver. His heart pounded not for fear of the gunfire whipping about but that the driver would discover the small package wrapped tightly in brown paper wedged beneath his seat. He considered moving it but thought it better not to draw attention to it. Besides, the driver seemed too frightened to notice much of anything as he lay curled up cringing with his eyes tightly shut.

The gunfire quickly subsided as more and more soldiers converged on the area. After a long silence, the driver found the courage to raise his head to see what had happened. He found himself looking at two SS guards pointing their Mausers at him.

"Out of the car! Now! Hands up!"

The driver sputtered, "I'm Dr. Mengele's—"

That was all he was able to get out before one guard struck him with the butt of his rifle. The driver fell to the ground still conscious but quite dazed. The other guard grabbed Jakob by the scruff of his neck and threw him to the ground beside the driver.

"What were you doing in that officer's car?" screamed the first guard.

The driver was unable to talk. The guard raised his rifle to strike him again.

"He is the driver for Dr. Mengele," Jakob said in a clear, articulate voice from his prostrate position on the ground. The guard's posture snapped rigid when he invoked Mengele's name. His courage and quick thinking had saved the driver from further beating and quite conceivably had saved his life.

"Who are you?" the guard asked.

"One of Dr. Mengele's twins."

"Get back in the car and do not move," the guard ordered Jakob and the driver, who needed assistance getting to his feet.

The squad continued sweeping the building rounding up members of the rebellious Sonderkommandos as they went. Finally, they found their way to Mengele's laboratory. Inside, they came upon Mengele holding his service pistol on Dr. Nyiszli and his assistant. Both were spread-eagle on the tile floor.

"Did you know about this?"

"What? The explosions?" Nyiszli asked.

"Yes! This revolt!" Mengele screamed.

"No, Doctor. We were both working on the autopsy of the Russian officer shot while trying to escape—just as you had requested this morning!"

"Why should I believe you?"

Pointing to the desk across the room, "Look at the typewriter. The report is only partially completed because I was typing as my assistant dictated the autopsy to me." Nyiszli offered the unfinished report as further proof of his noncomplicity. The nervous Nyiszli elaborated. "We stopped and lay on the floor when the explosion happened."

Mengele lifted the sheet of paper still in the typewriter and read it. Indeed, it did look as though the report had been interrupted midsentence.

"Take these two outside with the rest," he ordered the guard.

The guard poked both doctors in the ribs with the muzzle of his Mauser. They rose and walked out of the tiled autopsy suite with hands on heads. Once outside, they were made to lie facedown and forbidden to look around. They complied quickly and joined the several hundred already stretched out prone.

Nearly half an hour passed before Mengele emerged into the courtyard where all the prisoners lay facedown. "All doctors rise and go directly to your rooms. Do not come out until you are directed to do so."

Six doctors stood shakily and walked directly toward their rooms with their heads down and not looking about. Before they had clearing the courtyard, two SS officers began shooting the remaining prisoners with small-caliber pistols. One bullet to the base of each head—the brain stem. Normally, Nyiszli's autopsy reports would describe the damage to the medulla oblongata, the pons, the midbrain. But Nyiszli's reports would never be made. Only ashes mingled with tons of other ashes would be all that remained of this rebellion.

Nearly an hour and a half passed before the doctor returned to the car. As he approached the car, he saw that the driver's head was bleeding and that he was sporting a large contusion at the left temple.

"What happened to you?"

The driver, a little more coherent, said, "We were forced from the car by guards, and they threw us to the ground. The boy explained who we were. They let us go to stay in the car."

"The boy explained?"

"Yes, Herr Doktor. I was too ... uh ... He saved my life."

"I see."

Mengele examined the knot above the eye. "You'll live, but you'll have a headache for several days." The doctor climbed into the back seat with Jakob.

"Tell me, driver, did you know about any of this? It was your sonderkommando group. You lived with them."

"Oh no sir! They hated me because I was not a Jew! I am not even a Hungarian. They hated me and would not have told me anything."

"I see," Mengele said with a hint of skepticism in his voice.

Jakob played about in the floorboard behind the driver. He got down as far as he could and stuck his arm up under the driver's seat. The boy's rooting about caught the doctor's attention. "What are you doing down there? Get up off the floor. You are not a pig."

Jakob complied and stood. He held a small package he had extracted from beneath the driver's seat and showed it to Mengele.

"What do you have there?" The doctor took the package and unwrapped it. He said nothing as he examined its contents. He stepped back out of the car and summoned the nearest guard. "Take that man," he said, pointing to the driver. The guard dragged the driver out of the car once again and threw him to the ground.

The lieutenant came over to see what was happening. "What is it, Herr Doktor?"

"This man was smuggling this radio in my car. He had access to just about anywhere in the camp as my driver, and this is the result."

The lieutenant examined the radio. "Ahh. Quite clever. A rusty razor blade for the crystal. What should I do with him?"

"I do not care. Shoot him along with the rest. Better yet, take him to Block eleven and have him interrogated to see who else was involved with this. Have them find out whom he conspired with. Find out how the explosives made it to the camp and into the crematoria."

The doctor got into the car and started the engine.

The driver protested his innocence. "I had nothing to do with it! I never saw that thing before. Ask the boy!"

Mengele turned a deaf ear and put the car in gear to drive away. The driver pleaded with Jakob in the back seat. Jakob smiled, winked, and waved at the driver as soldiers dragged him away.

LATE OCTOBER 1944-JANUARY 1945

Zvi Spiegel, Zwillingsvater, had found himself standing in the entrance of the barracks much more the previous week. From far off to the east, waves of rumblings reverberated through the camp not unlike approaching summer storms. At first, the rumblings were heard perhaps two or three times a week. They were almost inaudible; they were felt more than heard, but their frequency and intensity built slowly each day. A palpable inquietude permeated the prisoner population and even more so the SS staff. News from smuggled newspapers stoked the rumor mill. The Red Army had driven the Germans back into Poland. Almost all of France had been liberated. Despite all attempts at censorship and rousing propaganda newscasts, Spiegel saw awareness of the grim realities all along the eastern and western fronts that had found their way into the psyches of the Auschwitz SS guards.

Hope was the rarest element in the Auschwitz universe. What should have been a herald of hope for the prisoners was actually taken as a bad omen. Spiegel felt a work gang of five hundred prisoners dismantling Crematoria II and III justified his apprehension.

The Nazis were erasing the evidence of the colossal crime called Auschwitz. Crematorium IV had already been destroyed by the revolt. Late one afternoon, explosions sent shock waves, smoke, and dust through Birkenau. Plastic explosives demolished what the work gang had not. Only Crematorium V remained intact. The talk was that its gas chamber and crematorium had been spared for the final purge of the last remaining witnesses before it too would vanish.

Mengele moved his dissecting laboratory into this last stronghold of death. Jakob and the other twins saw less and less of the doctor, and the result was less spoil for the barracks.

The apprehensive mood soon pervaded the boys' barracks as well. Just one day after Mengele returned from a leave home, all the boys were moved across the road to the former Gypsy barracks. The following day, the twin girls were moved in with them. Spiegel was certain such a change at Auschwitz could not be for anything but bad. The entire Gypsy camp had been liquidated in a single night from those very barracks.

Regardless of the looming threat, Zwillingsvater saw Jakob was excited at the prospect of seeing his sisters Leah and Rachel again. He watched his euphoria give way to despair when told by one of the older girls that they had been taken away one morning about two months earlier and had never been seen again. He watched Jakob withdrew into a dark and lonely corner within himself.

Early one morning soon after the consolidation of the girl and boy twins, a new SS doctor, Dr. Thilos, entered the barracks and ordered everyone to assemble. Guards recorded the numbers tattooed on the children's arms. Once the numbers were recorded, Thilos left. Soldiers barred the doors afterward and posted guards. A van would be by later to transport them to their demise.

The boys ran about frantically. One thirteen-year-old sharpened his stubby pocketknife vowing to kill at least one guard. Most just wailed. Zwillingsvater had to keep his wits about him. Somehow, perhaps miraculously, Zwillingsvater managed to persuade one of the guards to let him out to find Mengele. The guard had been around long enough to know the value Mengele placed on his twins.

Zwillingsvater risked his life by running to Mengele's relocated laboratory. Running drew the attention of the tower machine gunners. He had no idea if the doctor was even there, but it was the only chance he had at saving the boys and girls from annihilation. Even approaching the guards seeking permission to speak to Mengele could quite easily have gotten him killed. Zwillingsvater's hope was that no guard wanted to be responsible for keeping an urgent message from getting to the doctor. He finally found Mengele and informed him of the impending executions.

Sometime later, the guards removed the barricades, opened the doors, and told the children they were free to go outside. A story about an SS obersturmführer doctor packing his bags that very evening for a new assignment at an eastern-front field hospital became grist for the camp rumor mill.

By November 17, a new item circulated for the prisoners' consumption. An SS radio operator had told Nyiszli that the camp was under new orders to cease the special treatment—the SS euphemism for extermination—of all prisoners. No one believed that and least of all Spiegel because of the thousands of lies that had preceded that last bit. That was until a small, five-car transport pulled onto the ramp.

Spiegel watched from the doorway of the barracks as about five hundred sick, debilitated, and disoriented prisoners fell and stumbled out of the short transport. The small transport appeared to be just so much more fuel for the furnaces. But oddly, the fans were not whirring. The fireboxes were not stoked.

Long discussions occurred among the SS officers on the ramp. Surprisingly, they were all marched to F Camp, the prison infirmary. Later that day, another short train rolled onto the ramp with another five hundred prisoners—mostly elderly and women with children. They were led with their belongings to D Camp. *Are the rumor been true? The wholesale, indiscriminant murders are to cease?* Spiegel wondered.

He studied the goings-on at the ramp for several days. Ever the practitioner of the divining arts regarding the vagaries of the camp, he wrestled with the meaning of this new development and most important, what it meant to the twins in his care. He guardedly concluded it was a good turn of events. *How can such a departure from the practice of killing transport arrivals not be good? But this is still the universe of Auschwitz, which is still under the control of the satanic SS.*

What was good news for most prisoners was not as good for the Sonderkommandos. They were the living evidence of the size, scope, and depth of the Third Reich's most damning sin. Their first tasks as newly arrived inmates at Auschwitz had been to dispose of the bodies of the previous Sonderkommandos just as that group had disposed of the group before them. They were the thirteenth sonderkommando group.

Spiegel had picked up the story of the thirteenth sonderkommando group. A little after two in the afternoon on a late November day with leaden skies came the order: "Alle antreten!" "All assemble!"

The entire sonderkommando group assembled in the courtyard from all their scattered workstations. The guards called the roll and verified an exact muster list ensuring all were accounted for. The heavily armed SS guards marched them into the crematorium and sealed the entrances and the fates of the 460 souls. The four doctors of Mengele's inmate staff were pulled from among the condemned. Later that evening, Sonderkommando 13 was marched into the nearby forest and executed by flamethrowers. Even in its waning days, Auschwitz was able to find a new level of cruelty.

As if unwilling to be outdone by the cruelties of war, Spiegel felt winter harden. Biting cold driven by howling winds extinguished any embers of hope growing in the breast of any prisoner. The tax of surviving another winter day left nothing for nursing hope.

Late one evening, well after lights out, another explosion rocked the camp. Zwillingsvater got out of his bunk to see what was happening. Off in the direction of Crematorium V, a glowing red light reflected off the snow and hovering shroud of fog. Another omen. *Good? Bad?*

Spiegel heard the SS guards assigned to the crematoria ushering in the new year with unusually unrestrained enthusiasm. Their newfound depths of drunken depravity had been no doubt goaded by the same apprehensions as their prisoners had. After all, they too were witnesses of the unparalleled sins of the glorious Thousand Year Reich. Were they as expendable as the Sonderkommandos had proven to be?

Right after the twins had completed morning chores, several SS guards entered their barracks shouting a new order: "Collect your things and assemble outside! Raus! Raus!"

The twins were thrown into panic. They bundled themselves as best they could. Jakob wrapped his blanket around his shoulders. Zwillingsvater ran about assisting as best he could. He clung to the hope that the order to take their meager belongings meant they were being moved to another barracks.

Once they were assembled and counted, an SS sergeant addressed them. "You older ones are to assemble at the main gate." The selection was left to the sergeant. He quickly walked through the ranks of children shoving those he deemed of sufficient size out of the formation.

To the remainder, he announced, "The rest of you are being moved to the main camp. Follow these guards. Do not lag behind."

Zwillingsvater risked his life once again. "Oberscharführer, Dr. Mengele has assigned me to oversee his younger children. Is that what you wish me to continue doing, or has Dr. Mengele made other arrangements for them?"

The other guards were silenced by this. They expected to see the sergeant pull his service pistol and shoot the insolent fool. That didn't happen though. Death passed over once again at the mention of Mengele's name. The sergeant simply relented and shoved Zwillingsvater back toward the smaller children.

The company of forty-one children fell into step and followed the three soldiers and Zwillingsvater for the two-kilometer march to the Stammlager, the main camp, Auschwitz I. The cold and wind showed no more mercy to the children than it did to anyone else. Zwillingsvater helped Jakob, the youngest, struggle to keep pace with the soldiers and the other children. Mercifully, it took only a little more than an hour.

At the end of the march, they were ushered into one of the redbrick houses, which were far more substantial than the rough wooden barracks of Birkenau and thus offered more protection from the elements. Whether the relocation offered them more protection from the other perils of the camp remained to be seen.

A few days passed before Mengele made a rare afternoon visit to the twins' new barracks on January 17, 1945. Rarer still was the doctor's attire. He wore civilian clothes with a leather jacket and a soft wool cap. He made the SS private with him carry all his files to his car. Before leaving, he cupped Jakob's chin and admired his Aryan features as he had so many times before. "Ahh, my intelligentsia! You have been such a good boy."

JANUARY 18, 1945

The twins' barracks came to life before daybreak the following morning in the usual manner. It wasn't until after the housekeeping and preparation chores had been completed that Zwillingsvater noticed the new sound of the surrounding camp. More specifically, it was the lack of sound that was new. No shouts of commands, no dogs barking, no whistles. Nothing. *Has the newly fallen snow muffled the sounds so well?*

Zwillingsvater approached the window on cat's paws. He saw no one in the streets, no tracks in the snow. In neither of the guard towers he could see from the window did he see any sign of the otherwise ubiquitous machine gunners. He opened the door to the interior corridor and peeked out. No one. Summoning all his courage, he snuck down the corridor to the doors leading out onto the street and cracked the door just enough to get a glimpse of what was happening in the camp. Again, he saw nothing—not even wisps of smoke from the kitchens, the SS barracks, or the offices. Opening the door a little wider, he looked at two other guard towers. Just as the others were, they too were devoid of the usual menace.

He closed the door and stood motionless in the corridor trying to decipher what had happened. Caution dictated a measured approach. Nine months of Auschwitz had taught him that the SS found great pleasure in toying with the inmates. It was not inconceivable that they were hiding out of sight to encourage the inmates to make a run for freedom. They would then have legitimate reason to slaughter the remaining inmates. At some point though, someone would have to venture out.

He looked back toward the door of the twins' quarters. At least half a dozen faces peered out at him through the crack in the door. He crept back into the room with the twins. He no longer had the older children to assist him in managing his younger wards. He looked about to find the most mature of those who were left. Two eleven-year-old boys were the best he could find for the task of keeping order while he forayed out into the camp.

"Listen. I must leave you for a little while to get food. These two boys are in charge until I return. You must obey them. You must stay away from the windows and be as quiet as possible," he said with the sternest face he could muster. They all nodded in compliance. They had all learned to trust Zwillingsvater without question. Even the young ones understood how many times death had passed over them because of Zwillingsvater.

The camp kitchen sat one street over from the twins' barracks with another row of barracks between them. Zwillingsvater stepped outside onto the steps glancing once again at the two guard towers at opposite ends of the street. Still seeing no occupants, he dashed across the street and ducked between two barracks and out of sight of the towers. He crept along the wall of one of the barracks and paused as he approached the courtyard separating the barracks from the camp kitchen. Normally at that time of morning, the courtyard would be full of SS guards and kapos raining abuse on the camp muster of prisoners as they stood at attention to be accurately numbered.

On that morning, however, all that lay between him and the kitchen were the gallows used to instill fear and obedience. Upon them hanged three unfortunate, snow-covered corpses clad in their striped uniforms still silently warning prisoners. Zwillingsvater examined yet another guard tower for signs of life. Nothing. Like a hare avoiding an attack from a hawk circling above, Zwillingsvater darted across the vacant courtyard and found cover against the kitchen exterior. Again, he paused to see if he had been spotted. Satisfied he had gone unnoticed, he cupped his hands on the kitchen window to block the snow glare as he peered into the kitchen. Nothing.

Up to that point, had he been discovered, he may have been shot or just beaten, but what he was about to do if he were caught would cause him to join the three silent sentinels hanging just a few meters from where he huddled against the wall. Zwillingsvater slowly applied torque to the doorknob to test whether it was locked. To his surprise and relief, it was not. He opened the door, entered, and closed the door behind him as quickly as he could. It took a moment for his eyes to adjust from the bright snow glare to the dim interior of the kitchen. After a moment when he felt capable of silently navigating the dimness, he crept among the unfamiliar rooms.

He came to an interior pantry completely hidden from view from the outside. Reasonably assured turning on the light could not be seen, he flipped the switch. Nothing happened. He flicked the switch several times. Nothing. He found another light and tried it with similar results. The power was off. He found a sink and turned the water on. There was water but little pressure. He felt growing confidence that the SS had indeed left during the night. They had not come back to round up everyone. *The Russians must be close,* he thought.

With his newfound confidence, he organized as much food as he could. He found a couple of aprons and made bundles of food out of them. He made ready for the short run back to the twins' barracks. Stopping at the door and looking through the window in all directions as best as he could, he saw other prisoners emerging from various barracks. Their hunger-driven minds had made them reckless. An open-top SS staff car wheeled around the corner. Two soldiers in the back seat, SS officers, stood and sprayed them with machine-gun fire. As quickly as they had appeared, they disappeared the same way they had come in.

Zwillingsvater ducked and sat motionless for quite a long time. He wondered if they had been watching all along or if they were just a cluster of fanatical SS soldiers perfunctorily carrying out their last orders. Long minutes passed as Zwillingsvater considered his next move.

The door burst open, and three inmates fell in. They clambered over each other in their scramble to get to their feet. Once they regained their footing, they pilfered the kitchen for whatever food they could find. One saw Zwillingsvater and lunged for one of his bundles, but Zwillingsvater kicked past him and ran out the door only to encounter two more food-crazed inmates. One successfully latched onto one of the bundles causing it to open and spill its contents. That attracted others for a fight over what lay on the ground. Rather than join in the fight, Zwillingsvater elected to use the confusion to cover his exit toward the twins' barracks.

Anxious faces greeted him when he entered the barracks. The younger ones hugged his legs. They had no doubt heard the machine-gun fire. Some were crying whether from fright or happiness at Zwillingsvater's return; he couldn't determine which. He showed them the fruits of his foraging. He warned them to wait until he could sort it all out before they could eat. There were quite a number of other surviving prisoners and only so much food left to be organized. He first barricaded the door as best he could. If it were discovered these children had food, they would all be attacked children or not.

Later that morning, Zwillingsvater stood watch from the window as he had since earlier feeding the twins. More inmates wandered about. He even saw one of those he had encountered in the kitchen double over as he climbed the steps to the barracks across the way. He collapsed and fell face-first into a pile of dirty snow. He lay there motionless. Zwillingsvater assumed he was dead. *Poison? No, his body wasn't capable of digesting that much food any more. Poor soul ate himself to death.*

Jakob joined Zwillingsvater at the window rubbing his tattoo. After a few moments of watching the inmates stumbling outside, Jakob asked without looking up, "What happens now?"

It was a question that sounded more as if it had come from an adult rather than a child. Zwillingsvater, still caught off guard sometimes by Jakob's ability to understand even the most complex human interactions, replied simply, "I don't know."

"They won't be back now, the Germans. Dr. Mengele is gone too."

"And what makes you think that?"

Jakob looked up at Zwillingsvater. "He won't be back."

JANUARY 27, 1945

Nine days later, during the lengthening shadows of three in the afternoon, men in combat uniforms bearing rifles moved through the camp. Few of the remaining inmates could take notice of let alone welcome the liberating Red Army. Some of the twins, those still ambulatory enough to venture outside, begged Zwillingsvater to let them go out. Zwillingsvater's cautionary nature yielded to a logical but chilling deduction: if these new soldiers were hostile, there would be no other chance of help coming and it would be best that they killed them all right then. Zvi Spiegel no longer had any capacity for hope. He released them.

Many of the children lay in their cots barely able to lift their heads to see what was happening. Jakob was among them. The lack of heat, food, clean water, and death passing over all about them had finally taken its toll on the twins. Typhus had many in its grip. Jakob was in the early stages of the disease. His relatively better diet up until the past few weeks had allowed his young body to fight off the disease until just a day or two earlier.

Looking in on the sick children before he stepped outside, Zwillingsvater caught Jakob's eye. "We are saved, Jakob."

Jakob managed a smile but little else.

Zwillingsvater walked up to an officer and showed as much respect as he could by saluting him. The Russian eyed him for a moment and asked, "Do you speak Russian?"

Zwillingsvater understood enough to reply, "Nyet. Ungarisch, Cesky, und Deutsch."

"Ahh, Hungarian." He turned to his aide who in turn summoned a young soldier to translate. Through his translator, the Russian officer asked, "What is this place?" He swept his arm in a wide arc.

Upon hearing the question, Zwillingsvater lost his composure and fell to his knees weeping. The officer looked at his translator for an explanation. The translator could only shrug. Zwillingsvater wept for a minute or two before he could gather himself sufficiently to talk. *How can I possibly describe Auschwitz?*

But he did gather himself and introduced himself as Zvi Spiegel. He said his job was to care for the twins who were reserved for medical experiments. He described all he had seen—the thousands sent to the gas chambers every day, the starvation and disease, the experiments. He described the entire camp system including Birkenau and Monowitz. Pausing only long enough for the translator to catch up, he continued. The officer finally held up his hand for him to stop. He said something to his translator.

"Comrade Beshinkev wants to know if you can guide him through the camp."

"Yes. But first I must take care of my twins. Some are very sick."

"He wants to know how many twins there are."

"Forty-one." Zvi saw the look of incredulity on the officer's face.

"Here. This way. I'll show you," he said and led them to the twins' barracks.

The officer stepped into the barracks and looked about but just for a moment. He walked back outside and shouted some orders from the top of the step. Soldiers dashed about. A doctor soon appeared and was ushered into where the sick children lay. Soon, nurses joined the doctor with more equipment and vials of medicine.

"You will show me the camp now?"

Spiegel nodded, looked at the children, and saw that they were receiving the help they needed even though for some it might have been too late. He turned to leave when one of the children screamed. Everyone looked to see what had happened. The doctor was poised with a syringe at the child's arm. Zwillingsvater rushed to hold the child and comfort him explaining that these were good doctors. The child soon relented. He explained to the officer as they left the building how the SS doctors had performed horrific experiments on the children injecting them and constantly drawing their blood.

Later, after night had fallen on the camp, Spiegel heard actual laughter with music. Russian soldiers treated the capable inmates to singing and music. A few inmates were so energized as to actually dance. Ever the protector though, Zwillingsvater stayed with the children and especially the sick ones. They had all received medicine—probably penicillin he thought—and some were already responding well. Jakob got up and moved about although Zwillingsvater limited him. By the morning, he would be even stronger.

Just after daybreak the next morning, a hot breakfast made of some sort of grain was brought directly to the twins' barracks. For the first time in many months, they were happy, even most of the sick ones. Jakob was up and about as well. Though there was no need to hurry, the children devoured the pasty meal as if it might be taken away before they were able to consume it. Old habits died hard.

Before the breakfast dishes could be cleared properly, a group of soldiers came in and informed everyone they were to be the subject of a movie. Most of the children did not understand. Zwillingsvater explained to them as best he could. A few nurses came in with bundles of striped prison pajamas. They were to wear them for the cameras.

Zwillingsvater held up some of the pants against the children to show how huge the clothes were. The Nazis had not made child-sized prison wear for obvious reasons, but that did not deter the filmmakers.

"Simply put on several layers and roll up the sleeves," they ordered. Cooperation was probably the safest route to take, so he cajoled all his wards to do their best and don the prison garb.

Once they were all suited up and inspected by the Russian filmmaker, they marched out into the cold to a narrow walkway between two rows of barbwire fence. The children balked at the wire, which to that point had meant death to touch. Zwillingsvater immediately saw the problem and demonstrated that the wire was safe by actually touching it.

They walked out of the fence line several times. A nurse held Jakob, who had not fully recovered; the two led the procession. Zwillingsvater saw Jakob looking over the nurse's shoulder watching two cute twin girls who were following right behind the nurse. As they made a turn to exit the fence, one of the girls stuck her tongue out at the camera. Zwillingsvater saw Jakob smile at her for her irreverence.

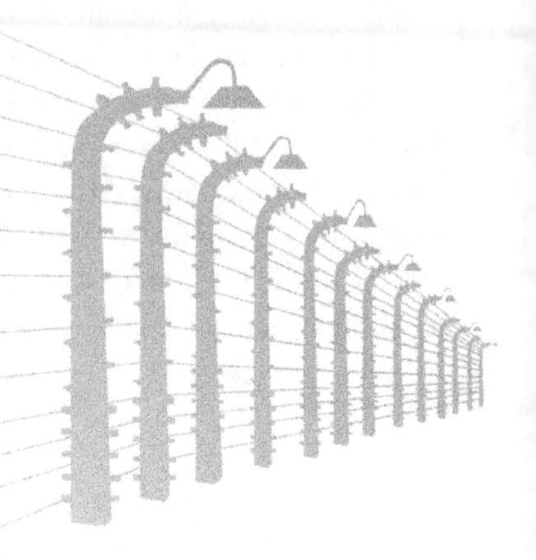

CHAPTER 8

MARCH 21, 2019

Malone caught a ride back to Saint Paul–Minneapolis with Pilsner, his advance work at the event site having been completed. A couple of hours later, he pulled in behind the state examiner's office and led Malone through the back entrance. Before heading to the mortuary, Pilsner took Malone to his small office so she could drop off her travel bag and heavy coat.

Chris could tell at a glance that Pilsner had been in that same office for decades. Tall stacks of journals, bulging file cabinets, and a well-worn carpet told the whole story. It was a familiar tale for most of the pathologists she had met in her career. As the old professional adage went, "There's no money in the dead," so most of them had adequate but meager accommodations.

They gowned up before entering the restricted area of the autopsy suite. Malone took note of the bodies on the gurneys parked along the wall. Even the state's capacity for the surge of victims was overtaxed. Fortunately, someone had lowered the temperature in the corridor.

Pilsner introduced Dr. Steve Olson to Malone. "Dr. Olson has been preparing the brain stem slides."

"I've been giving some thought to that very phenomenon, the on-off effect. I wanted to take a detailed look at the physiological components that control the autonomic functions. Breathing, heart rate, that sort of thing. So I called back here yesterday to have Dr. Olson take a closer than usual look at the tissue in the brain stem area, particularly the medulla. If something is disrupting the autonomic functions, perhaps we'll find something in the brain region that controls those functions," Pilsner said.

"I'm a little rusty on my anatomy of the brain. The part of the brain that drugs affect is what part?" Malone asked a little embarrassed for not knowing.

"The VTA, the ventral tegmental area, is where the highs come from. The reward center. Dopamine, a neurotransmitter, gets dumped into the system and gives that feel-good sensation."

"If I remember correctly, the VTA is part of the midbrain, correct?" she said hoping to save a little face.

"Yes. It's actually on the floor of the midbrain, kind of at the boundary layer between the pons and the midbrain."

"The midbrain, the pons, and the medulla along with the VTA between the midbrain and pons all make up the brain stem, correct?" Chris asked.

"Yes."

Malone grasped at a tenuous connection in her mind. "The other consistent puzzle piece is the drug histories of just about all the victims."

"But drugs weren't found in their systems," Pilsner said.

"I know, but that doesn't eliminate the histories."

"True. So what are you saying?"

"I'm not saying anything—just trying to take the only two puzzle pieces we have to see if they fit together. The victims died as if their autonomic functions had been disrupted. They had histories with drugs. Autonomic functions are controlled by the medulla. Drugs affect the VTA. The medulla and the VTA are part of the brain stem just millimeters apart."

Pilsner turned to Olson. "Have you found anything unusual?"

"I have. Dr. Malone may be on the right track. Let's go into the lab."

Olson led them into the lab, where he continued with his findings. "All but one victim showed signs of extensive hemorrhaging throughout the brain stem."

"Your one exception—was that the elderly woman?" Malone asked.

Olson flipped through his notes for a moment. "Uh, yes ... yes it was. What led you to that?"

"She didn't have anything else in common with the others. It looks like it was just her misfortune to die at the same time as the rest."

"Anything else?" Pilsner asked.

"I'd already started looking at the whole stem and the cerebellum before I got your message. Let me show you what we've gotten on the slides so far." Olson crossed the room to a bank of flat-screen monitors and pulled up enlargements on four of the screens.

"These are slides from the parts of the brain stem—the pons, the medulla oblongata, and the midbrain. This fourth one is from cerebellum tissue. Notice the damage to the cells on all of them except the cerebellum. The cerebellum is part of the hindbrain as are these other components, but it's not a part of the stem."

"Did this thing attack just the stem? Did you look at other regions of the brain?" Chris asked.

"Not yet, but that's next on the agenda now that I've seen these. It'll be interesting to see if the damage is limited to the stem alone. That'd be a pretty specific pathogen if that's the case."

Malone studied the images a little longer. "Can you test for foreign material at the cellular level?"

"Sure. It'll take a little longer," Olson answered.

"It'll go faster if we know what we're looking for. What'd you have in mind?" Pilsner asked.

"The other puzzle piece—drugs," Malone answered. "I know nothing showed on the tox screens, but tox screens are taken from blood samples. Let's see if these two puzzle pieces make the picture any clearer. Something tells me drugs are at the root of this."

"I'll get on it right away. I'll take samples from the victim who's on the table now," Olson said and headed off to some other part of the lab.

Malone looked at her watch. "I have to get to the airport for my flight to Atlanta. Can you send me any information you get as soon as you get it please? I have a meeting with my boss to discuss the other two incident sites. My understanding is they don't have any more that we do."

"You got it," Pilsner replied.

"Thanks. Can you take me back to your office to get my things? I've held you back from your work long enough."

Chris got the next-to-last seat on a flight that had been delayed for two hours. A cold front moving across the Plains had kicked off severe storms over a thousand-mile line. Being the last passenger to book, she had a middle seat between two large gentlemen. The same front that caused the initial delay passed over northern Georgia about the same time the flight was due to arrive, and that provided for an exciting ride and another forty-five-minute delay. But being the veteran traveler she was, Chris didn't care. She'd be home soon and would sleep in her own bed that night with Sam.

She got a text from Patterson after she landed.

Meeting tomorrow morning with FBI, DHS. 10:00 a.m.

The taxi dropped her off at her house at nine thirty. Chris found Sam in the kitchen fixing her a cucumber sandwich, her favorite. "How was your flight?"

"Great except for a two-hour delay, being seated in between two guys who looked like they could have been tackles for the Atlanta Falcons, and three hours of turbulence. Other than that it was great." She leaned over the counter and kissed him. "How was your day?"

"Not bad. Typical work problems."

Chris took a bite of the sandwich. "Mmmm. Thank you. Comfort food."

Sam came around from behind the counter and gave her a proper hug and kiss that he followed up with a two-handed shoulder rub. Chris felt much of the stress of the road leave her body.

"And how's Erika?" Chris asked dreading an answer that would kill the mood.

Sam drew a deep breath and exhaled. "No big flare-ups today. We had dinner together and a wonderfully engaging conversation about current events, her ambitions for college ... that sort of things."

"Really?" Chris asked in envy.

"Are you kidding? She barely said two words, but that trademark pissy attitude of hers was there. She's been in her room since."

Chris laughed at her gullibility a little embarrassed, but the desire to have her only child back was just too great. "Silly me."

"She'll be back. This is pretty typical. At least that's what they say," Sam said, hugging her again.

"I'll go up in a minute and poke my head in."

"Be careful she doesn't bite it off."

Chris savored her sandwich and the taste of home. Afterward, she pulled her dirty clothes from her travel bag and dropped them in the laundry room. Anyone familiar with the situation might have thought Chris was stalling. She was in fact mentally preparing herself not to overreact to whatever her daughter said or did. She didn't want to be baited into another battle.

Chris climbed the stairs to her daughter's room. The door was closed, so she knocked, "Erika? You in there?"

"What?"

"Are you there?"

"No, this is the next-door neighbor."

Chris ignored the attempted insult. "Can I come in?" She tried to open the door but found it was locked.

Momentarily, it unlatched, abruptly leaving Chris to open it enough to enter. She carefully picked her way across the clothing-strewn floor and resisted the urge to pick stuff up. "I got in just a little while ago. I just wanted to come up and say hello."

Erika looked up from her cell phone. The look on her face said, *Okay. You've said it. Now leave.*

Chris persisted. "You have a birthday coming up in a couple of weeks. Sweet sixteen. Any ideas what you'd like?"

Clearly exasperated with her mother's presence, Erika looked up from her cell phone again. "To be left alone?"

Chris resisted the urge to snatch the phone from Erika's hand and smash it on the floor. Instead, she chose to retreat but was unsure if that was cowardly or wise. Recent experience had taught her such encounters just metastasized into diatribes that highlighted her many failings as a parent. Chris was honest with herself; she knew that at that point, she simply didn't have a reserve of emotional capital to spend. The past three days had simply been too taxing. Chris closed her daughter's door behind her. She heard the lock click as she descended the stairs.

MARCH 22, 2019

Chris tore herself away from the Minnesota prairie. Lost somewhere over the snowdrifts stretching to the horizon, her daughter called out to her, "What's that buzzing?" The frozen prairie melted away to her own darkened bedroom. She reached for the persistent alarm. Normally, she'd be awake ahead of the alarm as her subconscious was already planning the day ahead and solving problems. Not that morning. Her body's fatigue overwhelmed the mind with its demand for rest.

Sam stirred beside her as she sat up and leaned back on the headboard. Her wakefulness erased most of the anxiety the dream had provoked in her. Most but not all. She savored the relief from having been in just a dream. But beneath the dream was the tormenting thought that Erika was involved with drugs. She told herself she was overreacting—projecting all she'd seen and heard in Minnesota onto the situation with Erika. *Just a mother's overprotective instincts*, she thought. *Erika knows better.*

She showered, got dressed, and fixed a breakfast better than usual with cut-up fruit, toast, oatmeal, orange juice, and coffee. Sam shuffled in, perched on one of the stools at the counter, and took a healthy portion of all that was offered. When Chris joined him, he reached around her, squeezed her shoulder, and kissed the top of her head.

"What's your day look like?" she asked.

"Oh you know, just another day for Atlanta's rising-star financial adviser who influences markets worldwide with every recommendation he makes," Sam replied.

"Whoa, big boy. You need to lay off those self-improvement courses. Your ego is plenty healthy."

"You're right. Let me give an answer based on reality. I'm meeting several couples in their midfifties who have suddenly realized they need to start saving so they'll have better than a dog-food diet in retirement. I'll probably be a little late this evening."

"Reality sucks."

"What about your day? They gonna give you a break and let you have an easy first day back?"

"Hardly. I'm going to try to take a couple of hours off this afternoon. Before that, though, I have a meeting this morning, and Homeland Security and the FBI will be there."

"Well, I think we've departed the usual couple's chitchat."

"Sorry. Too abrupt?" Chris was teasing him.

"No. I'm just wondering how many other couples in America start their day talking about their meetings with the FBI and Homeland Security."

"Yeah, this is a big one. Really weird. Lethal. Not sure yet, but drugs may be at the root of it."

Chris was about to expand on what she and Pilsner had discussed when Erika slunk into the kitchen.

"Good morning. You're up early. I fixed a nice breakfast for you."

Toast and juice were all she took before shuffling out.

"You know, in polite society, people greet each other," Sam said, annoyed.

"Gotta get ready for school," Erika retorted over her shoulder.

Sam began to say something else, but Chris put her hand on his arm. "Let it go. Dark side of the moon," she said, alluding to their running joke they had christened the Apollo Effect, a reference to the communications blackout the Apollo astronauts and ground control experienced when the command module traveled around the far side of the moon. Most parents of teenagers understood the reference as that period of anxiety, dread, and hope for the restoration of communication.

"So waddya think about having another one?" Sam asked.

Chris spewed a mouthful of coffee across the counter. She slugged Sam on the shoulder. "How 'bout we get you castrated?"

"Not the right time?"

"You wanna be dealing with this crap in your sixties?"

"I see your point."

Chris's mirth faded as she considered her daughter's disaffection.

Sam saw her melancholy. "She'll come back to us. It's just that phase designed to drive parents crazy."

"Promise? I just want my little girl back. It's such a dangerous world," Chris said.

Seeing his opportunity, Sam ventured into the territory of a sensitive subject. "Do you think they're going to pull you off the road now?"

"I think they might. Hope so anyway," Chris replied but that time without the edge of defensiveness. She had had enough of travel.

"I think you've earned your stripes by now," Sam said. "It's someone else's turn."

Chris didn't respond, but she did agree. She had indeed earned her stripes. She hoped this current assignment—coordinating the investigations from Atlanta—would be the start. Some travel would no doubt still be involved, but it would not be nearly on the same scale. If not, maybe it was time for a career change. Perhaps academia.

Sam looked at his watch, "Gotta run." He gulped the last of his coffee.

"Yeah. I need to get going as well. You taking Erika to school?"

"One of her friends is picking her up."

"A friend?"

"Lorrie. The one who's a junior and has her license."

"Lorrie? As if I needed something else to worry about."

"What? You don't like Goth or Visigoth or whatever that look is?"

Chris sighed in defeated resignation.

Chris arrived at the CDC campus at about eight thirty. The meeting with the FBI and DHS wasn't until ten. The team leaders from the three affected sites were to be present via teleconferencing. She'd use the time before the meeting to contact them for status reports. She didn't like the idea of having outside agencies or for that matter her own administration people present when updates were given. If there was a surprise, she wanted to know about it first. More important, she wanted a solution ready should a problem arise. Management was more easily managed from below if they were well prepared with solutions for any problems. A "We'll get back to you" response was always an open invitation for upper-level meddling.

"Good morning, Lawrence. How are things in sunny Minnesota?"

"Looking up. It's supposed to break above freezing today. We should complete the SEI interviews by the end of the day, tomorrow at the latest."

"Are you seeing any obvious patterns?"

"Well, the interviewees who seem most open and straightforward have indicated drug histories for the deceased. I asked the sheriff's office to confirm, and they all had some record of drug activity except the old lady."

"Yeah, that's what I suspected. I hope to have some tox screenings from brain tissue today. Perhaps we'll find our missing drugs there."

"There's one other thing that's shown up but only in about twenty percent of the cases. Six of the deceased had participated in the same drug-recovery program before dropping out."

"Really? Which one?" Malone asked.

"That national one, the Campaign for Hope. Tudos more or less sponsored it."

"Just twenty percent?"

"Yeah. I know it's not across the board, but it's statistically significant."

"Significant but not a smoking gun. But we'll throw it in the mix and see if there's any correlation."

"I was just wondering. I got a call last night from the DEA inquiring about what we're finding. Thought it kind of odd."

"DEA?"

"Yeah. At least that's who they said they were. I didn't give 'em too much info. Could've been a reporter."

"Probably wise. Wonder if they'll be at the ten o'clock meeting." Chris paused to ponder a moment about this latest bit of information. "Thanks, Lawrence. Gotta catch the other two team leaders before ten. Talk to you then."

"See you at ten." Lawrence hung up.

Chris knew the other two teams leaders but not as well as she knew Lawrence. Accordingly, she was a little more formal with them in her conversation than with Lawrence. She was mindful of the potential for resentment for her having been selected to be the national coordinator, but she detected no hint of umbrage. She confirmed the victims in the other areas had also had drug-related offenses. She asked they confirm that with the local authorities. Before ending the conversation, she asked them if they had been contacted by the DEA. Glenn Wallace from the Renovo, Pennsylvania, site affirmed he had done that the evening before.

She was done with the calls to the field by nine. After a quick scan of her emails, she saw one from Pilsner with attachments. His lab had found opiates in the brain stem tissue and trace amount of something else. Lead. She downloaded the information onto a thumb drive so she could present it at the ten o'clock meeting. For the remaining forty-five minutes, she sketched out a presentation even though it was not her meeting. She included in the slides a diagram of the brain from the internet with just the right amount of detail before running to the meeting.

The conference room buzzed with indistinguishable chatter as Chris entered. Seated at the center of the table was Patterson, her boss. He was leaning over toward the person in uniform to his right, none other than the head of the CDC, Dr. Michael Weinstein.

Good Lord, Chris thought. *This is higher profile than I'd imagined. Too late now. Better cinch up the saddle nice and tight. Could be a wild ride.*

Patterson saw her and motioned her to the remaining empty chair at the table. Chris made her way through the crowd and took her seat beside him. As soon as she settled in, Patterson rapped on the table with his knuckles. The room fell quiet.

"Okay, folks. Let's get started." The three field team leaders identified themselves and joined in by way of video conferencing. "Fine. Thank you for joining us. I'd like to make some introductions before we get going with the discussions. First, most of you know Dr. Weinstein, head of the CDC. He's here this morning to be brought up to speed on these recent incidents." Weinstein nodded to acknowledge his introduction, and Patterson continued. "We also have Special Agent Wayne Abbott from the FBI, Jim Crabtree from Homeland Security, and Robert LaCosta from DEA."

Chris's ears perked up when the DEA agent was introduced. Clearly, someone somewhere suspected a link to drugs before she had gotten her information from Pilsner. She roused herself from her speculations regarding the DEA when Patterson asked, "Dr. Malone, can you give us an update on the investigations please?"

Chris cleared her throat and pointed at the IT technician still in the room. "Could you help me download some images please?" She handed him the thumb drive.

The technician readied the projector and the controls; Chris addressed the room. "Apologies for not having prepped for this earlier, but I received some of this information less than an hour ago. I would remind everyone we've been aware of this incident for only a little more than a hundred hours."

Chris displayed a map of the US with three red dots showing the incident sites. She reviewed the nature of the events and the sudden deaths.

A voice from one of the teleconferencing speakers interrupted. "This is Lawrence Sanders in Minnesota. We've not found any more victims, but I asked the local authorities to let me know if they get any reports of missing persons. There is a report that came in yesterday afternoon of a fellow who's been missing for a little more than three days now. That puts it in the same time frame as the other deaths. They're searching the hunting camps and ice-fishing shacks. Lot of remote areas up here."

"Thank you, Dr. Sanders." Chris returned to her normal speaker's voice before continuing. "Dr. Sanders hits on a commonality of all three of these sites. They are all in sparsely populated areas. All three have one-industry economies, timber or mining. All three are in more-wintry climes."

For the benefit of those with less-scientific backgrounds, Chris began her presentation by giving an anatomy refresher with an elemental diagram of the brain. But not wanting to throw too much information at her audience, she focused on portions of the brain germane to the early findings from the autopsies. Specifically, she explained the location and makeup of the brain stem.

Confident everyone had a grasp of the brain's anatomy, she showed the slides of the damaged brain stem tissue Pilsner had provided. She introduced the results of the drug screening done on the victims' brain stem tissue.

"The VTA is directly adjacent to the brain stem area, and it's where drugs have their effects. The loss of the brain stem would also lead to a loss of autonomic functions such as breathing and heart rate. And this is why I presume Agent LaCosta from the DEA is with us this morning," Malone said.

Agent LaCosta shifted in his seat as the attention of the room turned to him. Chris rescued him for the moment by continuing. "From Dr. Pilsner's chart, you can see these victims were *not* drug-free as originally thought. Just their blood was drug-free. Blood screens for drugs could not detect the drugs present at the cellular level. Connecting the dots, we can now build a picture of some sort of drug involvement."

The room buzzed for a few minutes as the attendees grasped the implications of Chris's revelations. Weinstein again injected himself into the discussion. "This aspect of drug-use histories—is it true for all three sites?"

Chris projected her question toward the speaking heads. "Renovo and Bonners Ferry, did you find similar histories with your SEI surveys?"

A pause ... "Bonners Ferry here. Yes we did, and law enforcement verified it."

"Same here in Renovo."

Again, the room broke into sidebar conversations. Chris raised her voice to be heard above the din. "Please have the medical examiners take a close look at the tissue samples from the stem sections."

"Will do."

The room fell quiet again as Dr. Weinstein addressed the DEA representative. "Agent LaCosta, as Dr. Malone has alluded to, your presence at this meeting suggests some prior knowledge or at a minimum a suspicion of some sort of connection to illegal drugs. Would you care to apprise this group of what the DEA knows about this situation?"

Though it was framed as a polite request, Malone knew a command when she heard one. The room waited patiently as LaCosta squirmed and cleared his throat. "Well, the DEA has been tracking a new phenomenon that's recently hit the streets. The street name is Smokey because of its grayish color. Lab tests show that the actual narcotic content of the drug is actually very low, much less than one tenth of one percent of the usual dose. But the intel on the street is that it provides the same highs. The other substance that is added to the street drug apparently targets the VTA as Dr. Malone has explained. One amazing side effect of this new drug is that the number of overdoses has actually fallen off by more than eighty percent in the last two months nationwide."

"But now, death is no longer taking a holiday," Weinstein said.

"By way of the FBI, we received a sample from the Minnesota site, and it proved to be Smokey."

"I see. What you've described as a drug capable of targeting specific portions of the body strikes me as involving a technology I find hard to believe drug cartels have the capacity to develop or manufacture. In fact, with that sort of sophistication, why not just go legit and still make billions without the threat of going to prison? A drug like that could revolutionize how chemotherapy is administered. If you could smart-bomb a specific area of the body, massive doses could be delivered without all the horrible side effects normally associated with chemo."

Malone was impressed with Weinstein's ability to so quickly grasp the significance of the drug with so little information.

"The DEA doesn't believe the cartels are making this themselves but have somehow obtained it from a legitimate source. This technology is the current Holy Grail of the pharmaceutical industry, and for the very reason you point out, it will indeed revolutionize drug therapies," LaCosta replied.

Chris thought a moment about the logistics of drug trafficking as she understood them and asked, "Have you seized any of this drug coming into the US?"

"No, just the usual types of drugs. But interestingly enough, the sizes of our seizures have also dropped correspondingly to the mixture ratio. We're not seeing the large caches."

"That would indicate to me that the targeting drug is mixed with cocaine, meth, heroin—whatever—once it gets here," Chris said, forming her own hypothesis.

"That's what we think. Yes, the cartels can maintain their markets with shipments that are magnitudes smaller than previous shipments and still satisfy demand. It requires only blending it stateside. Their risk of detection and seizure is minimized."

"Have you made any seizures of the targeting drug anywhere?"

"Only in small quantities that are already mixed with the other agent drug like what was recovered at the site in Minnesota. Please remember, this is a new drug. Our standard methods of detecting and locating drugs, primarily dogs, aren't picking up on this unless it's blended with the actual narcotic. Until we retrain our dogs, boatloads of this stuff could be moving all over the country."

Weinstein asked, "Have you pursued the pharmaceuticals?"

LaCosta answered, "Yes. Well ... the FBI has. Perhaps Special Agent Abbott would like to respond to that."

Abbott fumbled briefly before replying. "There are three companies currently marketing targeting-type drugs." He looked at his notes a moment, "Astra Medicinals, Tudos Pharmaceuticals, and Century Pharmaceuticals."

Scribbling furiously, Chris asked, "What was that second one?"

"Tudos Pharmaceuticals. T-U-D-O-S. *Tudos* is Hungarian for 'savant.'"

Malone recognized the name from what Sanders had told her earlier about the number of victims who had been a part of the Challenge for Hope program. She thought about mentioning that but thought better of interrupting Weinstein.

"What has your investigation turned up?" Weinstein asked.

"I'm sorry, but I can't discuss details of an active investigation in a group such as this."

Weinstein did not reply immediately; he stared blankly at the FBI agent before asking, "Are the three field teams still on the call?"

They all replied they were.

"Thank you. I'd like you all to disconnect now please. Don't worry. I'll make sure Dr. Malone briefs you thoroughly on whatever else you need."

Three clicks from the speakers punctuated the muted room.

"Now Mr. Abbott, the only people who will hear what you have to say regarding the investigations are in this room. I assure you that whatever information you have will stay with them. I do not want to hear coming out of your mouth any nonsense about a need to know. I assure you that everyone in this room has a need to know. I will not have this investigation hamstrung by interagency turf battles. Seventy-four people died in less than a twelve-hour period in a way we've never witnessed before. Something tells me we haven't seen the last of this whatever it is.

"I'm at a point in my career now that I no longer have to concern myself with political fallout. If necessary, I'll call a press conference this afternoon and complain about the lack of cooperation from other agencies and specifically the FBI. I believe in today's parlance that's called bad optics. Some might call it the nuclear option. Whatever, I just want an unencumbered path to getting to the root of this and figuring out a way to stop it from happening again. I have no qualms about using anything at my disposal to obtain that unencumbered path."

The room fell quiet again for another insufferable pause. "Now, Special Agent Abbott, what have your investigations revealed about these three pharmaceuticals?"

Abbott cleared his throat and explained that none of the companies had distributed any of the finished products to any recipients other than legitimate destinations. All those destinations had accounted for their on-site stores. "However," he said, "Tudos had a problem accounting for the proper disposal of a rather large volume of out-of-spec material, several batches that had been contaminated in some way. And a large shipment destined for a licensed disposal facility didn't make it. The truck was hijacked, and it appears a shipping clerk tried to falsify the records to cover it up."

"Thank you, Special Agent Abbott. I look forward to a cooperative working relationship between our two agencies."

Chris broke the tension by sharing what she had gathered from Sanders regarding the victims who had participated in the Tudos-sponsored rehab program. "It may just be a series of coincidences, but it's still nonetheless odd."

"I don't believe in coincidences," Weinstein shot back. "Any more pieces to this puzzle?"

Malone sensed Weinstein was drawing the meeting to an end. "Just one. Also discovered in the medical examiner's findings was the presence of lead in the sample tissue though in small amounts, only slightly higher than typical background."

"Lead?" Weinstein asked.

"Yes sir. It's a consistent characteristic that appears in all the Minnesota victim tissue samples taken so far. The other victims will be sampled as well. Probably happening as we speak."

Weinstein's assistant leaned over from behind him and whispered something in his ear. He looked at his watch, collected his notepad, and rose. "If you will, please pardon this disruption. I must leave for another engagement. Thank you, Dr. Malone. Quite informative." Before exiting, he leaned down and whispered something to Patterson.

Patterson dismissed the meeting; before Chris could escape, he caught her by the arm, "Chris, Dr. Weinstein would like you to join us for lunch in his office at one o'clock. Are you available?" Chris understood framing it as a polite request was just a courtesy.

LaCosta approached her just outside the conference room. "Dr. Malone, Robert LaCosta, DEA. Sorry I didn't get to introduce myself earlier." He held out his hand.

Chris regarded him and shook his hand. "Agent LaCosta."

"About your last point about the presence of lead in the tissue. I wanted to let you know we've found small amounts as a precipitant in our drug tests. It drops out whenever we test the Smokey drug."

"Thank you, Agent LaCosta. That seems to be a characteristic with growing consistency."

Chris headed back to her office. She checked her email for any brushfires. Satisfied there was nothing that couldn't wait, Chris typed "Tudos" into the search engine. She didn't believe in coincidences either.

More than ninety thousand responses came back. Many were articles from trade journals and business magazines. Several from Holocaust websites appeared farther down the list. She started her education by reading the company's website to see what they had to say about themselves.

> About Us → Our History →
>
> The story of Tudos Pharmaceuticals began in 1978 during the worst recession since the Great Depression. It was a period of double-digit inflation, unemployment, and skyrocketing interest rates. It was not a time to be launching a new company—at least that was the conventional thinking of the day. However, a very unconventional thinker saw things quite differently. A young Hungarian immigrant and survivor of Auschwitz saw an opportunity when he took his entire fortune and purchased a nearly bankrupt pharmaceutical company. Using its existing infrastructure, he turned it into an internationally renowned producer of innovative pharmaceutical products. The story of Tudos Pharmaceuticals is really the story of Dr. Jakob Bauer.

Chris thought it odd that in a company's description of itself, so much emphasis was placed on its founder. Intrigued, she clicked the Dr. Jakob Bauer link. Several more links appeared under his name—nearly as many as for Tudos itself. She clicked on one that looked like it would be a general biography on a website not associated with the company.

She read with interest about Bauer's Auschwitz experience, his being a Mengele twin, and his numerous brushes with death. Chris felt her admiration for the man grow as she continued reading about his trials and triumphs through the postwar years. During the seventies, the roots for the current pharmaceutical empire took hold. Indeed, *innovative* was the proper adjective to describe the company's advances in drugs.

Hunger pangs brought her back around to the task at hand—becoming as well informed as possible before her working lunch with the two top people in the CDC in the next few minutes. She decided to indulge her fascination with the Jakob Bauer story later. Going back to the Tudos website, she clicked on "Products." She scribbled furiously in her composition notebook the names of the company's drugs and a brief description of their use, but nothing jumped out at her. A tinge of anxiety goaded her; she was wasting precious prep time. Another link looked promising: "Emerging Technologies Research." *Pay dirt,* she thought. The descriptions of half a dozen research projects filled just the first page. Rather than take notes, she printed it all out, three pages worth.

She quickly did the same for the other two companies; her pink highlights adorned nearly all the printed pages. But there was one description on her Tudos pages that really caught her eye: "Powering Nanobots with Radio Waves." Buried in the description was the phrase "lead peroxide crystals" *Lead.* She circled the section briskly in pink.

Chris checked her watch and saw she had just ten minutes to get to Weinstein's office. She gathered her notes and printouts and headed out the door only to get twenty feet down the hall before turning back. She dug her old address book out of the bottom of the drawer. Joyce Ellis. *It's been so long since I talked to her that I don't have her contact info on my phone.* She typed in the email address and banged out a message.

> Hi Joyce, Can't talk right now but will get back to you in about 2 hours. Sorry, but I desperately need your help. What can you tell me about any new drugs or procedures Tudos Pharmaceuticals has into the FDA

for approval? Sorry for all the mystery. Talk to you in a little while.

Chris hit send and ran out of her office at a pace a little slower than a sprint. She reached Weinstein's receptionist at 1:05. "Go right in. They're expecting you."

Swell, Chris thought.

"I'm so sorry I'm late. Something came up just as I left my office."

Weinstein reassured her it was perfectly okay; he said he and Patterson had been talking about their March Madness brackets. Patterson said nothing choosing to convey his annoyance at Chris's tardiness with a glare.

"Grab a sandwich and join us at my worktable," Weinstein said, pointing to the service cart with a platter of sandwiches, chips, canned sodas, and water.

Until that moment, Chris hadn't realized how hungry she was. She repressed the urge to stack several sandwiches on her plate choosing instead a meager half sandwich of tuna salad and some carrots. She joined the two men still standing as they waited for her to sit. *Old-school guys.*

"What's happened since this morning's update?" Weinstein inquired.

Chris, sandwich poised inches from her mouth, cleared her throat. "I don't think this is a biological pathogen. Given the drug histories of the victims, I'm leaning toward some sort of toxin. Also, I don't think biologics would behave in such a way. At least none I'm aware of."

"I think that's a valid estimation of the situation," Patterson said. "I think we should pursue that theory unless and until some new evidence says otherwise."

"I think the toxin theory is even more frightening," Weinstein said flatly. "A biological pathogen holds out the possibility of coming from natural origins. Toxins tend to fall more in the realm of human origin. Many of them are created specifically for harmful purposes."

Chris, finally having taken a bite of her sandwich, ruminated a moment on what Weinstein had said and what she had learned that morning. Some things seemed to be linked logically—cause and effect—like the damage to the brain stem and the observed symptoms. Other things were too implausible to occur naturally.

Wiping her mouth, Chris blurted out, "What's the oddest fact about these events we have so far?"

Patterson and Weinstein looked at her incredulously as if to ask, *What do you mean? All of it's odd.*

Chris saw she was overextended. She rallied to explain her question. "We've seen pathogens attack sections of the brain before. We've seen multiple victim incidents. But where have we seen events occurring almost simultaneously before?"

"Nine eleven," Weinstein said flatly.

"Human origin. Terrorism. Three separate events hundreds of miles apart require coordination, communication—"

"Funding," Weinstein interjected.

"God help us," Patterson said.

"Indeed," agreed Weinstein.

"After what the DEA guy LaCosta said, I was hoping that the worst case was that some bad drugs had made it onto the street," Patterson said. "I had the same hope the first plane hitting the Towers on 9/11 was just an accident. Right up until the second plane struck."

Weinstein slumped into his chair and sighed. "I think you've just articulated what we were all dreading but didn't want to face. What do we know about the three pharmaceutical companies the FBI guy Abbott named?"

Patterson said, "Well, Tudos, Savant, is right. Jakob Bauer really is one. Some of the things his company has come up with have really been due to out-of-the-box thinking. He has a knack for attracting the brightest minds to work for him, but if what I hear is true, he's really the brains behind many of the innovations. Not all of them pass over FDA hurdles, but they're clever."

Chris jumped in. "I found some info on some of their new research that may have a tie-in to what we're looking for. Something to do with powering nanobots some way that involves lead peroxide. The medical examiner mentioned tiny amounts of lead in the tissue samples. Agent LaCosta told me after the meeting that they were finding tiny amounts of lead as a precipitate in their drug-testing regimens. It's thin but worth pursuing." She made a mental note to have the medical examiners check for elevated lead counts in the victims' bone marrow.

"Run it to ground and see if it leads anywhere," Patterson said.

"An old college friend works for the FDA. Just before coming here, I sent her an email requesting any info she had on applications from Tudos. It's why I was a little late getting here," Chris said.

"See if she has anything on the other two. We don't know anything for sure yet. Let's not get tunnel vision or start any rumors," said Weinstein.

"I seem to remember some Wall Street talk a few years back about one of those big pharmas having some sort of bloodless coup in the boardroom. Maybe it was Tudos. I can't remember the details," Patterson said.

"My husband's a financial adviser. He lives and breathes that stuff. If he doesn't know some corporate secrets, he's pretty good at ferreting them out."

Weinstein looked at Chris for a moment and turned to Patterson. "See if you can find Dr. Malone here an assistant, someone who can be discreet. She's going to be very busy in the next few days."

"I think we can find someone suitable."

Weinstein rose and dismissed the meeting politely. "Now if you'll excuse me, I must leave for a meeting over on Emory's campus."

Chris stood as well but not before picking up her sandwich in a napkin. She flushed as she saw Weinstein smile at her and wink.

She walked out with Patterson. Before heading toward her office, she said, "I need to leave a little early this afternoon. Things back up at home when I'm on the road. I can do most of this work from home."

"Sure. I remember those days. Take whatever time you need."

By the time she returned to her office, all that remained of the sandwich was the napkin. She saw Joyce's reply on her cell phone but wanted to call her in the privacy of her office.

"Hello?"

"Joyce! How are you?"

"Chris! So good to hear from you. It's been a while. You doing all right?"

"Yeah. We're all doing fine, but I need some help with a case I'm working."

"Not sure what I can do, but I'll give it a try. So what's all the mystery about? You sounded stressed."

"Sorry about the cloak-and-dagger stuff. I was on my way to a meeting with my boss and my boss's boss when I got the idea to hit on you for some info. Thought you'd be a quicker source than searching what's in the public domain."

"There's a lot of proprietary info I can't talk about. A lot of agencies look over our shoulders. Some big money pivots on what happens with some of these drug applications."

"Oh sure, I understand that, and I wouldn't want to put you in a bind in any way, but I need some help understanding how these new targeting drugs work."

"What's this related to? Why would the CDC need info on that?"

"We've run across an unusual case that may have some connection to those drugs or something like them."

"Yeah. I caught your news conference a couple of days ago. You're big-time now, girl. Must be making the big bucks. Is this anyway related to all of those deaths up in Wisconsin and those other places?"

Chris paused before replying. "Uh, I have to get official now. I can neither confirm nor deny that assertion. However, it wasn't Wisconsin. It was Minnesota."

"Oh, I see. The reason I ask is there's some buzz going around about the FBI knocking around here asking some of the same types of questions."

"Yeah, they were at my meeting this morning, but you didn't hear that from me," Chris said.

"Hear what?"

"I'm looking for info on Astra Medicinals, Tudos Pharmaceuticals, and Century Pharmaceuticals, specifically anything to do with drugs designed to target specific parts of the body."

"Give me a minute. I'll look it up."

"You can call me back if you need some time."

"No, I got it right here. It sounds more like what we call a medical device than a drug. That's under the Center for Devices and Radiological Health Devices. That's not the division I work for, but I can probably still access some of the info."

Chris didn't respond; she understood her friend was actually just talking to herself as she worked her magic.

"I got two submission abstracts. One from Astra and the other from Tudos. Looks like the one from Tudos has been pulled back. There's a note that they pulled it and submitted an improved version."

Joyce mumbled something unintelligible as if she were reading to herself before she exclaimed, "Wow. This is really something."

"What?" Chris asked.

"These are nanoscale robots. Nanobots. You know what a nanobot is?"

"Apparently they're the future."

"Sure sounds futuristic ... Orwellian."

"More like Huxley's *Brave New World*."

Joyce mumbled some more before summarizing the matter. "They pulled the first application because of concerns regarding lead peroxide. Guess they would. Wow. The updated version uses zinc peroxide."

"Can you send me those files or at least the links?" Chris asked, feeling her gut tighten. "You probably saved me an entire afternoon of knocking about on dead ends. This is great. I have something to work with now. Sam can help with some of this corporate stuff."

"Give him all my love."

"Will do. Thanks, Joyce. One day, we'll have a real talk and catch up. If I ever go to DC, we'll meet up."

CHAPTER 9

JANUARY 28, 1945

By midmorning, the Russian film crew released the twins but only after several takes of the children marching out from behind the barbwire fences. The twin boys went with Zwillingsvater to their barracks. After the midday ration of potato soup and bread, the boys gathered around Zwillingsvater.

"You promised to take us home, Zwillingsvater. You promised!"

Zwillingsvater stood perplexed among the boys. Indeed, he had made such promises. At the time, they had been merely words to comfort scared children. He never really believed that the opportunity to fulfill his pledge would ever come. Another prisoner, one his own age, implored Spiegel to go with him.

No one could fault him if he did strike out on his own. He felt he had done more perhaps than anyone had to keep the boys alive up to that point. To take the boys home would take him in the opposite direction from his home. Had he not risked being shot when he ran to get Mengele when the boys had been selected for termination by Thilos? Tormented by such thoughts, Zvi Spiegel, Zwillingsvater, made his decision.

So it came to pass on the afternoon of January 28, 1945, thirty-six children walked out of Auschwitz led by their Zwillingsvater. Five were simply too sick to go any farther and would be for months. Those were left in the care of the Russians.

He carried a list of the boys' names and hometowns in his vest, food in his pockets, and four-year-old Jakob Bauer in his arms. The raggedy band, as big as an army platoon, headed east in the vague direction of home.

The war still raged to their west, and the roads in the liberated sectors of Poland were already choked with all manner of refugees, former prisoners of war, conscripted laborers, and concentration camp survivors. All were destitute. All were dejected. All were determined to go home. All nursed the fragile hope that they would find enough of their shattered lives in the ruins to build a future.

Thankfully, Zwillingsvater organized a small handcart along the way to carry Jakob when the boy grew too weary to keep up with the older children. At night, the group sheltered in barns and sheds along the road. Not knowing what to make of the children, the locals offered neither help nor mistreatment. Perhaps they were ghosts not to be vexed.

Zwillingsvater navigated his way east by keeping the Vistula River on his left. He knew the river eventually flowed into Krakow, where he hoped to find relief. Perhaps the Red Cross operated shelters there. Perhaps the boys would find surviving relatives. Perhaps the trains ran. Regardless, Krakow lay in the direction of their homes, and they would be that much closer there.

Other survivors joined the traveling band. Twelve women perhaps looking for their lost children were the first to throw in with them. Small groups of men joined them and parted company along the way.

By midmorning of the fourth day of their flight from Auschwitz, the ragtag collection of weary souls had swelled to 153 as they entered the outlying areas of Krakow. Military vehicles with red stars jammed roads. Expressionless soldiers stared out from the back of trucks as they rumbled by. In spite of their pace slowing because of the congestion, Spiegel's rabble army reached the south side of Krakow along the southern bank of the Vistula by twilight.

They took shelter that night in a walled-in sector of the city. The rounded tops of the wall panels reminded Zwillingsvater of the stones marking his grandparents' graves. He surmised this had been the Jewish ghetto and had yet to be reoccupied. That evening, they shared the last of their meager rations.

Fog along the river basin delayed the full light of day until midmorning. The stragglers who had joined them and had been with them for the past few days managed to get up and move on. Zwillingsvater made note of their departures. Perhaps they had been mere apparitions. Despite awakening to the shuffling noise of those departing, many of the children remained snuggled together fending off the cold as best they could. Fatigue, cold, and hunger had sapped them all of any typical youthful exuberance.

Zwillingsvater failed to rise as well. He lay thinking about what to do next. Should he leave this place with all of his wards and seek help in the city? Or would it be less risky to leave them there while he went in alone? He could cover more ground without them. Realizing there was no truly good option, he decided to take Jakob, the smallest, and one older boy, Simon Arie.

Simon concerned Zwillingsvater because of his penchant to harass Jakob, but he was the one mature enough to find his way back to the others. He reasoned he'd be with them both and could control the situation. If he found a safe refugee camp, he'd send Simon back and bring the others.

Once the boys were awake, he gathered them to explain he was going out to look for food and help. He appointed a couple of the older boys as task leaders to keep the others occupied and together. He told them he'd be back before dark at the latest. They were to listen to the older boys and not wander off. He watched their faces to see if any was going to cry, but none did. As young as they were, they still understood the necessity of survival.

Zwillingsvater struck out north toward the heart of the city with the two boys; Jakob was riding in the cart. Optimism required the cart for the food he planned to bring back. The winter daylight, dull as it was, gave witness to scattered, burned-out buildings. Other buildings sadly displayed pockmarks caused by machine-gun fire stitched across their facades. Something terrible had happened there. Zwillingsvater pressed on toward the bridge leading into the city.

Although it was somewhat ragged looking, the neighborhood just on the other side of the bridge appeared to have once been much more prosperous. It too had burned-out buildings but not nearly as many. Of the few he saw, Zwillingsvater recognized from the shape of their charred skeletons that they had been synagogues. One such building not burned served as a stable for draft horses. Judging from the scattered large mausoleums, he thought that an open field just to the east of the street was a Jewish cemetery; all bore the Star of David. *But where are all the other headstones?* Zwillingsvater pondered without breaking stride.

They saw people, but none of them seemed to take more than scant notice of the scarecrow man with two boys. Seeing only Polish civilians,

Zwillingsvater kept moving in hopes of finding a refugee camp or even an army camp.

Half an hour later, Zwillingsvater caught a whiff of something that caused him to stop short with his nose in the air.

"What is it?" Jakob asked with alarm.

"I smell food!"

They crossed through a park with many soldiers headed in the same direction up a narrow street lined with various shops. The street opened out into a grand courtyard. The centerpiece of the plaza was an ornate, rectangular building with porticos along the length of its two long sides. It was crowned with all sorts of odd, even grotesque, statues.

Buildings five or six stories tall rimmed the courtyard. Thousands of soldiers filled the immense space. Many were working on vehicles of every description. Some scurried to and fro, but most were queued up. Zwillingsvater followed the queue with his eyes to its head. Smoke and steam billowed out the top and sides of an enormous brown tent. He felt his legs weaken at the sight of food being served.

Zwillingsvater laid a restraining hand on both boys when he sensed their impulse to run for the food. These were soldiers—not SS guards but soldiers nonetheless. They too were hungry and no doubt equally adept at handling anyone thinking of stealing food. He studied the crowd and how it moved. He saw soldiers cleaning their mess kits at some oversized barrels about a hundred meters away.

Both boys fell in with Zwillingsvater's urgent pace as he pulled them toward the barrels. He figured food scraps were the best hope for the near term. It wouldn't be nearly enough, but it would have to do for the present. Zwillingsvater felt his heart sink as they reached the waste barrels and peered inside. Soldiers, especially those fresh from combat, didn't waste much food. There were only a few rejected morsels that he picked out and shared with the boys.

Jakob, revived somewhat from the meager crumbs, walked a little farther up the line crying out in Hungarian, "Kerem!" "Please!" He pointed with all his fingers of one hand toward his mouth.

Grim-faced soldiers stared at the little boy as they continued to shuffle by. One tossed him the last bite of stale bread and then another.

"Koszonom!" "Thank you!"

Seeing Jakob's success, Zwillingsvater grabbed Simon and whispered in his ear, "Go help Jakob but say nothing in German. Nothing in German."

Within fifteen minutes, the two boys had a sizable bundle and were having difficulty managing it. Zwillingsvater hung back knowing soldiers were more willing to give up part of their food to a child but less so for an adult. The boys' pleases and thank yous became less urgent and tended more toward a perfunctory drone resulting in diminishing results.

"You boys there! Run along. Leave these soldiers alone." A young officer speaking Hungarian and waving a short stick approached the two boys. "You have more than enough! Get out or I'll thrash you!"

Before Zwillingsvater could intercede, Jakob stepped toward the threatening officer and replied in his native tongue, "It's not for us, sir. It's for all the other children."

The officer drew up short of the boy. "What do you mean all the other children?"

Zwillingsvater reached Jakob and pulled him to his side. "Please forgive him, sir. He's only four and trying to find food."

"Who are you? You're Hungarian as well I take it."

"Actually, I'm Czech, but I speak Hungarian. I am watching over a number of boys. We are from the camp to the west of here, Auschwitz. Please forgive us." Zwillingsvater removed his cap.

"How many boys?"

"Thirty-six."

"Thirty-six? Where are they?"

Not daring to look up any farther than the officer's knees, Zwillingsvater explained, "I left the rest just over the river in an abandoned building. We just arrived last night from walking four days from the camp."

"How did you end up with so many children? Where are their parents?"

"They are all orphans. All twins."

"That doesn't answer my question. How did *you* end up with them?"

Zwillingsvater struggled for an answer. "There was no one else."

"All Jews?"

Zwillingsvater nodded.

"Relax. I'm a Jew as well. We've heard rumors coming back from forward areas about camps. They must be true." The officer turned his attention to the two boys. "Would you like more food for your comrades?"

Both boys eagerly nodded and said, "Igen!" "Yes!"

"Then get your bag of crumbs and come with me."

The conspiracy of hunger and exhaustion overwhelmed any reticence Zwillingsvater had harbored. Not knowing where they were going, the trio followed the young officer, who walked with a confident stride. They pushed their way through the mass of mud-brown uniforms to a building on the far corner of the plaza. It too was filled with uniforms, but less-coarse men filled them. Most of them sat at desks furiously hammering away on typewriters or cranking printing presses. Zwillingsvater took notice of the cameras and tripods just like the ones he'd seen filming the procession of children coming out of the camp's fence line.

"We are an intelligence company assigned to document for the world the many atrocities committed by the cowardly German fascists. I would like to see the children you say you have."

Zwillingsvater started to say something about the other film crew at the camp but thought better of it. "Certainly! I can take you there whenever you like. But I'd like to go as soon as possible to get this food back to the boys left behind." He held the bundle up to the officer.

The officer shouted some orders in Russian to several soldiers. They grabbed two cameras on tripods and carried them out the door to a couple of trucks. They came back in and lifted several crates that they carried to the trucks as well.

"You and your two young friends will lead us to these other children. We will feed them, and you will tell me their story."

Zwillingsvater nodded enthusiastically. "Yes! Yes!" He was still surprised at his good fortune. "I think I can find my way back. There was a large Jewish cemetery along the way. The boys are across a bridge not far from that."

"I know where it is. They are in the Jewish ghetto. Or it was until the Nazis liquidated it nearly two years ago. You ride with me and the driver. The boys can ride in the back with the others."

"Yes, yes of course," Zwillingsvater replied, hiding his apprehension about leaving the two boys alone with the soldiers. He had already left the other thirty-four on their own.

Zwillingsvater turned to them and addressing Jakob directly. "I am to ride up front with the driver to show them where the others are. You will ride in the back with these good soldiers. You must not be afraid. You understand, Jakob?"

Without hesitation, Jakob took Simon by the hand and led him to the rear of the truck. Zwillingsvater watched as two soldiers lifted the boys into the back and seated them among the crates and equipment. Jakob stared back out at Zwillingsvater as if to say, *I understand.*

The sun had burned through the morning fog; its light crested the rooftops as the trucks left the plaza. The trucks moved along at a speed only slightly more than a walking pace. Zwillingsvater watched the human flotsam and jetsam part and quickly fill the street again in the wake of the trucks as they made their way up a river of refugees.

Interrupting himself occasionally to give directions to the driver, Zwillingsvater related to the officer the story of the twins, the hell of Auschwitz, and the factory of death. He started hesitantly, but as if a dam had ruptured, his words came in torrents. He spoke until his throat tightened shut. He was thankful the officer didn't probe him for more.

As the trucks neared the cemetery, the Russian officer asked, "Did you notice that most of the headstones were missing when you passed the cemetery?"

Zwillingsvater nodded.

"The Nazis had them removed to make a road at the Plaszów work camp not far from here."

Even the dead were not safe, Zwillingsvater thought as he looked out over the derelict cemetery.

The trucks entered and stopped in another courtyard, one that was not nearly as large as the one they had just departed. At one end, a mountain of broken furniture partially buried under gray snow and cinder filled a corner. To the side of that stood what looked like a ghost town. Burned-out shells of buildings lined the street. Many of the buildings bore the pockmarks he had seen earlier that morning.

The soldiers sprang from their languor and dropped the tailgate with a bang. The two boys were lifted to the ground along with the other cargo. The brightening sun created tiny rainbows in the frost of everyone's breath. Zwillingsvater sent both boys down the deserted street to fetch the other children.

Zwillingsvater stepped back from the soldiers' activity. He watched as they mounted the tripods on the cabs of the trucks. Red flags appeared. Crowbars wrenched the crates open exposing dark loaves of bread. The soldiers pulled two large kettles off the back and mounted them on stands with burners underneath.

Zwillingsvater saw Simon emerge from a building midway down the street at the head of a column of boys five abreast just like in the camp. All went well until the soldiers waved bread beckoning them to come get it. The orderly column melted into a mob as it rushed and engulfed the truck with hands held out begging for the bread. Cameramen atop the trucks cranked the camera handles recording the chaos as the young officer shouted orders and pointed where to aim the lens. Zwillingsvater watched as Jakob, lagging behind the others, joined in. He appeared to have been crying and was a little scuffed up. He received his food and found a place to sit away from the others.

The melee subsided as the last of the boys received their meals. Zwillingsvater ate last. The officer came over to him and offered a cigarette. His hands too full to accept, he declined but thanked the officer profusely.

"There is a rabbi near here who is working with relief efforts. I think he is working with the Red Cross and some other agencies. I will have him come look you up. Will you be here?"

Zwillingsvater, caught with a mouthful, swallowed hard and replied, "I suppose. We just found that empty building last night and stayed there. I don't know if we will be allowed to stay."

The officer grinned. "Don't worry. All the locals think this place is cursed. The only ones who come here now are DPs."

"DPs?"

"Displaced Persons. You're a DP. You and your merry band are just a handful of the millions of DPs already wandering across the repatriated territories. And the war isn't even over yet. There'll be millions more."

Zwillingsvater made no reply. The soldiers began breaking down the serving equipment. They gathered the remaining bread into one of the boxes and gave it to Zwillingsvater. The young officer told him to take the leftovers. A moment later, they mounted the trucks and sped off in the direction they came.

The boys all gathered tight about Zwillingsvater seeking direction. He had some of them gather the food, and he herded them back toward their building. He had others gather as much scrap wood as they could find and carry. A short time later, they all disappeared into the building to hide out and wait for the rabbi.

Later, a small fire in the fireplace drew the boys tightly together for the warmth. Full bellies and fatigue soon overcame the children. After settling them in for the night, Zwillingsvater stole away to another room not wanting the boys to see him break down and sob. For the first time since his imprisonment, he allowed himself to grieve the loss of his own family—his parents and the others. He was ashamed to be alive. He wept until his sides ached. Eventually, he regained his capacity for rational thought. *Could it be true what the officer told me? Millions? The boys and I are just one more sad story in a sea of sad stories?*

Jakob curled himself up into a corner away from the others. It wasn't that he was cold, but his body hurt. And he hurt all over—not just where Simon had punched him in the ribs. On their way back from the army camp, the soldiers in the back of the truck had given both boys an extra loaf of bread. When Zwillingsvater sent Simon and him to retrieve the other boys, Simon had knocked him down and took his bread to show the other boys what the soldiers were offering.

As the night dragged on, taunts of "Golden Junge!" mixed with the delirium of his fevered mind. He alternated between bouts of profuse sweating and shivering. It was how he had felt when the Russian doctor had helped him at the camp, but this was much worse.

Jakob thought about his mother but couldn't remember her face. He knew he had to get Zwillingsvater to help him. Before rising to find Zwillingsvater, Jakob fumbled around in his bundle of possessions and pulled out the heel of a loaf of bread he had saved. He licked the piece front and back before returning it to the bundle. He pulled himself up and with great effort stumbled through the building looking for Zwillingsvater.

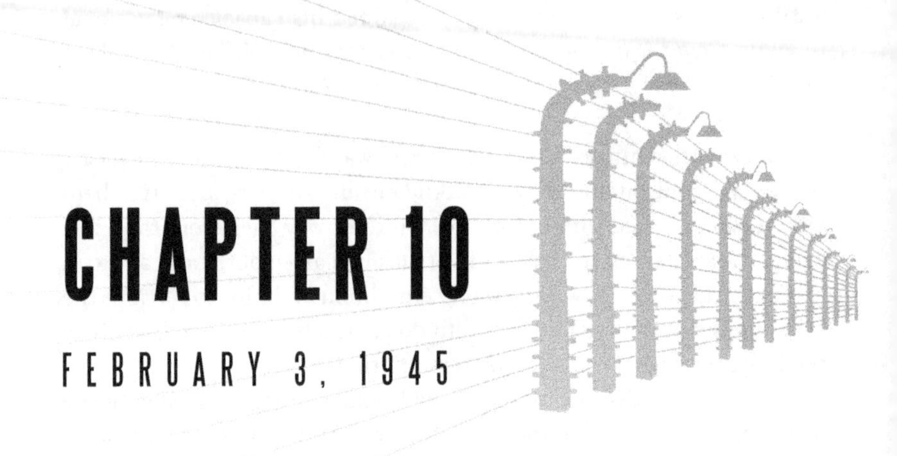

CHAPTER 10

FEBRUARY 3, 1945

Someone was yelling outside the door. Zwillingsvater roused himself in the dim light of the room. All about him lay the boys in his charge. He got up as quickly as his stiff body allowed not wanting to wake the others. Careful not to step on anyone, he stumbled to the broken doorway to meet the possible new threat.

Opening the door just enough to peek through the splintered doorframe, Zwillingsvater replied in Hungarian, "Igen?" "Yes?"

"Rabbi Stern. Mowisz po polsku?"

Zwillingsvater shook his head understanding he had been asked if he spoke Polish. He replied with his own question, "Beszelsz magyarul?"

The rabbi, not knowing Hungarian, shook his head. "Deutsche?"

Zwillingsvater nodded in resignation. "Ja."

The rabbi nodded. "Well, we'll just have to talk like two dogs barking at each other."

Zwillingsvater smiled sheepishly as he opened the door to let the rabbi in.

"I am Zvi Spiegel. The boys call me Zwillingsvater—Twins Father."

"Rabbi Chaim Stern. The Russian officer told me about you and your boys."

Spiegel shook the rabbi's extended hand. It was the first time since having been placed in the ghetto more than two years earlier that he had greeted another man in such a civilized manner. "The Russian officer told me about you—that you work with the Red Cross," Spiegel said. "I really need your help. I have all these boys. I have one who fell sick last night. I think it's typhoid. The Russians had given him medicine, and I thought he was well. Can you help me get food for these boys?" Spiegel said hardly taking a breath.

The rabbi held out his hands as if he were trying to calm a runaway horse. "Slow down. We'll get you help. You have a sick boy?"

"You can help me with the sick boy?"

"Yes. There is a pharmacist, Mr. Pankiewicz, not a Jew, but a good man. He saved many of the Jews when this was the holding ghetto. He's not far from here."

"Can we take him now?"

"You can leave your boys?" Stern asked.

"Yes. They will behave."

"It's just a couple of blocks from here. We will be back shortly. Then we'll see about some food for the others."

Spiegel turned to the small group that had gathered just beyond the light. "You boys stay here. I'll be back after I take Jakob to get some medicine. Then Rabbi Stern here will help get some food."

"Golden Junge," the boys tittered. Spiegel ignored them. He gathered up Jakob in his arms and headed out the door. He gave the boys a warning to mind themselves until he came back.

The pharmacist took the boy to a back room and asked the rabbi and Spiegel to remain in the front room while he looked at the boy.

"He's a good man—the closest thing we have to a doctor," Stern assured Spiegel. "The officer said you had thirty-six boys, twins? So many."

Spiegel relaxed a little. "Yes. I've had hundreds. But the camp ..."

"Zvi, you did what you thought best, right?"

Zvi bowed his head and nodded.

"What is the boy's name?"

"Jakob. Jakob Bauer. He's special. You'll find he's very intelligent when he comes around."

"So where are you from, Mr. Spiegel?"

Zvi regarded the rabbi for a moment and called upon his dimmed recollection of what civil conversation was supposed to be like. He tried to estimate the man's age, something nearly impossible to accurately discern of survivors. Camp life typically aged a person by years in a matter of months. *He's perhaps late thirties. Maybe forties?*

"I am from Munkacs, Czechoslovakia. For the last year or so, I have been at Auschwitz. How about you?"

"This is my home. My family has been in Krakow since King Kazimierz. I was in several camps. The last was Plaszow. Not far from here."

"Family?"

The rabbi sighed. "I did. Now ..." He shrugged.

They fell silent.

The rabbi drew a resolute breath and declared, "Well, let's see what we can do to help with all your boys."

MARCH 12, 1945

Zwillingsvater got up earlier than the boys did. He and they had been in Krakow a little more than a month. They had fixed up their temporary home enough to make it comfortable with items organized from other buildings. They had even started doing their lessons again.

The previous day, before Zwillingsvater returned from his daily trip to check on Jakob, Pankiewicz had handed him an envelope with real coffee beans. Zwillingsvater was determined to make a cup of coffee and linger over it as a free man might. He inhaled the vapor as it rose from the pot and savored the memories of mornings in his mother's kitchen long gone.

The warmth of the cup penetrated his cold hands as he held it and leaned against the wall. It was getting light earlier, and the boys would soon rouse, but that moment was his. The call of responsibility beckoned him, but he did not want to answer it just yet. He wanted to contemplate his future—the one after the boys were taken home. He found it difficult to even conceive of such a thing. Every step toward the east took him farther from home. To look so far over the horizon, to nourish hope, felt blasphemous.

Eventually, his other responsibilities crept in and captured his musings. He had lost one boy, Simon Arie, to typhoid. The boy had fallen ill soon after Jakob had. Jakob was doing better, but Simon had not responded to the medicine. He had seen hundreds of boys die in the camp, but for some reason, Simon's death bothered him more than did the deaths of the others. Jakob had been sick in the camp and probably hadn't fully recovered. Simon, though, had gotten free of the camp. Simon had been cruel to Jakob, but he had been just a child who had been placed in a savage world.

Zwillingsvater drank the remainder of his coffee, stood, and stretched. It was time to roust the boys and get them involved in their daily routines.

MARCH 15, 1945

The morning began well before dawn; the building was shaking so violently that Zwillingsvater got the boys up and made them run outside into the cold in fear it would collapse. Zwillingsvater and the boys were awestruck as they lined the building front. Tanks. Hundreds of them. Maybe thousands. All of them new with fresh paint and manned by soldiers in fresh uniforms. Headed west toward some new offensive against the hated Germans.

One of the older boys shouted, "Kill them! Kill the Nazis!"

Others joined the chorus. "Kill them! Kill the Nazis!"

Soldiers stared back vacantly at the band of manic children along the road. The boys continued their rage until the last tank turned the corner past them. Many slumped to their knees crying uncontrollably, totally spent. Zwillingsvater watched them.

The days were growing longer and warmer. The tide of DPs swept through Krakow in growing numbers. Keeping the boys focused and out of mischief was becoming too much for Zwillingsvater to manage. They were restless. It was time to continue their journeys home and face the next chapter of their lives.

Later in the morning, Zwillingsvater left the boys to their chores and went to the Pod Ortem pharmacy. The white-smocked Pankiewicz came from behind the counter and greeted him.

"Ahh, Zvi. Out and about. Such a nice day. Winter will soon be a memory."

"Yes. And from the looks of it so will the Third Reich."

"It woke me as well. So many tanks. It will be over soon."

"How is Jakob?"

Pankiewicz shrugged. "He improves every day, but he's still quite weak. He tries to help me here in the shop. Such a clever boy. Do you know he can speak a little Polish now? He reads my son's old children's books to me at night. And so young!"

"Yes, I believe it. I told you he was intelligent. Do you think he will be able to travel in a day or so?"

Pankiewicz pulled his pipe from his pocket and stuffed it with tobacco from a can on the counter. "Forgive me. I traded some medicine for this tobacco just yesterday. Such a pleasure since not having had any for so long. But to your question, I don't think so. He tires after just a few minutes of exertion. He's fine after a short rest, but I don't think he could sustain the effort you propose."

Zvi nodded. "I thought that would be the case."

"What are you planning?"

"Well, spring is nearly here. The children are growing restless. This morning, I saw in them … They want to go home."

"And you my friend? What do you want?"

Zvi paused. "I want to go home as well. I want to find my sister, my family …"

"Then you must go. You have done more than should be asked of any one person. You saved all those lives."

Zvi could only nod; such was his struggle not to cry.

Pankiewicz placed a hand on Zvi's shoulder. "Jakob can stay here for as long as he needs. I have grown used to having him in the shop."

"Is he in the back? I'd like to talk to him, explain things."

Pankiewicz gestured toward the door to the back room. Zwillingsvater found the boy on a tall stool at a small workbench crushing pills with a mortar and pestle.

"Good morning, Jakob. Helping Mr. Pankiewicz make his medicine?"

"Yes. He says I do a good job of crushing the hard pills into powder. I like doing it."

"Jakob, we need to talk a moment," Zwillingsvater said, placing his hand on the mortar.

Jakob ceased and looked up at him as if to ask, *About what?*

"You're getting better from your illness, but you are still not fully recovered. All of the other boys want to leave here and go home. The weather is beginning to turn warmer, and …"

"You want to leave as well."

Zwillingsvater, again caught off guard by Jakob's perceptiveness, confessed, "Yes. Yes I do. I want to find my family."

"But I'm not strong enough to go yet."

"No. But you will be in a few more weeks."

"Then go."

"You understand. I must help the others."

"Yes. I am just one. The others are many. Do what is best for the many."

Jakob resumed crushing pills with the pestle. Spiegel had no reply.

MARCH 28, 1945

Jakob's only companions were Pankiewicz and the rabbi. The pharmacy was filled with endless curiosities for him. Pankiewicz often showed him many science tricks when the shop was not busy. He preferred the company of the two adults over that of the boys. However, he did miss Zwillingsvater.

Alone at night in the bed Pankiewicz had made for him, Jakob thought of his parents and sisters. He even thought of Mengele. The doctor had shown him special attention. He struggled to remember their faces.

Rabbi Stern came to the pharmacy that morning as he did three or four times a week. On that day, Jakob was to go with the rabbi.

"Tomorrow is a very special day for us Jews, Jakob. I will need your help preparing for Passover. Do you know what that is?"

Jakob recalled something from the year earlier in the ghetto. Although his mother had not been Jewish, she was distressed at not being able to get some sort of bread and a few other things. Jakob's father had made a game of sorts pretending to eat the missing items. He made a face of delight at the savory items and a sour face at something called a bitter herb.

"I remember a story. A king was bad to the children of Israel, and God made bad things happen to him. There were frogs and big grasshoppers that made all the king's people scared. Then God sent an angel to kill a lot of the king's people. Then the king let the children of Israel go."

"You remember all that, Jakob? You are a clever boy."

"My father told me we are the children of Israel. Why do people call us Jews? Why do they hate us?"

The rabbi fumbled with an answer. "Children of Israel is, uh, an old, old name. It's more formal. More endearing. The name Jew means the same thing. As for why people hate us, I don't know. Perhaps because God chose us to be His people."

"Am I chosen?"

The rabbi roared with laughter. "Yes, Jakob, indeed you are. You are chosen for the future! You are chosen to do great things! And today, you are chosen to help me!"

"Were my sisters chosen?"

The rabbi's buoyancy imploded. "Yes. And so were my beautiful daughters."

Jakob took the man by the hand and left the pharmacy. Neither spoke as they headed to the synagogue on the other side of the Vistula River. Midspan on the bridge, Rabbi Stern picked Jakob up and held him in a tight embrace. Jakob offered no protest as he felt the rabbi sob.

The following evening, Rabbi Stern led Jakob to a large hall near the synagogue. Twenty or so people sat tightly packed in the cramped space. Most were men who were in scarcely better health or condition than the pajama men scarecrows who had populated the camp had been in. These men, however, spoke with lively gestures and expressions.

Looking around the dimly lit room, Jakob saw he was the only child there. He found himself in that situation quite often wherever he was in the old Jewish quarter of Kazimierz. He asked if Pankiewicz was there but was told Pankiewicz was not a Jew and would not be attending that evening. Seeing no other familiar faces, Jakob stayed close to Rabbi Stern.

The rabbi raised his hands to hush the gathering. "Please, please! Find your places. I could not locate any Haggadah or enough paper to write one out, so I apologize. You will have to rely on my feeble memory this evening. So let us settle and come together now as we commemorate this Festival of Freedom."

The room fell silent except for the shuffling of a few into their places.

"The words Festival of Freedom have new meaning for us now, do they not? We celebrate our ancestors' freedom, and now we celebrate our own. Let us remember those not yet freed and those who have been taken from us."

Also relying on dimmed memories, the assembled replied at Rabbi Stern's prompting, "Let us remember the Feast of Unleavened Bread. Let us remember our history from some thirty-five hundred years ago. Let us remember our history from just yesterday."

Rabbi Stern continued. "We tell the Exodus story. We tell the story of yesterday. We tell the story of freedom. We ask our questions. We remember our lost loved ones."

The room settled. "We begin with the lighting of the candles and the Kiddush."

The most elderly woman in the room stepped forward and lit two white candles on the front table. Jakob saw some continuing to cry—not sob but weep nonetheless.

"Blessed are You, Lord our God, Ruler of the universe, Creator of the fruit of the vine," the rabbi prayed.

"Blessed are You, Lord our God, Ruler of the universe, Creator, Who has chosen us from all peoples, and exalted us above all nations, and sanctified us with His commandments."

Jakob started when a man from the next table jumped up holding his head and ran from the room out into the twilight.

Rabbi Stern paused a moment before returning doggedly to the prayer. "You have given us, O Lord our God, with love festivals for happiness, holidays and seasons for rejoicing, as this day of the Festival of Passover, the season of our freedom. For you have chosen us from all peoples and sanctified us with Your holy festivals. Blessed are You, O Lord, Who sanctifies Israel and the festivals. Repeat after me the sheheheyanu, thanking the Lord our God for continuing to give us life, sustaining us, and bringing us together this night."

The congregation responded again with prompting, "Praised are You, O Lord our God, Ruler of the universe, Who has kept us in life, and allowed us to reach this season."

Jakob saw more weeping. Some of the scarecrows covered their faces. Another man stood and left the room.

The rabbi cleared his throat, drew a deep breath, and steeled himself as best he could for the next segment. "In Seders past, in our homes, we may have blessed our children, laying our hands on them, beseeching the Almighty to protect them."

The rabbi paused retrenching his resolve to continue. He wiped his eyes, cleared his throat, and took another deep breath. "But our children are gone. We are all who are left of our families. We must start over again. We must ask our Lord, God of the universe, to bless the children of the future."

Jakob stiffened as Rabbi Stern heaved him up to stand on the table and placed his hands on his head. The rabbi prayed, "May the Lord God bless you as Abraham, Isaac, and Jakob were blessed. May you have health, happiness, and a long and satisfying life."

Jakob recoiled as others at the table reached and laid their hands on him as well. Muffled weeping broke into open wailing. Jakob jumped off the table and clung to Rabbi Stern's leg.

Rabbi Stern allowed the lamenting to settle into a whimper before continuing with the Vareheha, a threefold blessing. "May the Lord God bless you and keep you. May He cause His spirit to shine upon you and be gracious unto you. May the Lord God turn His spirit unto you and grant you peace."

Many of the guests wiped their eyes with handkerchiefs or otherwise collected themselves. Rabbi Stern continued. "Wine is the symbol of joy and thanksgiving, and we drink four times during our Seder. The four cups are filled with red wine to remind us of the blood that was smeared on the lintels and doorposts of the Jewish homes in Egypt on the Seder night, the night of the tenth plague. The blood was the sign for the Lord's angel of death to pass over that house while the family huddled inside. HaShem protected them."

Jakob's head snapped up. That was a name he had heard before at the unloading ramp. The pajama man had whispered it to his mother. That's what he had called Mengele—the Angel of Death.

"It is a reminder of the Jewish blood shed by Pharaoh. And now, for us, it is a reminder of the blood shed by this terrible tragedy inflicted upon us by the Nazis. Through this red wine, at this Seder, we express our prayer that HaShem will continue to protect us."

Weeping renewed throughout the hall and again subsided. They mumbled in ragged unison, "The four cups of red wine stand for the four promises HaShem made to us: I will bring you out of Egypt, I will release you from the bonds of slavery, I will redeem you, I will make a covenant with you."

Stern resumed. "Let us begin this service by sanctifying the name of HaShem our Lord and proclaim the holiness of this festival. We usher in the Sabbath and all festivals with the blessing of the wine."

The congregation responded, "Praised are you oh Lord, Ruler of the universe, Creator of the fruit of the vine."

"Let us each put a drop in Elijah's cup so that we all contribute to the act of redemption," Stern instructed. "Further, in the tradition of the high priest of the temple, we wash our hands, the U-r'hatz, as a form of purification not as the removal of dirt from the body but to make our spirits clean helping us feel that holiness."

A hubbub of activity filled the room as the participants ceremonially washed their hands. Jakob looked on and imitated as best he could all that the adults did. Several of them sought to help him. Many of them simply stared at him. There was no malice in the stares. Sadness maybe. Perhaps reminiscence. Possibly longing. Nonetheless, it made Jakob uncomfortable.

Rabbi Stern continued with the ceremonies, but Jakob ceased listening. Every eye in the room was on him, or so he thought. *Quit looking at me!* he wanted to scream.

Jakob thought the ceremony would never end. Rabbi Stern had coached him the day before and earlier in the day as well regarding his role in the Seder. The rabbi had said nothing of these people fawning over him, examining him, studying him as they were. He withdrew as best he could, rubbing his tattooed arm furiously.

Jakob's interest was engaged again as he heard the rabbi tell a story he remembered his father telling during the Seder in the ghetto. A man with his name, Jakob, had many sons. He had two wives, Rachel and Leah, just like his sisters' names. Jakob felt a wave of sadness, of reminiscence, of longing pass over him. Tears welled in his eyes. More and more, he thought of his sisters, his womb mates. They were gone and he was not. A new emotion had gained a foothold in the bedrock of his soul—shame.

The Passover story, the maggid, continued; it was the primal story of the Jewish people as Rabbi Stern called it. Jakob's mind, having drifted to thoughts of his lost sisters, snapped back to the story upon hearing the mention of HaShem's Angel of Death on the night of the tenth plague. "I will pass over you," HaShem had said.

There was the pajama man's words again, Angel of Death. Had the angel killed his mother and father? His sisters? Had Doctor Mengele been the Angel of Death? Had he killed them?

More ceremony passed. A song, "Dayenu," was muttered through. Only Rabbi Stern was loud and articulate enough to be understood. Some food was taken. There was a bone, three *matzot,* and *maror.* Rabbi Stern explained the significance of each. Jakob found the maror, the bitter herbs, to taste awful. He wanted to spit it out but mustered enough control to swallow it although it made his eyes water. This amused the many faces watching him.

The rabbi held up three pieces of matzah, breaking one and wrapping it in a napkin. This he handed to a young man, who then left the room. Jakob, still trying to get the bitter taste out of his mouth, recognized the gesture as the part of the ceremony he had rehearsed earlier that day with the rabbi.

Rabbi Stern had called the wrapped piece of unleavened bread the *afikomen*. It was Jakob's job to go find where the young fellow had hidden it. It was a task that would be easy; Jakob had been shown the hiding place. Rabbi Stern had explained to Jakob that the youngest child was to find it and negotiate a ransom for its return.

A meager dinner was then served—meager due to the difficulty of finding kosher food. The Jewish community of shops and rabbis no longer existed. Fish made up most of the meal. It made little difference to the survivors in attendance and certainly not to Jakob.

When Rabbi Stern discerned everyone had eaten, he whispered to Jakob to go find the afikomen. As he dashed off, Jakob heard a woman crying. More remembrance. He returned in short order holding the napkin.

"It is now time for the afikomen that will draw our meal to a close," Rabbi Stern said. He turned to Jakob. "Jakob, did you find the afikomen?"

The boy held it up as he had been instructed to do. The congregation uttered their adoration of the child. The woman's crying grew louder, but it was tolerated.

"What is your ransom demand?" the rabbi smiled.

Jakob looked around the room at the fawning faces all projecting on him a precious memory. The weeping of the woman was all that could be heard.

Jakob turned back to the rabbi and in a loud, clear voice, "I want my sisters. I want Rachel and Leah."

Even the wailing woman ceased. Silence hung over the room. Rabbi Stern stood dumbstruck unable to respond. Jakob broke and ran for the door taking the afikomen with him. No one tried to stop him.

Outside in the cool air of the late March evening, Jakob ran with abandon past the cemetery and over the bridge. He ran all the way to the Pod Orem, Pankiewicz's apothecary. As the old man opened the door, Jakob fell empty into his arms.

"Jakob!"

Later that evening, the rabbi came by looking for the boy.

"Is he here?" he asked as Pankiewicz opened the door.

The old man nodded and gestured for Stern to come in. "He's asleep in his bed. He was crying for his sisters."

The rabbi nodded. He said nothing.

CHAPTER 11

APRIL 13, 2006

Ilsa Bauer-Monsinger welcomed him at the door of her New York brownstone. "Hello, Dad. Your trip down from Boston was okay?"

Before entering, Jakob Bauer reached up, touched the *mezuzah* with his fingertips, kissed them, and mumbled a prayer. "Yes, I was worried the flight would be delayed because of the weather. You know, springtime storms. But here I am."

"Let me take your raincoat and bag, Dad. You really should get the limo service to bring you down."

"That would cost a fortune!"

"Dad, I think you can afford it. If you don't want all the hassles of flying or driving, take that fast Amtrak train. There's plenty of room, and you can get up and walk around."

"I don't like trains," snapped Jakob.

Ilsa saw her father rub his left arm, and she reddened.

Realizing his brusqueness, Jakob sought to soothe Ilsa's feelings. "It's okay. I'm just a grumpy old man."

"I don't see why you live in Boston anyway. You're the CEO, and your headquarters is here. You wouldn't have all of this going back and forth."

"I like being near the laboratories, that's why."

"So stubborn. You should have stayed in the lab."

"Don't think I haven't thought about it." Jakob straightened himself and smoothed back his silver hair in the hall tree mirror. "Well, you look radiant, my dear."

Ilsa hugged and kissed her father. "Don't try to smooth-talk me. I know better. Aunt Helen and Uncle Miles are here with the kids."

"Wonderful. A Seder is not complete without children." Jakob smiled with effort.

Helen was his wife's younger sister and could easily have passed as her twin. He would never let Ilsa know, but it grieved him to look at Helen—such was her likeness to his deceased wife. Regardless, he would power through for that one evening.

Jakob entered the living room, and the conversations ceased as everyone looked up. Sarah was the first to get up and embrace him.

"Who is this? It can't be that little girl named Sarah. She can't be more than ten!" In truth, Sarah was nineteen. And in truth, Jakob really was surprised at how much she had matured.

His nephew, Ben, rose and shook his hand as a man would.

"Benjamin? My word! You're big as a mountain! Such a man!" Jakob declared without counterfeit.

Miles greeted him shaking his hand. Helen emerged from the adjacent dining room, and Jakob repressed an urge to embrace her as a wife. Instead, they exchanged a slight hug and kisses on cheeks. Jakob did feel another sensation, one he allowed full rein. The sensation of warmth from home and family passed over every part of him even to his soul.

"Dad? You all right?"

"What? I'm just fine."

"You froze there for a minute. You all right?" Ilsa asked.

"Oh yes, I'm fine. Just lost in thought. I was just thinking that every person on earth I care for is in this one room."

"Dad, you're such a romantic," Ilsa replied.

Minutes later, Randall, Jakob's son-in-law and Tudos's chief financial officer, materialized from somewhere in the back of the house. Jakob and Randall regarded each other for a moment. "Jakob."

"Randall."

"I need to help Ilsa in the kitchen," Randall said and disappeared again.

Jakob watched him depart before turning to Sarah. "So you've finished your first year of college? NYU, right?"

The living room fell into the buzz of family conversations. Jakob caught up on the exploits of his nephew and niece—always a source of pride for him. He fended off some subtle attempts by his brother-in-law, the broker, to extract some insider information.

Jakob came prepared having suffered the inquisition before. He gave Miles some unsubstantiated rumors regarding a couple of Tudos's competitors, nothing outside SEC boundaries but enough to keep Miles at bay. Jakob actually enjoyed playing Miles. He just hoped he didn't do something stupid with the information. Even if Miles did, Helen and the kids would be okay. Unbeknownst to them, Jakob had put safety nets in place for them.

Ilsa stepped out of the dining room. "We're ready. Everyone find your places. It's getting late."

Everyone dutifully headed to the dining room. Randall was standing behind his chair at one end of the table. Ilsa lit two candles, said a prayer, and took her place at the other end of the table. Jakob waited for Helen to be seated so he could sit on the same side of the table. Sitting across from her and seeing the image of his wife would prove too difficult. He ended up sitting next to Ilsa. Opposite from Ilsa sat the prophet Elijah's goblet. To his delight, Sarah sat on his other side and Ben to the other side of Elijah's cup; they were the three people he most wanted to be with. He loved talking with the younger ones with their ideals not yet compromised.

The ceremonies proceeded as they had for nearly four millennia, but Jakob never grew tired of them. This was for him connective tissue to so many who had been lost. He loved the symbolism, the message of freedom and justice, the story of how the Jews were redeemed from Egypt, God saving his people. He loved being with his family small as it was.

During the festival meal, Jakob, Sarah, and Ben discussed the two kids' ambitions—what they saw themselves doing in five or ten years. Ben planned on pursuing a science degree, perhaps in chemistry or biology, that would best give him the foundation for med school should he decide to go that route after graduating. If not med school, he saw himself doing research and being fulfilled. He had no interest in engineering though.

Jakob listened to the boy and marveled at the seventeen-year-old's maturity. To have such a clear vision for what he wanted out of life at his age pleased Jakob deeply. Even if plans changed, the boy had a grasp of reality rare in most his age.

"If you need help finding a summer internship, I have a pretty good connection with the owner of a company that does a lot of research," Jakob offered with a wink.

Sarah described her curriculum as putting her in the field of drug counseling. She conceded she wouldn't get rich with such an ambition, but she too believed the importance of having a sense of fulfillment during one's working life. She had witnessed the tragic downward spiral of a friend's older brother. In the end, they found him in a back alley with a needle stuck in his arm. It had devastated her friend and her family. The girl's parents ended up getting a divorce.

"The drug problem is out of control. We don't see it as much up here, but it is everywhere. There are not many families that aren't affected. I'd like to help," Sarah said.

"You're aware of the drug program my company partnered on with Health and Human Services, aren't you?"

"Are you kidding? The Tudos Campaign for Hope. That's all some of my professors talk about. Tudos can do no wrong as far as they're concerned. In their eyes, you're the model for the rest of corporate America. Apparently, having your Dopanoncessemin drug available at such a low cost has enabled the clinics in the hardest hit areas make a dent in the problem."

"That's wonderful."

"Yeah, Uncle Jakob, it's pretty cool for me to listen to them talk about the impact it's having all the while thinking, 'Yeah. I know that guy.'"

The three of them laughed with such abandon that the others stopped eating and stared at them.

"Sarah! Ben! This is not the time for carrying on like that!" Helen said.

"It's my fault. Don't blame them. They are just so passionate about what they want to do to help our fellow humans. Isn't that what a Seder celebrates?"

"Perhaps Ben and Sarah should get MBAs after graduating so they will know how the real world works, how all those great ideals get funded."

"Randall, not here," Ilsa seethed.

"It's okay," Jakob said, patting his daughter's hand. "Randall has a right to his opinions. He and I have a strongly opposite opinion regarding certain business decisions lately."

"Giving up a revenue stream worth potentially billions is not a business decision. It's business suicide."

"It's my company."

"Not all of it. You have an obligation to the other shareholders. You can't just walk away from that responsibility."

"Enough of it is mine. I have made a tremendous amount of wealth for our shareholders including you. What I did with Dopanoncessemin was my way of giving something back to this country, which has been so good to me. The company didn't lose any money from the drug program."

"The company spent nearly fifty-two million dollars developing that drug. It's the best thing on the market by a wide margin."

"Is it so bad for Tudos to be viewed as a stellar corporate citizen? Did you hear what they're saying about us in academia?" Pointing to his niece he said, "Tell him what you just told me, Sarah."

"Well, I hope you're prepared to fight off a class-action lawsuit. Win or lose, that's still a losing proposition."

"Randall! Dad! That's enough. You're making a spectacle of yourselves. We have guests."

"Forgive me, all of you, for my boorish behavior. It is inexcusable," apologized Jakob, furiously rubbing his left arm.

Randall simply held up his hands as if to surrender without saying a word.

"If you two Neanderthals are done, I have an announcement I've been saving for a special occasion. Despite our differences, we are family, and for me, the only family I have. But that will all change in about six months. Randall and I are expecting!"

The room erupted in a raucous exchange of congratulations and well wishes. Ilsa lifted her hands and waved everyone to quiet down so she could continue with her announcement. "Not only are we pregnant, we're pregnant with twins!"

The room erupted again. Jakob was beside himself. His eyes brimmed with tears. He wiped them with his napkin. Sarah smiled at his vulnerability.

Ilsa took her dad's hand and whispered in his ear, "Dad, they're girls. We are going to name them after your sisters, Rachel and Leah."

Jakob's reserve shattered. He fell into uncontrolled, unashamed sobbing.

CHAPTER 12

MARCH 22, 2019

Chris did leave work early—technically. She had envisioned leaving well before the Atlanta rush hour swelled the arteries out of town. As it was, she managed to leave only half an hour short of a full eight hours. Still, that was better than her usual ten- to twelve-hour day. She tried escaping the CDC campus using the Michael Street exit, but apparently, everyone else had had the same idea.

She and Sam had bought their home in Doraville for its relative proximity to the CDC campus. Locals describe their neighborhood in Doraville as ITP—Inside the Perimeter—referring to the I-285 loop circumnavigating Atlanta. The immediate neighborhoods around the CDC campus were too expensive while the ITP side of Doraville was just twenty minutes away—an acceptable compromise or so they thought.

Lately, traffic had been stretching the average commute to forty minutes, and that day was shaping up to be an hour's drive. Traffic reports on the radio detailed an accident on northbound I-85 just north of the intersection with the Perimeter. To make matters worse, it was Friday afternoon. The only thing missing was an ice storm. Even the side-street escape routes were clogged.

Surprisingly, she didn't mind sitting in traffic as much as others might have. It was the only time she truly had to herself. Usually, she utilized the time to contemplate things whether problems at work or a home project. However, improving cellular technology had encroached on her me time. Her cellphone synched with her car's sound system.

Hands-free even if the rest of her was anything but. There simply was no escaping the constant connectivity.

Her phone vibrated and the call connected through the car's speakers.

"Hello?"

"Did you forget me?"

"Oh crap! Sorry, Lawrence. I was supposed to call you back. Pretty busy day."

"What was all that with Weinstein and the FBI guy?"

"Epic! Weinstein went nuclear on the guy. The best part was how he did it. He didn't scream or rant. He just gave the guy an ultimatum in a kind of Clint Eastwood way to either cooperate or he'd call a press conference and tell the world how obstructionist the FBI was being."

"I'd like to have seen that. This thing must have gotten some folks in Washington stirred up if Weinstein is sitting in on status meetings."

"I think you're right. Lots of agencies. Lots of egos. Weinstein was pretty effective though because the guy folded like a cheap lawn chair. Weinstein's in the perfect position. He's at the end of his career, so he doesn't care if they fire him or if he quits."

"Sounds like an enviable place to be. I can't wait for my turn so I can tell off my boss. What a slave driver."

"Hey! You ain't there yet, pal!"

They laughed, and Chris relaxed a little. She really did enjoy the camaraderie of the troops in the trenches.

"Anything new in Minnesota?"

"Well, they found another body this afternoon sure enough just like we thought we might. He was in an ice-fishing shack. Body was frozen. It's on its way to Minneapolis for autopsy. Had to put him a big cardboard box because he'd frozen in a sitting position. Wouldn't fit in a body bag."

"A box?"

"Yeah, used a hand cart to roll it across the frozen lake to the ambulance."

"Now that's a mental image. Sheriff's department give you any background?" Chris asked with a slight chuckle.

"Yeah. The guy fit the profile. Sheriff said they found drugs in the shack as well."

"Did he die in the same time frame?"

"They're not certain yet, but probably so. The time on the missing persons report puts it right in the ballpark. Being frozen like that screws up the estimates. They hope to have a more accurate time of death this evening."

"Hope you're right. Pilsner's pretty sharp, and I'm sure he's seen his share of frozen bodies in his day. He'll have the report as soon as possible. We don't need another outbreak. Is the team about done?" Chris asked as she crept forward in the turn lane to turn left onto Clairmont Road.

"Everyone's leaving tomorrow morning on commercial flights except me. I'm going to interview the family of this last victim before I catch a flight home. Anything else come out after we were told to disconnect?"

"After Weinstein finished ripping him a new one, the FBI guy told us there was some sort of discrepancy in one of the company's shipping manifests for a large quantity of out-of-spec material. Apparently, it never showed up at the waste-disposal facility."

"I'm not sure I understood the connection with the legit pharmaceuticals."

"It has to do with the sophistication of the targeting drugs. It's doubtful the drug cartels could develop and produce drugs with the capacity to carry therapeutics to specific organs in the body. So the logical place to look would be the legitimate drug companies."

"They think big pharma is into street drugs now? They trying to capture that market too? Sounds to me like someone's tinfoil hat is on a little too tight."

"No. They've already got a license to extort money from drug-dependent people. But it seems that expertise has made its way into the cartels' hands somehow," Chris replied as she accelerated through the intersection onto Clairmont.

"I can't remember when you got booted out of the teleconference. Did you hear the part about the lead?"

"Lead?"

"I guess you didn't. Yeah. Pilsner also found elevated amounts of lead in the hindbrain tissue samples. I got another email from him this afternoon telling me that similar amounts were found in the other victims' tissue samples. Apparently, it's found only in the hindbrain tissue, not in other organ tissue."

"Lead? Were they all a bunch of paint eaters? How'd it not wind up in the liver or kidneys?"

"Not sure. The levels aren't that high, but they're higher than typical background levels; I'd say this is definitely another commonality. We just have to figure out where it fits. Oh shoot! That reminds me. Can you call Pilsner and ask him to take some bone marrow samples? See if there's any lead there. I think I'm losing my mind. Can't remember anything anymore."

"Need to check you for lead?"

"Hilarious."

"Hey, what's the weather like back home?"

"You know, one of those nice early spring days, a little cool but not cold. Midfifties. Sunny. Soft breeze."

"Well that's about fifty degrees warmer than here. I'm ready to get out of here."

"Come by the office when you get back on Monday. Maybe we can have lunch. I'd like to meet with the other team leaders. I think the CDC can spring for a few sandwiches."

"Sounds good. If I get thawed out by then."

"Good. See you when you get back."

Chris disconnected. Traffic was at a standstill, so she found the number for Glenn Wallace in Renovo, Pennsylvania. She'd talk to him before she called Sherrie Cunningham in Idaho since it was later in the day for him. She dialed the number.

"Hello."

"Glenn, Chris Malone. How are things up there in Pennsylvania?"

"We're ready to wrap up tomorrow and send everyone home. The interviews are done. No more incidents."

Chris recognized the road fatigue in his voice.

"There haven't been any missing persons reports from the time of the initial wave of deaths? They found one more body in Minnesota. The guy's family filed a report at about the time frame the other victims died. They're confirming time of death to make sure it's not another outbreak."

"Yeah. I checked with the sheriff's department, and there was nothing. I'll give 'em a call after I hang up to make sure nothing's been filed since I last talked to them."

"Gotten anything from the medical examiner's office regarding the tissue samples?"

"They called me right after they got results on the first sample. Just like you suspected, opiates in the brain stem and VTA samples. They're working up the rest of the samples."

"Have them check for lead," Chris said, embarrassed she hadn't called sooner.

"Lead? What?"

"Yeah. Lead was found in the Minnesota samples but only in the stem and VTA tissue. The levels are not much but still more than background. If we find it in the Pennsylvania and Idaho victims, we'll have something. Just not sure what."

"Will do. Anything else?"

"No. Just I'd like to have a working lunch with you and the other two team leaders when you all get back on Monday."

Chris called Sherrie Cunningham in Idaho. She also had the same reaction as her colleagues regarding the lead issue. It was unanimous. The Idaho team was about to wrap things up as well. Samples would not be forthcoming for at least another day or so.

After disconnecting, Chris pondered the matter of the lead. She'd made her way on to Buford Highway. *Just a few more miles.* She needed to give Joyce, her friend at the FDA, another call to see if she might get her to push the boundaries on what she could divulge. She looked at her watch. She'd wait until she got home and email Joyce. No point in ruining Joyce's weekend with a late Friday afternoon request.

The curtain in Erika's window flicked back as Chris looked up from the driveway. A moment after she entered the kitchen by the side door, she heard the footfall of two people upstairs. Suspicion grew as all of the scurrying overhead ceased. The toilet flushed, and then it was quiet again. A number of scenarios ran through Chris's mind—none of them good.

Dread filled Chris as she sighed and started toward the stairs. At the top of the stairs, Erika's door opened. She emerged with another girl, the one Chris really did not care for, Lorrie DeWitt. Both girls skulked past Chris into the kitchen without saying a word.

Chris stood at the bottom of the stairs in a storm of emotions. There was relief. It hadn't been a boy and her daughter trying to turn her into a grandmother, but she was suspicious. *What were they doing up there that they had to cease as soon as I got home?* She felt betrayed. *Why is this daughter of mine doing this to me?* Then there was anger that eclipsed all the rest. Chris felt something burst inside.

In the kitchen, she found the two girls whispering and laughing by the side door. When Chris walked in, they giggled and were unable to stop it.

Taking her cue from Weinstein's performance, Chris did not raise her voice, but there was no denying her malice for the girl. "Lorrie, I'd like you to leave. Now."

That stopped the giggling. Erika looked as if she had been slapped. Lorrie just rolled her eyes and opened the door. Chris resisted the impulse to snatch her bald.

"Mom!" Erika implored. "That's my friend!"

"You know you're not supposed to have friends here when your father and I are not here. What were you doing up there that you had to stop as soon as I walked in the door?"

"None of your damned business! I'm not a child anymore. This is my life."

"It *is* my business when it's under my roof!" Her cool, wizened Weinstein persona vanished. Cold objectivity gave way to fury. "I'm sick of your snotty little attitude. We're not your doormats. Everything we do is for you. We do without so you can have the best of everything."

"Spare me the martyr routine. It's not like you're scrubbing toilets on two jobs so I can have shoes. You're gone for weeks at a time because you love your career! Dad and I are just here."

That last sling hit home, but Chris refused to let it show. "I do it for you!"

"Listen to yourself. Who are you trying to convince? Me or you?"

Chris dug in. "You're either going to get your act together around here or—"

"Or what?"

"You can find other accommodations." Chris couldn't believe what she had just heard come out of her own mouth.

Erika folded her arms and held a long pause. It was her turn to deploy cold objectivity. "Fine."

Erika pushed past Chris and headed upstairs. Chris listened to the shuffling and banging coming from the room above her.

What did I just say? Chris asked herself in tears.

A moment later, Erika stormed downstairs with a knapsack slung over one shoulder. Out the front door she flew. Chris collapsed onto a chair at the table, lay her head on her arms, and sobbed.

Sam walked through the side door about an hour later and found Chris still at the table. She wasn't crying at that moment, but her red-rimmed eyes betrayed her.

"What's wrong?"

"Oh just the usual mother-daughter blowout. Is there some rule that mothers and daughters have to tear each other's guts out during adolescence?"

"Couldn't tell you. I only had brothers. Did you and your mom fight back when?"

"Yes. And you're not making me feel any better."

Sam walked over, pulled Chris up, and hugged her. "Tell me what happened."

Chris told him about coming home early and finding Erika and Lorrie upstairs and acting peculiarly. How they said some pretty sharp things to each other. "Then I did the stupidest thing of all. I gave her an ultimatum. Then she walked out the door."

"An ultimatum? What was it?"

"Either get her act together or find somewhere else to live."

"Ow! You may have jumped ahead too far. You gotta be able to back up your ultimatums."

"Yes, I know. Why do you think I've been sitting here crying for the last hour?"

"It's all right. Nothing bad's happened yet. It's Friday. No school tomorrow. Plenty of time for everyone to cool down. Lots of families have these little dramas. We'll get through ours."

"Should I go after her?" Chris asked.

"It's only been, what? A couple of hours?"

"Not even that."

"Well, all right. She's probably somewhere cooling down just like you. Give her some space. She's probably at a friend's house. Give it a little time and I'll go look for her."

"I want to go."

"Probably not a good idea. Maybe we should look into some sort of counseling before this gets too big."

"I just want my little girl back. The one who helped me bake cookies."

"She'll come back. Remember the Apollo Effect."

Chris hugged Sam. She straightened herself up, took a wet towel, and wiped her face and eyes. "What would you like for dinner?"

"How about I just go pick up some Chinese takeout from the Golden Dragon? It'll only take a few minutes."

Usually, Chris would have opposed the idea but not that night. "Sounds good. Lo mein and egg rolls. Get something for Erika."

Sam pulled out his phone and called the Golden Dragon. Chris heard him tell them to deliver and give their address.

"You're not going?"

"Thought I'd stay in case—"

"Erika calls?"

Sam shrugged. "Well ..."

"Probably best."

"Why don't you go watch TV or something to take your mind off things for a while?"

"Not in the mood for TV. I need to do some laundry from my trip."

She left for their bedroom. She returned a few minutes later with a basket of her clothes and headed to the laundry room. Sam was in the study waiting on the delivery guy.

Chris came back out and asked him, "What do you know about Tudos Pharmaceuticals?"

"Solid company. Blue chip stock."

"What do you know about their internal workings? Their management?"

"I don't know much right off the top of my head. I could do a little research and see what I come up with. Why?"

"Their name came up in association with some of the stuff happening in Minnesota. I just wanted some background."

"Something criminal?"

"No, but some of their product may have slipped into the wrong hands. Or some of their technology did."

Sam pulled up one of his brokerage websites and searched away. Chris set about doing her laundry. Half an hour later, the doorbell rang giving Chris an impulse of hope. It was the delivery guy. Sam paid him at the door. They sat in silence as they ate. Erika's order sat on a plate in little white boxes.

Chris slipped away afterward with her laptop to their bedroom. She arranged the pillows behind her head and back as well as under her knees so she could sit up in bed. Before starting on the computer, she made note of the time, 7:10. Any real progress in digging out information was slow in coming. The clock beside the bed demanded it be observed every couple of minutes.

Sam came up to the bedroom around nine with a handful of printed articles.

"Found several bits of info on Tudos. Pretty interesting stuff. Unusual."

"How so?" Chris asked laying her laptop aside and giving the clock another furtive glance.

"Well, until recently, control of the company rested with the founder's family—just him and his daughter. That's kind of rare these days. There are a couple of big corporations like that. Mars, the candy maker, is one of them."

"Yes. Patterson and Weinstein were talking about him at lunch. What's his name? Bauer?"

"Yeah, Bauer. You had lunch with the big guys today?"

"Yeah. Just the three of us. In Weinstein's office. I was having a pretty good day. Until I got home."

"Wow. Good for you. Anyway. Bauer's daughter was killed in some sort of drug gang shootout a few years ago. Apparently, they didn't have a very good lawyer to set up the daughter's estate prior to her death because the son-in-law got control of her shares of the company. Bauer lost control. The daughter always voted with the dad. The son-in-law, however, went against the old man."

"Family feud, huh?"

"All of this occurred after a big battle with the board of directors over something Bauer did before his daughter died that they didn't like. The company developed a drug to treat drug addicts. It kills the cravings addicts have for drugs so they have a shot at getting clean. It could have been a bonanza for the company. Bauer, however, made the drug available at cost to clinics across the nation. The company just broke even. After that, he lost controlling interest."

"Imagine that—a pharmaceutical company with a heart."

"Anyway, after wrangling in the courts for a couple of years, the old man still held forty percent. He came to the board with a proposal to settle things. He'd step aside as CEO on the condition he be allowed to be the director of research and development. He was still their single biggest shareholder and could damage the company. The publicity was already pulling the stock below the waterline."

"The board went with that?" Chris asked surprised.

"What else could they do? The situation was killing everyone. But it gets better. He then sells back to the company another twenty percent, buys a struggling electronics company with the capital, and runs it and the R and D department at Tudos at the same time."

"What is he, some sort of Superman?"

"He's supposed to be some sort of genius when it comes to the technical stuff. Tudos has now branched off into nanotech, the next big thing. They went out and bought a couple of small start-ups, funded their research, and now they're on the cusp of some pretty whizbang products. Their stock is back up, and everybody's happy. But guess who owns the company that makes the equipment that powers the little nanobots?"

"Pretty clever. Sounds like he's one of those guys who can play ten chess masters at the same time and not lose. I saw a publication today about using radio waves to power nanobots that Tudos developed. I had time only to read the abstract," Chris said.

Sam flipped through a couple of the articles in his hand. "Yeah, it looks like Bauer's lab figured out a way to animate the nanobots with an external power source, radio waves. The equipment used for that was from his other company. That was a huge breakthrough for nanotech. The vehicles don't have to carry their own power, like batteries. This article says it reduces the size of the little critters by an order of magnitude," Sam said, showing her the stapled article.

"It actually called them little critters?" Chris teased.

"Uh, yeah. That's the new scientific name for them. Little critters."

"How old is he? I saw something about him being a Holocaust survivor."

"I don't think he's turned eighty yet, mid to upper seventies maybe," Sam said with a shrug.

"I don't think I want to be empire building when I'm eighty."

"I think you're safe."

The conversation stalled. The elephant in the room had to be acknowledged. "It's after nine. Shouldn't we call her friends?" Chris asked.

"Still pretty early."

"I'm not cut out for this tough-love jazz."

"Give it a little longer. She's not stupid."

"No, but she's mad. And that's just as bad."

Sam crossed the room, lay down beside Chris, and embraced her. Sleep crept up on them both. At the first ring of the phone, they jumped straight out of the bed as if it had been hit by lightning. Chris looked at the clock with disbelief. Eleven thirty. *How could we have fallen asleep like that?*

"Hello?"

"Is this the Malone residence?"

"Yes."

"This is DeKalb County General Hospital ..."

"Hurry!" Chris implored.

"I'm going as fast as I can. We'll be there in a few minutes," Sam snapped back.

A glowing blue sign instructed drivers to turn right for the ER. The Malones worked their way across the waiting room to the receptionist's desk. A drowsy security guard looked them over as they approached.

"How may I help you?" asked the receptionist.

Sam stepped forward. "We're Sam and Chris Malone. We received a call about thirty minutes ago that our daughter was here."

"What's her name?"

"Erika. Erika Malone."

After a moment, the receptionist looked up from her monitor. "Can I see some form of photo ID?"

"Uh, sure." Sam fumbled and patted himself all over looking for the bulge of his wallet. In the rush to get out of the house, he had forgotten it.

"Here." Chris stepped forward and handed the woman her CDC identification.

The receptionist took the badge from Chris and puzzled over it for a moment because usually folks handed over their drivers' licenses.

"The CDC is an agency of the federal government. It's a valid form of ID," Chris asserted in an even tone.

"I ... I suppose it is. Let me call back and have someone from the med staff come out and talk to you. You can have a seat over there. I'll call you when they come out," the receptionist said.

Chris scanned the room hoping to find two unoccupied seats. The best she could do was an empty seat at the end of a row with a blank wall to one side. One of them could lean against the wall as they waited. Chris preferred standing. Although standing was not the most accurate word. She preferred to pace. And wring her hands. And bite her lip. The typical ER waiting room mini-dramas playing out all about the room piqued no interest in her. She was caught in one of her own.

After an eternity of just twenty minutes, the receptionist spoke with a nurse and pointed in their direction. Sam tugged on Chris's sleeve. As the nurse approached them, Sam stood and held Chris.

"Are you the Malones?" the nurse inquired as she approached.

"Yes."

"Your daughter's stable now. Sorry it took so long to get free and come talk to you. As you can see, this evening has been a madhouse. Before I take you back, let's step into one of the privacy rooms and I'll explain the situation to you."

The privacy room was tiny, barely large enough to seat the three of them around the little round table in the center. It was nonetheless a welcomed escape from the crowded waiting room. Chris was in no mood to discuss her daughter's problems in the presence of a hundred strangers.

"As I said, your daughter is stable. The EMTs administered Naloxone before she arrived. It probably saved her life. There was another girl brought in with her who was not as lucky."

"What?" Chris asked not quite grasping what the nurse had said.

"Was your daughter acquainted with Lorrie DeWitt?"

"Yes! She was just at our house this afternoon! What are you saying?"

"The EMTs didn't get there in time to save her. Both girls seem to have taken quite a dose. Tox screens are in the lab now trying to figure out what we're dealing with."

"Take us to her. We want to see her now!"

"Sure, I will. She's still under the effects of whatever she took. We're waiting for a room on the Critical Care Unit so we can admit her. She'll need to stay at least a couple of days. She's still getting a slow drip of Naloxone to counter the street drug until it clears her system."

Chris struggled to hold herself together. Given all she had witnessed during the past week, one thought pervaded her mind. "I need to speak to the pathologist performing the autopsy on the other girl," she blurted out.

"Excuse me?" the perplexed nurse asked.

"Chris, what are you talking about?" Sam asked equally perplexed.

Realizing how she sounded, Chris paused to explain herself to the nurse. "Look, I'm a field investigator for the CDC. I just spent this last week in Minnesota looking at a roomful of bodies. The cause of death is suspected to be related to drugs of a sort we've not seen before. One of the commonalities in all of the autopsies so far is a slight elevation of lead in brain stem tissue. A CDC alert about this will be coming out in the next twenty-four hours."

"Uh ... let me take you to your daughter first. Then I'll get the charge nurse to come talk to you."

The nurse led Chris and Sam past numerous bed stations to the far corner of the ED to two bed stations that were actual rooms. Another security guard sat not far away at a small station. *This must be where they bring the ones who get out of control,* Chris surmised.

The Malones walked in and were faced with the specter of their unconscious daughter restrained to the bed railing and with an IV tube in her arm. A monitor displayed their daughter's very life essence in blue-green lights and a rhythmic, regular beep. Chris rushed across the room to her daughter's side.

"Are these necessary?" Chris asked pointing at the restraints binding Erika's wrists and ankles. A large belt across her abdomen would have prevented her from thrashing about.

"They're a precaution should she regain consciousness. When she does, she'll likely be confused and combative. They're for her protection to keep her from pulling out the IV and flailing around," the nurse answered.

Chris couldn't muster the energy to argue. Perhaps it was for the best that her daughter was constrained in such a manner. She stroked Erika's sweaty hair away from her eyes. She wanted to cry but couldn't. Sam stood beside her with his arm across her shoulder.

"I'll be back with the charge nurse as soon as she's available," the nurse said as she exited the room, pulling the door closed behind her.

Chris reached for Sam's hand. "What did we do wrong, Sam?"

"Nothing. We've given Erika everything we have, and I don't mean just material stuff. We've made her the center of our universe."

"Then why do I feel so guilty? As if I've neglected her in some way."

"Come on. Don't do this to yourself."

The charge nurse came into the room. "I understand you have a question about the drug screening?"

Chris rose. "No, it's not about the drug screening. I requested to speak to the pathologist performing the autopsy on the other girl, the one who died of the overdose."

The nurse didn't respond immediately, but Chris could read the nurse's puzzled expression. She drew a deep breath to compose herself. "I am a field investigator for the CDC. No doubt you've seen the news regarding the multiple deaths in Minnesota, Pennsylvania, and Idaho."

The nurse acknowledged her awareness of what had been in the news.

"Well, I'm in charge of those investigations. We have reason to believe all those deaths are related to some sort of new street drug We're finding slightly elevated levels of lead in the brain stem tissue. There will be a CDC alert coming out tomorrow morning advising emergency care facilities to look for elevated lead levels in any fatal overdose cases."

"Ms. Malone, I'm not sure—"

"Doctor."

"What?"

"Doctor Malone. I'm an epidemiologist."

"Dr. Malone, I think you need to talk to the attending physician."

"It is imperative that Lorrie Dewitt's autopsy include sampling for lead in the brain stem tissue."

"You're going to have to talk to the attending."

The charge nurse left them in the room as she went in search of the attending physician. Chris turned to her daughter and sat beside her again holding Erika's cold hand to her cheek. Only a few minutes passed before two men came in without knocking. Sam stepped back suddenly, and Chris rose.

The older of the two held up a badge. "I'm Detective Allen from Homicide, and this is Detective Joyner from Atlanta PD's Drug Enforcement Task Force. You're the Malones?"

"Yes," Sam answered.

"You are aware that your daughter's friend died of an overdose? That your daughter was there at the time?"

"Yes. They told us that. You're not implying our daughter killed Lorrie, are you?" Sam blurted out.

"At the moment, we're just asking routine questions so we can determine what actually did happen. When there's an unnatural death, it gets looked at as a homicide until proven otherwise."

Chris and Sam nodded.

"How well did your daughter know the victim?"

"The past few months, she and Erika were spending quite a bit of time together. After school. Weekends. Like they were a secret society or something."

"Secret society?"

"You know how teens are sometimes. Sneaking around. Very secretive. Never talking to us about what they were doing. Barely talking to us at all about anything," Sam confessed.

"When was the last time you saw the two of them together?"

She knew her answer was going to cause trouble, but Chris said, "This afternoon. They were at our house. In Erika's room."

Detective Allen looked over at Joyner, who broke his stoic stance. He acknowledged the last bit of information with a question. "Will you give us permission to search your daughter's room?"

"Search her room?" Sam repeated weakly.

"We can get a search warrant if necessary. Things go a lot smoother without having to go to a judge."

"Now? It's nearly one in the morning. Our daughter is unconscious in a hospital bed," Chris said.

"We can do this tomorrow, but we need to do this, and we will one way or another."

Chris regarded the two detectives for a moment. They had her off balance. *Perhaps a different approach.* "Tell me, officers, have you heard anything about a new street drug called Smokey?"

Detective Allen shrugged, but Chris recognized a glimmer of recognition in Joyner, the drug enforcement guy.

"Why are you asking about Smokey?" Joyner asked.

Chris relayed her credentials for a third time and her recent encounter with the deaths in Minnesota. She explained her team's suspicions and the possible link to lead.

"What does that have to do with your daughter?"

"I hope nothing. But if you request the testing in the autopsy, it's more likely to happen."

"We're seeing Smokey more and more, but I don't think that's what your daughter and the other girl OD'd on. I've yet to see a single Smokey OD. And we found drugs at the scene where they found the two girls. What we found was something we call Reaper. It's a super-hot dose that's a mixture of a number of opioids."

"You're sure?" Chris asked finding it odd that she felt relief Erika had probably taken a hot dose of a drug other than Smokey.

"We've seen an increase in ODs of casual or inexperienced users in the past few weeks. Narcotic naïve is the term used to describe them. We believe the distributors are having a fire sale of their old inventory. They seem to be pushing it off on people like your daughter."

"Can you request the test for lead anyway? To be certain?"

"We'll ask."

"Thank you. If you can give my husband a lift, he can let you into the house for you to do your search of our daughter's room."

"I want to stay with Erika until they move her to a room," Sam protested.

"It'll be okay. She's going to be out of it for another several hours. No point in both of us being here," Chris said calmly.

The strained edge was gone from her tone. Sam yielded and left with the two detectives.

Chris sat by Erika's side for the next three hours before a bed on the CCU opened up. In that time, the attending physician stopped by and Chris explained her reasons for making the request for the fourth time. To her surprise and relief, the doctor said he'd ask the pathologist to perform the test on Lorrie's tissue.

The sun was still somewhere below the eastern horizon when Chris walked out of the hospital into the cool, breezy morning. She remembered nothing of her drive home. She crawled into bed beside Sam having only removed her shoes. The euphoria of sleep embraced her without hesitation.

Erika called out for help from somewhere across a frozen prairie, the wind carrying her plea off in a dozen directions. Chris searched the horizon in all directions while panic rose in her chest. Her eyes stung from facing the frozen blasts of air.

"Erika!" she cried out. Chris struggled to walk toward the sound of her daughter's cries, but the snowdrifts seized her and held her back. The landscape shifted again until it wasn't a landscape at all. It was her bedroom. Chris's heart pounded from the helplessness she felt. It was that dream again.

She lay motionless allowing her breathing to settle. Chilled from her sweaty clothes, she pulled the blanket up to her chin. *Where's Sam? What time is it?*

Blinding sunlight stabbed the room from along the edges of the curtains. Chris held the alarm clock in disbelief. It was almost noon. In reality, she hadn't slept that long, but the thought of having slept until noon distressed her. *Where's Sam?*

After a quick shower and a change of clothes, she headed downstairs to find Sam. What she found was a note.

Gone to the hospital. Decided to let you sleep. Call me when you wake up.

Chris couldn't decide if she should be angry or grateful. In the end, she defaulted to gratitude. She didn't have the energy for anger. She fixed a cup of coffee and ate a couple of pieces of fruit. She saw her reflection in the toaster. *I'm quite a sight.* But she couldn't muster enough emotion to care.

A considerable amount of time passed as Chris sat nursing her coffee. She didn't mind that it had turned cold. It was after one when she picked up her cell and dialed Sam.

"It's me."

"You okay? I thought you could use the sleep."

"I'm fine. How's Erika?"

"She's conscious now. Not very pleasant."

"You talked to her?"

"A little. She's still restrained." Sam paused. "They want us to have her committed for psychiatric evaluation. They think she's a risk to herself. It will probably only be for a couple of days."

"Do it."

"What?"

"Have her committed. Do whatever's necessary. You don't need me there."

"Chris?"

"Sam, I can't."

"Well, okay. Sure you don't want to come down and see her?"

"No. Not yet. I have to go to the office. Bye."

CHAPTER 13

MAY 15, 2006

Jakob sat at the enormous conference table as quietly as a condemned man before the gallows. He had not made a single comment during the entire weekly executive meeting. The subject matter so far had been pretty routine, but what would follow would be anything but.

"That brings us to the last agenda item this morning—the one titled Confidential Discussion," announced Randall Monsinger.

Turning to his assistant on his left, he leaned over and whispered, "We won't need minutes for the rest of the meeting. You can leave."

The men seated around the oblong table patiently held their collective tongues as Randall's assistant gathered his laptop and walked out. As soon as the door closed completely behind the young man, Randall continued. "I'm sure most of you have heard the rumblings regarding a lawsuit against us over the Campaign for Hope program. At this point, it's just a rumor, but we need to position Tudos as best we can against the possibility."

"Against the probability," said Jim Baines, Tudos's senior vice president for marketing. "It's more than a possibility. I think the aggrieved parties have such a strong case that a lawsuit is a near certainty." Baines was a well-groomed, middle-aged man whose salt-and-pepper hair perfectly accented his golf tan.

The room murmured in agreement. Jakob Bauer remained silent. His tattooed forearm ached to be rubbed, but aware it was common knowledge that particular tic would telegraph he was under duress, he sat as motionless as a statue. He looked across the table at Stuart McInnis. Jakob had brought Stuart into Tudos at the beginning when he first bought the company. Jakob considered him a friend. All Stuart could do when their eyes met was to look away.

"Gentlemen, before we proceed any further with our discussion, let me introduce an attorney we have brought onboard to help position ourselves better. Some of you may already know Jim Holloway." Randall motioned toward the lawyer seated at far the end of the table. Holloway nodded.

"Jim is here for a couple of reasons. First, his presence makes this discussion a conversation protected by attorney-client privilege, so none of us can be subpoenaed to testify regarding what is said here today. Second, Jim is an accomplished veteran of lawsuits from shareholders. Don't let his folksy, southern manner fool you. He's going to help us build our defense starting now. Jim, would you like to address the group?"

Holloway removed his glasses and tossed them on his notepad. "I agree with Mr. Baines. This is a tough case against Tudos. But"—he paused for emphasis—"it's not completely a lost cause."

Jakob took notice of the offered ray of light but continued to sit motionless.

Holloway continued. "We can have our freewheeling conversations and debates within these walls until we're all blue in the face. But outside of here, beyond my presence, you must not, you cannot, you will not speak a word to anyone, not even each other. I cannot make this point strong enough. Do not talk about this to your bartender, your personal assistant, your wife or girlfriend, not even your mama. How many times have we all seen someone high up on the totem pole torpedoed by some secretly recorded video? Don't be that guy.

"Now, this lawsuit is not a lawsuit ... yet. It is as Randall said a rumor. But we are going to treat it as if it were an active suit. When we get served notice, and please note I did not say *if* we are served notice, we'll already have had a campaign working on the public psyche for weeks. We're going to discuss, debate, fuss among ourselves about all the bits and pieces, but first, we're going to discuss our offense."

Jakob brightened. Those were exactly his thoughts. Go on the offense. He saw others in the boardroom beginning to fall under Brother Holloway's gospel spell as well.

"We're starting with this discussion now because I don't need or want a client who has already lost the battle in his mind. I want you to be fully engaged believers in your own cause. So how do we go about such a campaign?" Holloway asked.

The room buzzed in hushed tones. Holloway paused before continuing to allow the uniformly dark-suited executives fan the spark of optimism themselves.

Holloway resumed his sermon. "Who are the parties rumored to be lodging this suit? Well, whoever they are, they'll surely be joined by others. So let's list the potentials."

Holloway walked over to a whiteboard and picked up a marker. The executives fell into an uneasy quiet like schoolboys hoping not to be called upon.

"Come on. It wasn't a rhetorical question. Who are the likely candidates to be coming after you?"

Randall got the ball rolling. "The rumor is that there are a couple of large funds and one private shareholder with substantial holdings."

"Okay. A couple of funds and a private party." Holloway wrote the two on the whiteboard far to the right side and with a large margin above the column he was forming.

"These two are external to Tudos. Now, I suspect every filled seat in this room could *technically* join in this suit as well. Not that they would, but they could. No doubt there are some end-of-year bonuses going to be affected by the break-even business plan for the drug program."

The room broke into a much louder buzzing of general agreement with a hostile flavor. Jakob sat stoically silent and resolutely unmoving.

Holloway wrote EXTERNAL above the right-hand column and started a column on the left side headed INTERNAL. Under it, he wrote Execs. "Who else internal to Tudos? Any researchers, techs, plant managers, secretaries, janitors ...?"

Randall spoke. "The research team that developed the drug specifically was to get some really nice bonuses over the life of the product. Generally, every vested Tudos employee gets a bonus based on salary and tenure."

"Let's start with what's probably the largest of these groups, the big funds. When combined, these guys typically hold the majority share. These are made up of ..." Holloway began.

A slight but noticeable commotion rustled through the room.

Holloway stopped and turned from the whiteboard. "Did I miss something?"

Randall said, "That's not the case for Tudos. We have one shareholder who controls a little more than fifty percent of the stock. Actually, there are two, but they vote as a bloc." Randall extended his hand in Jakob's direction. "Jakob Bauer, our founder and CEO, and his daughter, my wife."

Jakob watched Holloway turn away from the whiteboard. He was certain that a high-profile attorney such as Holloway would have already done his homework and thus knew that. *This is theater.* Jakob thought.

Holloway looked at Jakob. "Well, all in the family. Mr. Bauer, I understand you are at the root of this situation. You are the champion of the drug rehab program."

Jakob acknowledged the charge with a simple nod.

"No doubt you're bearing much weight on your shoulders because of this. Fortunes are at stake—college funds, summer homes, yachts. You're the scapegoat in all this. Mr. Bauer, a prophet is without honor in his own household. You no doubt looked at the epidemic of drug addiction, death, and mayhem and said to yourself, 'Something has to be done.' I promise—you are going to come out of this the hero."

Jakob remained stoic in his demeanor; the New Testament reference escaped him completely, but he fully grasped that his vindication was at hand.

Holloway returned to the whiteboard. "Let's look at this likely second-largest group, still, the largest group likely to sue. The group comprises mutual funds, pension funds, and the like. How do we undermine their high-ground position as the aggrieved party?"

Again the room was silent.

"Not a rhetorical question, y'all." Holloway stopped and made evident he would wait until kingdom come or until someone proffered a response before continuing. The pause gained mass as it hung above their heads.

"You make it so that anyone who dares cast reproach on this program to cure the world of drug addiction will be perceived as soulless schmucks, pariahs," Jakob said. He was standing.

Holloway smiled. "And how precisely do we go about making the public at large perceive them as such?"

"A PR campaign showcasing recovered addicts with their families—kids extolling the virtues of the program and expressing their undying gratitude to Tudos for helping them. We showcase the growing statistics of the positive effects. We get community leaders talking about the comeback the communities are beginning to see."

Grinning even more broadly, Holloway asked a leading question, "Is that all we're going to do, Brother Bauer?"

"We're going to market to funds that tout themselves as socially conscious. Get them to buy into what we're doing and shore up the stock. We're going to make it a moral imperative to hold our stock—a badge of honor for the socially aware."

Jakob took a breath and continued. "We're going to give out the bonuses to the research guys because they earned them, but we'll roll that cost into the break-even number. We in this room are going to give up our bonuses because it's the right thing to do. And we're going to let the world know we did."

Clapping and raising his hands as if he were at a tent revival on a hot, sultry night in backwoods Georgia, Holloway exclaimed, "Halleluiah! Preach it, Brother Bauer, our prophet! As we say back home, better blow your own horn before someone else turns it into a spittoon."

The room laughed at the metaphor but seemed enthused nonetheless. All except Randall. Jakob saw that the growing optimism was not sitting well with him. After all, it was Randall who had brought Holloway in on this problem. Now, the man was making Jakob the savior.

The strategy session ran longer than anticipated. Numerous schedules were wrecked because of it. Lunch orders were taken so the participants could carry the planning into the afternoon.

By two o'clock, a fairly comprehensive game plan had emerged. Even budgets for the various elements had been worked out. The executives there were broken down into various teams with specific tasks. Jakob and Randall were left to coordinate with Holloway the execution and progress of the teams' tasks. Holloway called it the plan of salvation.

Holloway was at the whiteboard reviewing the team assignments with the whole group when Randall's assistant burst into the conference room. Holloway paused midsentence at the interruption.

"I told you we were to be left alone!" Randall snapped.

"Yes, I apologize, but it's the police. It's about your wife."

CHAPTER 14

MARCH 24, 2019

Chris stood with the two Atlanta PD detectives at the end of a long hospital corridor at the entrance of the psych unit. Out of respect for hospital decorum and privacy, the conversation was hushed but nonetheless intense. Detective Allen handed her an envelope.

"We got the pathology report from the medical examiner. There was no trace of lead in the victim's brain tissue, Ms. Malone."

Chris regarded the two policemen as they stood between her and the psych floor entrance. "That's good. Probably safe to assume Erika didn't take any of that new street drug either. Thank you for the update."

"Ms. Malone, Georgia law now considers anyone who sells or distributes drugs to a person who then dies from an overdose to be guilty of first-degree murder. If the victim is underage, the death penalty is then recommended. Don't you want to see justice for Lorrie DeWitt? For your own daughter?"

"Officer Allen—"

"Detective."

"What?"

"It's Detective Allen."

"*Detective* Allen, asking that our attorney and a doctor be present during your questioning Erika is not too much to ask. And believe me, no one on this planet would like to see whoever sold them the drugs given a lethal injection more than me," Chris stated with a cold evenness.

"But, Ms. Malone, that could take hours."

"It's Doctor."

"What?"

"It's Doctor Malone." Chris paused. "I have your number. We'll call you."

"Look, we found more of the drug in your daughter's room. It's possible your daughter could be viewed as an accomplice in the death of Lorrie DeWitt."

Chris absorbed the information. "All the more reason to have an attorney present. Now if you'll excuse me, I must look after my daughter."

Chris brushed by the two detectives as the door to the psych floor opened for her. She walked to the nurse's station and identified herself. Chris handed over her purse and cellphone to have her things placed in a locker. The nurse gave her instructions about what she could and couldn't do while on the floor. Chris nodded as she looked back through the glass doors to see if the two detectives were still hanging around.

A second door opened, and Chris stepped into the patient area. She was struck by how Spartan the hallway appeared. No paintings on the walls. Nothing that could be used as a projectile or a makeshift weapon. No light fixtures on the walls. No place to hang yourself. Solid ceiling, not a suspended ceiling, so no elopement above the ceiling.

Erika's room was midway down the hall. Chris passed the day room where a few patients sat and talked. Others sat and stared out the window or muttered to themselves. All the patients' rooms she passed were unoccupied. Chris paused a moment at Erika's room, gathered herself, and entered.

She found Erika asleep. Chris, torn between waking her and letting her sleep, could only stand there looking down on her only child in a hospital bed. At least she wasn't strapped to the bed like a felon as before. After some time, Chris elected to leave, but Erika stirred as she turned away.

"Mom?"

"Yes dear."

"Are you leaving?"

"No. I'm here. How are you feeling?"

"Like a prisoner."

"Well, it's just for a short while. Until ..." Chris halted, unable to find the right words.

"Until what? Until I detox? Until I get my head on straight?"

"Erika ... your father and I—"

"Had me committed. I know the law. If I was over eighteen, you'd have no say."

"Erika, whatever we do or have ever done has been for your good."

"Like locking me up in this nuthouse? Do you think I'm crazy? Or just an inconvenience?"

Chris, desperately trying to engage without being drawn into a fight, replied softly, "You nearly died, Erika. Your friend, Lorrie, did die. I ... we ... just wanted you to be safe. To take a pause from whatever it is you're going through."

Erika said nothing, but she gathered her legs up under her body and sprang at Chris like a striking snake. The force of Erika's whole body hitting Chris in the upper trunk knocked her through the open door and into the opposite corridor wall.

Recovering instantly, Erika pounced again on her mother grabbing her hair and pounding her head repeatedly against the floor shrieking with each blow, "I hate you! I hate you!"

Chris, stunned, offered no defense to the savage beating. Two nurses pulled Erika off her. The nurses struggled to restrain Erika as she repeatedly lunged at Chris.

"I hate you! I'll kill you!"

Two more staff members and a security guard arrived finally subduing the out-of-control Erika. Chris could only watch as they dragged her demonic daughter down the hall to a special room. She watched as they struggled to close the door as if on a wild animal.

"Oh Erika." Chris's vision narrowed as if she were looking through a shrinking tunnel. And then it went black.

Chris fluttered her eyes open to see a dimly lit room unfamiliar to her. She tried to lean forward, but a blindingly sharp pain kept her head nailed to the pillow.

"Whoa, settle back."

It was Sam.

"Where ... What ...?"

"You have a concussion. They want you to stay the night so they can observe you."

"What day is it? How long ...?"

"It's Sunday, a little after four in the afternoon."

Chris looked at the television and saw a muted Atlanta Hawks game underway. The screen appeared out of focus. For that matter, so did Sam. Her head throbbed along with every heartbeat.

"Can I get something for this headache?"

"You're already maxed out on the dosage."

"It's not working. I feel sick."

Sam held up a small basin. "Do you want to throw up?"

"No. I'm afraid if I lean over, my head will split and fall off my shoulders. Maybe it'd stop throbbing if it did." She raised her hand to her head and felt the bandage wrapped around her head. "What's this?"

"You hit your head pretty hard on that wall. You have several stitches."

"Ugh. This just keeps getting better. Did they shave my head?"

"Just a little."

"How did I hit …?"

"You don't remember?"

"I remember going to see Erika and getting stopped by those two cops. After that … I don't …"

"Erika attacked you."

For a moment, Chris saw the edges of the tunnel again, but she resisted. Sam held her hand and squeezed it tightly.

"What are we going to do, Sam?"

"I don't know."

Despite her condition, Chris heard the defeat in his voice. It wasn't as if he had said, "I don't know, but we'll figure something out." He was completely drained of hope. The tunnel closed in again, and she offered no resistance.

Sometime later, the fog lifted as Chris opened her eyes again. The room was darker that time. The muted television was the only source of light. Her hand felt wet and restrained. She looked down and saw Sam, asleep, leaning over from the chair beside the bed. His head rested on her hand as he still clutched it.

Tears. He's been crying. That's why my hand's so wet. She tried not to disturb him, but her hand hurt. She slid her hand away from his clasp and stroked his hair. He aroused and raised his head.

He was confused for a moment. "Guess I fell asleep."

"What happened?" Chris asked.

"You blacked out. They came in and worked on you."

Chris noticed the IV tubes in her arm and the active monitor beside her bed. She looked at Sam. "It won't happen again."

"They took you back downstairs for another CT. They thought it could be swelling on the brain."

"That's not what it was."

"That's what they said. How'd you ...?"

"I'm going to be all right. We have to be strong for Erika."

"She tried to kill you, Chris."

"That was the drugs." Sam didn't respond. Chris continued. "We have to find her a program. Something with a good success rate. Something for kids her age."

"How are we going to pay for that?" Sam asked clearly distressed.

"There's more. I recall now what those two detectives said. They hinted pretty strongly that they could make Erika out to be an accomplice in Lorrie's death. We're going to need a good lawyer as well."

"Geez, Chris."

"We can make it all work. My health plan will pay for some of it. Thanks to your investing, we have a pretty good college fund."

"Her college fund?"

"Sam, the college boat has sailed. There won't be any college if we can't get her through this. There won't be anything."

Despair clouded over Sam's face again.

"We're going to come out of this, Sam—with Erika."

Sam embraced her and wept.

Midmorning the following day, after much protest from Sam, Chris aligned with her doctor's recommendation that she go home. She promised not to overdo it. By early afternoon, she was looking out at the bird feeder beyond her patio.

Later that evening, she read through mountain of work emails. She sent Patterson an email telling him about an accident in the kitchen and said she would have Sanders cover for her for a couple of days; she would be back in a day or two.

By eleven that evening, she was completely spent.

In the kitchen the following morning, Sam asked, "How're you feeling? I'm not sure it was such a good idea that they sent you home yesterday." He poured cereal into a bowl for her.

"I'm glad to be home. Besides, hospitals are the best places to pick up other bugs."

"Need anything?"

"I sure could go for a cup of strong coffee."

"Not yet. Doctor's orders."

"No coffee? Well, at least now I have an incentive to get better."

"Really? How are you doing?" Sam looked at the back of her unbandaged head.

"Better. Much better. I don't have a headache anymore. My vision is back to normal. I want to go out this morning. The walls are closing in on me."

"You can't go back to work, Chris. Not today. Besides, we're supposed to meet with Erika's attorney this afternoon."

"I didn't say anything about going to work. I want to go to the hairdresser. See what she can do to cover up this hole in my head."

Sam chuckled. "The difference between men and women. Men would go around with a head wrap the size of a turban to get sympathy, and you want to hide it. It really doesn't look that bad."

"Okay, smart guy. I'll just tell everyone you hit me."

"Hey, don't even joke like that."

"Seriously, I slipped on a wet spot in the kitchen and hit my head on the floor. If anyone asks, I slipped on the floor and banged my head hard on the floor. Let's get our stories straight. No one needs to know about the thing with Erika."

"I agree. Got it. Happened Saturday morning while we were getting ready to go to see Erika."

Chris took a bite of her cereal and looked out the window onto the backyard. "But I am going to work. Tomorrow. I need to get back. This last incident ... And for my own sanity. There's nothing I can do for Erika by being with her. She just blows up when she sees me, and I can't just sit here. I'm ready to go back."

"Chris, you can't do your ten- or eleven-hour days. It's only been two days since you whacked your head. You need to take it a little easy."

"It's how I cope, Sam. It's like the comfort some people get by working on a giant jigsaw puzzle. Only my puzzle doesn't come in a box with a picture on it. Don't worry. I won't overdo it. I'll play the sympathy card so they'll cut me some slack."

"Promise?"

"Promise."

"Would it do any good for me to put my foot down and say you can't go?"

Chris only laughed in response.

"Yeah, I thought not."

The following morning, Chris sat in her car in the CDC employee lot to gather herself before walking into work. She practiced her story and even thought up a few quips to make light of it. She checked herself again in the mirror and headed for the building.

"Hey! Look who's back from the dead."

"Good morning, Wiley. Glad to be back from the frozen north?"

"Am I ever. Give me Dixie. My blood's too thin to live any farther north. So, the accident." Wiley stretched out her hands as if to draw the story out.

"It's embarrassing."

"Even better."

"There was water on the kitchen floor. We were rushing around to go out the door and *wham!* I'm on the floor."

"Well, that's not so bad."

"Unconscious, slight concussion, five stiches."

Wiley looked up at Chris's head. "Can't see them."

"They're there. I had my hairdresser work on me yesterday."

"You feel all right?"

"I'm fine. Do me a favor and give everyone the official version so I don't have to repeat it a thousand times today."

"Will do."

"Thanks. Are Lawrence and the rest of them back? I need to catch up. Two days and I feel like I'm behind a month."

"Most are already in this morning. Tony will be here in a few minutes. He has to drop the kids off. Let me get you a cup of coffee."

"You know, normally I'd say no, but that really sounds great. Thanks."

Chris made her way back to her office. The message light on her desk phone blinked incessantly. Twelve messages. She tapped a key on her computer keyboard, and the monitor came to life. Two hundred and seven new emails. "Oh my head," Chris muttered.

A knock on her door and Lawrence Sanders stuck his head in. "Welcome back, Chief."

"Good morning. Anything earth shattering shake out while I was indisposed?"

"Wiley came up with a name to call this thing, whatever it is. The PAMNID incident."

"PAMNID?"

"Yeah, for Pennsylvania, Minnesota and Idaho. PA-MN-ID. PAMNID."

"Clever. Got anything a little more substantial?"

"We've been crunching the data from the SEI surveys. Tony and Kyle are trying to tease out some more specific times to get a better focus on our time lines."

"Getting anywhere?"

"The majority of the responses were vague, but there are two victim time lines from Idaho that are kind of interesting."

"How so?"

"It appears they expired right at the tail end of the time line. We were able to narrow down the time by their time cards. Also, they were the only ones in Idaho who actually made it to the hospital. It suggests perhaps they'd received a reduced exposure to whatever the vector is. At least that's one possibility."

"Anything else peculiar about them?"

"Just that they fit the profile of all the others—drug histories. And there's another oddity about the Idaho site. When we plotted out all the victims' locations—their residence versus where they were found—the locations of where the bodies were found formed a sort of semicircle. The Pennsylvania and Minnesota sites were more or less a full circle."

"Really? Got a map showing the plots?"

"Yeah. I just sent you a file."

Chris turned to her computer and scanned for the email from Lawrence. It was the most recent one. She opened it and clicked on the file. A map came up with red and green dots scattered across half the grid. Green showed the victims' residences and red where their bodies had been found. Each dot had a number. Most of the numbered dots were paired red and green at the same location while a few were scattered. Two green dots sat outside the semicircle.

Chris zoomed in so she saw the number inside the dot. Lawrence knelt beside her to see the screen as well. They both scanned the area in the semicircle to find the matching red dots. After a moment, Lawrence pointed to both of them. "There they are. Both of them together. Their green dots are outside the semicircle and the red ones inside."

"Is that telling us a story?" Chris asked.

Lawrence shrugged. “Maybe. It’s certainly worth a closer look. There are no red dots in this whole other region.”

“Is there a river there or something? That line looks pretty distinct.”

“It hard to tell from this map,” Lawrence said.

Chris accessed the internet and went to the US Geologic Survey website. With a few clicks and some input, she pulled up a topographical map of Idaho. It took a few minutes, but eventually, all the lines and features filled in. Chris zoomed in on the Bonners Ferry area trying to match the same area the victims’ map covered.

“That’s about right,” said Lawrence.

Chris and Lawrence both peered intently at the screen running their fingers down a ridgeline that ran roughly northwest to southeast. The higher elevations, up to sixty-five hundred feet, were on the western side. Chris flipped back to the other map to locate a couple of crossroads to use as reference points on the topo map. They readily saw that the ridge was the line of demarcation.

“That’s really odd,” Chris said. “There are just as many houses on both sides of the line. Nobody died on western side of the line.”

“The map is telling us something but what?”

“Is Sherrie back from Idaho?” Chris asked.

“Yes. She got back yesterday. I haven’t seen her yet this morning.”

Chris called Sherrie Cunningham to let her know they had uncovered something regarding the Idaho site. After hanging up, she said, “She’s on her way. Can you get one of the interns to work with the graphics folks to make a large-scale print of this map overlaid on the topo map? Get one for all three sites.”

“Sure. It’d be a good little project for one of them.”

“Stick around until Sherrie gets here. Let’s pick her brain together. Anything come up while I was out?”

“That FBI special agent, what’s his name, was here yesterday. Wanted to talk to you.”

“That’s probably one of those messages blinking on my phone. Did he say what he wanted?”

“Said he’d call today to talk to you.”

“I’ll give him a call after talking with Sherrie. Maybe he has something.”

Five minutes later, Sherrie poked her head in. “How’s your head? Wiley caught me on the way over and gave me the story.”

"My head's fine."

"So what's up?"

"Lawrence has pulled together some preliminary data into a picture that suggests an interesting story about the Idaho site. I wanted to get your thoughts on it." Chris turned her computer monitor a little so all three could crowd around the screen. "Lawrence, why don't you show her."

Sherrie listened and studied the maps on the screen. "I can see your point. The half-circle with red dots kinda looks like half a pepperoni pizza."

"Great. We'll call it the pizza theory," Chris quipped. "How was your working relationship with the local sheriff's office when you were there?"

"They were cooperative. Happy to have someone there," Sherrie answered.

"Do you think we can still get cooperation from them?"

"Sure. What do you need?"

"I'd like to develop a map of the affected area, the same scale as these two. I want to put a dot on the location of every known active drug user that the sheriff has information on, and not just the dead ones."

"What are you looking for?"

"I want to see if there are any known users in this area of the pizza that has no victims. If there are users living in that area, why aren't they dead like the rest?"

"That might be a tall order."

"Yes, I know. It would probably be best if you went back in person and worked with the sheriff's office directly. Show him a copy of these two maps. Get his input. One of the interns is working on getting a larger map. Take a couple with you."

"It's a she."

"What?"

"The sheriff's a woman."

"Even better. How soon can you leave?"

Sherrie looked at her watch. "Let me get back to you on that."

After Lawrence and Sherrie left, Chris turned to her next task. She pondered whether to divulge the patterns at the three locations to Abbott. She decided to take a show-me-yours-and-I'll-show-you-mine approach.

She called him. "Special Agent Abbott, sorry I wasn't here yesterday when you came by."

"Yeah. Dr. Patterson told me you'd had an accident."

"Slipped on some water in the kitchen. Bang. Unconscious. Concussion. Five stitches." *What's the penalty for lying to an FBI agent?*

"Ouch."

"I'm good to go now. Anything new on your end?"

"Actually, we do have some more information, but not sure you'd call it evidence."

"Anything would be appreciated. Let's meet and I can show you what we're working on. Can we do this tomorrow morning?"

"Nine o'clock work?"

"All right. Got it on my schedule. I'd like to have two of my three team members there. The third one will probably be on her way back to Idaho."

"I'd rather just have you. I'm kind of stretching protocol talking to you during an active investigation."

"Okay. I can live with that, and we can still keep Dr. Weinstein happy. See you tomorrow."

A couple of hours later, Sherrie poked her head in again. "Got a minute?"

Grateful for a break from the tedium of triaging emails, Chris spun around. "Sure."

"I'm set to go tomorrow morning. I had to wait a little while before I called Sherriff Ross. Time difference. I didn't want to sandbag her by just showing up. Anyway, I told her a little bit of what we found and what we were looking for. She told me something I thought you might be interested in."

"I'm interested in anything that will help explain this."

"When I described the half-pizza footprint of the victim locations, she said her department had a similar problem with their radio communication system. The ridgeline blocks out the transmissions to half her area. They have to use repeater towers scattered across the area to send their radio signal over the mountainous terrain."

"Of course! A radio shadow. No line of sight. Makes perfect sense. Just like the Apollo Effect."

CHAPTER 15

JUNE 6, 2007

The small, utilitarian lobby of the Tudos research building felt cold to Stuart McInnes. The cleaning crew was the only sign of life. The whirring of a floor buffer echoed off the hard-surfaced walls. He stepped over the power cord and made his way to Jakob Bauer's office.

McInnis knocked and entered without waiting for an invitation to enter. "Jakob, you working late or just come in extra early?"

Jakob looked up from his desk to see who this intruder was before answering. "Does it matter?" he smiled. "Good to see you, Stu. You just get in?"

"Yeah, a little while ago."

Jakob removed his glasses and rubbed his eyes. "Must be serious for them to send you up here to Boston to do the deed, or did you just draw the short straw?"

Stuart held up his hands. "Don't worry. It's not that. If they could have gotten rid of you that easily, they'd have done it months ago."

"How'd you know I'd be here?"

"Geez, Jakob, we've known each other for a long time. Where else would you be?"

"So to what do I owe the pleasure of your company?"

"Let's just say two old friends need to talk through a problem to their mutual benefit."

"All right. Let's talk. Can I pour you a drink? I think there's a bottle somewhere around here."

"No thanks. I had one at the hotel."

"Needed a bracer before coming to talk to me?"

McInnis looked about for a place to hang or lay his coat but found no available spot. He settled by laying it across the back of a chair intended for visitors. "I saw the cleaning crew outside. Maybe you ought to let them in here once in a while."

"Very funny. To me, there is order to all this. My daughter used to berate me about it all the time. Called me a hoarder."

The banter paused awkwardly for a moment before McInnis said, "I'm so sorry about Ilsa. I know it's been more than a year, but I still can't get over her being gone. I remember that when she was just a kid, she'd call me Uncle Stu. I guess I was at your house all the time when we were starting Tudos."

Jakob rubbed his forearm vigorously and sighed. "Thirteen months and those dope-dealing punks are just now going to trial."

"It's just stunning, Jakob. You institute a multimillion-dollar drug program to salvage lives hooked on drugs and your daughter gets killed in the crossfire of two street dealers fighting over territory. It's just not ... It's just not ..."

"That day ended three lives—Ilsa and my unborn granddaughters. She was pregnant with twin girls you know. It robbed me of ever having grandchildren." Jakob reached out and patted his friend on the shoulder.

McInnis slumped into the visitor's chair. "I think I will have that drink."

Jakob sat behind his desk and rummaged through a bottom drawer until he came up with a bottle of cognac. He crossed the room to a coffee maker and found two relatively clean mugs. Jakob poured a generous portion into each. "To better days."

Each man swallowed a healthy slug and said nothing for a long moment. Stuart savored the burning passage of the amber liquid down his throat, the slight burning in his ears, the fire as it hit the stomach. It was a vice both men had sworn off many years before upon doctors' orders. But Jakob knew the cognac was medicine for their souls.

Jakob broke the solemnity. "Let's get to it, Stu. This is not a social call. You're here on a mission."

Stu took a deep breath. "Jakob, the board wants your resignation. That's why they sent me up here. They thought I'd have the best chance of talking you into it."

"I hear the lawsuit against us is not going so well for the plaintiffs."

"That cockamamie campaign that lawyer Holloway cooked up seems to be taking hold. A number of those socially aware funds are buying our stock. The initial losses are all but recovered. That takes some of the steam out of their argument that the drug program hurt the bottom line."

"And it makes it harder for the board to can me."

"Yes it does," McInnis concurred.

"I don't watch much news, but I also hear Randall approved of using my daughter's death to draw sympathy from the public. Is that true?"

McInnis took another slug and nodded.

"Randall. Knows the price of everything and the value of nothing."

"Well that may be, but he has Ilsa's shares now, and without them, you no longer have a majority bloc."

"But the board doesn't want the spectacle of a knife fight in the front office, so they'd like me to retire and fade away," Jakob stated as if building a case.

"True. Nobody wins with that."

"Stu, do you know what I like to do in my spare time, my hobby?"

Stu thought a moment. "Actually, I don't think I do."

"I don't either. A life of leisure has no appeal to me. My entire life has been a series of problem-solving tasks. From the moment I stood in front of Josef Mengele and impressed him with what little I knew about classical music until now, I have solved problems. I do it as naturally as I breathe."

"That I do know about you, Jakob. Every corner we were ever backed into, you were able to puzzle us out of it."

"So you see, just walking off into the sunset to play golf or fishing or whatever else retired people do just wouldn't do me any good. I may have been able to do it if I had grandchildren to lavish my time and attention upon, but I don't have even that now."

McInnis cast his gaze to the floor sensing he had failed in his mission.

"Stu, I have a counteroffer for you. One that I think avoids the appearance of boardroom mayhem."

McInnis brightened up a bit but was a little confused. "A counteroffer?"

"Yes. I think it will make everyone reasonably happy, even the plaintiffs in the lawsuit. After all, it's me they're so hot to punish. My proposal will take me out of the boardroom."

"Now you're losing me. How do you remain engaged then?"

"Hear me out. First, the company buys out half my holdings in Tudos. That still leaves me with a twenty percent share, not enough to control anything but enough to still have some sway. Second, I step down as CEO *but* be made the head of Research and Development, Third, I be allowed—"

"Jakob, why would you want to do that?"

"R and D has been floundering for a couple of years now. Nothing new, at least nothing groundbreaking, is in the pipeline. The targeting drug project is stuck on zero. I think I can dislodge it. I have an idea for curing cervical cancer using a targeting system that's not even a drug. There are a couple of other new technologies I want to place Tudos in the forefront of. Just like the old days."

"Jakob, I don't know if they'll go for letting you run R and D."

"They better or I'll go to one of our competitors. Tudos will end up looking like a bunch of pikers."

McInnis began to say something but only opened and closed his mouth like a goldfish before motioning Jakob to continue.

"Third. I want to start a new company outside Tudos. Actually, I want to buy an existing company that's struggling."

"Jakob, you realize you're in your sixties now, right? I mean, the amount of work for what you're proposing would kill a thirty-year-old. Maybe the labs, but turning around a company on the ropes ... Don't you remember all the work we had to do to get Tudos solvent when we took it over? What's this other company do?"

"They make electronic instrumentation."

"So do a thousand other companies."

"I have an idea."

"Yeah, and me too."

"Stu, I want to get back to what I love most and do best, and that's innovate. I hated the business end of this industry. I just want to spend what time I have left working toward something that will really benefit people."

"Okay, Jakob, I'll take it back to the board. They really want to avoid bloodshed, so they might go for it."

"You know, Stu, I could really use someone with experience in reviving a company."

"I don't think Tudos would be happy with you headhunting before the ink's dry."

"Just something for you to think about."

"No, I'm about done. I *do* know what I like to do in my spare time."

"I understand. Actually, I envy you in that respect. But this is something I have to do."

Jakob raised his cup to toast again and drained the last measure.

CHAPTER 16

MARCH 28, 2019

Chris turned the office lights on. Not even Wiley was in yet. Lawrence's intern had come through with the three maps by the end of the day. Chris wanted to remember to say something to her. By the time Wiley poked her head in Chris's door, she'd had nearly half an hour of uninterrupted time to pore over the maps.

"Morning, Chief. Aren't you the eager beaver?"

"Got these late yesterday. Didn't have time to study them in detail then. I have a meeting with that FBI guy this morning. I'm hoping I can squeeze something out of them."

"Well good luck," Wiley said. "Looks like you're off to a good start."

The dots on the Pennsylvania and Minnesota maps made a sort of loose cluster circular in appearance like a whole pepperoni pizza. Chris took a ruler and measured the north-south and east-west diameters. The diameters ranged from forty-five to fifty-five miles. Taking a straightedge, she crisscrossed the map and made a small *X* where the two lines intersected. Using the *X* as the pivot, she drew a rough circle with a twenty-five mile radius.

Wow, Chris thought. All the red dots, the places where the bodies had been found, were within the circle. She went to her computer and pulled up the satellite images again. Zooming in on the center *X*s of both sites confirmed her suspicions. At the Pennsylvania site was a small coal-mining operation. At the Minnesota site, it was none other than the heart of GenStar's operations.

Chris felt her pulse quicken. She pulled the Idaho site map, the half-pizza one, over to the work table. She hastily drew a semicircle also with a twenty-five-mile radius. Just as with the other two, all the red dots fell within the boundary. Again, she located the *X*. A sawmill operation was nearby it.

Chris checked her watch and saw she had another forty minutes before her meeting. She desperately wanted a cup of coffee. After getting one from the lunchroom, she stopped by Wiley's desk and asked if anyone was scheduled to be using the small conference room. She gathered all the maps and her notes and laid them out on the conference table there. Sipping her coffee, she stared at the maps trying to make sense of it all. *How much is coincidence? What do the three manufacturing companies have in common? Were there any other deaths similar to the two outliers in Idaho?*

After locating two green dots in Pennsylvania and three in Minnesota that were outside the rough circle, Chris made notes of the numbers. She'd check them out after her meeting. Better yet, she called Lawrence from the conference room phone, gave him the victim numbers, and asked him to pull up the details.

Right at nine, Wiley called the conference room. "Special Agent Abbott is here to see you."

"Can you bring him back? Thanks."

A moment later, Abbott knocked on the door.

"Special Agent Abbott, good to see you again," Chris said.

"Dr. Malone. You seem to be recovering well."

The two shook hands.

"I found something interesting this morning I wanted to bounce off you and get your take on," Chris said.

"Sure."

Chris laid all three maps out side by side and explained what they were and what the dots meant. Careful to show Abbott the circular pattern at the Pennsylvania and Minnesota sites first, she then showed him the half-pizza site in Idaho. She explained the significance of the first two green dots outside Idaho's semicircular site. She then showed him the other similar green dots at the other two sites. Wanting to see if Abbott would pick up on the ridgeline boundary, Chris said nothing of what the sheriff had said about the radio problems in that area.

Abbott studied the maps as he tried to follow along. "So what are you saying regarding the two victims in Idaho?"

"The victims were either already in the perimeter or had crossed into it during the twelve-hour window. From their timesheets, we know they must have crossed into this semicircle sometime at the end of the attack."

"Attack?"

"Incident, whatever it was. It was as if they'd stepped into an area under some sort of umbrella."

"You're thinking there's some sort of external component to these deaths, not just the drugs?"

"Not necessarily. I'm just saying those two deaths are anomalies. There are five others similar to them at the other two sites. We're trying to run down more information."

She showed Abbott what was at each of the *X* locations. She watched his face as he leaned over to take a closer look but saw only skepticism.

"I'm not seeing it," Abbott declared momentarily. "Mines and sawmills aren't very high-tech operations."

"It's only a working hypothesis at this point," Chris replied, disappointed in Abbott's response. "What have you got?"

"I'm afraid what we have is pretty thin. We sent agents to all three pharmaceuticals that market the targeting drug. Nothing out of line in any of them except the truck hijacking I mentioned in our first meeting. The shipping clerk in question has a record including felonies. However, everything we could find on the guy points to him getting his life straight. He jimmied the records after the hijacking because he was afraid it would come back on him. Stupid. Just made it worse."

"You said earlier that the truck was bound for a waste facility. Where?"

"In Mexico. That's where it was hijacked as well."

"Did you talk to the police in Mexico?"

"We had some folks from the DEA make inquiries. It's kind of a sensitive area. Relations are bad enough already."

"Why hijack a truck of useless waste?"

"The truck and the trailer haven't surfaced. It could very well be that they were the target."

Chris shook her head. "That makes no sense either. Why steal a truck full of useless crap you'd just have to get rid of instead of waiting for the truck to unload and then steal it?"

"You're assuming they knew what the contents were. Quite likely, it was just a target of opportunity."

Undaunted, Chris asked, "Why'd Tudos hire an ex-con? I mean, I'm in favor of rehabilitating people, but turning one loose in a place that makes drugs is a little too progressive, don'tcha think?"

"Yeah, we had the same thought. We spoke to their HR department about that. Turns out Jakob Bauer submitted his name and vouched for him."

"How'd that happen? Bauer's the founder of Tudos. Wouldn't think they'd travel in the same circles."

"We asked Bauer the same question. Turns out the shipping clerk, Ron Kaiser, is the son of a longtime Tudos employee. Bauer became aware of the kid about the same time the trial for his daughter's killers was going on."

"You talked directly to Bauer?"

"Yeah. After we talked to HR, Bauer called us."

"What was the contaminant?" Chris asked.

"What do you mean?"

"At the first meeting, you told us that several batches of the targeting drug had been contaminated and sent for disposal. Did you ever find out what caused the contamination? I'm sure it must have cost them a boatload to lose several batches. Surely they put a great deal of effort into finding out what caused the problem."

"No, we didn't ask. Does it matter?"

Chris felt her jaw tighten, but she held her tongue for a moment before answering in the best civil tone she could muster. "In a case like this with more questions than facts or answers, it could be."

"We could always ask some follow-up questions if you'd like."

Chris started to reply, stopped herself, and then said dismissively, "Never mind. Probably just another rabbit to chase. Is there any chance you could have your field offices go to the industrial sites and inquire if they have equipment that broadcast radio or Wi-Fi signals?"

"I'll just have someone check with the FCC to see if they have a license on file for a system that can broadcast that far."

Still masking her frustration with the agent, Chris sought to end their meeting as quickly as possible. "No, those are the most promising leads we have so far."

"Like I said, I can kind of see the pattern, but the umbrella thing seems too farfetched."

"Perhaps you're right. Well, if you'll excuse me, I must get ready for my next meeting." *That's my second lie to the FBI in less than a week.*

"Of course. I'll find my way out."

Back in her office, Chris sat at her desk sipping a second cup of coffee while staring into space. The coffee had grown cold by the time she picked up her phone and dialed an internal number. "Wiley, can you please get me the contact information for Jakob Bauer please? If you have to, get that intern who did the maps to help you. It may take some digging. Oh, and see if you can find a flight to Boston today, the earlier the better."

Grateful for an aisle seat and a direct flight on such short notice, Chris sat with her laptop open on the pull-down tray. The intern had come through again with the right stuff. Knowing she wouldn't have a lot of time to research the popular media material on Bauer, Chris had had the intern download as much background information on him as she could find. The kid had come through; every article had good information. She had done more than just cut and paste the information; she had read and filtered it before sending it. Chris made a mental note to herself to see what programs and scholarships were available that would bring this kid into the CDC fold.

The man had an impressive story. He was a triplet with two identical sisters. Particularly impressive was the fact he had survived Auschwitz and Mengele though his sisters had not. His mother was a non-Jewish German married to a Jew. Bauer's parents had fled Germany to Hungary shortly after the Nuremburg Laws were passed. The laws were designed to marginalize Jews in German society. Among many other things unthinkable today, mixed marriages were forbidden. No one from even his extended family had survived the camps.

Orphaned after the war. Adopted to the United States by a childless Jewish couple from the Bronx. PhD in pharmaceutical sciences. She teased out of several other articles that he had married sometime shortly before he bought into the company that became Tudos. Had had one child late in life, a girl.

The last article she read was from the *Boston Globe* that detailed how Bauer's daughter had been the innocent victim of a shootout between two drug-dealing street gangs in a nondescript New York City neighborhood. Bauer's daughter happened to be at a traffic light in a taxi when a car going the other direction stopped and shot over the top of her cab at a cluster of people on the corner. Some of the people on the corner returned fire, and Ilsa Bauer-Monsinger was struck in the upper chest. The cab driver acted heroically and tried to take her straight from the scene to a hospital, but she bled out in the back seat of the cab before reaching the emergency room.

The plane descended into Logan. She had to put away her laptop.

Chris caught a cab and gave the cabbie the address of the Tudos laboratories. When she searched the location on her computer, Chris was surprised they were not out along the Route 128 corridor. That stretch of highway was renowned for the many biotech and drug companies that lined it. The Tudos labs were in the same neighborhood as the campuses of Harvard and MIT, where they had been from the beginning.

Chris landed squarely in the middle of a Boston traffic jam. Drizzly rain made the road slippery. It would be a while before she would arrive, so she settled in for a long cab ride with her laptop hoping the battery would last the trip. The slapping windshield wipers provided a rhythm that suited her somber mood.

The dreary, wet scenery held no interest for Chris. Instead, she read the articles Sam had sent her regarding Tudos. As she had already heard, Jakob Bauer had been the messiah of the company. Article after article heralded therapeutic breakthroughs one after another.

> Chris opened a second email from Sam that read in part,
>
> Talked to a friend who knows a guy who knows a guy who says there's a rumor floating around that Bauer is sick. Possibly cancer? I don't have any verification on that but something to keep in mind.
>
> A third email from Sam read simply,
>
> I'm meeting this afternoon with our attorney, Erika's doctor, and the police at the hospital. Talk to you when you get back tonight. No matter what happens, no matter how bad all this gets, I still love you.

Chris turned her computer off and stared out the window for the remainder of the cab ride.

The cab arrived at the address having taken an hour to go just seven miles. Chris was underwhelmed by the building. It was of a modern design favored in the sixties that contrasted jarringly with the surrounding Boston neighborhood. The presence of the building must have been used by incensed Bostonians to justify future zoning laws and preservation commissions. It wasn't even an attractive example of sixties architecture. It did, however, look utilitarian, almost factorylike.

It took some time and effort, but she was eventually escorted to Bauer's office. Chris noted that the interior's utilitarian look matched that of the exterior. The man's office looked like a hundred other offices at the back of laboratories she had seen around the country.

He had no receptionist. Bauer greeted her directly after dismissing the security escort. "Dr. Malone. I'm Jakob Bauer. It's a pleasure to meet you."

Chris shook Bauer's extended hand. "Dr. Bauer, I've heard so much about you. It really is a pleasure to meet you. My husband will be so jealous. He's a great admirer of all you've accomplished. And please call me Chris."

"Certainly if you will call me Jakob." He smiled pleasantly.

Chris noticed the man's crisp, clean features. Even in his seventies, his hair was as full as that of a man half his age though it was no longer golden. He was no taller than she was, but he seemed much taller. Perhaps it was his slim frame or his posture that created that illusion. But the most stunning feature, what really grabbed Chris's attention, was his eyes. They were as young and as lively as a sixteen-year-old's. There was no hint of their seven decades. And they were bluer than any she had ever seen, as blue as a tropical lagoon.

"Please come in. May I fix you a cup of coffee? Tea perhaps?"

"No thank you." Chris shed her raincoat and found the one visitor's seat.

Jakob took her coat and laid it across a stack of journals. He crossed behind his desk and sat as well. "The FBI was here a few days ago asking questions regarding a missing shipment or something to that effect. I'm not sure what else I can add."

"As I said when I called to arrange this meeting, and thank you so much for meeting with me on such short notice, I am with the CDC, and we have some more ... perhaps technical questions is the best way to phrase it."

"What sort of technical questions?"

"Your company is one of only three companies with well-developed targeting drugs. I was wondering if you could walk me through the nuts and bolts of how they work."

Jakob paused a moment before replying. "I can provide an overall perspective of how they work. Some of the specifics are closely guarded trade secrets. Proprietary stuff. I'm not sure, however, how any of that relates to the missing shipment."

"According to the manifest, the shipment was apparently a large quantity of contaminated targeting drug material."

"I fail to see why the CDC would have an interest in such a thing," Bauer said.

"I'm not at liberty to reveal too much either, but we have a working theory that the material may be a part of one of our investigations."

"A working theory you say."

Chris cleared her throat. "Yes. I'm here to get a better understanding of the product to better develop the theory or throw it out altogether. With your cooperation of course."

Another pause hung over the room before Jakob answered, his blue eyes boring into hers. "I will help as much as I can. How about we walk around the lab and I can show you some of what else we are working on as I answer your questions. I find that I think more clearly when I walk about."

"I'd like that very much," Chris replied.

"Do you know what our first attempts to create a targeting system were, Chris?"

Chris shook her head. "No."

"We looked for natural homing devices already existing to deliver chemotherapy drugs to the cervix. It wasn't a drug at all. Can you guess what we hit upon?"

Again, Chris shook her head.

"Sperm. All those little swimmers. All hell-bent on one destination. But we've still not found a way to get the chemotherapy drug to effectively adhere to the sperm cell."

"Wow. That's very"—Chris groped for the right descriptor—"out-of-the-box thinking."

"Yes it is. That's where real progress resides," Jakob agreed, smiling.

He led her down a hallway to a small anteroom with white coats lining the wall. He took one with the word Visitor stitched on it and handed it to her. He gave her a hairnet, a pair of overshoe booties, and a pair of safety glasses from the shelf. Once they were fully garbed in the safety attire, Jakob led her into the lab.

"This used to be our production facility when we first began, but we outgrew it. It is now our research laboratory."

Chris was genuinely impressed by the size of the room. "You do all your research here? Where are your production facilities?"

"Yes, and we do bench-scale production here. A full range of production scales are done at our other facilities scattered across the country."

"Where are the targeting drugs produced?"

"Here in Boston. Waltham actually. Not far from here."

"Can you explain how they work? Without giving away any proprietary information of course."

Jakob led her over to one of the many whiteboards and drew the classic shape of an ordinary house key with jagged teeth. "Imagine the targeting drug as a key with this particular pattern for the teeth." Then taking a different colored marker, he drew a sort of blob with a jagged edge along one side that fit perfectly to the jagged pattern of the key. "This blob is a specific type of organ tissue. Now we have the targeting drug molecule bonding to the particular tissue cell just like a specific key fits a specific lock. Now imagine this key has another shank with another tooth pattern." Jakob extended the key on the opposite side of the first shank and gave it a jagged tooth pattern. He then drew a second blob of a slightly different shape that fit perfectly to the second key pattern. "Now this second blob is the therapeutic you want to attach to that specific cell. The targeting drug is really not a drug. It has no therapeutic value in and of itself. It's more of a targeting transport than a drug."

"So if you are administering a highly toxic chemotherapy, let's say, with the targeting drug, it goes only to the cells with cancer or whatever," Chris said.

"Precisely. And as we find the keys to more and more specific cell structures, the more types of cancers we'll be able to treat."

"How many types can you treat now?"

"Not nearly enough. Perhaps twenty."

"Seems like quite a few. Did you start with the most common forms of cancer and work your way down to the rarer forms?"

"That would seem to be the logical approach. The story of how we got the twenty or so we have now is a little more complex. Some cells gave up their secrets much more readily than do others. Some forms of cancer are less deadly than others or currently have better treatment options than others do. In large measure, our approach was guided by an effort to save as many lives as possible as soon as possible. So we first went after the cancers with the less-effective ranges of treatment options and higher mortality rates. Triage of a different sort."

"I'd think that would open you up to all kinds of criticism. We get criticized every year trying to predict the strain of flu we need to fight with the annual flu vaccine. We don't always get it right."

"Eventually we'll get them all. I believe that. Firmly."

"Have you developed targeting transports for different brain tissues?" Chris asked and watched carefully for Jakob's reaction.

Without pausing, Jakob answered, "As a matter of fact we have, but not all. As it turns out, several of the neurological structures were among the tissue types most readily identified and mimicked."

"Really? I would have suspected they would have been among the more difficult to crack."

"It's been a fortuitous development for people with the more common forms of inoperable brain trauma and tumors. We can now deliver very powerful doses of therapeutics to very small, specific areas. One of my staff described it as the difference between carpet bombing and using smart bombs."

"What parts of the brain can you target?"

"Oh, the basil ganglia, temporal lobe, the—"

"Any of the brain stem parts? The VTA?"

"Actually, that work is our most promising. You're aware of Tudos's cooperation with the Department of Health and Human Services program for addicts? The basis of our portion of that program is a drug we developed called Dopanoncessemin. Another big benefit here is the ability to administer prescription opioids for pain management with a miniscule amount of the actual narcotic. Cut down on the side effects like constipation. And patients are less likely to develop addictions."

"I've always been intrigued by how drugs get their names," Chris quipped, attempting to keep the conversation in a friendly vein.

"A blend of Latin and biology. *Non sesse.* To cease. Dopamine. The reward circuitry of the brain. *Dopamine non sesse.* To cease dopamine. Dopanoncessemin."

"Clever."

"Anyway, by coupling a variant of the Dopanoncessemin drug and a targeting transporter, we will be able to increase the efficacy of the program."

"Are you able to couple the transporters with the nanobots you're developing?"

"Why Dr. Malone, I do believe you must be reading my mail. You've done your research. The nanotech research is the next frontier for medicine. I'm sure you're aware of my departure from the executive structure of Tudos. No need to be coy about it. They were going to can me."

"Yes, I had my husband do some research on Tudos. He's a finance guy. He told me all about the war at the front office."

"In retrospect, I'm glad it happened. More important, I'm glad I was able to get back into the lab. It's where I am most content. I'm an old man. Whatever time I have left, I want to leave one more transformative gift to humanity."

"You've already done so much. I'm surprised the Nobel Prize committee hasn't called on you."

"I don't think that will be in the cards. What I'm trying to achieve probably doesn't rise to that level."

"I wouldn't be so sure, Dr. Bauer."

"Would you like to take a look at some of our nanotech research?"

"Absolutely."

Jakob lead her to another section of the facility. "We have to suit up in bunny suits for this part of the tour. You also have to wear special conductive shoes. It's part of the measures necessary to mitigate static discharge. Most things in this area can't handle static electricity very well."

After donning the suits, Jakob and Chris stepped out of the airlock into a type of laboratory Chris had never experienced before. The floor looked quite different.

Seeing Chris's reaction, Jakob explained, "The whole floor is conductive. That's why you have to wear the special conductive shoes. Any static buildup is grounded to the floor."

Jakob led Chris to the workroom. In the middle of the room was a device with two independently rotating arms shaped like the letter *C*. Both arms had a bulbous head at one end, and a small cone protruded from each head toward the interior of the *C*'s radius. The plate at the base of the device read Bauer Electronics.

"What do you know about the function of radios, Dr. Malone?"

"Next to nothing I suppose. Why?"

"Did you ever hear stories about prisoners and GIs in World War II making radios out of rusty razor blades and such?"

"Razor blades? No, can't say I've ever heard of that."

"Well, it's true. The rust, ferrous oxide, formed the crystal structure needed in primitive radios. And those same principles are used to power the nanobots we make. The little bots are nanoscale radios of sorts. Specific frequencies excite the molecules causing motion. The radio frequencies from outside the bot are what make the whole technology possible. If the bot had to have a battery of some sort, it would simply be too large. And even if a battery small enough could be developed eventually, it would lose power."

Chris listened intently trying to absorb and digest what Bauer was telling her. In her mind's eye, she pictured little spherical shapes vibrating about crazily. She couldn't quite grasp how that would be of any benefit. "So what does all that motion achieve?"

"Imagine all that motion occurring in the proximity of carcinomatous cells. It'd be like they were standing next to a whirling dervish with knives. Targeted destruction."

Jakob powered up the device. He manipulated a series of knobs and two joysticks, and the two heads orbited about a central point.

"This is the heart of what makes the nanobots work," Jakob stated. "Notice that the two heads can rotate around a central axis. Each head produces a separate, very specific radio frequency and projects it in a narrow beam. The two heads are aimed along separate lines that intersect. That point of intersection is as small as a pinhead."

Chris imagined nasty-looking cells being shredded by spinning vortexes.

"Are you familiar with harmonics, Chris?"

"Two frequencies combine to create a third frequency with a higher or lower amplitude."

"Precisely! And that is the purpose of the two heads. Two frequencies intersect at a tiny, targeted area in the body creating a third frequency only at that spot. And—"

"The third frequency is what turns the nanobots into the whirling dervishes," Chris offered.

"Very good."

"Why not just use the targeting transport and expose the patient to the third frequency en masse?"

"Such a quick study! But we can't do that for a couple of reasons. If a large area were suddenly exposed to the destructive work of the nanobots, it's probable the destroyed tissue could not be expunged from the body quickly enough. The buildup of necrotic tissue would lead to infections and so forth. Working small areas allows the body's natural systems to do the removal work. Second, we swim in a sea of radio frequencies. By using a binary system, we can control what the patient is exposed to."

"Is there potential for using it on nontissue targets?" Chris asked.

"Nontissue targets? Such as?" Jakob asked clearly intrigued.

"My husband's had several bouts with kidney stones. Could your little nanobots—"

"Destroy just the stones?" Jakob injected excitedly. "That's brilliant! How could we have missed that potential? Kidney stones. Bladder stones. Gallstones. Noninvasive treatment. Much better than lithotripsy."

Jakob pulled out a notepad from his coat pocket and scribbled away. "I'm sure I'll remember your suggestion, but at my age, I wouldn't want to chance losing such a great idea."

Chris said nothing as he wrote out his notes.

"Dr. Malone, if you ever get tired of the CDC, come see me!"

"Well thank you, but I think I just gave you the only thing I would ever be able to contribute. I'm an epidemiologist. The chemistry of pharmaceuticals is well beyond me."

"Oh don't sell yourself short, Dr. Malone. I already have chemists and pharmacologists. I need someone who fully comprehends the maladies that plague humanity, someone who has seen them at the front lines. Someone who can help us point our guns at the real enemy."

"You're really serious," Chris said, taken aback. "I'm flattered, but I'm quite content engaging in that battle from where I am."

"I understand. Perhaps as a consultant sometime in the future."

Chris, seeking a graceful way to steer the conversation back to the issue at hand, asked, "What's the base material for your radio receivers? The little nanobots?"

"Well, just like the old razor blade radios, we use ferrous oxide, rust. Gallium oxide for some. Zinc peroxide is one of the best."

"Ever use lead?"

"Oh yes. We used lead peroxide for our proof-of-concept experiments. Tried to get approval to use it on a larger scale, but the FDA couldn't get past the thought of lead poisoning. We tried to explain to them that the amounts we were talking about were well below the *de minimis* levels. It's actually a better material for our purposes. That wasn't the main reason we dropped it though. Turns out the military and Homeland Security are developing a new interagency communication system that will use one of the two frequencies that make lead peroxide jump. It will be pervasive over most of North America. It's called the Dominion Project."

Chris felt her face flush at the mention of lead peroxide. She jerked her head toward another direction and faked a sneeze hoping Jakob didn't notice her reaction. She turned back to Jakob.

"Gesundheit! Good that you're all suited up with a mask. Couldn't be the dust. There isn't any in here."

Chris met Jakob's eyes. *Does he know what I'm fishing for?*

The meeting with Bauer lasted a short time longer before Bauer was pulled into a meeting with several researchers. Chris left for Atlanta on an early evening flight. Before boarding, she checked her emails. One marked Urgent was from Patterson.

Be in my office first thing tomorrow morning. Under no circumstances are you to have further contact with Jakob Bauer or other officials from Tudos. Leave that up to the FBI.

Somebody sure made some fast phone calls. Must have struck a nerve, she thought.

CHAPTER 17

THE SAME DAY—MARCH 28, 2019

As trigger jobs go, Gerald LaRouche thought this one looked fairly simple. He had done enough jobs though, and he knew how to avoid falling into the trap of complacency. He would be thorough as always. That's why he was in such demand and in turn could demand a better-than-average fee.

He sat with another man in a plain white utility van less than half a block away from the DeKalb County General Hospital. It was a tree-lined street curving along the perimeter of the hospital grounds. This section of the hospital grounds had been cut into a slight hillside giving the road about a fifteen-foot elevation above the grounds. A residential neighborhood of redbrick homes, azaleas, dogwoods, and towering pines occupied the high ground above the street. From less than a half a block away, LaRouche could look down upon the psychiatric unit's fenced-in outdoor recreation area through the van's rear windows.

"Just like clockwork, they let the loonies out every day at one fifteen right after lunch," LaRouche said. He continued watching the activity below through the zoom lens. "The staff pretty much stays by the door and lets the patients wander around. Our little lady goes and sits on the picnic table the farthest away from the staff."

The other man said nothing but made note of the time and activity.

"Looks like today our little lady has company. Maybe her dad. Maybe a lawyer and a doctor. Those last two are definitely cops." LaRouche took several photos zooming in as closely as possible on each face. The two he suspected of being police had their backs to him, so he got only profiles of them.

"You sure? How can you tell?"

"It looks like they're the ones asking all the questions and the others are discussing among themselves before they answer."

"She's going to tell them where she got her stuff. The man in Juarez is not going to like that."

"Looks like we'll be coming back tomorrow," said LaRouche.

"Is the weather supposed to hold? If it's cold or rainy, they'll stay inside."

"The weather is supposed to be about the same for the next couple of days—upper sixties, lower seventies."

"Good," the other man said.

"This looks to be as good a place as any to do it. Get here early before all the other cars show up. Park the van there, a little less than a car length in front of that hydrant. Less likely someone will pull up too close behind you. That'll give you a full view of the yard. Have all the equipment in the van before we park and leave it. Come back to it an hour or so before they let the wackos out in the yard."

LaRouche watched the meeting with his target. After about twenty minutes, the two cops got up and left. The others talked among themselves. The girl didn't seem engaged. All but one of the others left shortly. *Has to be the dad.* He saw him give the girl an awkward hug, say something, and leave.

The two men searched the recreation yard and the side of the hospital for security cameras. They spotted three, but none was pointed out toward the street.

"What do you think—twenty-two mag? It's less than a hundred yards. Probably not more than seventy-five," LaRouche asked.

The other man thought for a moment. Made his own estimate on the distance. "You think a twenty-two mag has enough energy to make a clean head shot?"

"A magnum will. It's not that far. It only needs to penetrate one side. I'm thinking about the noise. A twenty-two's much less noisy. Let those staff guys get to talking to each other and they might not realize anything's happened until they're ready to go back in."

"Shoot from inside the van. Get a couple rolls of insulation to absorb the sound. Nobody will take notice of the shot noise. Besides, a twenty-two won't exit. It'll just rattle around inside the skull. Doesn't even have to kill her. Just scramble her brains," the other man said, agreeing with the logic.

"Drive away nice and easy when all the commotion starts."

"Let's check for other security cameras on our way out of here."

"Sounds like a plan. Let's get out of here," LaRouche said.

MARCH 29, 2019

Erika heard her keepers, as she called them, coming down the corridor rousting the other patients out of their postlunchtime lethargy.

"Okay everyone, let's get ready to go outside and enjoy the sun. It's a little breezier today, so zip up your jackets."

The patients all fell into line complying fully with the directives to the best of their abilities. All save Erika.

"Come on, Erika. The fresh air will do you good. Sunshine on that pretty face will cheer you up."

Erika rolled her eyes and snapped the sweatshirt hoodie over her head obscuring her face. She was loath to show it, but going outside really was the highlight of her day. Mealtimes were miserable and made worse by the company. Visits with the doctors were just inquisitions. All the rest of the day was just an endless plain of boredom. She hoped her dad would show up.

Outside, she headed for the picnic table farthest from the door. On her first trip outside, she had considered dragging the table closer to the fence and using it to scale the fence. She discovered someone had thought of that and had anchored it firmly to the ground. She had seen the staff watching her and laughing.

On that day, Erika simply sat down facing outward toward the freedom she imagined on the other side of the fence. She looked at the line of cars parked along the street above and saw the rear door of a white van crack open slightly, but she didn't see anyone. *That's odd,* she thought. A robin landing on the top strand of the barbwire in front of her drew her attention. Her head snapped back. All went black.

Sam stared at the long line of red taillights ahead of him. He hadn't moved an inch closer to the hospital in five minutes. He resigned himself to having missed Erika's free time outside. Though she'd never admit it, he could tell she enjoyed the time with him. It was the only time he ever caught a glimpse of the old Erika—his little girl.

He pulled his cellphone out to see if he could find some traffic information. Before he could start his search, it rang. Caller ID showed DeKalb General Hospital.

"Hello?"

"Mr. Malone, this is Emma Rogers from DeKalb County General. We need you to come to the hospital as soon as possible."

"I've been trying to get there for the last forty-five minutes! I'm stuck ten blocks away. What's going on?"

"There's been an incident involving Erika."

"What happened? She all right? What's wrong? What kind of incident?"

"We'll explain in detail as soon as you get here, but your daughter's been shot."

"Shot? Oh my God!"

"Mr. Malone, you need to compose yourself. She's being prepped for surgery. Do we have your permission to perform the necessary procedures to save your daughter?"

"What? Of course. Do what you have to do. Save my daughter!"

"Can you park your car and walk the rest of the way here? The campus is locked down. Traffic is not going to clear anytime soon."

"Yes."

"Good. I'll meet you at the main gate entrance. Call me back on this number when you get close. I'll be wearing an orange vest that reads Incident Response Team. I'll get you through the police line."

Sam pulled the car to the curb. Before starting his trek to the hospital, he called Chris. When she didn't answer, he left a voice mail and a text message telling her to go to the hospital immediately. He said nothing about Erika having been shot.

The police were breaking down their equipment just as Sam reached the front gate. Ms. Rogers found him right away and led him to a counseling office on the surgery floor. She asked if his wife was coming. Sam explained he had not been able to get hold of her but had left messages.

As if on cue, Sam's phone rang. It was Chris.

"What is going on, Sam? Has Erika attacked someone else?"

"Chris, there's been a shooting. Erika's been shot. I just got here."

Sam pulled the phone from his ear because of Chris's scream. "Chris! Chris! Shut up for a minute! I just got here. I haven't talked to anyone yet. All I know is she's in surgery. Get here as fast as you can."

Sam sat alone in the small counseling office trying to convince himself Erika was going to be all right. Nearly an hour later, a security guard escorted Chris in. Sam rose to embrace her.

"It's not good, Chris. She was shot in the head. She's been in surgery for two hours."

Emma Rogers came in a minute later. She extended her hand to Chris. "I'm Emma Rogers. I'm here to assist you in any way I can."

Chris turned on her. "How could this have happened?"

"The police could find no evidence that the shooter was on campus. The shot must have come from off campus. Erika was outside in the psych unit's outdoor recreation area. No one heard the shot."

Rogers was describing the extent of the gunshot injury to Erika's head when there was a knock on the door. Allen and Joyner, the two detectives, stepped in. Sam had to restrain Chris from attacking them. He couldn't restrain her from screaming at them though.

"Get out! Can't you leave us alone?"

"We're here to let you know what happened."

"I already know what happened. You two clowns left our daughter hanging out to dry. Were you using her as bait?"

"We had no idea they would come after your daughter," Allen confessed.

"This is on your heads! Now get out!"

The two detectives retreated hastily and left. Sam got Chris to settle a bit as they waited suspended between heaven and hell. Barely a word was spoken. Time ceased.

Sometime after six o'clock, a young doctor came in and introduced himself. "I'm Dr. Twiggs. I did the surgery on your daughter. She's going to survive. However, there was quite a bit of damage to the brain. How that will manifest itself remains to be seen. We won't know until the swelling subsides and we can bring her back to consciousness. That will most likely take several days."

"She's in a coma?" Chris asked in a shaking voice.

"Of a sort, yes. We induced it. Her body needs time to heal itself. And we're reducing her core temperature to ninety-two degrees to minimize swelling."

"We'd like to see her," Sam said.

"Sure, I understand, but I must caution you, her appearance right now may be shocking. She's attached to a lot of monitors and equipment that look pretty scary. Just prepare yourself for that."

"Yes, we understand."

"Very well. I'll take you over."

Sam and Chris followed the doctor. Sam felt as if he were walking on lead legs. He wanted to be by Erika's side but was terrified of what he'd see.

Twiggs opened the door. The light from the array of instruments illuminated the room in subdued blues and greens. His daughter was unrecognizable. Beside him, Chris broke down crying. Only his quick grasp saved her from crumbling to the floor.

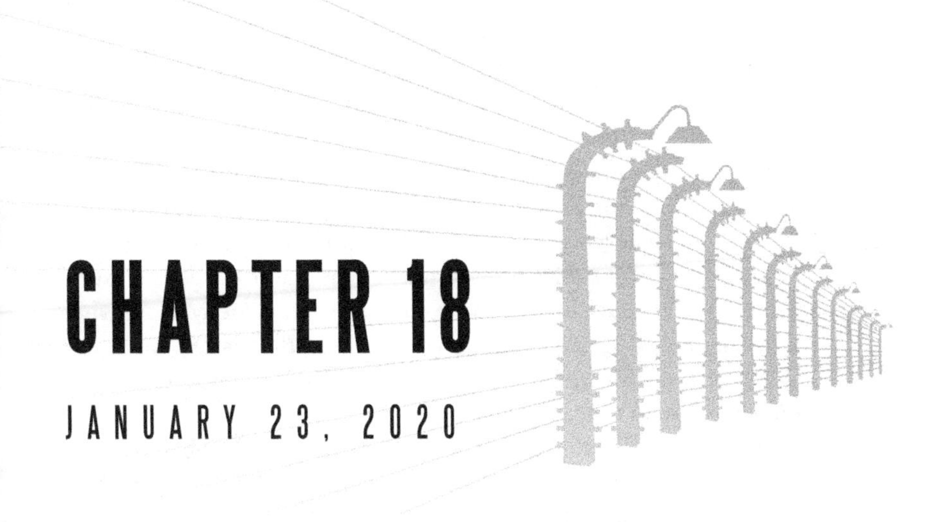

CHAPTER 18

JANUARY 23, 2020

Sarah closed the tour guide she had been using to occupy herself on the long flight from New York to Poland. Day was breaking on the horizon. The cabin lights came back on. She looked over at her Uncle Jakob still sleeping in the seat beside her.

"Uncle Jakob, Uncle Jakob, we're going to land soon. Did you get some rest?"

Jakob roused from his slumber groggy, blinking, trying to get his bearings.

"You must have been in some deep sleep. Are you okay?" Sarah asked.

"Yes, yes, I was really out. I feel fine. We're about to land? That was quick."

"You were sound asleep for a long time. It'll be another forty-five minutes or so. I thought you'd like to get up and stretch before they make everyone stay in their seats."

"Yes I would. I need to use the restroom as well. Thank you for waking me early. What time is it?"

"It'll be about seven in the morning when we get to Warsaw."

Ben, Jakob's nephew, leaned over from across the aisle. "Good morning. We have a connecting flight at nine to Krakow. We should be settled into our hotel by noon Krakow time."

Jakob gathered himself and went to the restroom.

Once she saw the restroom door close behind her uncle, Sarah turned to her brother and said, "He looks a lot more frail than usual. Do you think talking him into coming here was a good idea?"

"He's older than the uncle we used to play with all the time. It didn't take too much to talk him into this, though. He resisted a little, but I think deep down he wanted to come back. Some sort of closure I guess."

"Maybe. I just hope it's not too much. He's never talked too much about it. The last few years, a few things have come out. Most of what I know about what happened to him comes from the history books I've read. I've pieced a few things together about what happened to him, his family," Sarah said.

"His life is such a sad story. For us, he's just Uncle Jakob. But if you step back and look at his life, it's just astonishing. I mean, what does a place like Auschwitz do to a four-year-old? Then you look at all he's achieved with his life. Then you look at all that's happened to him since. An amazing, sad story."

The door of the restroom opened. Jakob made his way back toward his seat, but he didn't sit down right away. "Feels good to get up and walk around," he said in hushed tones in consideration of the other passengers still struggling for snippets of sleep.

Jakob walked up to the front of the first-class section and back a couple of times before he sat. The flight crew started stirring about, so he got out of their way.

"I'm glad we came a few days early. Gives me a chance to acclimate to the time change. I don't adjust as easily as I used to," Jakob said.

"You do pretty well for someone your age. I have friends my age who don't get around as well as you do," Ben said in jest.

"Ben, you shouldn't lie to an old man just to make him feel better."

Sarah took his hand and said, "It's not that big of a lie. You're still pretty spry."

"You too?"

She squeezed his hand.

"There's another reason I'm glad we came early. I want to show you some of Krakow. I know it's going to look a lot different than when I was last here seventy-five years ago, but I bet I can still find some of the places."

"Uncle Jakob, I can't think of anything I'd like to do more than that. Ben and I were just talking about how little we know about your life."

"I want to show you something of the good that happened. I want to show you the Pod Ortem Pharmacy. Mr. Pankiewicz took me in. Had he not done so, I don't know what would have happened to me in the chaos that followed liberation. He's the reason I went into pharmaceuticals."

"You see? That's something right there we didn't know about you. We want more!"

"I had someone locate some of his family. Mr. Pankiewicz passed away a long time ago. One of his daughters and several grandchildren still live in Krakow. I've arranged to have dinner with them."

"That's great," said Ben.

"I'm glad you two talked me into this. It's something I've needed to do, something I've wanted to do for a long time. But quite frankly, my courage failed me every time I thought about coming back. So many ghosts. I think I've been trying to outrun them my entire life. It won't be long before I join them."

Sarah shot a glance over at her brother before she interrupted Jakob's moment of unguarded soul baring. "Oh Uncle Jakob, don't talk like that." She tried to make her rebuke sound lighthearted. In truth, though, his display of vulnerability frightened her.

Jakob smiled at her. "You're right. I'm turning into a maudlin old man. Forgive me. I want this to be a trip full of good memories." He rubbed his arm, and the conversation withered. Thankfully, the flight attendant came by and interrupted them.

The flight landed right on schedule in Warsaw. Sarah and Ben shepherded their uncle through customs and onto the connecting flight to Krakow with just-in-time efficiency. Just as Ben predicted, the trio arrived in their hotel suite about a quarter after twelve. The first order of business was to call room service to bring up a light lunch. They unpacked and made themselves comfortable while they waited for the knock on the door.

Afterward, Jakob went into his room to rest. Sarah was determined to force her biological clock to reset to local time. She busied herself answering texts and emails. She searched out the Pod Ortem Pharmacy, translated as Under the Eagle, and Tadeusz Pankiewicz.

The man's pharmacy had sat at the edge of the Jewish ghetto during the Nazi occupation. He was the only non-Jewish civilian allowed into the ghetto. Pankiewicz supplied medicine to the ghetto with the Nazis' permission. The Nazis were afraid of being engulfed in one of the many epidemics common to the cramped, squalid ghetto. What the Nazis were not aware of was the other assistance he rendered such as contacts to the outside world.

Pankiewicz had been enrolled in the Righteous among the Nations by Israel for what he did during the war. There was no mention of Pankiewicz's work after the liberation in any of the internet articles. No mention of her uncle. Something else lost to history. Something good done that no one would ever know about.

Sarah peeked in on her uncle and found him by the window looking down on the street below. A streetcar rumbled below as it passed over a switch in the tracks. She debated saying something, but he turned to her and said, "It's very different from what I remember. The streets aren't full of soldiers."

Sarah crossed the room to stand beside him and look out as well. "It looks really cold," she said.

"I remember it as a very pretty city in the spring even in the midst of war. Tomorrow, I'd like to walk around."

"It will be awfully cold. Are you sure?"

"The places I want to go are not that far away. I can take the tram to some of them."

"Would you like some company?"

"Absolutely. Ben too if he wants to come."

"I guess the two of us can navigate our way around. There are usually enough people in Europe who speak English, so you can knock about well enough."

"Oh, I speak Polish, but not well," Jakob said offhandedly. "It's been a while. But probably well enough."

Sarah gave her uncle a sideways hug. "And something else I didn't know. Where did you learn Polish?" Before the words cleared her lips—"Oh Uncle, I'm so sorry. Stupid of me."

"Sarah, please. I don't want you walking around me like you're on eggshells. That sort of thing just wears everyone out. All of the things that happened, they're all in the past. And the past is what it is."

Sarah just smiled and shook her head giving Jakob another embrace.

JANUARY 24, 2020

Jakob looked up from the news he was watching to see Ben and Sarah walk into the living room bleary eyed and disheveled.

"Dzien' dobry," he greeted them in Polish.

"Brushing up on your Polish? I assume you said good morning," Sarah said.

"As a matter of fact I am. I've been watching the local news. I'm not as rusty as I thought I'd be. And yes, it is a good morning."

Ben looked at the screen and saw a protest of some sort. "What's everyone so worked up about?"

"Nazis, anti-Nazis," said Jakob.

"There are Nazis in Poland? I would think the Poles would hate the Nazis."

"Those are German Nazis. Only they don't call themselves Nazis."

"So what are those non-Nazi Nazis upset about?" Ben asked.

"This is the seventy-fifth anniversary of the final days of the Third Reich. They're protesting all of those milestone events from seventy-five years ago," Jakob said.

"You mean like the liberation of Auschwitz?"

"None of that ever happened. At least according to them."

"Do you think there'll be protesters at the ceremony?" Sarah asked.

"What if there are? I'm too old to be afraid of them any longer," Jakob said flatly.

Ben sighed and muttered something to himself.

"Ben, you up for some wandering about the town? Sarah's going," Jakob said, trying to change the subject.

"I need to work on my thesis."

"You shouldn't be missing school. Education is too important," Jakob scolded.

"School will always be there. This will come only once. And like you said, education is important. But not all education comes from a book or a classroom. Besides, my research is done. All I'm doing now is trying to make sense of it. Anything I need from school is online anyway. I can do it from anywhere in the world."

"Oh, Mr. Wise Man. When did you get so worldly?" Jakob teased him.

"Let's go down to the dining room for breakfast. It'll take longer. That'll give it time to warm up outside from frigid to just freezing," Sarah said.

"Okay by me," Jakob said.

"Guess I need to go powder my nose and make myself presentable then," Ben said resignedly.

Ben joined Sarah and Jakob several minutes later in the dining room.

"We were about to go back to the room and look for you," Sarah needled him.

"Sorry. I was talking to the concierge. He can arrange for transportation for you two so you don't have to be out in the cold so much."

"Yes. I am aware of that option. We can bundle up enough. Besides, we need to get acclimated for the activities on Monday. All of those ceremonies are going to take all day I'm sure. Most of them will probably be outside," Jakob said, displaying his stubbornness.

"They promised to have some sort of tent for shelter—at least for the returning survivors."

"That may be, but it's still going to be cold. Besides, I want to get there early—before the crowd shows up."

"The camp doesn't open to the public until ten," Ben said.

"But they'll open it early for special guests and substantial donors to the preservation fund. We'll be there at eight."

"Okay." Ben held up his hands in surrender. "I suppose we need to leave here no later than six thirty."

"Good. Settled. Now let's eat a nice big breakfast. Sarah and I have a big day ahead of us, and you have your thesis."

They all returned to the suite after eating. Sarah and Jakob bundled up in their winter wear including fashionable insulated footwear. Jakob showed Sarah his heated vest.

"That's not fair. Where's mine?"

Jakob disappeared into his room for a moment and brought out two more vests matching his. "Here, one for each of you. Figure out which one is which. Here are the extra batteries."

"You sly dog! Always something up your sleeve," said Sarah.

Ben examined his vest and said, "Maybe I'll go with you now."

"Oh no! You are sentenced to writing that thesis," Jakob said, mocking sternness. Jakob's tone turned more serious. "We will be back no later than three thirty this afternoon. Shabbat starts early here, just after four. I've arranged to have our Shabbat dinner here."

Jakob felt no need to explain his sudden desire to be observant.

Downstairs, Jakob picked up a map from the concierge's desk. Standing on the sidewalk just a couple of steps in front of the hotel, he turned the map to orient it in the same direction he was standing. Sarah thought about pulling out her cellphone to use the GPS but then thought better of it. *This is his day.*

"Diagonally across that intersection and about two blocks beyond is the Cloth Hall on the Market Square." Jakob pointed in the direction he wanted to go. Then as a side note, he pointed in the other direction down the block from the hotel. "Two blocks that way is Oskar Schindler's old apartment." He headed out across the street toward the Cloth Hall.

Sarah and Jakob entered the square at the southwest corner. Jakob stopped to get his bearings. Before him was a church, small by European standards. Beside it was a man's enormous bronze head lying on its side. It must have had a three- or four-meter diameter. It was hollow with hollow eyes. The neck was open and large enough to walk in. The bronze was polished bright around the eyes where children no doubt crawled in and out of the head.

Jakob stood staring at it for quite some time before he said, "Well, that wasn't here the last time I saw this place." Turning 360 degrees to take in the charm of the square evident even in the depths of winter, Jakob said, "The last time I was here, it was packed with the Red Army."

Sarah hooked him by the elbow to get him past the shocking art. "Is that the Cloth Hall over there?"

"Uh, yes. That I do recognize. It's been restored somewhat."

They crossed the deserted courtyard to the side entrance of the rectangular building. Jakob pointed up at the grotesque figureheads that adorned the top. "Those things used to scare me when I was here before."

"Wonder why they always placed things like that on the top of buildings all over Europe?" Sarah asked.

"Old Europe. Superstitious. Dark Ages."

"And anti-Semitic."

"True. But Krakow was something of an exception though. Jews had been invited here by King Boleslaw. The king desired to build a commercial center here. Jews were known for being literate, having a business sense, industrious. So the good king opened the door."

"Sounds like stereotyping."

Jakob laughed. "Social norms have changed over the last eight hundred years. It was a mutually beneficial arrangement." Jakob walked into the cavernous interior of the hall. "And it lasted up until eighty years ago," he concluded somberly.

Jakob sensed that Sarah wanted to steer the conversation from where it was heading when she suddenly walked to the nearest market booth displaying dinnerware. All the pieces had intricate patterns in cobalt blue. "Look at these! So vivid! This is what I want for my home—when the time comes."

"Is there something you haven't told me?" Jakob asked.

"No. It's just that girls dream of stuff like this. Most important to me though is that I want my Prince Charming to meet you." She hooked Jakob's elbow again.

"I would like that very much. You and Ben mean the world to me. To see you grow up as you have, becoming such decent people, has been my life's greatest pleasure."

Jakob and Sarah wandered from booth to booth for the next couple of hours. The couple drew the attention of several shopkeepers. They were practically the only ones there other than the shopkeepers themselves. Jakob practiced his Polish on them. They bought several gifts and made arrangements for the items to be sent back to the States.

By one o'clock, Jakob was nearly spent. Drained though he was, something deep within felt revived. Something he had considered dead for longer than he could remember.

He was hungry as well, and that gave him a perfect reason to leave. Before leaving, the two stopped at a café on the perimeter of the square.

"The square must be a wonderful place to spend a pleasant summer evening—a place to spend a honeymoon," she said as they stepped out of the raw cold and into the warmth of the café.

By two thirty, they were back at the hotel. An exhausted Jakob napped until room service delivered their evening meal. Jakob roused himself from his slumber and inspected the delivery. Finding all he had ordered including two candles and a white tablecloth as well as a bouquet of flowers he had not ordered, he tipped the three delivery people. He knew it was not so much the custom to tip in Europe, but he explained to the trio how pleased he was. He instructed them to share it with all those who had helped procure all he had requested. They offered no resistance to Jakob's generosity.

After the wait staff had cleared their service equipment and left, Jakob turned to Sarah and asked, "Will you light the candles and pray?"

"I've never started Shabbat before. I'm not sure I know what to say."

"You've heard your mother do it a thousand times. You know what to say. It's in you."

Sarah did as she was asked. Her voice trembled slightly during the prayer, but it didn't falter. When she was done, she squeezed Jakob's hand, "Thank you, Uncle Jakob."

"See? It was in you to do. Never doubt yourself. Now let's sit and enjoy our time with each other."

The three did indeed enjoy themselves. They talked about all manner of topics. Ben and Sarah had long since outgrown the usual sibling rivalry and had become friends. Jakob saw himself as a sort of proxy parent but was careful not to usurp their real parents' position. Jakob probed them for their thoughts always wanting to know more of how they felt. The two usually turned it back on Jakob and got his opinions.

After nearly two hours, the conversation petered out. It wasn't an awkward lull so much as simple exhaustion from talking and laughing. Jakob savored a sensation he rarely ever experienced. A tear formed in the corner of one eye, built up, and then breached to run down his cheek.

Sarah caught sight of it. "Uncle! What's wrong?"

Jakob quickly wiped it away. "Oh nothing. I'm just becoming a sentimental old fool. I don't think I've ever been more content."

Sarah leaned over and hugged him.

Jakob straightened himself and took a long drink of the wine. "Forgive me. I must tell you two something." He paused and took another long drink before continuing. "About two years back, I experienced some really powerful headaches. It got to the point that I went to the doctor to be examined." Jakob paused briefly before continuing. "To make a long story short, I have a tumor in my brain."

Sarah gasped. "No!"

"It has remained almost dormant for several months, but recently, it has begun to grow quite fast. So far, there are no signs it has metastasized, which would normally be good news."

Ben, more composed than his sister, asked, "What are the treatment options?"

"There are no options. Nothing. It's inoperable."

"Can't the nanobot technology Tudos developed be used to cut it out?"

"That is one of those bitter ironies in life. My tumor is fairly rare, and Tudos has not yet developed the proper targeting system for this particular form."

"Can't they push it? Get something to work?"

"Afraid not." Jakob spared Ben his next question. "Three to four months. Five at most."

Sarah jumped to her feet knocking over her chair and ran crying to her room.

Jakob looked at Ben and rested his hand on his shoulder. "It comes to us all. It's just my time to pass over."

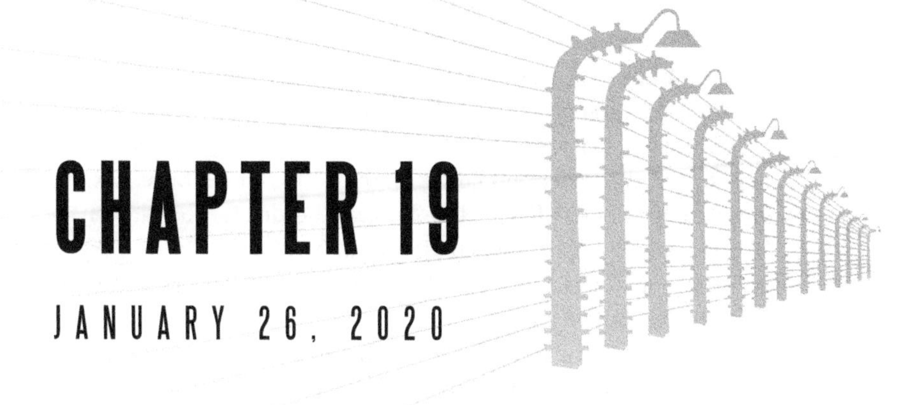

CHAPTER 19

JANUARY 26, 2020

Chris sat across from her daughter at the kitchen table. "Just a few more, Erika, and you can go take your nap. You're doing really well. Now open your mouth slightly and push your tongue into the gap between your front teeth." Chris paused to demonstrate. "Now breathe out across your tongue." Another pause to demonstrate how to make the *th* sound. "See? The. There. Them. Thanks."

Erika repeated each one in succession with exhausting intensity.

"The the the the the the the the the," Chris said in rapid fire.

Summoning all her concentration, Erika repeated as fast as she could.

"Three thousand three hundred and thirty-three milliliters of theophylline."

Erika started to say that but realized it was just one of her mother's geeky jokes. That drew a smile. "Very funny."

Chris smiled back. Erika's palsied smile still pained her. "That's enough for now. Feel like resting?"

"Yesh." Erika nodded.

Chris rose to help her daughter to her feet. Erika waved her off wanting to do it herself. She made slow progress down the hallway from the kitchen to what had become her bedroom after having been her father's office. The stairs were just too daunting at that stage in her rehabilitation.

After seeing Erika to her room, Chris found Sam in the family room reading the Sunday paper.

"She's making progress, don't you think?" Sam asked.

"Yes, slow but sure. Day by day."

"Yeah," Sam agreed vaguely from behind the paper.

"Is this a good time to talk?"

Sam folded the paper and laid it on the coffee table. "Sure. Let me get another cup of coffee first." He got up and headed for the kitchen.

"Fix me one too," Chris called after him.

A few minutes later, he returned with two mugs. "Well, what do you think of what we talked about?"

"I've rolled it around in my head. Do you think you'd be happy going to work for them?" Chris curled up beside Sam after he sat on the sofa.

"I like what I'm doing now, but I think I could adjust to corporate life easily enough. The health insurance is the big thing. It's as good or better than yours."

"The college fund is just about gone," Chris stated.

"All of those modifications to the house weren't cheap. That handicapped bathroom cost almost half of what we bought the place for," Sam said.

"She gets better every day. It's just going to take a lot of time and hard work," Chris said.

"Chris, do you think you'll be happy staying home watching Erika?"

"Let's be real here. We're no longer in a position to pick and choose options based on personal fulfillment. We're looking at simple, long-term survival now."

Sam put his arm around Chris. "Yes, you're right. But there's nothing wrong with trying to salvage as much as we can to make it a little easier."

Chris sighed. "It'll take some getting used to. Right now, it's almost what it was like when Erika was a baby, when childcare cost us almost what I was bringing home. I can do a lot of the rehab with her myself. Save a lot on that. That will help ease the pain of going down to just one income."

Sam nodded. "We could sell the house. Move farther out. If you're not at the CDC, there's no reason to stay in this neighborhood. Take the equity and buy something cheaper. Reduce the mortgage."

"Sam, we're not selling the house. This is our home. Besides, we just poured a boatload of money into it. We'd have to modify any other house just like we did this one if we moved. I don't think I have the energy for that."

"Yeah, I know. Just thinking out loud."

"I can't continue like this at work either. I simply can't put in the effort I used to. And it shows too. Everyone has been understanding and gracious and all, but there's still a mission the CDC must fulfill. They're not just a bunch of government bureaucrats pushing a bunch of paper around. People die if they don't do their job. And I'm not cutting it."

Sam nodded. "The good news is we don't have to make a decision today. Nothing is going to happen until the company makes its expansion. I can stall them a few more weeks."

"Good." She sipped coffee. "You know, there is one plus to all of this. Erika doesn't hate me now."

"Chris, she never hated you. She was just being a teenager, just acting out from all those raging hormones."

"The mother-child reunion. The Apollo Effect turns into Apollo 13. Houston, we have a problem."

Trying to be upbeat, Sam said, "If it doesn't work out here with you and Erika, you can always go back to the CDC."

"No, I don't think there'll be any going back from this. That will be our new reality forever if we go down that road."

Sam squeezed Chris tighter. "We're going to make it. It's not what we dreamed about, but you and I are still good, right?"

Chris buried her head against Sam's chest. "Yes, we're still good."

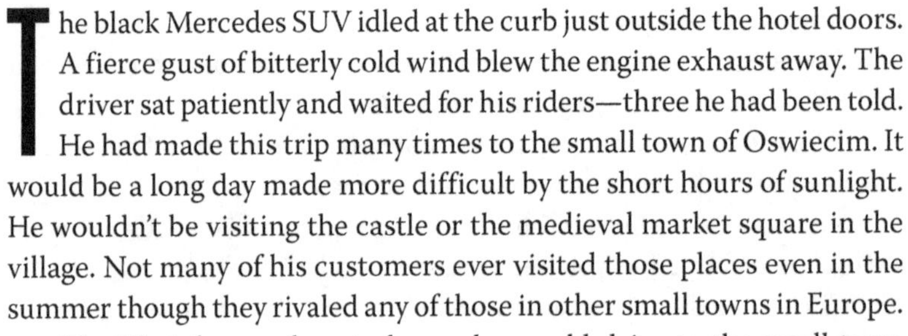

CHAPTER 20

JANUARY 27, 2020

The black Mercedes SUV idled at the curb just outside the hotel doors. A fierce gust of bitterly cold wind blew the engine exhaust away. The driver sat patiently and waited for his riders—three he had been told. He had made this trip many times to the small town of Oswiecim. It would be a long day made more difficult by the short hours of sunlight. He wouldn't be visiting the castle or the medieval market square in the village. Not many of his customers ever visited those places even in the summer though they rivaled any of those in other small towns in Europe.

No. That day as almost always, he would drive to the small town the Nazis had renamed Auschwitz. It was a special day—seventy-five years after the liberation of the camp by the Russians. His opinion of the Russians was not much higher than his opinion of the Nazis. He had been born well after the war, but the corporate memory of his family had kept alive the stories of Nazi and Soviet atrocities alike. He had no doubt his fares that day were Jews who had come to pay homage.

He had no opinion of Jews—he didn't know any personally—but their demand for his services gave him employment, and he was grateful for that. His excursions to the camp were almost always the same. Drive his passengers westward along the Vistula River for a little more than hour. Drop them off at the original camp, Auschwitz I, where most of the indoor exhibits were. After they had lunch either under the trees outside the gates or across the street at one of the restaurants, he would transport them to Auschwitz II, the camp called Birkenau. In between, during his wait to pick up his passengers, he would meet with several of the other drivers and while away the time in leisurely conversation.

Later in the afternoon or early evening, he would pick up his passengers again for the trip back to Krakow. That was typically a quiet journey devoid of conversation or questions. He had learned to keep tissues available in the back seat and even small plastic bags should one of the passengers become nauseated.

When his fares for the morning, an elderly man and two others, appeared in the otherwise deserted lobby, he jumped out of the warmth of the vehicle to open the door for them. Even the short distance from the hotel door to the car door was enough to let everyone know it was going to be a painfully cold day.

Jakob looked at his watch and saw it was already six forty-five, later than he had hoped. But given the wind-driven cold weather, he doubted they would linger long over any of the places he wanted to show the children. It wasn't lost on Jakob that the weather was exactly how he remembered it as a child. There were no battery-operated vests or warm vehicles to hide in or heavy coats or winter boots. He wanted to remember to make that point to his niece and nephew when they toured the camp.

Sarah pulled three cups from the sturdy bag of food the hotel kitchen had prepared for them. "Anyone want hot cocoa or coffee? There are some pastries and bagels as well."

"That sounds wonderful," Jakob said. He turned to the driver and asked in Polish, "Driver, excuse me. What is your name?"

"Tad," the surprised driver answered.

"Tad. Would you like some coffee or hot chocolate?"

"Oh, no. Thank you. Thank you very much."

"Are you sure? We have plenty, and my niece would be happy to pour you a cup and put it in the cup holder for you."

Tad relented and nodded. "Okay, okay. Coffee, please. Thank you very much."

Within a minute, a cup of hot coffee sat in the cup holder within arm's reach of the driver. Ben declined all offers of food or beverage in favor of reclining his seat in the front in an attempt to get a little more sleep.

Sarah handed Jakob his hot cocoa and a bagel. She fixed the same for herself and ate in silence. He ate silently as well watching his niece from the darkness of his corner of the back seat.

"You've barely acknowledged my existence since Friday. You said nothing at dinner with the Pankiewicz family last night. What's wrong?"

Sarah looked over at her uncle for a long moment. The streetlights were bathing him in constantly changing angles of light. Finally, she replied, "You know what's wrong."

"Yes, I suppose I do. It's nothing I can fix though. I can't even apologize for it."

"Do Mom and Dad know?"

"Yes."

"For how long?"

"I told them not long after I found out."

"Why did you wait so long to tell Ben and me? Because we're just children?"

Jakob reached across the seat for Sarah's hand, but she pulled it back. "Truthfully, probably so. I confess I still see you and Ben as children. It's not a judgment on your maturity. It's just that I care for you so much that I can't help it. If it's any consolation, I thought of Ilsa the same way, right up to ... well, right up to the end. Still do. Someday when you have your own children, you will understand."

Sarah reached across the seat and took Jakob's hand. "I'm still mad at you," she said as she squeezed his hand.

"Right or wrong, I didn't want you to have to deal with this any longer than you had to. There's enough sorrow in the world. I'm just sorry I will be a source of it for you."

The two of them sat holding hands as the big SUV passed over the Vistula and cleared the outer suburbs of Krakow. Dawn broke red along the lower edges of the sky. Jakob gazed out the window looking for anything familiar as the car motored on. A little farther along, as they neared the town of Oswiecim, they saw rail yards that paralleled the road in several stretches. Some were active with massive locomotives going about the business of the day. The intersection of multiple rail lines had been among the most important reasons the Nazis had chosen this place—easy rail access to and from all over the Reich.

To Jakob, some of the yards appeared to be railroad junkyards; rust was the dominant color. At the end of one of the yards sat three short, squatty wooden boxcars. Visions held securely away for seventy-five years ruptured and filled his eyes.

Sarah took his hand again. "Are you all right?"

Ben turned in his seat and studied his uncle.

"I'm fine. Just weary of driving. I think we are close now."

Indeed, they were at the entrance of Auschwitz I within a few minutes. As the big SUV pulled up, a small delegation walked out to meet them.

Ben leaned over and whispered to Sarah and his uncle as they exited the vehicle, "How much did you donate?"

"Enough," Jakob whispered.

Jakob stood for a moment and looked around to get his bearings of a place he had not seen in three-quarters of a century. Only a vague sense of recognition came to him. He looked beyond the brick and mortar and noticed the armed figures in black attire all about. He felt his pulse quicken, but he forced himself to show nothing. *They are here now for my protection*, he thought.

The welcoming group quickly ushered everyone into a conference room in the visitors' building. It had been administration offices during the Nazi era, but it was then serving as a visitors' center, educational facility, and administrative offices for the historic site.

Inside was a table set with a breakfast spread. Neither Sarah nor Jakob were hungry, but Ben availed himself. The delegation filed into the room and took their positions at one of the tables. A senior-looking fellow, Director Hausner, stood and welcomed Jakob's family. He introduced their guide for the day, a pretty, smiling woman about Sarah's and Ben's age. He explained there would be enough time that morning to tour the grounds before the crowd developed.

"Dr. Bauer, will you please come forward and allow us to present you with a token of our appreciation for your very generous gift. It will be a great help in the preservation of this important site. Because of your gift, future generations will be able to come to this place and gain an understanding of the price of intolerance and hatred," Hausner said.

Jakob rose to accept the gift, a crystal globe with the words Never Again etched into the glass all over the surface in nearly every language. It was very heavy, and Jakob nearly dropped it. Someone snapped a photo of the occasion. The small audience applauded.

As he was unprepared to give a speech, Jakob cleared his throat stalling to gather his thoughts. He managed to string together a few platitudes and clichés appropriate for the occasion. Everyone applauded warmly when he concluded.

Hausner approached Jakob and pumped his hand vigorously, "Dr. Bauer, we cannot express enough how much your endowment gift means to the future of this museum. There are so many preservation projects ahead of us that we thought we would lose to the elements."

"It's important that the world not forget what happened here, Director," Jakob replied politely.

"Dr. Bauer, I am embarrassed to ask this, but we have a problem with the ceremony today."

Jakob stiffened a little. "Yes?"

"One of our speakers, a survivor like yourself, has fallen ill and cannot be here. It has left a huge hole in our program."

"Are you asking me to speak? I have nothing prepared. This is too solemn an occasion to just throw something together. I don't see—"

"Please, Dr. Bauer. That the world may know and remember that the victims here were real people. They existed. They had families. They were just like every other human on the planet. Please. It doesn't need to be elaborate."

Jakob sighed. He knew what he had to do. The curse of responsibility. To be a *mensch*. "Very well."

The director grabbed Jakob's hand and shook it furiously again. "Oh thank you! Thank you, Dr. Bauer. I will do the introductions. You will be pleased."

"Please keep your remarks about me to a minimum. Please don't go overboard."

"Overboard?"

"It's an American expression. It means don't go too far, say too much, exaggerate. All I want is a simple introduction. Who I am. A survivor. And please tell them I had only a very short time to prepare for the speech. I want to manage everyone's expectations."

The director nodded and pledged his compliance.

"What language should I use to address the audience? I'd like to speak in English so my niece and nephew can understand better."

"English is fine. We have interpreters available, so English is fine."

Ben and Sarah sidled up to their uncle after the director hurried off.

"What was that about?" Ben asked.

Jakob smiled and slapped him on the back. "Nothing. You'll see. Later. A surprise. Now what say we get on with our private tour?"

Their guide stood patiently by the exit waiting for the small ceremony to wind down. As Jakob approached, she stood erect and greeted him with a warm smile. "Good morning, Dr. Bauer. I am Sasha, your guide. I am here to make sure you have access to wherever you wish to go."

"What time should we be where the ceremonies are?"

"They start at two. That's the warmest part of the day. The tent is heated though. We should be there at one thirty or so."

"In that case, I'd like to start here at this part of the camp, Auschwitz I, and show my niece and nephew what I remember of it. Perhaps we can have lunch before we head over to Birkenau. Do I need to call my driver?"

"Oh no. We have transportation for our honored guest. And lunch will be provided here whenever you are ready."

"Thank you. Sounds like you have thought of everything. Would you please make sure my driver is made aware of where we will be? And would you make sure he gets lunch?"

"We certainly will, Dr. Bauer."

Jakob turned and pulled Ben and Sarah forward. "These are my niece and nephew, Sarah and Ben. They are my companions for this trip."

Sasha shook their hands in greeting. "So happy I can be of service to you today. If you have any questions, please feel free to ask me."

Sasha led them out a side door to a small open area. Across the way loomed the main gate with the infamous Arbeit Macht Frei iron archway. Sasha led them in that direction. Just in front of the gate sat a small, enclosed golf cart large enough for four.

"We have transportation for you for within the confines of the camp if you so desire, Dr. Bauer," Sasha said, pointing to the cart.

"Maybe later. I'd like to get some exercise."

"Very well. I can summon the cart anytime. Where would you like to go?"

"I was not at this camp very much. I was taken several times to a building and tested over and over."

"That was probably Block 10. It is at the opposite corner but not a far walk."

Sasha led the group a couple of streets ahead where they turned right. On either side were the entrances of the brick barracks.

"If it were not for the barbwire and knowledge of what this place was, you'd think this was some sort of campus, a school or something," Sarah said.

"Good eye. Originally, this part of Auschwitz was barracks for the Polish cavalry before the Nazis invaded. The first commandant, Rudolf Hoess, converted it into a prison camp for Polish prisoners of war. The Nazis built the barracks on this street when they thought there would be only a few thousand prisoners. Later, Russian prisoners of war were sent here. The mission of the camp grew from that."

Sasha pointed out the buildings on their left as current museum exhibits and displays of different topics. They reached the end of the row of barracks. The last two were connected by a court wall.

"Why are these two barracks walled in?" asked Ben.

Their guide drew a breath before answering. "These two barracks, Blocks ten and eleven, are probably the most infamous of the buildings here at Auschwitz one except perhaps Crematorium one. Block eleven, there on the end, was called the Death Block. It was used for the punishment of prisoners. Cyanide gas from Zyklon B was first used there on Russian prisoners to test its suitability. Many other forms of punishment and torture occurred there."

Sasha paused allowing what she had just said to be processed.

"Block ten is where medical experiments were performed particularly on women and ..." She stopped abruptly.

"Women and twins. This is where Mengele did his research on living subjects," Jakob said to finished Sasha's discourse.

"Forgive me, Dr. Bauer. I didn't mean to be so insensitive."

"Not at all, Sasha. There is no way to be delicate about what happened here," Jakob said reassuringly. "This is where I last saw my two sisters."

Ben broke an awkward pause by asking, "So why the connecting wall?"

Rather than answer, Sasha walked over to the iron gate, opened it, and beckoned them into the courtyard formed by the two barracks. At the far end stood another wall festooned with wilted flowers and burned-out candles. Two large leaning posts stood a few feet away from Block 10. The windows of the Block 10 building were shuttered.

"This courtyard was a place of torture and execution as well. The two posts you see were used to lift prisoners with their hands and arms bound behind them. The guards lifted them up by their wrists from those hooks you see at the top. They were suspended a few centimeters from the ground until their arms pulled out of their shoulder sockets. That wall you see at the far end was the backstop for firing squads."

Sarah cried silently at first, but she then buried her face against her uncle's chest and wept deeply. Jakob embraced her and stroked her hair but said nothing. Eventually, she sobbed herself out. Sasha handed her a tissue from her satchel.

"I'm sorry. This is all so overwhelming. I've heard about all of this my whole life, but when you see it, it just ..."

"Don't be embarrassed, Sarah. If you felt nothing here, you wouldn't be human," her uncle said to comfort her.

Sasha pulled her radio from her satchel. "I can have the cart brought up to take us all back to the visitor center," she said.

"No, please. I want to see more. I'm fine. I've had my cry. I'll be fine. Really."

"Are you sure?" asked Jakob.

"Yes, I'll be fine."

"Perhaps we can go into some of the exhibits," Sasha suggested.

"Yes. Let's get out of this wind," Jakob said.

Sasha led them to one of the exhibits a few doors down in the direction they had come. Ben and Sarah studied the exhibits intently and with newfound interest. Jakob could think only about how sanitary it all looked as an exhibit. In his mind, nothing could convey the stench of the place. Nothing could portray the feel of vermin crawling on you constantly. And certainly nothing could replicate the constant psychological burden of knowing death could befall you at any moment for any reason or none at all. He held his thoughts to himself.

In Block 4, at an exhibit titled simply Extermination, Jakob felt his pulse quicken and chest tighten. Sarah and Ben walked and listened to Sasha. Jakob begged off not wanting to see again the scenes he had seen every day for months. He found a book in a room set off by itself. It was no ordinary book though. It sat atop a pedestal and wrapped around its perimeter. If it were straightened, it would perhaps be three meters thick, he thought. The pages bore all the names of known victims of the Holocaust. Millions.

Jakob found the section with names that started with B. He found an Isaak Bauer, but the birthdate did not match. There was no Ilsa Bauer. His parents were not listed. They had gone to their demise without registering with the Nazi machine. He did find Rachel and Leah Bauer. The birthdates were the same as his. *My sisters.*

Jakob felt a stabbing pain shoot through his head. His vision narrowed to a tunnel. Breathing became difficult. He closed his eyes to make the room stop spinning. Gradually, his equilibrium was restored. The knifing pain subsided.

"Are you all right, Uncle Jakob?" Ben asked gripping his elbow.

"Yes. I am now. Just a sudden headache. The ones I told you about."

Without asking, Sasha got on the radio and summoned the cart. "Let's head back to the center and take a break. Hot coffee and cocoa."

"That sounds like a wonderful idea," Jakob said.

As they left the room, Jakob saw Sarah looking at where the book was opened. He was sure she saw the names.

Sasha returned them to the conference room where they had gathered earlier that morning. Apparently, it was serving as an operational center for coordinating the day's events. Menacing men with weapons and in the black uniforms stood by the entrance. More were inside talking on radios and studying maps.

At one end of the room sat an unoccupied table. Jakob and his entourage sat and rested. Sasha brought them carafes of coffee and hot cocoa. She encouraged them to get something to eat. It would be a long day and increasingly difficult to get something to eat as the crowd gathered. They all made an attempt to take advantage of the spread of food; only Ben ate with any enthusiasm. Jakob and Sarah nibbled out of courtesy but had no real appetite.

While Sarah and Ben watched the goings-on in the room, Jakob pulled his little notebook and jotted down a few things for the speech he would give later. He checked the time and put away his notes. "We probably should be heading out if we want to see any of Birkenau," he announced.

"Are you sure you want to do that, Uncle?" Sarah asked concerned the effort and emotion of the day would be too much for him.

"Yes. I've gotten my second wind now. I feel fine."

"We could delay our return home and just come back here tomorrow or the next day after you've rested."

"No. Thank you for your concern, but I will not be returning to this place again."

Hearing the discussion, Sasha offered a compromise. "There is a way you can see the whole camp from one spot without having to get out and walk around. I can take you up into the tower at the main guardhouse. You can see nearly everything from there, and it is right where the ceremonies will take place. You'd be able to show your family what you want to point out without having to exhaust yourself."

"That's a great suggestion," Sarah exclaimed.

"I do want you to see what my world was. What I overcame."

"Uncle Jakob, I don't think we will ever be able to fully grasp that. Please do this for me. I'm worried about you. I promise, Ben and I will return here."

He knew his niece was right—no one could ever really understand. And he was nearly spent. Jacob conceded. "Very well. For you. But you promised to return."

A van pulled up to the curb. One of the armed guards opened the door for them. Jakob pulled back.

"This is our security escort for the rest of day. There have been protests and threats. This is just a precaution," Sasha assured them.

Jakob mastered his emotions again and got into the van. Sarah and Ben climbed in behind their uncle. The guard was the last to get in. Jakob noted that the driver was armed as well.

A short drive of barely two kilometers and they were there. Jakob had difficulty recognizing anything. A colossal white tent as large as any circus ever employed sat immediately in front of the iconic guardhouse. It straddled the rail spur where it entered the camp. The van stopped at a security checkpoint before continuing to the entrance. More black uniforms and even armored vehicles scurried about.

Jakob watched Sasha hop out, flash her ID card, and speak to the two guards at the gate. The van proceeded through the arched opening, passed through the building, and entered the interior of the most infamous of all the Nazi concentration camps.

"How big is this place? It's enormous!" Sarah gasped clearly awed.

"One hundred and seventy one hectares. More than four hundred acres," Jakob said.

Not far from where the van sat, the rail line passed through a different archway directly beneath a tower. Sarah remarked how the tower reminded her of an airport control tower because of the windows all the way around the perimeter of the top floor. The rail line split into three lines as soon as it entered the enclosure.

Sasha turned in her seat in the front. "This is the tower I was describing. You can see almost the entire camp from here. We have provided some binoculars for you. Dr. Bauer. There are two flights of stairs to the top. But you'll be out of the wind, and it's warm inside. Do you want to make the climb?"

"Certainly. I've come this far."

"Then let's get started."

Sasha helped everyone out of the rear of the van and gave them a moment to straighten themselves. She led them to a door on the other side of the tracks watching that they all stepped carefully over the rails and ties. The stairwell was narrow and wound its way to the top. Jakob was winded, but he forced himself to appear otherwise.

They discovered that what Sasha had said was true; they could see the entire camp from the tower. It was a vista new even to Jakob. Several sets of binoculars sat on the tables in front of the windows. Ben picked up a pair and adjusted them as did the others.

From their vantage point, they could see how the rail split into three parallel lines that merged again at the far end nearly a kilometer away. The camp was clearly bisected by the rails.

To the right of the rails sprouted a forest of chimneys, hundreds of them. Along the front fence line, only one row of tar paper shacks remained intact. To the left was a considerably smaller section of the camp.

"The right side was mostly male prisoners. The women were kept on the left," Jakob explained.

"The women's side is much smaller," Sarah observed.

"The Nazis had less use for women laborers," Jakob said matter-of-factly.

"Straight ahead is where Crematoriums two and three are located, or at least their ruins. All the way across diagonally to the right is where four and five are located. That wide-open area between the two right-hand rail lines at that railcar is called the Ramp. That is where the transports stopped and the people got out. The new arrivals were selected to live a little while longer as laborers or exterminated right away from there. That is where I last saw my parents," Jakob explained mechanically, devoid of emotion.

"All the way to the far end of the fence line on the right of the tracks, that single chimney standing there, was my barrack. Just before you get to that was the Gypsy camp. We had full view of every transport train that delivered its passengers. We could see the selections as they happened and watched the ninety percent or so who were destined for the chimneys walk to one of the crematoria. We knew when a transport was about arrive because the big incinerator fans started up to stoke the furnaces."

Jakob sat his pair of binoculars on the table, turned to Sasha, and said in the same flat, emotionless voice, "Is there somewhere I can go until it is time for the ceremonies? You can take the children with you and tour some of the camp. I would like some time by myself if that is possible please." Jakob massaged his arm.

"Dr. Bauer, I will make that happen for you. Give me a few minutes and I will find a place for you." She pulled her radio from her satchel and called someone. There was some back-and-forth discussion. In a short time, another guide appeared.

"I want to stay with you, Uncle Jakob," Sarah said.

"Please, Sarah, I would like to be alone for just a little while. Please try to understand. I just need a little time. Go with the guide and walk around. I'll be okay."

Sarah said nothing; she left the observation room and walked down the stairs. Ben followed without a word. The other guide left with them.

When they were gone, Jakob looked at Sasha. "I'm sorry. This is more than I thought it would be. You have some place for me to rest? I need to gather my thoughts if I'm to speak."

"Yes, come with me. We set aside some rooms because we knew there would be some elderly survivors who may be in need of a place to rest. We made a few of the old offices privacy rooms."

"Thank you, Sasha."

Jakob stood by the window and looked out on the gathering crowd. They arrived by the busload. Some arrived in official-looking motorcades. The security forces arrived in military vehicles. All but the security guards ducked into the large circus tent to escape the wind and cold.

A knock on the door. "Dr. Bauer? It's Sasha. Are you awake? It's getting close to the time for us to gather in the tent."

"Yes. Come in, Sasha. I'm awake."

Sasha entered. "Your niece and nephew are already there. They have front-row seats."

"Are they still miffed at me?"

"I don't think they were mad at you—just concerned."

"Tell me, Sasha, where are you from?"

"Israel, sir."

"How did you end up here as a guide?"

"Part of my studies. My mother's father was a survivor from here."

"You're keeping his memory alive?"

"I suppose. This place, what happened here—it must never be forgotten. His survival, my existence—they are linked to this place."

"Indeed." Jakob turned from the window. "Shall we go?"

Sarah and Ben were indeed in the front row in a section cordoned off from the rest of the seating area. Jakob walked to the seat beside them. Before sitting, he leaned over and kissed both on their heads. He sat in the seat next to Sarah, and Sasha sat on his other side.

The interior of the tent buzzed with unintelligible chatter. A small party of dignitaries ascended the stage. The crowd grew quiet. Director Hausner walked to the podium.

"Ladies and gentlemen, welcome to this solemn occasion, the seventy-fifth anniversary of the liberation of the death camp, Auschwitz ..."

Jakob's mind wandered off as the director introduced various state officials onstage. He pulled the notes from his pocket, looked at them briefly, and ripped them in two. Sarah looked over at him. He patted her arm. "It's okay."

A few minutes later, still lost in his thoughts, he heard his name from the podium. Sarah and Ben turned to him in astonishment. He stood. He leaned over and whispered, "This is that surprise I was talking about."

He had earned the nickname Der Sturm, the Storm, from his men because of his fierce rhetoric. Of late, the name rested on his covert acts of violence against what he saw as the greatest enemy of the Aryan people—the eternal Jew. Today would forever seal his place among the immortals of the cause. That day, his name would stand beside Himmler's, Heydrich's, and those of the martyrs of the 1923 Munich *Putsch*. The day's act would rally like-minded Aryans everywhere to the cause.

Der Sturm pulled the van over to the side of the road at a spot nearly four kilometers east of the entrance to Birkenau. He watched as three men in brown fatigues scrambled out the back and unloaded its content onto the pavement. In less than thirty seconds, three drones, each more than a meter across, came to life with loud whirring. A two-kilogram explosive device hung beneath each one. The three operators donned VR goggles linked remotely to the drones and exercised the levers on the handheld controls.

Roughly the same distance from the camp to the south and north, two other teams, also under the command of Der Sturm, scrambled to get their drones operational. In less than two minutes, nine armed drones at three sites sat on the ground, motors revving, awaiting the order to execute their mission. All three team leaders confirmed their readiness.

Der Sturm shouted into his radio, "Launch the drones! Launch the drones!"

The three drones from his team and the six from the other teams sprang from the ground and flew away like avenging angels. As the drones sped away, a black truck raced toward his group. Der Sturm saw armed men in black uniforms standing on the exterior running boards. "Halt! Get down on the ground!" blared the vehicle's loudspeaker.

The gunner on top of the security vehicle opened fire at the parked truck. The three operators stood their ground directing the drones away as fast as they were capable of flying. Der Sturm pulled his pistol and returned fire. He was cut down immediately. The three operators continued even as the truck pulled up beside them and the black-suited men jumped them. Rifle butts cracked each of the operators in their heads.

Jakob ascended the stage, stood a moment before stepping up to the podium, and rubbed his arm. He stepped closer and grasped the sides of the podium.

"Good afternoon. My name is Jakob Bauer. And as Director Hausner said, I really was asked to speak just this morning. I have spent much of the intervening hours thinking about what I would say on such a solemn occasion. I am not a great orator, but fortunately, I did take a course many years ago during my sophomore year of college in public speaking. It has proven to be an elective course that has served me well over my lifetime. I remember one maxim for a successful speech is to keep it short.

"As I wrestled with the many things I could say here today at this seventy-fifth anniversary, the one thing I definitely will say at the outset is that I will not speak at the one hundredth anniversary no matter how nicely you ask, Director Hausner.

"I certainly don't mean to be glib or disrespectful regarding these proceedings, but there will be a one hundredth anniversary and a two hundredth anniversary and so on into the future. This anniversary, this remembrance, is the seventy-fifth. What will all of those future anniversaries be like? It's not likely there will be any survivors with their eyewitness accounts.

"How will the future regard this place? How will the future interpret the events of this particularly sad chapter of human history? Even today, before the last eyewitness has passed over, there is a thriving community of denial that challenges the reality of what happened here and all across the rest of the Third Reich.

"Today, we gather at these gates to commemorate the seventy-fifth anniversary of the liberation of this camp. For me, the seventy-fifth anniversary I remember more vividly happened a few months earlier, in the early morning hours of June 17, 1944. The train transporting my family passed through that portal and deposited us into the netherworld of Auschwitz. My sisters and I were handed over to the control of Dr. Josef Mengele. Any trace of either of my parents vanished up the chimneys within an hour of our arrival.

"Auschwitz became our reality. Within a couple of months, even my sisters were gone. Today, that four-year-old boy now stands before you to say yes, it did happen. Hatred and intolerance must never again gain a foothold.

"I ask my niece and nephew, who are with me here today, and their generation to hear what I have to say. Some twenty-five hundred years ago, another uncle, a fellow by the name of Mordecai, a Jew, went to his niece, Queen Esther, to warn her of a plot to annihilate all the Jews held captive during the time of the Persian Empire. He wanted her to go to her husband, the king, and expose the plot. She was hesitant. He warned her that if she remained silent, she too would be among the victims. Her status as queen would be no protection. Mordecai concluded his plea for the queen's intervention with this question—'Who knows whether you have been brought to this place for such a time as this?' And so I conclude my plea to my niece and nephew, to their generation, and to you all with the same question. Who knows whether you have come into this world for such a time as this?"

Jakob stood a brief moment at the podium looking out over the silent audience before turning to walk to his seat. Before he reached the steps, the smattering of applause erupted into a roar. The listeners rose as one. Director Hausner came over to shake Jakob's hand. Looking down from the stage, Jakob saw Sarah and Ben with red-rimmed eyes beaming at him.

There was a flash. A bang. The back of the tent collapsed under billowing smoke. Another explosion. Screams emanated from the cloud of dust and smoke. Jakob froze trying to comprehend what he was seeing.

Someone tackled and dropped him off the stage. Whoever it was landed on him—Sasha.

"Stay down! It's an attack!" She pulled a machine pistol from her satchel. Sensing Jakob's question, she said, "I'm Mossad."

Jakob looked about for Sarah and Ben. They were just a few feet away huddled under the stage. Another blast detonated just above them. Heat and smoke enveloped them. An eternity passed before Jakob could breathe again. Sasha lay heavily on him still shielding him.

"I can't breathe! You have to get off." Jakob pushed hard against Sasha. "I can't breathe! Get off!"

Sasha slumped off of him and lay awkwardly. Jakob saw the flowing blood running from a large gash in her temple. Her eyes were fixed, staring at nothing. She was dead. Sarah and Ben crawled out from under the stage to drag Jakob back under its shelter.

A fourth blast detonated on what remained of the tent. Ben cried out and grabbed his leg. His pants were immediately drenched in his blood. Sarah ripped open his pant leg at the seam exposing the wound. She unbuckled his belt, stripped it from his waist, and wrapped it tightly around the leg above the gash. Ben cried out again in blinding pain before he slumped over unconscious.

After long minutes, bright beams of lights came scanning through the smoke and dust. People moaned and cried out for help. Sarah stood and screamed in the direction of the lights, "Over here! By the stage! I have two wounded! My brother is bleeding out! Hurry!"

CHAPTER 21

FEBRUARY 12, 2020

Chris sat pensively across from Patterson in his office. She had known this time would come. It was something she had relentlessly turned over in her mind almost daily.

"Chris, I wish I could give you a better performance evaluation. I know you've done the best you could considering your daughter's tragic situation. To be honest, I really admire how you've managed as well as you have, but it just wouldn't be fair to all the rest who have taken up the slack."

"Dr. Patterson, I'm not contesting your evaluation of my performance. I know I'm not performing up to the levels I'd like. When that last round of anthrax exposures cropped up, I wasn't able to answer the bell. To be honest, I think you graded me higher than I would have myself."

"Chris, no one expects you to lay aside your personal life every time there's an outbreak. That's why we have multiple teams to spread the load around."

"Still, I don't have an answer for the PAMNID cases. I'm just glad it hasn't reared its head again. I don't have an answer."

"Well, before you came onboard just after 9/11, there were anthrax attacks going through the mail system. After all these years, it's still a mystery who sent them. You've been one of the best investigators I've ever had, Chris. I'm certain you'll bounce back once things settle down at home."

"I wish I shared your optimism. Erika's making progress, but there's so much more to do before she'll be independent. I know I've thanked you before, but I'm really grateful for how much the CDC has worked with me to get through all of Erika's operations and rehab."

"You've earned your stripes. I don't think the folks who filled in for you minded so much. But let me change the subject. I think we're done with the evaluation. This morning, I got a call from none other than Dr. Jakob Bauer."

Chris eyes widened. "I've had no further contact with him just as—"

"Relax. He didn't call to complain. He wants to meet with you."

"Meet with me? I'd think he'd be recuperating after what happened in Poland."

"He did sound weak, but then, he's pretty old. He left his private number. He says he has something that may help your investigation. Can you schedule a day trip to Boston? He didn't want to trade emails."

Chris thought for a moment about her routine with Erika and Sam's schedule. "Let me check with my husband and see if he can pick up Erika after her rehab tomorrow. If so, I can go to Boston tomorrow."

"That would be wonderful."

"Seems a little odd, though. I mean requesting me specifically."

"He's an eccentric."

"You don't have a problem with my going?" Chris asked.

"I'd send you on the Gulfstream if I thought I could sneak it past the bean counters."

"Okay. I'll call him as soon as I clear it with my husband."

"This is the address, lady," the cabbie said, looking at Chris in the rearview mirror.

Chris looked up the hill at a large Victorian house. She looked at the other houses. Most were Victorians as well. The snow made the scene look like a Christmas card, one that read, "From our house to yours, Happy Holidays." A really nice neighborhood well out of her price range but not what she would have expected for a billionaire's residence.

"Could you wait until I'm sure this is the right place? Here's an extra ten if you can."

"Sure, lady," the driver answered, stuffing the tip into his coat pocket.

Chris made her way up the driveway to the front door. She rang the doorbell and waited. She shivered as a gust of wind swept across the porch.

"Dr. Bauer is in his study. This way," the man said, pointing toward a room just off the vestibule. "May I hang up your coat?"

Chris glimpsed the man's shoulder holster when he pointed. She took her coat and scarf off and gave them to him. He hung her coat on an old hall tree that was nearly as large as any closet she'd ever seen.

"Dr. Bauer? Dr. Malone is here to see you."

There was no answer. The man knocked. Still no answer. He cracked the door, peeked in, and went in. Chris stayed in the vestibule and felt the heat escape the room. She saw the old man slumped in his large chair at a desk. The man nudged him. To her relief, Dr. Bauer roused awake.

"Dr. Malone is here to see you," the man explained to the blinking Dr. Bauer.

"Bring her in. Bring her in. I just nodded off. I'm all right."

Chris stepped into the overheated room as the man beckoned her in. Cherry paneling, overstuffed chairs, and dim table lamps set on end tables adorned the study. The man withdrew and left her alone with Dr. Bauer.

"Dr. Malone. Good to see you again. Please forgive me if I don't get up. I'm nursing a broken rib and a number of bruises. I don't bounce back like I used to."

"Quite all right. I heard about what happened in Poland. Terrible."

Bauer's hands appeared swollen. Even his face and head were swollen making him appear cherubic.

"Please have a seat. Pardon the untidiness. I'm more or less living in this room now as I recuperate. I can have William bring you some coffee or tea if you'd like. Water perhaps?"

"No thank you."

"You probably want me to cut right to the chase and explain why you are here."

"Yes. This is quite unusual."

"Very well. I requested you to come here because I can't travel. The trip back from Europe nearly killed me, so I couldn't go to Atlanta. I wanted you because you were the only one asking the right questions."

"What do you mean?"

"About what happened in those small towns. I believe you refer to it as the PAMNID incident. Catchy name."

"Helps us discuss the subject a little easier to have a name."

"Yes I suppose so. Have you figured it out?"

"No. The CDC, FBI, DHS—everybody got overwhelmed when that anthrax showed up in the mail again. I got sidelined with some ... uh ... personal matters. There were no more outbreaks, so it got put on the back burner."

"Yes. I heard about your setbacks."

"You heard? What do you mean?"

Jakob smiled. "You've met William outside there. He's part of my security team. They are quite good at what they do. I had them check you out. Nothing sinister. Just public-record stuff. They told me about what happened to your daughter. I'm sorry."

"You spied on me?"

"No. They never had you under surveillance or anything like that. It was all public-record stuff as I said. Not much more than a background check you can get off the internet," Jakob answered defensively.

"Dr. Bauer, I am more than a little upset with you. That's my private life! You have no right to that!" Chris felt blood rush to her face.

"I can see that. And you have a right to be. Please hear me out though. I had to understand you."

"How long have you been spying on me?"

"I had your background checked when I got back from Poland."

"And the reason?"

"I need your help. The PAMNID contagion is not over. It's just dormant."

"How do you know that?"

"I initiated it."

"You? How is that possible?"

"It wasn't that difficult. I just let human greed and depravity take their course."

"You're not making any sense, Dr. Bauer."

"I suppose I'm not. It doesn't even make sense to me now. Let me ask you. If you were the emperor of the world, how would you stop the drug epidemic happening in this country?"

"I don't know. Personally, I'd like to see every dope dealer hunted down and locked away forever."

"Yes, given what's happened to your family. That's the supply-side approach. I've given the question a great deal of thought. I underwrote the Dopanoncessemin program as a kind of demand-side attempt. It had some success, but not what I hoped for. After my daughter was killed ..."

Chris shifted uneasily in her chair.

Bauer continued. "After my daughter was killed, an innocent bystander caught in a drug shootout, I wanted to hurt the drug culture to its core—especially the ones profiting from it. Hurt's not the right word. I wanted them to suffer."

"It's too embedded. It's even too big for the federal government to have any real effect. It *is* the government in parts of South and Central America."

"That shipment of the targeting drug—do you know why it had to be disposed of, what it was contaminated with?"

"No. I don't think that was ever answered."

"Nanobots. The kind developed for tumor-tissue destruction. Just about a perfect blend of fifty percent."

"The targeting transport drug. What was it targeted for?"

"You probably already know the answer to that," Jakob replied.

Chris thought for a moment. Then it hit her. "The VTA—the hindbrain!" Chris blurted. "You targeted the VTA?" Chris paused a moment struggling to grasp the full scope. "Why fifty percent blend?"

"The other half would transport whatever was added to it."

"You gave that to the drug cartels?"

"No. Remember, Ron Kaiser, the shipping clerk with the criminal record? I hired him and put him in that spot for a reason. I knew the temptation would overtake him. I even took up smoking a pipe again so I'd have an excuse to go to the loading dock and smoke. We met and talked nearly every day. I told him how powerful the targeting drug could be. How it could be so effective in managing pain with opioids. Next thing I know, an entire production run is contaminated with lead peroxide–based nanobots. Nature simply took its course."

"You set it up! You knew what would happen."

"I simply arranged for an opportunity and the worst of human nature to come together."

"How much is out there?"

"Enough to destroy fifteen to twenty percent of the market. Historically, that's been enough to collapse any market. The cartels will go to war to recover their lost market shares from each other. Cartel wars are fairly medieval."

Chris paced back and forth. "Collapse a market? These are people! How many people?"

"Perhaps six million."

"Something like this can't happen. Six million? Are you out of your mind?"

"It will pass over harmlessly the millions more who don't use drugs. Sacrifice the few for the many. Create the fire break that's needed to protect the innocent."

"It's not possible."

"It is possible. It will happen. And I need you to stop it. Homeland Security is about to commission the Dominion Project. It's a network of geosynchronous satellites linking all their secure networks. It's a hardened system designed to work in the wake of a spectrum of disasters. It will blanket the entire country. The frequency it uses is one of the two frequencies needed to create the third harmonic. The other frequency is ever-present in our modern world. The two frequencies together animate the lead peroxide nanobots. If they start the system, you'll see what you saw at the three test sites happen across the nation. It'll all happen within a twelve-hour period coast to coast."

"I don't believe you. There's no way you could distribute those drugs to the entire country. And, and … and why haven't there been more incidents?"

"I didn't have to distribute. There's already a thriving distribution system. The cartels did it all."

"Why'd those people in those three towns die if it hasn't activated yet? Why'd they die and nobody else?"

"The nanobots are animated by a specific frequency. I showed you that in the lab. Those three towns have industrial companies that recently purchased equipment from Bauer Electronics. They bought transmitters to connect their remote sites to their central control system. There's a link to our service center so we can monitor the equipment. For a twelve-hour period, I was able to make it transmit a specific frequency."

"Why would you do that?"

"It told me that the contaminated nanobots had saturated the country when it made it to those backwater areas."

"You killed all those people?"

"I didn't steal the targeting drug, I didn't distribute it, nor did I inject it into anyone's arm."

"You just pulled the trigger."

Jakob had no immediate response to that. "Yes," he whispered finally.

Chris couldn't think of anything to say. *The enormity!* Her head felt as if it were about to burst. *Who could conceive of such a thing? Who would believe it?*

"Auschwitz had its Angel of Death—*Malekhamoves.* Now, I am Malekhamoves. When Ilsa was murdered carrying my twin granddaughters, I wanted revenge. I wanted blood. I wanted to kill the pathogen, the parasites."

"Dr. Bauer, why are you telling me this? Why me? Why not the FBI?"

"You understand. You know the pain I suffered when those bombs went off during the ceremony at Auschwitz, when I saw my nephew nearly die. A young woman died saving my life. When I saw the terror and suffering, it came to me. A moment of brilliant clarity. I'm the evil one. Me! I'm no different than Mengele or Himmler or any of the rest of them."

Jakob stopped talking and mopped his brow. He appeared even smaller to Chris.

Winded, nearly spent, Jakob continued, subdued. "Evil is a contagion—a pestilence. Revenge is the horse it rides."

Jakob pulled himself from his chair and crossed over to his desk. Chris was alarmed at how furiously he rubbed his left arm. He pulled a cement-block-sized binder to the edge of the desk but was unable to lift it.

"These are my notes. Everything is in here. I need you to make people understand. Stop the Dominion Project from starting up."

Jakob collapsed to the floor. Chris rushed to the door to call the security guard. An ambulance arrived and carried Jakob away, unconscious and on oxygen. The security guard told her she'd have to find her own way out.

A cab arrived and took her back to Logan Airport. Before going through security, Chris bought a large white canvas bag from one of the airport kiosks to carry the cumbersome bundle of Bauer's notes. It would draw less attention from the TSA.

She thought about reading through the notes after she settled into her window seat. Wrestling with the bombshell Bauer had handed her was all she could manage though. An older woman, a grandmotherly type complete with photos, sat beside her. Chris pulled the file bundle out and leafed through it in hopes of avoiding mindless chatter for the next three hours.

Undeterred, the woman persisted, detailing the setting and circumstance of each photo. The photos were all of just one grandchild, a boy. They spanned the full range of a young life, infant, toddler, pumpkin-toothed grin from kindergarten and the rest, all the way to the prom. The exhibition outlasted the preflight safety demonstration, the taxi to the runway, and even the takeoff. Chris was trapped.

Her last picture showed a lean but muscular young man in football pads holding the ball as if he were about to throw a pass. His smile could have been used to sell toothpaste. At that point, the woman broke down, cupped her face in her hands, and wept. Chris, knowing nothing else to do, hugged her shoulder.

The sobs played out after a few minutes. Chris asked if there was anything she could do to help. "No. It's too late. He's dead. I'm going to his funeral."

"I'm sorry for your loss. Really."

"Thank you." The woman straightened herself. Wiped her eyes. Apologized.

"Not at all," replied Chris. "The loss of a child is probably the worst thing there is."

"He was injured playing football. Broke his leg and really tore up his knee. They gave him painkillers. It wasn't long before he was hooked. When he couldn't get the prescription drugs, he started in with heroin to kill the pain. And … well, that was it."

The woman barely spoke another word for the rest of the flight. It was the longest flight of Chris's life.

Back in Atlanta, Chris picked up her car from the short-term lot and drove home. Dark of the winter evening had already fallen. Sam had set out the trash cans for the morning's pickup, making it difficult to pull in. Annoyed, Chris got out and pushed them to one side before driving up to the house.

From the back stoop, she saw Sam through the window. He was working with Erika on her balancing exercises. Chris crept through the back door as quietly as possibly so as not to disturb them. She watched her daughter strain to master each exercise.

Erika caught a glimpse of Chris watching. "Mom! I'm getting better!" she exclaimed, smiling her crooked little smile Chris had come to love and hate with equal measure.

"That's my girl, baby."

Sam and Erika continued for another half hour. Chris settled at the kitchen table with Bauer's notes. The evening slipped into the late hours before she read even one of the files. Her mind could not focus on the whys and hows.

Sam came in after finishing up Erika's rehab routine. "I don't know about Erika, but I'm sure getting a workout." He kissed Chris's forehead.

"I've been watching. She's really intense."

"She told me she wants to do a 5K run in March. Some sort of benefit," said Sam.

"She'll be ready. I can see it."

"She gets that from you, Chris. That pitbull tenacity."

Chris took Sam's hand and held it to her face. Sam kneaded her shoulders.

"So how was your day? You went to Boston, right?"

"You wouldn't believe me if I told you. I went there to meet with Jakob Bauer," said Chris.

"You're kidding! I just saw something scroll across the bottom of the business news that he died."

"Died? I was with him when he collapsed. They took him out in an ambulance." Chris opened up her laptop and accessed the internet.

"Chris, you were meeting with Bauer. About what?"

"Remember the PAMNID incident?"

"Yeah. I didn't think that one was active."

"It's not. He just wanted to talk about it."

"Well?"

"I don't know. He was pretty banged up from that terrorist attack in Poland. Confused." Chris got up for a cup of water. "I think I'll go to bed. It's been a long day."

"Yeah. Me too."

Later, long after retiring, Sam found himself awake. Chris's side of the bed was empty. He went to the bathroom. Outside, the trash cans banged around. Looking out, by the glow of the streetlight, Sam saw Chris drop a sizable white bag into one of the cans that landed with a thud.

Sam pulled on his bathrobe and went to investigate. He found Chris at the table with her laptop open. "What's going on? I saw you throw something out."

"Couldn't sleep. Thought I'd get rid of some old files. Didn't want to miss the pickup."

Sam walked around behind her and put his hands on her shoulders. "Chris, you're really cold!"

"I feel fine, now. I'm working on my resignation letter. It's time, Sam."

ADDENDUM

Many of the scenes and characters braided into this story were based on actual events, places, and people. I included these details to strike an accurate depiction of the hellish world known as Auschwitz. The Auschwitz story is too dire a warning to humankind not to be told and retold often in the hope of reaching as many as possible. It must not fade or be driven from our collective psyche.

Research for *Passover* encompassed numerous books, documentary films, site visits, and personal interviews. Two books proved most helpful for providing insight into the daily life of Auschwitz. *Auschwitz: A Doctor's Eyewitness Account* by Dr. Miklos Nyiszi gave an up-close account of the operation of the crematoria and Mengele's research. *Children of the Flames* by Lucette Matalon Lagnado and Sheila Cohn Dekel provided glimpses into the daily lives of the twins during their time as wards under Dr. Mengele.

I would be remiss if I did not mention the immeasurable contextual information I gathered on a tour of Auschwitz sponsored by the CANDLES Museum in Terra Haute, Indiana. I was fortunate enough to interview Eva Moses Kor, a surviving Mengele twin and cofounder of CANDLES. Ms. Kor is the subject of at least two documentaries. She and her sister, Miriam, were the first two twins being led out of the camp in the iconic Russian documentary film about the liberation of the camp. My visit with the CANDLES group to Auschwitz profoundly affected my understanding of the Holocaust.

The following is a list and brief description factual details incorporated into *Passover*. This is by no means intended to be a scholarly work. I provide these descriptions merely as an aid to the reader who may want to know more. I encourage all to educate themselves about the larger subject of the Holocaust.

PLACES

Auschwitz

Probably the most notorious of Nazi concentration camps, Auschwitz is the German name imposed on the Polish town of Oswiecim. It was actually a regional complex of forty-five subcamps. The original camp, sometimes referred to as the Stammlager or Auschwitz I and home of the infamous *Arbeit Macht Frei* gate, was by no means the largest. One of the industrial labor camps was Buna-Werkes operated by I. G. Farben. Birkenau, named for the birches common to the area, was the largest, some four hundred acres and once destined to grow even larger.

Birkenau, once operational, is where the rail transports deposited their victims for selection. Roughly 90 percent of the new arrivals at Auschwitz-Birkenau were selected for immediate disposal in gas chambers and crematoria. Four of the five crematoria in the Auschwitz system were at Birkenau. The other one was at the Stammlager. Most of those not selected for immediate disposal were made to work, rendering the last ounces of their lives' value to the service of the Third Reich. A tiny fraction, including twin children, were selected for medical experiments.

During its operation from June 1940 to January 1945, 1.3 million were sent to Auschwitz; 1.1 million did not survive. One million of those were Jews. At least 200,000 were children.

Other specific, factual locations within Auschwitz were Kanada, Blocks 10 and 11. The Ramp, the rail line that had two siding tracks, bisected the Birkenau camp. Crematoria II and III stood on either side of the track's terminus. The twin boys' barracks was located in the southwest corner of the men's side of the Birkenau camp closest to Crematorium III, the Ramp, and the Roma (Gypsy) camp.

Krakow

More than a millennia old, Krakow is a beautiful ancient city. It was spared most of the destruction from World War II common to other parts of Europe. At the heart of the city are the Main Market Square and the ancient Cloth Hall that has housed merchants for more than eight hundred years.

Kazimierz, the Jewish Quarter, houses some of the oldest synagogues in Europe as well as scars from the Holocaust. A short distance from the Kazimierz is the Jewish ghetto as seen in the movie *Schindler's List*. Portions of the tombstone-shaped walls can still be found in some sections of the perimeter. Many of the actual tombstones from the Kazimierz Jewish cemetery were removed to be used as pavers for the Plaszow labor camp.

Plaszow

Not far from Krakow was the Plaszow labor camp (also depicted in *Schindler's List*). The camp commandant was Amon Göth, a particularly notorious war criminal with a reputation for inhuman cruelty. Göth was also in charge of the liquidation of the Jewish ghetto in March 1943.

EVENTS

Summer 1944

Auschwitz was at its lethal zenith during the summer of 1944. All the components—gas chambers, crematoria, rail lines, operational procedures, and deceptive practices—blended harmoniously to achieve a maximally efficient killing machine. As many as ten thousand per day were "processed." The Jews of Hungary bore the burden of feeding the machine.

August 2, 1944

On the evening of August 2 and into the early morning of August 3, 2,897 men, women, and children of the Roma (Gypsy) camp were rounded up and sent to their deaths in Crematorium II. Over the operational life of Auschwitz, 23,000 Gypsies were imprisoned and 20,000 perished.

October 7, 1944

Using explosives smuggled in from the Buna-Werkes and weapons from Polish partisans, prisoners revolted and destroyed Crematorium IV and damaged Crematorium II. The prisoners, called Sonderkommandos, were tasked to perform the grim work in the crematoria.

During the lifetime of Auschwitz, Sonderkommando groups were rounded up and executed after four months or so as the Nazis did not want witnesses to their genocide.

Immediately after the rebellion, all 853 members of Sonderkommando 12 were executed. Beyond the damage they did to the two crematoria, Sonderkommando 12 killed seventy SS officers and men.

A few days later, Sonderkommando 13 was formed from a transport to keep the remaining crematoria operating. Not too many weeks later, they were rounded up and executed by flamethrowers.

November 17, 1944

Dr. Miklos Nyiszi, a Jewish pathologist assigned to Dr. Mengele, received information from a noncommissioned officer that killing prisoners was henceforth forbidden. Nyiszi's skepticism was assuaged when he witnessed a small, five-car transport of five hundred sick and debilitated prisoners arrive; they were taken to the camp's hospital in Camp F instead of immediately being sent to the crematoria. It was an indication of how badly the war was going for the Nazis, who were at that point showing concern for retributions for their war crimes.

January 27, 1945, Liberation Day

Units of the Soviet Sixtieth Army appeared at the gates of Auschwitz at about four in the afternoon. What the soldiers found astonished even the most battle-hardened of them. The Red Army invested considerable time and effort documenting the evidence of Nazi cruelty and inhumanity.

PEOPLE

Marc Berkowitz

Born in 1932 in Slovenia, Czechoslovakia, Marc and his paternal twin sister, Francesca, arrived at Auschwitz in March 1944. Marc became Dr. Mengele's errand boy. However, this did not exempt him from suffering from Mengele's medical experiments.

Dina Gottliebova

Born January 21, 1923, in Brno, Czechoslovakia, she arrived at Auschwitz with her mother in 1943 from the Theresienstadt concentration camp in Czechoslovakia. Mengele took notice of the surreptitious artwork she had done in a children's barracks and enlisted her for a special task. Before agreeing to work for Mengele, Gottliebova negotiated her mother's safety. She was tasked to paint the portraits of Roma (Gypsy) prisoners. Mengele, interested in racial features, was not satisfied with the ability of photographs to capture the unique features and coloration of the Roma people.

Dr. Miklos Nyiszli

Born May 5, 1901, in Szilágysomlyó, Austria-Hungary, he died on his birthday in 1956. Prisoner tattoo number A-8450. Under compulsion, Dr. Nyiszli worked as Dr. Mengele's pathologist performing autopsies and prepared slides and reports for the Kaiser Wilhelm Institute at Mengele's behest. He worked in Crematorium II and was an eyewitness to the mass murder of thousands. In March 1946, he wrote a book describing his experiences as a member of the Twelfth Sonderkommando, *Auschwitz—A Doctor's Eyewitness Account*. The 2001 film *The Grey Zone* is based on Nyiszli's account of events leading up to the October 7, 1944, prisoner revolt.

Tadeusz Pankiewicz

Born November 21, 1908, Pankiewicz operated the Pod Ortem (Under the Eagle) pharmacy at the edge of the Jewish ghetto in Krakow, Poland. He managed to get some medicine into the ghetto when the Nazis became concerned about typhus outbreaks. He allowed his pharmacy to be used by many of the captive Jews to meet and have contact with the outside world. His actions for helping the Jews were punishable by death. On February 10, 1993, he was declared as "Righteous among the Nations," an honorific, by the State of Israel.

Zvi Spiegel

Born January 5, 1915, in Budapest, Hungary, he later moved to Munkacs, Czechoslovakia. Perhaps the oldest set of twins under Mengele's control, Zvi and his sister, Magda, were twenty-nine when they came to Auschwitz. Although he suffered from mysterious spinal injections at the hands of Mengele, Spiegel was also tasked to manage the twin boys' barracks.

Zvi was known as Twins Father to the boys. He often risked his own life helping the boys in his care survive. Such was the case the day Dr. Thilos ordered the boys' barracks liquidated in the gas chamber. Spiegel's actions that day saved the entire barracks.

The author took some historical liberties in telling how Spiegel helped return the boys to their homes. Spiegel returned thirty-six boys to Hungary within six weeks after liberation.

Irma Grese

Born October 7, 1923, she was hanged for her crimes at Nazi concentration camps December 13, 1945, at age twenty-two. She was captured April 7, 1945. Grese was known for her exceptionally sadistic cruelty with women prisoners especially prisoners she viewed as having retained their attractiveness. Her cruelty earned her the nickname Hyena of Auschwitz. She was rumored to have had several affairs with male camp staff members including Dr. Mengele.

Josef Mengele

Born March 16, 1911, in Günzburg, Bavaria, he drowned on February 7, 1979, after suffering a stroke while swimming in Brazil after having eluded justice for thirty-four years.

Mengele came to Auschwitz in May 1943. While only a captain (Haupsturmfürher), Mengele is perhaps the most notorious of all lower-level Nazi criminals. He performed bizarre and monstrously barbaric medical experiments on the Holocaust's most innocent victims—children. He was known to prisoners as the Angel of Death.

Mengele was an educated man with a doctorate in anthropology and a doctor of medicine degree. He came from a wealthy, cultured family and was considered poised and charming. Even some of the female prisoners regarded him as attractive.

Dr. Heinz Thilo

Born October 8, 1911, he committed suicide May 13, 1945, after capture. Oberstrurmfürher (Lieutenant) Thilo was sent to Gross-Rosen concentration camp after Auschwitz. The author took some historical license in having him sent to the eastern front.

During the summer of 1944, while performing his selection duties on the Ramp, Thilo's image was captured in one of the photographs from the Lili Jacob Album.

CPSIA information can be obtained
at www.ICGtesting.com
Printed in the USA
LVHW111610280120
645065LV00003B/375